INTO THE LIGHT

Book One of the AXE DRUID Series

Written by CHRISTOPHER JOHNS

© 2019 Mountaindale Press. All rights reserved. No portion of this book may be reproduced in any form without permission from the publisher, except as permitted by US copyright law.

This is a work of fiction. Names, characters, places, and incidents either are the products of the author's imagination or are used fictitiously. Any resemblance to actual persons, living or dead, businesses, companies, events, or locales is entirely coincidental.

MOUNTAINDALE PRESS

Table of Contents

Dedication 5
Acknowledgments 6
Chapter One 7
Chapter Two 16
Chapter Three 49
Chapter Four 57
Chapter Five 69
Chapter Six 96
Chapter Seven 119
Chapter Eight 138
Chapter Nine 153
Chapter Ten 162
Chapter Eleven 167
Chapter Twelve 187
Chapter Thirteen 201
Chapter Fourteen 209
Chapter Fifteen 220
Chapter Sixteen 233
Chapter Seventeen 262
Chapter Eighteen 274
Chapter Nineteen 284
Chapter Twenty 292
Chapter Twenty-One 306
Chapter Twenty-Two 320
Chapter Twenty-Three 325
Chapter Twenty-Four 337
Chapter Twenty-Five 345
Chapter Twenty-Six 359
Chapter Twenty-Seven 367
Chapter Twenty-Eight 385

Chapter Twenty-Nine 423
Chapter Thirty 447
Chapter Thirty-One 462
Chapter Thirty-Two 470
Chapter Thirty-Three 490
Chapter Thirty-Four 503
Afterword 512
    Author's Note 512
About Christopher Johns 514
About Mountaindale Press 515
Mountaindale Press Titles 516
    GameLit and LitRPG 516
    Fantasy 517
Appendix 518
    The Good 518
    The Bad 520
    And The Ugly 521

Dedication

In loving memory of Jaken "Warmecht" Fox, loving and doting father, friend, and confidant. I hope that your little moon can someday know the man I did.

We miss you, bud.

Acknowledgments

Thank you to Nick Kuhns, Jay Taylor, and Lucas Luvith for your amazing editing skills! You guys are some serious editing monsters, and I truly appreciate your willingness to slog through my world with me.

I would like to thank the lovely folks at the GameLit Society for being there to help me along and supporting my dream alongside me. That, and giving me plenty to do!

Thank you to all my supporters, my awesome friends—without whom this book would never have been possible—and my loving fiancée for constantly telling me I can do it.

Specifically, to a certain Mr. Wilson, who for the entirety of this series has acted as that neighbor over the fence. Giving odd wisdom, insight and support in your own way since the beginning. You are a light, sir. And not nearly as dim as you portray yourself to be. With deep respect and profound—and surprising—kinship in this new world. Thank you. You know who you are.

You all rock.

Chapter One

"Hey, man. Wasn't Aaron supposed to be getting on tonight?" I asked into the headset. A quick button press and my character dove into a forward-shoulder roll.

The in-game knights we were fighting were difficult, and dodging was the easiest way to defend. I growled as another of the hulking suits of armor stepped forward, entered the fray, and swung at me. I must have walked inside his aggro—aggressive action—range and pulled his attention.

"You know how he can be sometimes, man," Erik's voice filtered through the speaker over my left ear. "He's so busy with life, his lady, and trying to get his shit in order that we don't hear from him for days on end. Things have been different since we got out. You know how it is."

I nodded, as I thought. *He's right.*

I had met Erik in the Marine Corps through a friend in my shop. Shop was a common term for any kind of small, business-like unit like ours, as public affairs Marines. As soon as we had met, it had been a fast friendship, simply because we had so much in common: interests and humor, what set us both off, and a love of photography, stories and of course, video games. Over the years, we had become brothers; hell, he'd even saved my life when I had hit a truly low point in my career.

So, here in this dank, blood-drenched cathedral of turmoil and suffering, we did what we did best: killed shit, looted, and kept trucking along. This was our way of bonding and staying in touch—video games. After a while, he had introduced me to Aaron, another Marine, who shared most of our same interests. We had been gaming together ever since.

We spent another minute or so mopping the knights up and healing before moving on. These types of games were great at first; everything was so new and intense that you can't help but be lost to the enchantment of it. But this was my second—or was it third?—time through this one area, and it was getting a little tedious. Hell, half this area in the game had been one "back-turn, secret hallway, here's-the-thing-you-didn't-know-you-needed-to-do fun." So much *fun*. Don't know why I let Erik talk me into these kinds of games; as fun as they were, they had some seriously scary bits in there, like when monsters, mimics, and other *numerous assholes* would just pop out on you and kill you in the most gruesome ways possible. Mmm, wholesome fun.

"You saw your boy today, right?"

Erik's voice brought me out of my small reverie, and I had to sprint away from the giant we had just started fighting. I'd retreated in order to get a better vantage point. It wasn't working.

"Yeah, man, took him to the park today," I said as I backed into a wall, then sprinted through the giant's legs. "He made a new friend with some little boy who doesn't like to climb very much, so he was showing off."

I'd spent the day with my son, the rambunctious, four-year-old boy running and playing at the park while I observed and encouraged him to try and make friends, climbing all over the jungle gym and giggling as I shook it a bit. Spending time with him was a joy, and I looked forward to seeing him again soon.

"Good shit, brother." I had to dodge once more and swung my great axe into the creature's leg. "I'm glad you're getting to spend some more time with him, man. I sent Aaron a text, still no response."

"Well, wherever he is, I hope he knows we are about to royally fuck this mini-boss up." I pushed my character forward a bit and dodged another blow from the giant. "Fuck, man. You wanna grab some hate? This guy has been riding my ass this whole fight, and he hasn't even *hinted* at dinner."

"Nah, son, you got it. Lemme get some time to heal real fast." Erik's character, a thin male with a katana in hand, drank from a flask before he headed towards the boss. "You have that dream again, man?"

I grunted as the giant we were fighting smacked me back and into some ooze. Slimes began to materialize from the liquid disgustingness and slowly glide toward me... if I couldn't get out fast enough, those little bastards would gang up on me and kill me. Not to mention they were ugly as sin. Their slime-like bodies were taking on grotesque and misshapen limbs that dripped and grasped at me, and *fuck if I wanted that on my beautiful avatar.*

"I did a few days ago, but it's always just before my damned alarm goes off." I tried to heal but got smacked again; my health had taken a beating. I was closer to dying than I was comfortable with.

"Gotta heal, man," I warned Erik.

He slashed at the giant's ankle and threw a Magic Shot at it which finally took enough of the hate from me. We were going slowly but surely. I retreated, healed, and waded back in.

A name popped up on the screen in the upper left corner, and my friend Jake, recent father and newest friend to our gaming circle, jumped into our chat.

"What's the haps, ladies?" His almost surfer-like voice flooded our ears, and I smiled.

"Killin' shit, puto, you?" Erik joked. "You gonna get on at all man?"

"I've gotta put little Luna to bed. She's been kinda fussy, but it's cool." Jake yawned and cooed to his daughter. We could hear her gurgling happily on the other end. "I'll be on in a little bit, though. Y'all still gonna be on?"

"I will be for a bit, but I gotta work tomorrow." I whooped as I watched the giant's health drop by a decent chunk when my flaming great axe hit his leg. "I'll be on after that, though. How about you, Erik?"

"I will be for a bit, but I gotta go do a thing with the wife tomorrow, I think. Leave or not, life doesn't wait." His normal tone became a bellow, "SHIT, GET THAT FUCKER."

I panned my view to the left; a small, goblin-like creature was running up behind Erik's character brandishing a jagged and rusted blade with teeth hanging off the pommel. A globule of flame flew from my left hand and hit it squarely on the chest. While it was stunned, I moved in on it and whacked it with my weapon once to end its pathetic existence.

"Got him. Here comes the rain of flame," I informed my partner and turned on the giant, his last quarter of life ebbing from the bar above his head. It began to swing the club in its fist as Erik dodged and I threw fireball after fireball. Finally, it fell to its knees and disappeared.

"HELL YEAH, BABY!" Erik and I shouted together.

He followed it up with, "That's what you get for fucking with the Overlord, man. You should've told him, bro."

"He didn't know," I shrugged and stated theatrically. "They all think that just because they're the size of a gigantic cathedral that we aren't gonna start some shit when they talk smack."

"You guys are nuts," Jake said. I heard Luna in the background starting to try and fight sleep a little. "Talk about the dream at all?"

"Yeah, he had it a few days ago," Erik informed him cautiously. "Wait, you know about it?"

"Yeah, he told me about it last night while he was helping me get through the last area you all had already cleared. I've been having a weird dream too, but it doesn't sound exactly like the one you guys are having."

All of us had had some kind of weird dream lately: someone was calling out for help. I had heard it in some nightmares, so I hadn't thought anything new of it—but it was a little weird when it happened during a dream about being able to fly. Aaron had mentioned he had experienced a similar dream too, but since he was always so busy, we hadn't had time to discuss it much.

"That's wild, bro." I couldn't help nodding at Jake's observation. Still, I needed to change the subject. It seemed like the more I discussed the dream or any dreams, for that matter, the more likely I was to have nightmares. Not that it mattered anyway—they were the most common thing I had going for me.

"Yo, I saw Jake—not you, ya big lug, the other one—and Evan at the gym today," I said as I stretched out my hands a bit. "Jake plays this game as well, and he's not too far off from where we are. Evan said that he would be getting it this paycheck so he could join in."

"Right on, man," Jake, Fox was his last name and what we called him if we played when the other Jake was online with us, sounded pleased. "What did you work today, man?"

"Cool!" Erik droned a bit, cutting me off before I spoke. "More people to play with since your ass is never online when I am."

"Hey, man, I can't help that my life is nuts, okay?" I teased him back. "And I hit up some shoulders and back. Got a new personal best on shrugs, four hundred pounds."

"Tight, man!" I could hear Jake clap on his side of the mic, and his daughter giggled.

"Yeah, yeah," Erik remarked. "If you were as good at gaming as you are lifting, you might be less of a scrub!"

Neither of us held it against the other when we couldn't play. It was just our way of showing brotherly affection. His schedule was almost as screwy as my own, but his joke at the end there had been what made me laugh the hardest. That was what we did; we ragged on each other. I muttered some choice curse words in his direction, and Jake started laughing.

"Well, you better fucking game it up this weekend fool," Erik warned. "Cause you know we're getting all the loot, kicking ass, and saving the day."

The three of us laughed, and we started to move through and systematically clear the area while we waited for Jake to finish what he was doing. This was why I gamed. These were my people, and damn if I didn't fucking love these assholes.

* * *

That night, I had the dream about the voice again. It called, but I was just in a dark room. It sounded a lot closer than it ever had before, but I still couldn't make out every word. It was like trying to listen to a radio in the car when there are multiple stations broadcasting on the same frequency. The sound would cut in-and-out, and it got garbled in the rest of the sounds.

My alarm chirped at me from beside my head, and I woke up with a groan. All I had to do was make it through my shift, not let anyone die, and then come home to game with the boys. But first, the gym. I packed my work polo, khakis, fresh socks, and briefs in my bag, followed by a towel and dressed for success in some shorts and my Viking-inspired t-shirt that said something to the effect of, "Your prince is my prey."

The gym was only a half hour drive, so I threw some tunes onto my phone and let the bass of crashing metal smooth my still-curious mind and my nerves. I tried to shuffle my shoulders a bit to relieve a bit of the tension as the houses on the side of the road blurred by.

I parked my car in the gym lot and walked inside. A few people were there, some on the elliptical machines and treadmills. I waved to the manager, and she smiled back.

"Hey, man!" A stout guy about my height at five-foot-six with a *nice* beard, a faded haircut, and man-bun waved at me from behind the other side of the counter. "How's it going?"

"Not bad, Evan," I grinned at him and stuck a fist out. "How you doin'? Work okay? Has the gym been busy?"

Evan was the quietest of the group. That didn't mean he was shy or that he wasn't important; he just knew when the time was right to speak up. He was observant and thoughtful, most times, but when he did decide to join a conversation, you'd either laugh or have your mind blown. The guy knows his stuff and has a lot of passion for his hobbies and interests.

"I can't complain too much. Work is work, and you know how the gym gets this time of day. Though, I didn't sleep too well last night. I'm sure you know how that is. You usually have trouble sleeping, right?"

I nodded. It was true; between the dream and the nightmares that seemed more prevalent after the Corps, sleep was broken at best. At worst—I stayed asleep and had to endure what I was seeing.

"Yeah, that's what leg day is for, bud. Give the nightmares no chance to run!"

We both chuckled, and he pointed to my other buddy, skinny, fit, and funny as hell— that was Jake. They both wore their purple gym work shirts and khaki shorts, and you could tell they worked out. Jake's curly hair bounced as he walked around near the spray bottles with a jug. Somebody had to refill them, right?

"Yo, Jake!" I waved over to him and he smiled back. Every now and again, we would all meet up here and have a meeting of the minds. Usually about a new song from a favorite band, a new game, or the newest movie. We all had a lot in common—hence the friendship. He had the beginnings of bags under his eyes, some dark circles. Was there something going around or what?

"Whattup broham?" A resounding clap rang out from our high-five greeting. "Leg day?"

"In full effect, man." I grinned. Leg day was a personal favorite of mine; as much of a pain as others found it to be, I enjoyed the struggle.

The man had almost no trouble making conversation with anyone. Probably why we got along so well, having that in common. Well, that and an unhealthy love of quoting random songs, games, movies and other pop culture.

"Go get it!" He chuckled. "We can chat about that game between sets and see how best we can get Evan here all caught up. Maximum Effort!"

I gave him and his best friend a thumbs up before turning toward the free weights and smith machines. I loaded my favorite smith machine with a few forty-five-pound plates on each side and tightened my black weightlifting belt. With my lower back problems, it helped a lot to have it on while I squatted. Then I switched to the leg press machine, racked my usual dozen forty-fives, six on each side, and began my warm-ups.

After I was good and sore, then freshly showered, I spent the next eight hours at work. Never really a bad time. I liked my coworkers, helping people is worthwhile, and there are long stretches where I may not have to talk to anyone. It was downright lovely at times for a desk job.

Once work was complete and my relief had arrived, I was on my way home to play. Erik and I got Fox all caught up to us after several hours of turmoil and struggle before it was time to go to bed. It was my weekend, and I was planning to try and sleep as best as I could. Hell, I even threw in a couple of melatonin chews to keep me asleep. Well, at least, I hoped it would help a little bit. We would see how that turned out. I laid there on my bed, staring at the ceiling for a little while, surrounded by pillows and waiting for slumber to take me as it normally did.

Chapter Two

"Help us, traveler," the otherworldly and almost androgynous voice pleaded. *"Our world can yet be saved, but the window is closing. You must make your choice. Will you come?"*

I stood there, basked in a pale blue light, waiting for my phone's alarm to wake me up for a day of gaming and general tomfoolery with my friends—but it never rang.

Now, don't get me wrong, like everyone else I've dreamed most nights my whole life. In the last five years, ninety percent of them have been nightmares... Five percent of those are so bad that Freud would probably fudge his Huggies.

It felt like a weight just fell from my shoulders when I heard the voices plea.

Excuse me for feeling more than a little relieved and curious about a dream that was asking for my help. Even if it had seemingly been invading my other dreams. Okay, wait, that seemed creepy. The light began to pulse, and the thought fell away to curiosity. A whole world needs my assistance? Sure, I'll bite.

No sooner had I made that decision, the dream stopped.

"Oh, COME ON!" I snapped as I sat up, light from the sun hitting my eyes.

Wait... light?

I had curtains that blocked the light, not blackout curtains by any means, but sure as hell more than that. I blinked my eyes, and I was surrounded by the blue light.

"Am I still dreaming?" I asked out loud. This was already so different from anything I had ever experienced, and my nerves about crapped out on me that I might receive an answer.

"Welcome traveler," the voice greeted me. *"We have been watching you for some time and have been pleased to see that you are familiar with the ways of our world."*

I am? I thought. *Maybe I would learn more from being silent like my aunt and uncle had always said.*

"We believe you refer to them as video games?" the voice continued. *"If you will take a moment to think or speak the command 'status', a screen will appear and you can adjust your basic statistics."*

"Status."

Sure enough, an opaque screen and keyboard popped up in front of my eyes. The screen itself was mildly translucent. I could touch it and feel it, but it didn't move from its place in front of my eyes.

Name:
Race:
Level:
Strength:
Dexterity:
Constitution:
Intelligence:
Wisdom:
Charisma:
Unspent Attribute Points:

It seemed pretty straightforward, but I'd had some games come with different definitions on stats.

"Can I ask questions?" I asked aloud.

"We encourage it," the voice stated.

"Okay, what world?"

"*Brindolla.*"

Odd name, I thought. *Oh well, I've heard worse.*

"Can I see what each of the individual stats means?" I asked, then followed it up quickly with, "Like, an abbreviated explanation of what they affect?" I didn't need a ten-page explanation on how each one worked.

"Yes, we will also allow you to know that we calculated what we gathered from your life and experience into your statistics as well."

"Interesting," I mumbled quietly.

***Strength** – Allows the traveler to lift more weight, increases melee damage with certain types of weapons, and increases defense. Base strength increased by 3 for time spent working out and practicing close-quarters combat techniques.*

***Dexterity** – Allows traveler to move faster and dodge attacks more effectively. Also increases melee and ranged weapons damage and accuracy. No increase to base dexterity.*

***Constitution** – Directly affects how much damage the traveler can take before death. 1 point of constitution equates to 10 HP. Also affects endurance and susceptibility to poison and disease. Base constitution affects regeneration of HP (Hit Points) outside of combat. HP recovers at .01% per second. Shapeshifted forms benefit from base statistics as well. No increase to base constitution due to increased levels of sickness in recent times.*

***Wisdom** – Responsible for recovery of mana and mana pool for healers. 5 points of wisdom equate to 0.01% of mana recovered every 5 seconds and 10 mana for healers. Also, higher wisdom assists with the perception of traps and lies. May further affect certain types of spells. Base wisdom increased by 2 for life experience.*

Intelligence – Responsible for the potency of most spells and increases spell damage and mana pool. 1 point of intelligence equates to 10 mana for battle casters. Base intelligence increased by 2 for the pursuit of knowledge when required. Base intelligence increased by 3 for advanced knowledge of lore for unknown worlds and mythological creatures.

Charisma – Affects others perceptions of the traveler and how they will interact with them. Increases potency of certain spells and abilities. Base charisma increased by 3 due to a willingness to and successfully interacting with others.

I read and reread each of the explanations. It seemed I had a lot of caster heavy stats.

A caster, as a lot of my fellow gamers called them, was a player who specialized in spell casting. There are several different kinds of casters, most usually dealing heavy damage with little to no healing ability, which sounded like me, to be completely honest. I usually play some kind of sneak-thief assassin build or a fireball-slinging caster when I played online with my friends.

But I don't know if that's what I wanted this time through. May as well see what else there was to offer.

"What does it mean with the race space being blank?" I asked. Before the voice could respond, I tapped the prompt that said Race and looked through some of the ones available. There were a few that reached out to me right away.

"There are many different races and subraces amongst the denizens of this world, many of them are tolerant with each other, if not friendly. Although, there are those who would seek the rise of their own race above the others." The voice paused, as to let me digest the information before continuing, *"We have*

translated the names of certain races into names like those you may have seen before."

I nodded and kept looking. They were the races and subraces you might see in normal fantasy or role-playing games, commonly referred to as RPGs. Dwarves, Elves, Gnomes, Halflings, Humans, and Orcs; those seemed to be a majority of the populace of the world. Next to each race's name there was a percentage. Looked like humans were doing what they did best and populating the world, making up a solid forty-three percent.

I saw a couple that grabbed my attention, though.

Fae-Orc – Made by the coupling of nomadic Orcs and Elves who came together when the plains and forests met. Fae-Orcs are a seemingly perfect blend of their parents. They typically boast well-developed muscles and lithe bodies with strength Elves cannot claim naturally. They also seem to have an affinity for magic that Orcs rarely have. Fae-Orcs often sport oddly colored skin and have different racial abilities based on their parent's lineage. Relations: Fae-Orcs are well accepted by plains-roving tribes of Orcs, forest-dwelling Elves, and most humans and other races. They are seen as inferior by High Elves and Northern Orc tribes. Increase strength by 2 and intelligence by 1.

Kitsune – Fae by nature, this race is a humanoid fox who can shapeshift at will between human and fox forms (humanoid and true fox). Kitsune have strong affinities for magic and stealth, although some have been known to become exceptional warriors. Kitsunes' fur color may change depending on their environment and region. Relations: Kitsune are seen as kindred spirits by most Sylvan, Fae creatures, and by Nature itself. Elves will often live in harmony with their fox-like cousins, and Beast-kin treat them with respect as they seem to be like them. Humans are leery of them at times, especially in the countryside where they are rarely seen. Some hunters and Northern Orcs have been known to hunt Kitsune for their tails. Increase intelligence, dexterity or strength, and Charisma by 1.

Beast-kin – The result of magical experimentation on animals, Beast-kin have varying forms and often live in tribes. Beast-kin typically do not have strong ties to magic, as their beings were formed by it; however, newer generations are being born with more magical abilities and are recruited as tribe shamans and spiritual leaders. Beast-kin have strong bodies depending on their animal forms and high magical resistances. Relations: Beast-kin have strong ties to the Kitsune and Fae races who understand they didn't choose their existence. They often have treaties and trade agreements with plains Orcs and some Elven tribes. Humans seem to be accepting of them, but some hunt the Beast-kin or enslave them for their strength. Older Beast-kin are wary or even hostile toward mages. Increase strength, wisdom or dexterity, and constitution by 1.

These races and subraces seemed to have good depth. I was loving this so far. The Beast-kin seemed cool, but I was already leaning toward more magical means. Their hostility toward magic users seemed like I was asking for trouble. The Kitsune looked intriguing; being able to switch between forms and the bumps to my stats played into my favor. And the Fae-Orc? Man, they seemed awesome as well. The strength boost was unsettling. I could be a well- rounded individual with that. Depending on how the classes worked, I could metagame the hell out of this.

I tried to click back to the classes, but a red X popped up.

I guess I had to choose a race first. *Hmmm...* Well, I was already kind of strong, I think?

"Hey, voice," I said out loud, "what is the average stat?"

"If you mean how powerful someone might be, the average person will be around a ten in any given statistic. A knight or mercenary might have a higher constitution and strength, whereas a mage or shaman may have exceedingly high wisdom and intelligence."

"Ah, thank you."

"You are welcome, traveler."

I chuckled to myself and chose my race. I used some sliders on the status bar to shift some of my avatar's features. I moved the color for this back and forth; it was interesting to see how certain colors stood out and looked better than others. There were a few advanced options that I didn't much care for like scarring and any kind of ritualistic tattoos that some races may have, but I didn't want any kind of marking that I hadn't earned. You know? One thing was for certain and would probably never change—I did really have a thing for playing creatures with tails.

When I finalized my looks as much as my stats would allow, I moved over to the class options and began to scroll through.

Same as before, they were the ones that you would typically find in an RPG. You had your sword-swingers like the Barbarian and Fighter and your sneaky and dexterous Thief and Ranger with their daggers and bows. The caster classes had a few more options. The healer everyone tries to avoid— the cudgel carrying Cleric. Mage—your spell-slinging juggernaut with next to no life, a real glass cannon. Wizard, no not like the ones in the movies, these guys usually read from a spell book—think magical librarian who lost his job for burning the library down that one time. We don't talk about that.

There were two classes that really stuck out to me, though, almost on a personal level because I had a lot of love for them in other games I had played.

Bard, the literal jack-of-all-trades. These guys can be shifty, shady, and loud—all kinds of amazing if played right. They can use weapons, spells, and buffs to cause some serious mayhem on and off the battlefield. I had a guy in one of my tabletop gaming groups who used a bard with crazy high charisma to seduce a Dragon instead of fighting it. It was beautiful.

Whoa, whoa, whoa! I thought to myself as I looked over the next one. This was one I hadn't seen in a while in anything I had played.

Druid. Mother Nature's personal warrior. Tarzan with a pet at times and better smelling. Sometimes. Druids can do all kinds of great things: shapeshift into animals, cast spells, heal, and do some *serious* damage when they need to. I've known a couple people to play them, hell I had when I first discovered PC gaming.

Ah, those were the days.

A brief glimpse at the class overview and description confirmed what I had already known, but it also reiterated the fact that transformations benefit from base statistics. I didn't understand that, though, and I raised my query to the voice.

"If you were to transform yourself into a bear, which has a typical strength of fifteen for an average sized bear, then you would be almost as strong as the average bear with your current base strength. The same could be said if you were to transform into something that is dexterous like a forest cat. You would be less agile than an average one with a typical dexterity of thirteen. Your base statistics will reflect in your transformations."

"Wow," I said. Some possibilities came to mind, and I liked the way they were playing out in my head. I chose the Druid as my class and went back to the stat screen.

It appeared I had some choices to make. Down in the right-hand corner, I noted that I had ten attribute points to spend.

"How do attribute points work?" I asked before I went and screwed myself up on the start screen.

"You, and those like you, will be as newborn babes to this world. With that in mind, we have armed you with the means to increase your stats to a more reasonable level.

"Attribute points are gained upon reaching the next level. Most of the citizens of this world gain only two per level to spend freely while one point goes automatically to one of their racial statistics that they use the most. You, as a traveler, will receive five at each level. Also, statistics can be improved by reaching certain milestones, upon completion of certain events, or as quest rewards—although that is uncommon."

I nodded to myself and got started. I pressed the strength stat and bumped it up by two. Next, constitution went up by five. Couldn't have someone one shot me, you know? That left me three points to play with. I grumbled to myself and finally decided to evenly distribute the last three points into dexterity, wisdom, and charisma.

That left me looking pretty good, especially after my racial bonuses.

Name:
Race: Kitsune
Level: 1
Strength: 15
Dexterity: 12

Constitution: 15
Intelligence: 16
Wisdom: 13
Charisma: 15
Unspent Attribute Points: 0

There was still the not-so-small matter of my name. I had a name I used for everything. Every time I played a character in a game, it was always my moniker. *Why change the formula*, I thought to myself. I selected the name tab, and a keyboard popped onto my status screen. I typed it in: "Zekiel Erebos". Then I hit enter. There, all done with that bit.

"So, what's the premise of this game, Voice?" I asked as I cycled through the settings to change some of the aspects of my avatar. I decided on one for my fur and my eyes. Excellent, this was going to be awesome.

"War has found my world." The voice took on a lighter, more feminine lilt and tone. *"I am the goddess Radiance, and I will be responsible for caring for the travelers. Throughout the time that we have become aware of this threat, we have evolved our world and its people to mirror facets of the video games from your world. We used some of the ones produced over the last few decades so that we might find better-suited champions. Thank you for accepting our request for aid, traveler."*

"Damn, this is one hell of a game," I muttered to myself. "What of the other gods? Where are they?"

"They watch over the world and prevent War from coming here directly while the travelers amass their strength. This is no game, traveler. It is the fate of my people. Please, save them from War."

"What?!" I shouted the question, but the voice was gone. The darkness claimed me.

* * *

I sprang to my feet as soon as my eyes were open. I looked around and slowly sank to the floor. The truth had come to light.

I was in another world.

This clearly wasn't my room. It was a *much* nicer room with wooden panels for walls and oak floorboards. The bed was a mat with what felt like fresh straw inside it and a simple, green wool blanket. The furnishings were all wooden as well. A small desk and chair in the corner with a window view—the whole room was a comfortable sixteen by thirteen feet and filled with a sweet scent of straw. The smell was so strong it was almost suffocating.

I saw a wooden chest at the foot of the bed and went to go for it when I caught a glimpse of the mirror near the doorway. The face staring back in horror and awe was my avatar's.

It—I—was a couple inches taller than I had been back home—five feet, eight inches with broad shoulders, a waist narrower than I had seen in years—like when I had just come back from boot camp narrow. I had muscle and looked like some of the bodybuilders I had envied growing up.

I mean... lifting the way I did, usually five times a week and for a couple hours at a time, I would never reach this kind of definition on my own. I was used to being strong and not cut, but this was nuts—I'd need a kick-ass trainer to reach this level.

Oh, did I mention I had a tail? I set about trying to wag it. It moved, the air causing the fur to wave like a flag, and I lost my mind. Don't hate.

I'm not proud, but it's what happened.

I looked again, noticing the black fur coating my body. It was sleek, and there was a slightly blue-tinted highlight when the light hit it. I looked to see if my choice of eye coloring had stuck, electric blue—so blue it was crazy—almost like they glowed.

My facial features were vulpine—a short muzzle with whiskers, sharp teeth like a fox's, and ears on top of my head. I could smell everything: the bed, the wood in the room, the musty scent in the air. I could hear more than I ever could in real life. The birds chirped and sang outside, and I heard a clanging and awed voices in hushed tones in what had to be other rooms.

I clacked my teeth together and practiced making different facial expressions. Smiling was equally funny and scary depending on the look in my eyes. I could pull my ears back and snarl almost convincingly, but it was going to take practice to refine the look. I closed my eyes and hoped that it would work, the last thing that could possibly go wrong.

"Testing. Testing one two," I said aloud. YES! Okay, I could talk. Time to test out the one ability I had. I closed my eyes.

"Shift!"

I watched the mirror intently and grunted. Nothing had changed. I may or may not have spent ten minutes trying to get the ability to work, but nothing I did seemed to get me to switch between my forms.

Oh, well that's some bull. Can't be overly picky, though, can we? I suppose that it might be unlocked later like in certain game tutorials that lock abilities until they're most useful. Moving on—time to see what's in the box.

As I was turning to look back at the chest, I noticed a small blip pulsing in the bottom right corner of my vision, and when I focused on it, an opaque screen sprang into existence before me.

> **ERROR!**
> *You have not yet unlocked the desired skill or ability that you are attempting to use. Further attempts are futile until you meet the required criteria.*
> *Criteria unknown at this time.*

I huffed a bit, but I guess I could be happy that my suspicions had been confirmed rather than simply going through an area blind. I'd done that before, and it had never been all that pretty. Knowing prerequisites were important, and it always helped to be conscious of them. Still, I could focus on that later. I looked toward the foot of the bed and rubbed my greedy mitts together as I stepped toward the chest.

I opened the chest, and some clothes were inside. A well-made, crème-colored tunic, brown breeches, and a black belt. Luckily, I had woken up with some small clothes on—basically, this world's version of boxers. My breeches even had a slit in the rear for my tail to fit comfortably through. I wagged it in appreciation. Gods, I will never get tired of that. I dressed and saw that the clothes provided no armor, but they covered me; that's what mattered, for now.

Next, I pulled out a large axe, a sturdy, wooden handle with leather bound around it for grip and the chopping portion of the thing about half the size of my head. It reminded me of the axe I used to chop wood for my uncle when I was a kid.

> **Beginner's Axe**
> *+2 to attacks with this weapon*
> *Also can be used to chop trees*
> *Weight: 10 Lbs*
> *A gift to the traveler from the Gods. Use it wisely.*

If the item descriptions were like this, the items alone would be worth collecting. I opened my menu to see if there was an equipment tab—which there was. I opened it up and equipped the Beginner's Axe. The axe shifted from my hand to my belt and hung there within easy reach. When I walked a bit, the haft bobbed and thumped my leg, but it wasn't uncomfortable. I practiced bending and moving in different ways to see if there was any discomfort or lack in range of motion; there didn't seem to be.

After that, I found a coin about the size of my palm at the bottom next to some boots that I put on. They felt great like they were crafted just for me. When I picked up the coin, the status screen popped up on its own.

Token of Radiance

Quest Item: Bring the token to your class trainer for beginner level training. Warning: All magic and combat abilities locked until training begins.

QUEST ALERT: ALL ABOARD THE NEWB TRAIN: Find your trainer to begin your walk in this world.

Reward: Class Training, 10 Experience points, 5 coppers

Huh, class training? Okay. Maybe that was why I couldn't shift? I thought to myself and shrugged. Again, things were making sense; it was just taking me longer than normal to understand. No wonder I got murdered in my sleep regularly. If I always acted like this, I'd be easy pickings. Not in this dream, though.

I checked the bottom of the chest and pulled out what had to be a sack of coins. It disappeared when I put it into my inventory. Five hundred gold had found its way into the funds portion of my inventory. Now, if this played like a normal game, there would be a ratio: a certain number of copper coins per silver, a certain number of silver to a gold coin, and so on.

If my suspicions were right, it was probably one hundred to the next coin. So, a hundred coppers to the silver and the same to gold.

If that was the case, daddy struck gold, boys and girls. No pun intended.

That was some serious cash to toss at a noob, even one with prior gaming experience. This must have been pretty serious. Then again, these were gifts from the gods themselves. They could probably afford to toss some chump change to someone who is needy and greedy like me.

But if they needed us to be so strong, why not just give travelers the best gear? I'm sure there's a reason.

I reached back into the box, sweeping my hand back and forth in case I missed anything—empty. I looked myself over in the mirror. The black fur of my body seemed to work well with the crème color of the tunic tucked into the brown breeches. The boots were black and matched my belt. I practiced my smile again and opened the door of the room.

The hallway was a little wider than your average one, large enough for two people to walk side by side. I moved down the hallway; my room was the last door on the right-hand side. There was a wall that matched flush with mine to my right, so it wasn't a secret room. Nothing sounded ominous in the place, and I could smell something that made my stomach gurgle and told me I needed to eat.

I walked down the hallway, slowly but not to the point where it looked like I was afraid.

First impressions, right, I thought sarcastically. *Gotta be the big guy adventurer, Head Honcho, Chief Traveler and all that. Can't go into the lion's den like a dumb lamb and expect not to come out naked and bleeding—or dead.* I had a sneaking suspicion that wouldn't be the case today. I hoped.

There were five doors on this side of the hallway. A few were ajar, but the final one was closed. I continued on into the medium sized room the hallway led to. Tables and chairs were strewn throughout. A small group of people stood at the bar chatting with the barman.

"Ah!" The bartender, a human man who looked to have seen some years and a healthy amount of sun, smiled wider and waved me over. "We have another. One more to go, and we can truly begin."

He looked over to the three individuals at the bar before him and continued to wipe down the mug in his hand, his gray eyes sparkling. I could see he was a good six feet tall and would've had a serious set of muscles in his younger days, but he seemed good natured. His gray hair was pulled back into a ponytail, he had a small reddish-gray beard, and I could make out a single scar along the right side of his face that started at his hairline and fell to his chin.

"Begin what?" I asked nervously as I walked over and joined the group. I'd since lost all of my first-impressions-are-everything swagger and tried to hold my now-jittery nerves in check.

The first figure to turn my way wore a blood-red robe. He dropped the cowl, and I could see his gray skin and long, shaggy, white hair over yellow eyes, high cheekbones, and pointed ears for the first time.

"No way, dude," said the figure in a voice I knew all too well. My brother-from-another-mother was here. He was in my dream!

"Erik!" I shouted and bolted over to pull him into a bear hug.

We both laughed, and I stepped back to look him over again. He had a slight build in real life, but don't let that fool you; he was fast and works out with a single-minded purpose every day. He's also my go-to for a lot of the newest games and reviews. He's the gaming guru I never knew I needed. He stayed true to himself and kept his avatar close to his real height of five-foot-six.

"Yohsuke, fool," he joked and strutted imperiously. "Jake and Evan are here too."

As he said their names, I looked over, and sure enough, the other two were standing there with huge grins.

"Hey, Broski," said the tall, lanky Elf who looked like he had hypothermia. I recognized his voice and mannerisms as my buddy Jake. "Long time, no see."

This just kept getting more and more unreal. I had just seen them earlier.

The Elf stepped forward, and we clasped hands. His pale blue skin was wrapped in black animal fur with traces of white streaking through hanging out of tan breeches. He had a bow slung over one shoulder and a quiver at his hip. Long, black hair graced the top of his head, with the sides cleanly shaven; the color was a startling contrast between his icy blue eyes and his hair. On his other shoulder perched what could easily be more hair, but it moved and "mrowed" at me.

"Tmont came with me," Jake said giving her a pat, and the little cat purred, closing her bright green eyes.

"That's awesome, man." I clapped him on the shoulder, and Tmont swatted at me. I loved that cat.

Evan stepped forward, and I pretty much started to fangirl right then. He was a Dwarf, but not just a run-of-the-mill one—Evan had chosen a Fire Dwarf as his avatar. He stood about four and a half feet tall, with a wide, stocky build under a singed, hooded cloak draped over him. The tanned skin was complemented well by the black and purple flames streaming from his chin and his head that looked like hair and a beard. He had given his avatar a scar over his left eye—it didn't hinder his sight from what I could see—and the fiery, green eyes that stared back at me sparkled with amusement.

The man could make an avatar, alright?

Did I mention my tail?

"What the hell are you guys?" I asked incredulously. *What other awesome races did I miss, or was this a 'they're limitless because it's only a dream and I haven't let my mind go to experience it fully' kind of deal?* I let that thought go and listened to my friend.

"I'm Yohsuke, the Abomination Spell Blade," my gray friend declared proudly. He brandished what looked to be a broken katana hilt in the air as he laughed.

"I'm Bakoj, the Ice Elf Ranger featuring Tmont," said Jake, striking a heroic pose that dumped his furry partner in a graceless pile on the floor. The tiny cat growled indignantly and stalked away. "Sorry, T."

"I would be Balmur, an Azer Rogue." Evan ducked into a pretty sweet battle position, plucking his dual hand axes into his grasp from under his cloak.

"And I'm Jaken Warmecht, a Fae-Orc Paladin of Radiance," stated a proud voice behind me.

I whirled around, and sure enough, there was a burly, six-and-a-half-foot-tall man. The guy looked the spitting image of my friend Jake, well Jaken—because that's what his real name actually was. Except his skin was purple, and his hair was as black as midnight. He even had the goatee and mustache combo he liked to sport back home. Even though we had just been gaming together, I was glad my friend could be in this world.

"Get over here, you hazel-eyed freak of nature!" I shouted. He complied and lifted me effortlessly off the ground.

We laughed as he playfully swung me back and forth as I patted him on the back. Then I felt a sharp pain in my tail and looked down to see an angry, black ball chomping on me.

"I'm not a feather duster, you furry ass!" I grunted as Jaken squeezed.

"Come on, T." The little monster's owner grabbed her, and I pulled away as she let go.

"This is the craziest dream I've ever had, bro." Erik shook his head.

"This is no dream, Yohsuke," said the bartender.

He set down his rag and the mug before taking his apron off and stepping out from behind the bar. He pointed us to a table in the middle of the room that had seemingly magically filled with food.

"Sit and eat," he advised. "We have much to discuss, and I don't want to have to speak over grumbling stomachs from you all."

We all complied; even Tmont had his own bowl of food. While we ate, the bartender explained.

* * *

Essentially, the threat to his world was real. Very real, and the only reason Radiance herself wasn't here to explain it was because she was needed to protect the barrier that kept War out. War, the great destroyer of worlds who sends minions of his army forth to weaken entire solar systems so he could enslave each planet at his leisure. Sounded pretty odd to me, pretty unreal.

"For now, the gods of this world have kept the worst of the horde out, but they can only last so long, and some are starting to slip through," he said at last. "With you lot here,

Radiance and her siblings can keep the barrier active while you hunt down the rabble who managed to sneak through."

After a minute, Evan looked up from the table and said, "If this guy is some eater of worlds, what can *we* do?"

It wasn't like all of us hadn't thought the same thing. Evan just had the courage to say what had to be said first.

"I'm Sir Willem Dillon." The bartender smiled and brought himself to his feet. He leaned up against the table with both hands and whispered, "I am a Paladin in service to Her Light, Radiance, and we have a plan. Follow me."

We all stood and marched for the back room, the Paladin leading the way with confidence in his steps. Once inside the cramped space, the older man closed the door, and a bright flash of pale blue light arced from door to wall.

"Now, no one can hear us," he growled. "Can never be too careful."

We all looked at him expectantly, and after a couple of seconds, he started from his thought by clearing his throat.

"When he arrives at a world, the gods are too weakened from fighting the spies and vanguard to be able to push him back or crush him. So he comes in, crushes all remaining resistance, and takes over." He chuckled slightly in spite of his apparent anger. "It's an ingenious strategy, really, monster that he is. He mops up and then enslaves the populace to feed his war machine. Turns whole planets into members of his ever-growing army, but against Radiance and the other gods at next to full strength?"

Realization dawned on us. If they were fit to fight, War might get his comeuppance.

"But why us, if all it takes is someone strong to beat these guys?" I shook my head a bit in disbelief. "You should have been able to wipe the map completely before it became an issue. Right?"

"If the bastards hadn't gone for the strongest and bravest of us first, yeah, we might have," he said quietly. "When they arrived, our best fighters were at the fore of the battlefield. Strongest there was. A whole army. All of them wiped out because the things were working together and still coming. That's when the gods sealed the world. There was a reckoning, oh be certain of that."

He paused to collect himself, as if reliving a terrible nightmare. The pain on his face visible to all.

"The gods were swift and brutal. They tore a huge swath of the creatures apart even as their numbers began to overrun our own. We thought they had turned the tide, but then stronger ones came, as if they were waiting for that exact thing to happen." He sniffed. "They destroyed what remained after the gods had left to focus on keeping the whole slew of War's creatures at bay. After, they scattered to do their bloody work sowing discord and hate, killing where they could but not too much. They were perfectly content to bide their time. They raise minions of their own and send them to conquer in their name until the job is done."

"And now here we are to try our hand, yeah?" asked Jaken.

The man nodded as he wiped his nose. Overcome with grief, a couple of tears fell from his eyes, but he ignored them otherwise.

"If we fall here, there is nothing to stop him from reaching your own world," Sir Willem Dillon said, after a moment. "With all that has been going on there, I can't say for sure that his minions aren't already at work, but it's at least a chance."

I could see how his statement was valid, but all I could think about was my son. Young, adorable, strong, and adventurous. He got all the good looks, and I'm not even mad about it. If I was going to do anything for him, it was going to have to be this. A knot began to form in my stomach, kind of like the nervous tangle of emotions you get before doing something mildly dangerous and stupid but also possibly fun.

I looked around the table and saw some of the same realization hit everyone. Jaken rose to his feet, a solemn but determined look on his face that I wasn't used to seeing there.

"I'm in," he said. "I'm not the best when it comes to these types of games—you all know that—but I've got people I love back home. I'm going to fight for them."

We all nodded in agreement. We would fight, and we would win, or gods knew what would happen to our families.

"Good," the bartender said simply. "For now, we have time. We will get you training, then get you out into the world to gather strength and face the evil that has befallen our land." He looked at us all steadily. "Once you do what you can, we can get you home."

We left the tiny room and gathered back around the table we had eaten at before. Sir Dillon told each of my friends where they might find their trainers. Turns out, he was actually Jaken's trainer, which was more than a little convenient.

He looked at me as my friends left. "Your trainer will be in the forest east of this village. If you open your map, you'll see the indicator on it. There may not always be one, but if you look at your compass, the red arrow shows your direction and the green shows the direction you need to head. Match the two, and you'll get there."

"What's my trainer like?" I asked. I imagined some grizzled, old hermit, living alone in the forest close to a swamp.

"I don't know," he said with a shake of his head, "but whoever it is, you belong to them for a week. Learn swiftly."

We both walked outside, and the whole group stood there in awe. I knew why, too; the place was beautiful. Green trees of varying types littered the surroundings, and people from all races gathered and mingled amongst stalls and shops. I didn't see any Kitsune, but I guess we stuck to more magical lands or deeper forests near Elven colonies.

I saw surly-looking Dwarves hawking their wares to Beast-kin—great, towering, bear-like men carrying supplies into a store off to my right, but they weren't just bears. I saw some wolf-kin and other species of Beast-kin working and humans together, too. The town was bustling, and I couldn't remember ever feeling such wonder in my recent adult life.

Small children ran and played together: human, Dwarf, and Beast-kin. There was no judgement or segregation that I could see. It was beautiful.

"See you guys later," I said after a glance at my compass. I turned so that the red and green arrows matched, then headed off to meet my trainer.

* * *

I walked for about an hour before I reached the indicator on my map. I called out into the empty woods for a couple minutes, hoping to draw my trainer's attention, before deciding to just have a seat and wait. The sounds of the forest came and went throughout the few minutes I sat there. The sun felt great on my fur, and I guess I dozed off.

I woke up to the sound of silence.

That's odd, I thought to myself and stood.

I stretched and looked around. Whenever the forest full of noisy animals got quiet in the movies, it meant there was some big bad nearby. I pulled my axe from my belt and searched the tree line. I couldn't see anything, but I had forgotten the crucial flaw of being the supposed apex predator on my own world.

A sleek black panther dropped from the tree above where I had been napping. The muscles on the big cat coiled with contained aggression. It paced around me in a slow circle, looking me over almost appraisingly. It eyed me with emerald-green orbs, the deadliest gems I'd ever seen.

The panther sat down and began to lick a paw, seemingly losing interest in me as fast as it had arrived. I took a tentative step closer to the creature. In the light, I could see lighter markings in the black fur that looked almost like a leopard's spots.

"Are you my trainer?" I asked in wonder. Would I be able to be as deadly as the creature before me?

"What would Sharo teach you, cousin?" said a sweet voice behind me.

I turned to see a lean Elf sitting in the tree to my right. I really needed to start looking up. "I was told to come here to receive training," I said as I fished the coin out of my inventory. I held it up to the light.

She dropped out of the tree and walked toward me with confidence and grace. Her lithe body moved so well, and the green tunic and trousers she wore moved as if painted on her skin. She wore no boots, which struck me as odd, but oh well.

I offered the coin to her, and she took it. As soon as it cleared my outstretched fingers, it glowed like a beacon. She gasped, and her body went rigid. I didn't hear a thing, but the panther sprung and knocked me onto my stomach. I felt the crushing weight of a paw on my upper back, and Sharo growled menacingly into the back of my neck. I could feel his teeth just there on my skin.

"SHARO, RELEASE HIM!" the Elf cried. Sharo backed off, startled, and lunged to her side. He stood on his rear legs and sniffed her, checking to see if she was injured.

He attacked because he was worried for her. I rubbed the back of my neck where he had held my life in his jaws. I felt the indents and a slight slickness. I brought my hand away and saw crimson on the small fur surrounding my pads. I confirmed, with my HP bar, that a little health had been taken.

"You are a traveler?" she said in wonder. She swiped the great cat out of her way and walked toward me. I felt my whiskers bend a bit as she touched my cheek. I leaned back as she leaned toward me. She seemed to be trying to see into me, as if I was a pond with hidden treasure at the bottom.

"Yes," I said slightly embarrassed at her sudden closeness.

She suddenly swept me into a hug so tight that I grunted and wondered how she hadn't broken a rib. She laughed. Her smile was as dazzling as the sun reflecting on a pond. She let me go and danced away. Sharo looked confused, but he played along and started to bounce around her and rub against her legs.

She stopped and looked at me again. "This is good. I was so worried for the forests and beasts of this world, but Lady Radiance has delivered our hope at last!" She smiled again and beckoned me to come closer.

"I will awaken your dormant Druidic power. Come." She had me sit in the middle of the clearing. "Close your eyes."

I did as she asked. Her slender hand on the top of my head shifted my fur aside and settled against my scalp. She began to whisper in a language I had never heard before. It sounded like a series of natural sounds: a growl, a snort, the babbling of a brook, and a whoosh of air.

A screen popped into view behind my eyelids.

Secret language learned: Druidic – the language of nature herself, all of nature's bounty understand the language.

"–Lady, mother of the wilds. Defender of the downtrodden prey and sacred master of the predator. This lone wolf wishes to join your pack. He wants to protect the bounty of your lands from the evils that pervert your creatures, those who drive them mad and enslave them. He will seek them and destroy them for you, in your name. Will you grant him your strength and grace? Will you relinquish your secrets to him?"

I hoped for the best and whispered, "Please. I want to help."

I felt warmth blossom in my chest and travel throughout my body. I could hear the trees gently swaying, moaning, and their leaves tickling the breeze. I could feel the comfort of the earth beneath me and the warmth of the sun for what felt like the first time. The animals all around the clearing seemed to find something nearby fascinating because they grew louder and louder until it was almost deafening.

There, amongst all the chatter and emotion in the forest around me, I heard it—a voice that sounded like a hundred breezes through a thousand leaves, an aged tone with an almost-frightening level of wisdom but still soft with tender love. I felt it more than heard it, my entire being enveloped in this soft, nurturing embrace that stated one thing.

"Welcome, my child."

I opened my eyes at last and saw that Sharo was sitting in front of me, but rather than his emerald green eyes, I saw violet and gold. It was nature herself looking back at me, her ancient wisdom pressed against my mind almost like a physical force. It was like water lapping up against me, soothing but a reminder of the deep pool I had dipped my feet into, like anything could be lurking beneath those waters and I might never be the wiser. It wasn't necessarily a bad feeling, oddly enough. It helped me know my place and gave me something to strive for—survival.

Then he blinked and his eyes were normal, and the pressure was gone.

The great panther bounced again and head-butted my shoulder in welcome.

"Welcome, brother." I looked up and saw the Elf looking down at me with pride.

She offered me a hand up, and I took it. The forest around us just seemed so much more alive. I couldn't believe how unaware I had been before.

I saw my notifications screen flashing at me, so I opened it up.

CONGRATULATIONS TRAVELER – You have unlocked the Class of Druid.

With the power of Nature's might, you can make your stand as a champion for the realm. Quest Completed: 10 Exp and 5 copper gained.

New Abilities Available

Shapeshift – Take on the shape and fighting capabilities of the form you choose. Restrictions: shapes are acquired in two ways: the Druid must have fought the animal or touched the animal for an extended period of time (2 minutes) in order to shapeshift into that animal, with the exception of any forms the Druid could take naturally otherwise due to racial abilities or traits. Base stats affect the transformation. Cool Down: 1 minute. Restrictions: Cannot shift from one animal form to another. Shapeshifting must occur from the Druid's natural form. Caster is restricted to certain types of creatures: no mythical or legendary creatures, no creatures not of the Prime Plane. (These restrictions can be lowered or nulled at higher levels or by meeting certain criteria.) Note: Any and all worn gear—to include weapons—and inventory items will be magically set aside for the Druid in animal form. They will return as worn upon returning to the Druid's natural form.

Animal companion – Acquire an animal companion through the "Nature's Bond" spell. A companion will assist the Druid however it can, in combat or otherwise. Restrictions: Only one companion can be had at a given time, and the bond last's until the Druid chooses to end the bond or the companion dies.

New Blessings Available

Nature's Love – Nature herself has decreed that you are of her children. Natural animals and creatures of nature will be less likely to attack unprovoked. Some of Nature's children will be willing to offer aid however they can.

Nature's Bounty – Nature herself has seen the importance of your mission and has bestowed her ultimate gift to you. Cool Down for shapeshifting waived. (Cool Down is zero seconds.) Increased experience shared through Nature's Bond with Animal Companion both ways. 25% EXP per kill increased to 50% per kill.

The last one seemed pretty amazing, if I said so myself. That meant my future pet and I might be able to level a little faster together.

The Elf and her friend watched me from the shade of the tree I had been under. They must have moved there while I was reading over the new abilities I had acquired. I winced, wondering how slow I had been, but she didn't seem to mind.

"I am Dinnia, and this is my companion, Sharo," Dinnia said, indicating herself then the panther. "We are the protectors of this forest, and now, we are also your trainers."

"Great," I said smiling. "Thank you. What should we learn first?"

"I will begin by teaching you how to take the form of an animal," she said as she beckoned me over to the shaded area.

We sat, and she talked me through the process. It seemed simple enough: just think of the animal I wanted to take the form of and will the change to occur.

"Don't I need to touch an animal or fight one to take the form of it?"

"You already have." She laughed and pointed to Sharo who hid his nose behind his massive paws.

"That was more like a surprise attack, but if you think it counts." I laughed and closed my eyes, trying to form an image of Sharo in my mind. Once I had it firmly envisioned, I willed myself to shift.

I felt warmth for a split second before the change came. I was sitting in front of my trainer but looking down at her from a little bit higher perspective. I looked down at myself and saw that it had worked! I was now a panther a little smaller than Sharo. Sharo looked and felt like he weighed about four hundred pounds, and I probably weighed around two hundred and fifty and reached about seven to eight inches shy of his massive five-foot height. His fur was a little lighter than mine, as well. Where his had a faint hint of spots, mine was just midnight black like my own fur.

I stood and paced around, assuming I would have difficulty moving, but I didn't. This form felt as natural as simply walking through the forest normally.

Sweet! None of that lanky, awkward teenage phase for me! I noted that there was another notification and opened it with a thought.

Abilities Unlocked

Kitsune Shapeshifting – Take the form of an anthropomorphic fox, human with similar features, or a fox as your natural shape. Transformations are indefinite until the Kitsune chooses to change forms. Each of these forms is considered a natural form, as all are the Kitsune. (All clothing, worn items, and gear remain a part of the Druid while in fox form.)

So this was how that had come about? Weird. Maybe I had needed to actually shapeshift before it came about, or was it because I had accomplished the prerequisites needed to unlock the ability? What if I had been a Paladin or a Rogue? How about a Ranger?

I shifted back—a lot easier of a process than that first shift had been—and raised the question to my mentor.

"Some abilities, like shapeshifting, do require that certain criteria be met," she explained patiently. "As the Kitsune are racially considered cousins to the Elves, I think I may know how you were restricted, but I'm not an expert so it may be an incomplete explanation. For the Kitsune to be able to transform for the first time, they need to unlock another ability. I think it has something to do with their trickster nature, children running off or playing as foxes and being hunted. The god of the Elves—and this is where it gets a bit fuzzy for me—put a condition on their ability to change form until they were mature enough to gain skills and abilities to protect themselves."

I could understand that to some degree. I still didn't see why that had meant crap to me, since I had *chosen* the race, but you couldn't expect the gods to drop something as heavy as a racial requirement on an ability for a single person, right?

I shook my head and thought to myself, *Listen to me wax philosophical over some rules. Bah, get on with your training, kick some ass, and get home. Kind of stupid that all we had to go on was, 'Hey do this thing for us, and it will save your people too—oh, and we'll get you home.' We had all volunteered for this. How bad could it be?*

I nodded once more, then shifted back into my panther form a lot faster this time.

Sharo looked over at me and seemed pleased by the representation. Dinnia clapped and smiled.

"Follow me!" She shifted into a wolf about the same size as Sharo.

Her fur was a motley of browns and grays streaked with black patches. She looked back at me with her normal green eyes, barked, and then took off to our left. It looked like we were heading further east.

I could tell that—even though we were moving quickly—Dinnia could have gone faster. She was allowing me the opportunity to get used to the speed I had at my disposal. No matter how natural it felt, practice would make perfect.

After a couple hours of running and a couple of rest stops for me, we arrived at what I assumed was the destination: a large ruin. It looked like it was a castle of some sort, but it had been destroyed, or at least, at one point, it had been attacked and left to the weather and time. The walls looked decrepit with piles of rubble strewn everywhere. Vines grew all over the walls that were strong enough to support them. If the outside looked this rough and overgrown, the inside must be worse.

"This old ruin was where Lady Radiance stationed her knights and Paladins," Dinnia explained. "We won't be going any closer, as you aren't yet ready to face the enemies who lie in wait."

"What happened?" I asked. I tried to see if I could see any of the enemies she spoke of but got nothing. Lame.

"About a century ago, when the dark forces initially struck, they took to the holiest places after slaughtering our best." She indicated the castle with her hand. "This was one such place. The General of the Sword, one of the great beasts who slaughtered our strongest warriors, took this castle and left his minions in his place as he continued to go about his foul mission of desecrating our world."

Hmmm... how did that make sense, though? If it was only minions, why didn't the locals just take care of them and take the place back?

"So, wait," I began and rubbed my temples a bit, "if you know that they're here, why not just go in and take care of it yourselves? You are much more powerful than me. With the other trainers, you, and Sharo, you could go in there and kick some serious tail."

"Were you not informed of our issue?" she asked incredulously. After I shook my head, she just sighed and looked up to the sky. "My people, native Brindollans, cannot go near them for two reasons. One being that if we are near them, they can sense us. Once they inhabit a world, they seem to grow accustomed to the people of it and use this to hide themselves. Two, if they so choose, the stronger ones can drive even the most stalwart warriors mad and bend them to their will. Some places like this will be crawling with minions of the dark; others may have men and women, children even, carrying weapons and guarding them."

My jaw dropped a bit at the fact that, since we weren't from here and we weren't here when they came, we were essentially invisible to their senses. Well, they could see us, I'm sure, but we would have a definite advantage. *Wait, there has to be some kind of catch.*

"Won't they get used to us as well?" I asked as doubt reared its ugly head.

"A working theory is that, with there being so few of you and so many of us, we act as a kind of cloak for you. We hide you from them by existing."

"So... what? Do I just head on in there and try to whoop some darkie butt?"

She laughed. "No. At least not until you and the rest of the travelers are ready. Lady Radiance believes that you all might be able to do it at a higher level."

"Well, how do we get that ball rolling?" I asked, slightly nervous but excited to try some things out.

"We fight what we can fight," she said. "The 'Darkies,' as you have called them, have enraged some of the animals here and driven them insane due to their close proximity. These insane animals are not like normal creatures, so you must be cautious. We will hunt and kill those animals until either you are strong enough to go into the castle or the week runs out. The others will be going to the inn nightly. You will not. My training will be harsh. I hope you are ready."

"Sounds like fun," I said as I stretched my back. "Let's get started."

Chapter Three

Our first encounter was with a wolf eating a rabbit in a nearby copse of trees. It only weighed as much as a German shepherd. The poor thing was foaming at the mouth, and its fur was matted and caked in blood and dirt.

I watched it closely for a while. After about a minute or so, the level and health bar popped up over its head and body. **Insane Wolf Level 2 with 80 HP.**

Not a bad monster to sharpen my teeth on. I was going to shapeshift but figured I should get comfortable fighting on two legs first, to see what my capabilities were. So far, a lot of what I did seemed natural, though in my world, it would be far from it.

I stepped into the clearing, my eyes glued on the wolf, and the rest of the world fell away. My palms began to sweat a bit, and my vision narrowed, excluding my surroundings except for the wolf. I was focusing too much; I needed to pull it back and be aware, so I glanced around and used my peripheral vision to see if I could catch anything out of the ordinary. Nothing seemed amiss.

I pulled out my axe slowly and crouched down. I walked as silently as I could behind it, trying to sneak like I would have if I were playing a Rogue class. It seemed to be working well so far. I was about four feet away when it went still. I stopped and slowed my breathing to the point where it almost felt like I wasn't.

After what felt like forever, the wolf went back to its meal. When I finally snuck close enough to attack, I slowly widened my stance and reared back to swing my axe overhead like I would chop wood. At the halfway point in my downswing, the wolf spooked, and I only scored a shallow hit on the rear leg.

It whipped around and snarled at me before it lunged. Somehow, I managed to put the handle of the axe between me and the wolf, and it snapped at the wood for all it was worth. A quick glance at its health bar told me about ten percent of the wolf's health was gone. I pushed to the left a bit, then snatched the axe back to the right to dislodge the handle from the toothy prison. I only had a split second before the wolf was lunging at me again. This time I swung the axe like a golf club and just aimed for the wolf's nose. Never was one for golf; I sucked at it.

The wolf was too consumed by its desire to kill me to really care about the axe, so I got my hit in; bad news was that it wasn't the cutting edge. The back portion of the axe clocked the wolf in the head, and it went down in a heap. With it stunned and laying there helpless, I lined myself up for my original shot. I brought the axe down with all my might, and the wolf's life bar dropped to nothing.

25 EXP gained.

I felt bad for the poor creature, but I knew there was nothing that could be done. Maybe if my friends and I could get those darkies out of the castle, the wildlife would return to normal here. The wolf didn't drop anything but experience. I was okay with that. I just wanted to let him rest in peace.

I turned, and there were three more sets of eyes watching me—none of them belonged to Dinnia and Sharo. Three more Insane Wolves came from the bushes in front of me—all level 2 and at the same health as the first. Shit, this was gonna hurt.

They lunged together, and all I could think to do was to drop as they jumped.

Shit.

As soon as they got within my range, they were already mid leap, so I dropped onto my back and brought the blade of my axe to bear. I caught the middle one in the stomach on its way over. The axe went deeper than I thought it might, and the muscle and flesh caught the lip at the bottom of the weapon wrenching it out of my hands. Shit, shit, shit...

I rolled to my feet just in time to dodge the one on my right, but lefty got me on my forearm as I set my feet. The pain was very real. It hurt like hell, and it threw me over the edge of my calm. I roared angrily and gouged my thumb into the crazy animal's right eye until I felt it give, and the beast let go.

I scrambled back a bit to try and create some room, but they stalked forward. I settled for keeping them in my line of sight and shapeshifted into my panther form. I roared angrily and barreled my way to them. The one with my axe still in his stomach was on the ground dazed and only had about sixty percent HP left, so I started with him. I dropped onto him with both my front paws and started to batter him. Each smack of my paw brought him down about fifteen percent; four swipes put him out of the fight.

The other two tried to harass me while my back was turned—nipping and biting at me—but they never did anything more than five percent of my health. Between that and the bite I took earlier, I was sitting at seventy percent or so. I donkey kicked one in its eye, and it flew against a tree with a crash and a yelp. His health bar was still above his head at around twenty-five percent, but he didn't seem to be able to get up.

The other wolf tried to take advantage of the distraction by attempting to leap onto my back. He got a good bite in, and that pushed me further off the deep end. I was at sixty percent now, and I started to buck as he scrambled to find purchase. After another couple of rough shakes, the little mongrel fell off me, and I fell onto him. My teeth dug into the back of his neck, and I bashed him with my right paw until I heard a loud crack;

his body went limp. I turned to go for the one that lay crumpled at the base of the tree. It was attempting to stand, but couldn't. I must've shattered its spine, but it didn't matter. It would pay for angering me.

I pounced one last time and landed both of my forepaws on his throat, crushing it and killing the lame animal.

75 EXP and 10 Copper gained.

New Abilities Unlocked.

Feral Rage – Fall into a murderous rage when in combat. Damage received halved, bonus 50% damage dealt. Ability ends upon exiting combat. Requirements: Animal Form and 20% or more damage received in one blow. Cooldown: 1 Hour.

CONGRATULATIONS!

LEVEL UP! Level 2. You have 5 unspent attribute points.

I smiled to myself as the rage slowly drained away a bit at a time. Maybe it didn't leave all at once. Maybe that was in case the fight wasn't truly over? I'd ask Dinnia in a minute. I needed to level myself.

In the last fight, I had seen that I was doing well enough. My strength was pretty high, and for my level, I probably had pretty good health.

After a moment, I decided to add one point to strength and two points to dexterity and constitution which left my stats looking a little more rounded. If I played my cards right, I would be a force to be reckoned with. Time would tell. I felt a difference immediately. I felt a little lighter and stronger.

Name: Zekiel Erebos
Race: Kitsune
Level: 2

Strength: 16
Dexterity: 14
Constitution: 17
Intelligence: 16
Wisdom: 13
Charisma: 15
Unspent Attribute Points: 0

I groaned as the soreness from the pain came back. I sat down against a tree and waited for Dinnia to show herself. A moment later, she came out of the trees to my left. I hadn't even felt her presence or any kind of indicator she had been there.

"You could have stepped in," I said softly.

I could've died in that fight. If I died here, was I going to die permanently? Shit. No one had thought to ask that question when we came here. This was something to ask the Lady if she ever graced us with her presence again. Maybe the Paladin would know?

"Yes, but what would you have learned?" she asked as she sat beside me. "You wouldn't have learned what you were capable of. You would have gone into every fight with the thought that someone will always be available to help you which is not the case. You have two of the greatest weapons known to this world—intelligence and will."

She was right, of course. I couldn't rely on everyone all the time. Did I have a party? Sure, but what if we were outnumbered and couldn't get to each other? What if we got separated?

Too many what ifs... I had to be the weapon, just like in the Corps. We are strong alone and strongest together, but Gods help anyone in the way of a Marine and his brothers and sisters.

"That's fair," I said at last. "I leveled up. Got Feral Rage too."

She looked at me sharply. "Already? How? What happened?"

I filled her in, and she nodded but still looked concerned. "That's a higher level ability usually only earned at level 10 or so, and you are correct—it stays in case there is something else that needs killing. You are a strange one. Once you ascend to level 3, I might be able to see about teaching you some spells that I know. Onto the next fight."

After failing to become a wolf, she informed me it was because they were no longer natural beasts. Something about being tainted by War's Generals or their minions made them dead to nature. The poor bastards.

We traveled a short distance away and found a similar scene: more wolves and more wolves killed. The same over and over again. Nine wolves later, I made it to level 3.

This time, I focused more on constitution and wisdom. I increased constitution by three to put me at twenty overall and I added two to wisdom putting me at fifteen. I wasn't using mana yet, but I wanted to be ready when I did. My shapeshifting ability didn't take any mana at all, so I was golden for now. I hadn't received any spells that would take my mana, but I had hoped I would be able to learn one now that I was level 3.

Let's see how this works, I thought as I looked through my notifications.

Abilities unlocked

Frozen Dagger – Summon and throw a blade of solid ice. Explodes upon impact. Cost: 5 mana. No cooldown.

Nature's Voice – Converse with all animals. Duration: 60 minutes. Cost: 40 mana. No cooldown.

I smiled at the sight of my first spells.

Dinnia had some spells she could teach me at my level so she opened her own menu, and after fiddling with some buttons or settings, a screen popped up in front of me. It looked to be the list of spells she knew. Sweet. That meant my friends and I could show each other our abilities. I'd have to ask her to show me how to do that.

Filgus' Flaming Blade – Summon a sword made of pure flame. Deals additional fire damage. Sheds light up to 20 feet. Duration: 10 minutes. Cost: 20 mana. 30 second cooldown. Dispelled when dropped.

Lightning Bolt – Summon and shoot a lightning bolt up to 60 feet. Damage boosted on armored enemies. Cost: 25 mana. 1 minute cooldown.

Regrowth – Boosts natural health regeneration. Heals target for 3 health per second. Duration: 30 seconds. Cost: 30 mana. 10 second cooldown.

"You can choose between those three," Dinnia explained. "I'll teach it to you, and then we can rest for the night. The sun is setting."

I hadn't noticed the dimming crimson light coming through the scattered tree branches and leaves. It was beautiful. I turned my mind back to the spells. Druids, by nature, always seemed to hit hard with their spells before resorting to fighting directly via a shape-shifted animal form. Is that where I wanted my utility to lay, though—being ordinary?

Hmm. For now, I could try these spells out and specialize later. Besides, these could help me decide, right?

Filgus' Flaming Blade looked interesting. I'd lost my weapon once already in a fight, but then again, I was already a potent weapon on my own.

Lightning Bolt... I mean, come on, need I say more?!

The regen spell looked nice, too. Part of the reason a Druid was so powerful was their versatility. They could both heal and deal damage. Three HP per second for thirty seconds? That was almost half my health at ninety HP, all said and done.

With a Paladin in our party, I imagined we would have some decent healing, but the capability never hurt... right?

"Do Druids get a lot of healing spells?" I asked.

"Some rely heavily on the arcane to heal others," Dinnia answered. "I only know the one, but that is simply because I only use that one and have opted for other spells as I got stronger. I learned this one around level 6."

Okay, so I didn't have to learn it just yet.

I indicated my choice by tapping Lightning Bolt.

"Oh, an elemental caster huh?" She laughed. "Prepare yourself, then."

She came over to me and brought her hands up to my temples. I felt immense pressure and had to fight the urge to drop to my knees. I didn't fight too hard, I guess, because once the pressure eased, I did just that.

"It gets easier," Dinnia said as her panther friend came over to nudge me and purr reassuringly.

I stood and realized that I knew the spell. It was as simple as trying to call out to a friend, like I had known it all my life.

"Don't do it." Dinnia had realized I was about to try it. I blushed a bit and nodded. It could wait.

We spent the night in a tree nearby. I slept in my panther form, which was odd but seemed to be a normal thing for my trainer and Sharo. It was nice.

Chapter Four

The next morning, we had a breakfast of berries and water—light fare but flavorful and filling.

After traveling a couple of miles, I began to catch the sound of running water, and I was rewarded with the sight of a waterfall an hour later.

It was beautiful. The waterfall crashed into a lake with rocks at the base that broke the flow of water as it spread, minimizing the waves. This allowed the sun's reflection to gloss over it, making it look as smooth as glass far from the pouring water. The lake itself looked to be guarded by moss-covered rocks along the water's edge, perfect places to fish if you were into that kind of thing. Aside from the crash of the waterfall, the place was serene. Birds called to each other in the branches overhead, and I could even see some large fish swimming under the crystalline waters.

"Why are we here?" I asked Dinnia, still shocked by the wonder I felt.

"Training," she said as she stifled a yawn. She went over to a tree nearest the water's edge and began to meditate, while Sharo didn't even try. He just laid down near the water and started to nap.

A few minutes later, a small bear cub—a grizzly bear cub according to the little name bar—wandered to the side of the lake. It snuffled the water and started lapping it up greedily. I watched in silence. It looked so cute. It must have weighed around fifty to sixty pounds, brown fur gleaming softly in the light. It romped and played at the edge of the water, attacking the lake and causing ripples to expand out, disturbing the glasslike surface. Fish scattered in fear, but the little thing carried on in its play.

The little bundle of fur and energy played its way over close to us. It sniffed at Sharo, then nudged Dinnia playfully before turning to walk in my direction.

The cub sniffed at me from about six feet away. I decided it was time to try one of my abilities. I thought about using it and triggered Nature's Voice. I felt a slight pull from the center of my being, and my mana drained by the cost of the spell.

"Hello, little one," I said softly as I reached out to her. She sniffed again and sneezed in surprise.

"Are you a bear?!" she asked excitedly. She barreled into me as fast as she could and knocked me over. I was wrong—around eighty pounds.

I laughed as we wrestled a little. "No, I'm not a bear."

"How do you speak like a bear?" She looked at me quizzically. "Strangest not-bear I've ever seen."

"Have you seen many not-bears, cub?" asked a deep, masculine voice. Sharo had wandered over and was looking at the cub like an indulgent uncle.

"No, Sharo, I haven't," she huffed. "What is he? He smells like home."

"He is a Druid," explained a lighter voice behind me. I turned to see the golden-brown eyes of a fully grown bear behind me less than six inches from my head.

I bolted upright and tripped over Sharo as I tried to backpedal. It wasn't pretty when I dropped onto my backside.

"Ah!" Sharo swatted at me from where he was and whined, "That was my tail! Kyra, you sneaky thing, do you have to tease the baby?"

The bear laughed and sat down. The ground shook a bit; she must have weighed a good thousand pounds. The cub squealed with glee and jumped toward the larger bear.

"You know I cannot help myself, Sharo," she said as she turned her massive head my way. "Well met, young Druid. My apologies for startling you, but that is part of why you are here, I suspect. Right, sister?"

Dinnia nodded and leaned back, content to let the bear explain.

"You are here because you lack the instincts inherent to the shapes you take. The Druid is a powerful fighter and magician, but only some have what it takes to master the way of beasts, to truly meld with their feral side. I am here to try and bring it out of you." She stood and bustled my way with her cub in tow.

"How will we be doing that?"

"The easiest way is to allow instinct to take over and one of the best ways to do so is to fight. Cubs and other young animals learn to trust their abilities through play fighting with each other and their parents. You would not have had these valuable lessons, obviously, so that is what we are going to attempt to replicate today. I see that you are level 3. That is good; it may help." She stood on her hind legs, and her full eight-foot height was impressive. I didn't want to fight her, especially not in front of her cub.

Kyra eyed me in amusement and then roared so loud the flecks of spittle that flew from her jaws reached me from four feet away.

I prepared myself for the worst, dropping into a battle stance, hands out and legs parted with my knees bent.

"You won't be fighting her," said Sharo. "You'll see who when she comes."

Moments later, the bushes off to my left split, and a monstrous black bear shot through—teeth bared to the world and searching for a threat.

"Auntie Marin!" The cub shot forward. The bear visibly relaxed. I looked at her health bar and saw her name change from Black Dire Bear level 5 to Marin level 5. A dire bear? Wow. She was huge! Her black fur glistened in the light.

"Hello, little cub," she growled at the bundle of playfulness. "You called for me, my queen?"

Queen?! Sure enough, Kyra's name changed to Bear Queen Kyra level 12. Holy shit, I had been ready to fight an opponent four times my level. Wow. That was stupid; maybe I should make checking that information a priority? Yeah. That will be a priority in future encounters.

"Yes." She tilted her head at me. "We needed a skilled fighter for the young Druid here to spar with. Care to help?"

"If my queen wills it. Although, I haven't been feeling well today for some reason."

"I see. Maybe Dinnia can help?" the queen suggested.

Dinnia raised her hand, and a green aura sprung to life around the larger bear. You could see some of the strain leave her features.

"Thank you, Lady Dinnia," Marin said as she approached me.

"Shift your shape, young Druid," the queen said as she sat back down and called her cub to her side.

I did as I was told and assumed my panther form. Then out of nowhere, Marin went on the offensive. She swung her massive right paw at my head, and I ducked back just in time. And that's how it went. She would attack; I would defend or dodge. I could tell she was trying to hold back.

"Good, little Druid," the queen praised. "Now, feel your body's natural responses. Let your mind open up to Nature and Her glories, and she will show you the way."

I wasn't quite certain what she meant, but I tried to be open minded. I heard the tree branches and leaves swaying in the breeze. I felt the earth beneath my feet and the thudding of my opponent's paws. It felt right. I lifted my nose to the air and scented the breeze. Trees, grass, moss, water and the scent of small prey animals wafted into my olfactory glands, and I could almost separate each one from the other like it was the easiest thing to do.

Then I caught another scent. One that felt... unnatural. It made my fur stand on end, and bile rose into my throat unbidden. This scent was wrong. Very wrong. It made the world around me feel weird, and I could hear the forest fall still and silent around me. Then I felt it, that thing that had caused me to feel this horrifying sense of being *unclean.*

A pack of Insane Wolves burst into our makeshift arena. Marin lost her mind and dove for the three closest Wolves. She swatted at the one to her right and bowled it into the two behind it.

The cub screamed in surprise and hid beside her mother. Dinnia and Sharo would have helped us, but it seemed they had their hands full with a pack that had sprung out near them. There were about twenty Wolves around the lakeside.

I tucked into the attackers nearest me. I brought my left paw down onto one of them and unleashed hell. It brought him down to about fifty percent after all was said and done. They were all level 1 or 2, but they had the advantage of numbers. I felt my fur stand on end and jumped straight up a good six feet—just in time, as a wolf sailed through where I had been and snapped into the wolf I had been fighting.

I dove into the two before they could untangle and dispatched the injured one, then turned on the other attacker. I snatched it up with my jaws and tossed it into the oncoming Wolves. I needed to move, or I would be surrounded; that was no good to anyone.

I looked around, saw a thicker tree branch, and leapt for it. I clambered onto it and shifted back to my natural fox-man.

"I'm going to start casting my spells," I shouted to the others. I didn't receive any response, but I had to trust that they had heard.

I held my hand out to point at a Wolf trying to sneak up on Marin and cast Lightning Bolt. My mana dropped by another twenty-five. So far, I had managed to eat my way through sixty-five MP out of my one hundred sixty MP. Time to test my other spell then get back into the fray .

I began slinging Ice Knives like it was the cool thing to do. No pun intended. I had managed to throw a good seven and killed a few more Wolves when I saw a few break from around Sharo and Dinnia and go for the queen. They were joined by a couple from our group, too. They made a dash for the queen and her cub.

I shifted again and roared as loud as I could. I tensed my legs hard as possible and pushed off the branch with all my might. I hit the group like a dark, angry shooting star. Teeth and claws flashed again and again. One of the wolves got me good on my right shoulder as another one got the opposite flank. It took me down by twenty-five percent.

Good, I thought. I let Feral Rage take me and ravaged the wolves around me.

I was death incarnate. I spun into one Wolf, breaking its neck with a paw to the temple, then took the eye of the Wolf next to it in the same swing and flick of my powerful wrist. The other three Wolves backed down for a moment to regroup. They came at me together but never made it. Marin slammed into the flank of the right one and killed their momentum. The one in the middle tripped, and I fell on it instantly. Sharp claws on my powerfully built back legs dug into its stomach with almost sickening glee. It yelped and flailed, but I pushed my paw into its throat and gripped before kicking my legs like I would to wipe the dirt off on a carpet. It yelped again, and I could feel the viscera and gore fleck my hide and flee the body beneath me. Deciding to end my fun, I sank my teeth into its neck. The Insane Wolf died with my teeth in its throat. I looked for my next victim.

Dinnia and Sharo finished their attackers then rushed to our aid. Once the final Wolf had been dispatched, we took a quick assessment of the damage. I had only lost about forty percent of my health in that battle, and Sharo looked a little rough, but he was healing thanks to Regrowth cast by Dinnia. She cast the same spell on me when all seemed clear, and I shifted back, my rage abating.

The fight had only lasted a little while, maybe a few minutes.

"You did well, young Druid," Marin said through heaving breaths. She didn't look too hot. Dinnia tried to cast Regrowth on her, but it didn't seem to stick. Once again, I caught the stink of something unclean, and it was originating from her.

"No!" The cub began to cry. She came over to the huge black bear and tried to rub against her, but Marin wasn't having it. She swatted at her and brushed her back to her mother.

"I am fading," she said in a pained voice. "My queen, please."

Kyra looked away, obviously in pain. Dinnia and Sharo sat in stoic silence.

"What's going on?" I asked.

"She has been infected by the dark ones," the cub mewled. "She's asking to leave our lands before it's too late, but it seems it already is."

"Can we stop it?" I asked in spite of the scent accosting my nose. I had always had a soft spot for sick animals, and Marin was a badass; I had no choice but to admit that. She could have easily stomped me in our sparring, but she had held back so I could learn. I looked at my trainer, and she shook her head. My heart sank, and tears began to form in my eyes.

"Druid, what is your name?" Marin asked softly.

"I am Zekiel Erebos," I said back just as softly. I looked up and could tell by the look in her eyes as the name hit her ears what was coming—my heart sank further into the pit of my stomach.

"Give me a warrior's death, please, Zekiel," she begged as she collapsed. "While I still have my soul."

QUEST ALERT: WARRIOR'S LAST BREATH –
Offer a noble death in combat to Marin.
Reward: Unknown.
Will you accept? Yes/No?

I sighed inwardly; I knew what she was thinking because I would want the same thing if our roles were reversed.

I tapped yes and looked at her. Truly looked at her. Her face was accepting, and she must have received a prompt showing my acquiescence to her wishes.

"Thank you for trying to pass on your knowledge, Marin," I whispered, fighting back outraged and indignant tears on her behalf. "Fight well."

I shapeshifted once more. I was at around ninety percent HP and still recovering, but she was at about fifty-five percent. My panther form coiled to spring; I waited for her to make her move.

She stood at last and came at me with all she had. I ducked under her blow and felt the wind on my back. I brought her near the tree I had leapt from earlier and used it as a springboard. I jumped off of it and onto Marin's back. I latched my claws into her shoulders and bit for all I was worth. I took about ten percent of her health before she dropped her weight and me with it. My back legs sailed up, and she swung me loose a bit. I let go and landed safely away before she could swipe at me.

She turned and growled at me. I growled right back. I wanted her to have her honor, but I wasn't going to die so that she could have it. We charged into each other. Well, I charged, and she just picked me up and slammed me down like a sack of potatoes. Ouch. That took me down to about eighty percent from the ninety-five percent I had regenerated to.

A thought came to me, and I shifted out of panther form—not into my fox-like human form but to an actual fox. I had been thinking about it the night before when I went over my stats and abilities. Shapeshifting allowed me to transform into any animal, within reason, and back to my natural form. The fox I turned into now was a natural form for me. I shot between her back legs and shifted again into my Fox-man form. I cast Lightning Bolt on Marin, and a small symbol like a lightning bolt appeared under her health bar. She was at about thirty percent and stunned. I was out of mana at this point or dangerously close to it. Time to get physical.

I shifted once more and laid into her with my panther claws. At about twenty percent, she was back up and pissed off.

A red aura permeated her being, and I could tell she was under some kind of attack boosting buff. She swatted at me, and I couldn't move fast enough. She caught me in the chin, and my sight blurred for a second. I shifted to fox just as she took another swipe.

This time, I jumped to her right and under her massive paw. I leapt onto her back and shifted back into a panther. My weight dragged her forward into the tree in front of us, and she fell over the roots. By the time she landed, I was batting at her. My claws sunk in, and even then, she managed to get to her feet one last time after shrugging me aside. Marin was on her last legs. Her health was below five percent.

She eyed me once more and charged with reckless abandon. I let her come to me, and when she was three feet away, I leapt up and over her. She tried to raise up to catch me, but I had turned my body in the air and clawed her in the side of the head. She couldn't compensate for the strike and ended up tripping as I landed next to her. With one, then two of my most powerful swings, Marin was no more.

I hurt and ached like hell, but I wasn't going to leave her side just yet.

QUEST COMPLETED: WARRIOR'S LAST BREATH – You have given Marin the death she sought. Reward: Increased reputation with Queen Kyra and her people, Marin's Pelt, 500 EXP.

CONGRATULATIONS!

LEVEL UP! Level 4. You have 5 unspent attribute points.

There were pressing matters to attend to—the loss of the warrior I just killed to help save her honor and the mourning that everyone might be going through—but I needed a second before I could deal with that. The ache was too familiar—too personal, too close to some of the emotions I had felt once upon a time when I had been younger—so I turned to my stats page for that breathing room.

I threw a point into intelligence and strength and three into dexterity. It seemed like speed and strength in equal parts would help me greatly if I were to face larger groups again, and now that I had some spells I could use, I would need to be able to deal some damage with those.

Name: Zekiel Erebos
Race: Kitsune
Level: 4
Strength: 17
Dexterity: 17
Constitution: 20
Intelligence: 17
Wisdom: 15
Charisma: 15
Unspent Attribute Points: 0

Just like last time, I felt a little lighter when I moved, but overall, my heart ached, my eyes drooped, and my fur was wet under my eyes due to the loss of such an amazing warrior.

"Thank you, Zekiel," said Kyra. She walked over to me with her still sniffling cub right on her heels. "You helped her spirit find peace."

"Does this happen often?" I asked. "Do animals and creatures get turned like this all the time?"

"No, it only occurs to creatures who dwell close to the ruins or who venture too close too often. We had to move our patrols away from that area to keep this from happening again, but she must have been going close to the ruins in an attempt to keep us safe. She's always been gone too often for me to ensure that she used the different routes our warriors travel now. She had always been stubborn about protecting our lands; I should have made her return to us more often. I should have done things differently."

She looked down at the body of the Dire Bear and sighed softly. "She must have thought herself immune... I should've known she might do these things."

The cub came over to Marin's body and cried on it silently.

"We need to stop this," Kyra said at last. "You are here to do just that. Please, will you go to the ruins and cleanse them?"

***QUEST ALERT: JUST LIKE NEW** – Queen Kyra has asked you to cleanse the ruins that Dinnia showed you. Reward: 2,000 EXP, status amongst her people for you and those who assist in the quest.*

Will you accept? Yes/no?

"Of course," I agreed, without hesitation. "As soon as my friends and I are strong enough, we will go to the ruins and cleanse the darkness."

"Thank you," she said and nodded to me. "You seem to have an easier time adapting to your beasts than most other Druids that I have met. I cannot provide much further aid, other than to tell you to always trust your instincts here. Good luck."

With that said, she and her cub left the lakeside.

CHAPTER FIVE

Over the next few days my training went without incident. By the end of my week with Dinnia and Sharo, after hours of hunting down the infected creatures and destroying them, I reached level 8.

As I went on and realized how much damage I could do with my spells, I decided to go ahead and round out my stat scores a little more. I bumped up everything but charisma to twenty, then halved the remaining six points I had left between strength and constitution. Sure, I could be a squishy, spell-slinging glass cannon like a lot of the caster archetypes in a few of the games I'd played at home, but that just wasn't me.

Dinnia and Sharo joined me on my way back to the village. She informed me that the name of the village was Sunrise. It seemed kind of fitting to have the people who first came here to save their world start in that town.

Sunrise came into view a couple hours after we left the lake. The air was filled with hustle and bustle of children playing while merchants hawked their warehouse and haggled prices with the shoppers. It was a nice sight after all the destruction and infestation I had been seeing.

When we reached the tavern, Dinnia and Sharo bid me farewell and left without looking back. I'd miss having the two of them around, but we all knew that they had done what they could to help our merry band on its way.

The only ones gathered so far were Jaken and I. He looked a lot more buff than when we had last seen each other. We shook hands, and he started telling me about his time training. Apparently, Sir Dillon was a cruel taskmaster. He had the poor Paladin wannabe lifting and working out every morning before taking him to a cemetery nearby to grind and quest.

He had reached level 8 just this morning after helping heal someone's lamed horse. He showed me his stat page.

Name: Jaken Warmecht
Race: Fae-Orc
Level: 8
Strength: 26
Dexterity: 16
Constitution: 28
Intelligence: 12
Wisdom: 28
Charisma: 13
Unspent Attribute Points: 0

"Why is your intelligence so low?" I asked. If he was going to be healing things, wouldn't that help? And his spells' damage would suffer.

"Intelligence doesn't mean anything to me, man." He smiled. "Well, not to my class anyway. Wisdom is the stat associated with being able to heal. My main stats are strength, constitution, and wisdom. Dexterity will just help me move a little faster is all. Not to mention my chosen weapon is the longsword and shield, so I have all that I need."

"Chosen weapon?" I asked dreading what was going to be coming. My friend just smiled and told me to share my stats page with him. He congratulated me on my stats and showed me what he was talking about. Just under my abilities tab was a combat tab. Shit. How long had I had this?!

Jaken must have seen the look on my face because he patted my shoulder. He had me open the tab and I saw right away that I only had three points. He explained that the tab opened and became available at level 5. That was why I hadn't noticed it. I had been too busy just leveling and grinding to explore my status screen.

I decided to go through that later and waited with my friend for the rest of our party to return. Next came Bokaj and Balmur. Both looked a little leaner than the last time we saw each other. Our greetings went much the same as mine and Jaken's. Balmur shared his stats with all of us first while Bokaj went to collect Tmont from outside.

Name: Balmur
Race: Azer Dwarf
Level: 8
Strength: 15
Dexterity: 25
Constitution: 18
Intelligence: 25
Wisdom: 10
Charisma: 13
Unspent Attribute Points: 0

"I'm going for a class specialization that my trainer told me about called an arcane trickster. It's a Rogue who can use some spells. I have a pretty sweet one that I can show you guys later."

I wondered what it looked like until I felt something tug on my tail and chomp down. My health went down about ten percent, and I whirled on my attacker. A panther purred at me innocently with big eyes.

"T, you dickbag!" I tackled her to the ground, and we started to wrestle a bit. Tables and chairs scattered. She had grown a lot in the time away; she looked like she weighed half as much as me in my panther form. I looked at her info and saw that she was level 5 in her own right. Nice.

"Come here, Tmonty!" Bokaj called as he walked through the door. The medium-sized panther sauntered her way over to her master and rubbed herself against his legs. I used my Nature's Voice spell quickly.

"Listen here, you little shit, my tail isn't a chew toy!" I growled at her and took a menacing step forward. "Chew on mine again, and I chew on yours!"

"I make no promises, Master's friend," she purred in a deeper voice than I expected from a cat her size. She paced forward and butted her head against my clenched fist before returning to Bokaj.

"Woah, man, what was that?" he asked as she sat back down.

"What was what?"

"You started growling and snarling just like a panther," he said. "Were you yelling at T?"

"A little," I said with a smile. "I was kind of miffed that she keeps attacking my tail."

"You can't do that, T. That's not cool, brah." He stroked the big cat's chin, and a new round of purring erupted.

"Wanna share your stats?" Balmur asked.

"Yeah, man, sure thing."

He pulled up his stat screen and sent it our way.

Name: Bokaj
Race: Ice Elf
Level: 9
Strength: 14
Dexterity: 30

Constitution: 25
Intelligence: 17
Wisdom: 15
Charisma: 20
Unspent Attribute Points: 0

I had to admit, I was more than a little jealous of his progress and stats. He told us all about how his trainer had come to him and had him help with a quest to take out a local group of monsters. Fish-like creatures had been turned savage by the infestation in the area, and it put him up two levels from that quest alone. The rest of the time they had spent hunting other various fish monsters and animals in that area that had been tainted.

We waited another hour, drinking and eating a little. The drink Sir Dillon gave us was sweet with a fruit I hadn't heard of with undertones of bitter hops. It was a little intense for my tastes—I usually preferred liquor at home—but it left me feeling pretty good. I knew it could really get me bad if I had too much, so I nursed one until our final companion joined us.

Yohsuke strode through the door, his clothes a little torn up and disheveled, but it didn't seem to bother him a bit.

"What the hell happened to you, brostein?" I asked and strode over to him.

"You know me, man," he said with a smile. "We get all the loot. We get all the EXP."

I looked up and saw what he meant. Level 10. That's Yoh for you. Leave it to him to never stop.

"But how?" I asked at a bit of a loss.

"I went and got every quest I could from this village," he said as he walked to the table and grabbed some food. He explained that Elves entered a trance-like state that they used for four hours to rest. His trainer was also an Elf, and they only had to rest when they were tired. He spent all his time fighting, killing, and questing.

"Sounds like you, bro," I sighed and clapped him on the shoulder. "Show us what you've got?"

"Yeah, man," he said and pulled his stats up. He never stopped eating the whole time; it was impressive.

Name: Yohsuke
Race: Abomination
Level: 10
Strength: 11
Dexterity: 32
Constitution: 20
Intelligence: 30
Wisdom: 28
Charisma: 9
Unspent Attribute Points: 0

Holy hell. Everyone had some awesome stats. Mine were well rounded, but I wondered what it would be like when we all fought together.

"I'm glad you could all make it!" Sir Dillon came out from the back. He smiled at us all, and we each took turns shaking his hand.

"A level 10 in one week's time?" he said with raised eyebrows. "And a level 9? Very impressive. Seven would have been above average, but the rest of you are level 8 it seems? Well done, all of you."

He brought out a map and laid it out in front of us. On it was a path to the same castle ruins that I had been shown at the beginning of the week.

"I know where this is," I said quietly.

"Good," he said and proceeded to fill the rest of the group in. He had a more general knowledge, and I filled in everything I could from what I saw.

"Well, if we're going to be effective and rid this area of the darkies, we'll need new gear," I put in. We all couldn't help but smile at the prospect of better gear. Every gamer lives for better gear, and we were no exception.

We all promised to spend the rest of the day kitting ourselves out in preparation for tomorrow, then meet back here when we finished.

As my friends left, I opened my menu and went to my Combat tab. I looked through and saw that there were all kinds of proficiencies: swords, shields, daggers, and bows. I scanned through until I saw my favorite weapons. I had been favoring the axe the last few games I had played through, and the one I had currently served me well. The bow, which was a personal favorite because when all else failed, kill it from afar. Daggers, I loved to dual wield when I could.

We already had three of the harassment types, though: Bokaj, Balmur, and Yohsuke, so that defeated the purpose of me needing a bow or to dual wield. They all hit fast and harried our enemies. Jaken had the tank role covered easily. He would have plate armor and a shield to help him absorb damage while we took out the enemies.

My role would normally be to heal or cast spells until my mana was spent, then fight on as an animal in a more traditional support role. Between the one healing spell I got from hitting level 6 and the several Jaken had at his disposal, we would be fine on healing for a while—I hoped.

What I wanted to do is hit hard when I had to use my weapon and provide more solid damage than the dexterity based attackers we had.

So, I threw a point into the Axe Proficiency skill.

AXE PROFICIENCY – Unlock weapon skills and damage boosts with axes. Bonus damage with axes +1%.

After unlocking that, I saw that there was another selection that became clear after that: Great Axe Proficiency.

"Oh yeah, son," I said out loud. This was me, right here. I had always played a strength build in a series of the harder games I played. It was my favorite weapon so far, and I could think of some situations it would help us.

GREAT AXE PROFICIENCY – Unlock weapon skills and damage boosts with great axes. Bonus damage with axes +2%.

It looked like you could put points into each one again to boost the damage they do, but each level took the level number as payment. Level two in either skill required two points, then three, and so on.

I closed the screens and left to look for my own new gear. From what I read, I didn't really have any kind of armor restrictions as a Druid, but I didn't want to wear heavy armor and have it get in my way. I looked at my own gear again, and it was still lacking. No armor whatsoever, and it was looking rough after a week of wear in the wilds.

I checked over my funds as well: five hundred gold, thirty-five silver, and fourteen copper.

I was golden. I went to the blacksmith over near the square where I had heard him beating metal into submission. I walked into the squat, plain, wooden building's front door. I couldn't see too much of the back as it was fenced in with a high fence. When my eyes adjusted, I noted all the swords and weapons on the racks. They looked great, like they would serve well.

I waited for the blacksmith to finish his current piece before he turned to me. He was somewhat tall for a Dwarf and built like a brick wall. Great slabs of muscle covered his body, and his calloused hands flexed on the tongs when he realized I was there. His black eyebrows raised and white teeth shined as he smiled. He set his tools down and walked over to me.

"HAIL TRAVELER!!" he shouted as he realized who I was. He came out from behind his counter and pulled me into a great hug. I'm fairly certain I heard my back pop no less than twelve times.

After, he put me down, and I caught my breath. With a small grunt, I stood upright and shook his meaty hand.

"How do you know what I am?" I asked. I thought Radiance would want to keep us and our mission a secret.

"Our village petitioned the Lady Radiance to allow her chosen few to come here," he said with a smile. "The closed off nature of our village allows us some privacy, but it also means we are alone out here with War's minions and their infection. We know who ye all are, and we appreciate what ye are willing to do for us. We will help ye how we can."

"Thank you, sir," I said with a smile.

"Oh no," he admonished me with a gentle swipe to the air. "None of that now. I'm Rowland. This here is me shop, and I will not be called 'sir,' as I clearly work fer a livin'. Now, what can I do for ye, traveler? A fine weapon, mayhaps?"

"A great axe, if you have one,"

He closed his eyes and seemed to be going through his inventory mentally before opening them again. "Sorry, I don't have one made."

My shoulders sunk a little, but he clapped me on the back in a brotherly way.

"Ye'll not be without a weapon, me friend," he said. "I'm a damned good smith, and I'll not be letting our world's hope go into battle without some of me cold steel. Ye come back in about, oh, a few hours, an' I'll have something made just for ye. Now, hold still. I need to measure ye."

He did just that. He measured my height, the length of my arms, and my hands. He even asked what my current strength was and if I was planning on raising it, to which I replied yes. He grunted and took some notes down.

"On your way to the armorer?" he asked. When I nodded, he smiled. "On your way, send that goofy-looking carpenter my way. We have work to do!"

I smiled as I left. I really liked this guy, and I wondered if everyone in the village was as cool as him.

I saw the sign over the shop down the way with a hammer and some wood on it. The building was red oak and well made. I poked my head in and was assaulted by the scent of fresh-cut wood and the sound of cursing. Now, I've heard my fair share of cursing—this was impressive.

"GODS-CURSED BASTARD OAK!" a voice shouted from the back. "YOUR MOTHER WAS A HAG OAK, SHE WAS, AND A TERMITE RIDDEN DRYAD WAS YOUR FATHER, YOU POXY FU–"

"Hello?" I called out as I stepped all the way in.

An instant later, a small, dusk-skinned woman poked her head out from behind the doorway. She was athletically built with a slim body but well-toned muscles. She stood about five-foot-six or so and had her short, brown hair swinging into her hazel eyes.

What? Rowland said goofy-looking carpenter. She was gorgeous! She took off her apron as she stepped fully through, and I was lucky to keep my jaw attached.

Oh, hello inner cartoon wolf.

"Oh, hello, traveler," she said with her cheeks flushed slightly. Whether in anger or embarrassment, I couldn't tell, but wow, it did wonders for her regal cheekbones.

She smiled awkwardly with full lips and looked away.

I was staring, wasn't I? No. SHIT. SAVE IT.

"Uhm, S-sorry," I stuttered. "I was just impressed by the creative cursing. Rowland asked me to swing by and ask you to go see him. I guess he needs help with a project—seemed pretty urgent."

She groaned and muttered about him being a goat-headed slave driver.

"Can I do anything else for you?" she asked finally. "Maybe stand still for a portrait?"

I blushed and couldn't even say anything, so I just shook my head and hoped I stopped staring at her. Though, if I had said yes, I'd have probably been on the receiving end of a hammer—whether from her or from Rowland I couldn't tell you.

"Have a great day then. I'll be on my way out."

I left and scurried away to the armorer. The armorer's building was a good three-minute walk away, just outside the square according to the four citizens I had to stop and ask. It looked large enough to be someone's business and home in one. That could be the case; it seemed the most economically sound. The base of the building was thickly cut brick and mortar, while the top was made up of wooden slats stuck together with mortar on the connectors.

The door to the building was open to the street. I walked in and saw a very friendly looking Bear Beast-kin. She had light brown fur, and her honey-colored eyes with obvious mirth in them. She smiled at me. It was a warm smile filled with rows of fangs close to how Kyra's looked.

"Hello, friend!" she said as I approached. "I'm Kynin. How can I help you?"

"I came to see about getting some armor," I explained. "I also wondered if you could do anything with this?" I pulled out Marin's Pelt.

"I can't, but wait here." Her eyes widened at the sight of the material, and she shouted, "Farrin!"

The bear disappeared, taking my pelt with her. A few minutes later, she came back downstairs with another Bear Beastkin in tow. He was holding the pelt looking at it in both wonder and rage.

"Where did you get this?!" he shot over the counter and had me in his hands, lifting me off the floor. "What did you do to my friend?!"

"You knew her? Marin, I mean?" I wondered; worry gnawed at my gut.

"She and I would play in the forest together when we were little," he explained through the threatening tears and strangled pain in his voice.

"My condolences for your loss." Sincere regret tightened my voice. "If you'll put me down, I will explain everything to you."

He grudgingly complied but stayed close. He might have thought I was going to bolt.

I told him everything. Well, everything to do with Marin. I didn't know how much the village knew about our mission, despite what Rowland had said, but it wasn't going to help the story. Hell, if anything, it would hurt it—my leveling and training would seem more important to me than his friend's life.

I told him how she had been helping me learn as a new Druid with her queen when we were attacked by the Insane Wolves. How she and I had fought together to preserve the lives of her queen and the royal cub. How she had begun to feel the infection take hold of her mind after prolonged exposure to the ruins.

As they both cried, I recounted the tale of our battle to give Marin an honorable death.

"She fought with honor and strength," I said quietly. "I've been surrounded by honorable men and women before, but her spirit was uncrushable. It was a privilege to help grant her last wish."

Farrin nodded and bowed his head into the fur in his hands. He sobbed quietly for a moment, and his sister joined him. They were quiet for a while, with tears and whimpers. I stood respectfully quiet. I knew what it was like to lose someone close to you. I had been through the same crushing guilt. *What if I had done more? Could I have done something different? Why them, and not me?*

Over the years, I had learned that people would do what they would, and there wasn't always a damned thing you could do about it but stand by and watch in either pride as they succeeded or horror as they went down in flames. It was these lessons that I had carried with me and helped forge me into the man I had become. Did it make it any easier to deal with loss? Fuck no, but I beat and punished myself a little less for someone else's choices.

After they had let it out, the Bears looked at me, and I shook the thoughts out of my head, the self-doubt falling away, if only a little.

"Kynin, measure him and get me the notes. I'm closed for the rest of the day." He came over to tower over me. I hadn't noticed before just how big and strong he looked, even when he had lifted me like a bag of groceries. "You come here first thing tomorrow morning, and I will have your armor prepared, Druid Zekiel."

Farrin squared his shoulders and nodded my way before leaving. Kynin got out her measuring cord and started my measurements. Half an hour later, I had told her some of what I was looking for, and she said it would be done. She also apologized for her brother's treatment. She finished it with a hug and a kiss on the forehead, saying that no one should have to take the life of a comrade.

I stepped outside, the sun shining down on me from above, the noise of the people in the village, all carefree and happy, filling the air. I envied their ignorance a bit. They may be a little privy to what may be going on, but they hadn't had to take the life of someone just doing their best to keep their loved ones and people safe. I had. That shit still tugged at my heart. I took a deep breath in, then released it, letting the angst and bitter feelings drain from me.

"Don't dwell. Marin wouldn't want you to," I growled at myself.

I had plenty of time before I had to go back to see Rowland, so I wandered out into the square and let the hawkers show me their wares.

They sold everything from food and delicious smelling sweet meats to jewelry and potions. I went to check out the jewelry first.

"Ah, good sir!" A human man stood behind the counter and swept his arm over his pieces. "Come look over my wares, and I can guarantee you will find something you like."

I did just that. A lot of his jewelry was lovely—only a few pieces were enchanted but nothing that would really benefit me or anyone in the party outright. At least, not that I knew of.

I guess the owner realized I wasn't interested and I wouldn't be talked into buying anything because he went back to hawking his wares and shooed me away. I went to the potions stand and wasn't disappointed at all.

The little girl behind the stand knew exactly what her prices were, and she sold her items to me straight. She even told me about her family a bit. Her mother made the potions as an alchemist and had a shop nearby, and her father gathered herbs in the surrounding forest. Though, she did say that he didn't go out as far any more due to there being dangerous creatures out there. Her father was taking care of business nearby, while her older brother had gone to get them lunch. She was responsible for the stand while he was gone.

Her little hands handled each item with care as she explained what the benefits of each potion were. Her blonde hair bobbed back and forth in little pigtails, and her freckles were adorable.

"Health potions replenish your vita-veetal... your health by twenty-five points. The mana ones replenish your mana by the same, good sir," she finished with a curt nod to herself.

"Excellent sales work." I clapped for her, and she smiled.

I got ten Health and fifteen Mana potions at five silver apiece. She had given me a discount since I was buying in bulk like that. All in all, I spent a gold and twenty-five silver for the potions and twelve copper for a kabob of sweet meats each for myself, the little girl, and her older brother upon his return.

The rest of the wares around the square were just things that I really had no interest in. After a bit, I remembered that my clothes were probably on their last legs and bought some more to change into right away. Then I bought some more to change into after a time. Three tunics and shirts, four breeches, and six pairs of underwear. Socks I bought in bulk. I spent another ten silver on all of it together, then changed into a green shirt and some brown breeches.

  I decided to take a walk around the village. It was nice out; the sun shone lazily behind a couple thin clouds, and the village seemed to be perpetually traveled by the villagers and residents. Everyone seemed to get along. There was music playing from a couple of spots around, some restaurants, and a few street performers, but something else caught my attention.

  I heard a muffled shout and a grunt of pain. One of the benefits of being a Kitsune was heightened, animal-like senses. I heard it again and decided that whatever it was, it was wrong. I shapeshifted into my fox form and bolted toward the noise as fast as my four legs would take me. I came upon an alley near the tree line and saw three figures. One was a young man who looked to have the same blond hair and freckles as the little girl at the potion stand.

  The other two were hulking Wolf Beast-kin. They had grey fur and weapons on their sides, like they could be mercenaries. One held a cudgel, a club but made of metal with teeth on it. It looked pretty threatening to me, especially under the boy's chin. Cudgel had his yellow eyes scanning his surroundings for passersby. His back was to the trees, and his friend was intent on the boy, so neither saw me behind a water barrel.

  "You're too good to buy two starvin' Beast-kin a meal with the coin you're flashin' about?" said Cudgel. "What're you too good to associate with us? We not good enough for your charity?"

"I told you—I only had enough to feed my little sister and me," the boy tried to explain calmly. He was brave, that's for sure. I wasn't going to stand for this. The two wolves were only level 4, but the boy was level 2. I could do this.

I snuck around the building behind them and into the bushes in front of me. Around the back of the houses, I noticed some storage crates stacked high enough for me to jump onto the roof. I leapt from my hiding spot to the boxes and made my way to the roof across from the boy. I shifted back to my normal form and waited until the boy saw me. His eyes widened a bit, but I shushed him with a finger to my lips and motioned for him to keep his eyes on them. They were saying something about paying a visit to his sister, and that was my queue to intervene.

I changed into my panther form and dropped onto Cudgel's back and hissed menacingly at the other wolf from my position. Cudgel's health was down a quarter of the way. I guess I had gotten a good sneak attack.

Yippee.

I transformed again as the wolf beneath me started to grunt and call for help.

"Hush, little wolf, or I'll make you," I said, dropping my voice a couple octaves and adopting a commanding tone. "I despise banditry in my village. Leave now, and you keep your lives. Stay or try anything—ANYTHING—near here or anywhere I can find you, and I will end you. Gruesomely."

I looked down at the wolf beneath my foot; the whole time he had been struggling fruitlessly to escape, but I kept him pinned.

"Return the child's money." The wolf in front of me stepped back a bit. "Ah, ah. Don't run. Return the money, then flee. Do anything stupid—I decide on how hungry I am and how into wolf stew I am. Do we have an understanding?"

They mumbled, and it kind of pissed me off, so I stepped a little harder on Cudgel's back. I heard some bones crack. The wolf in front of me tossed his coin purse at the boy and sprinted past me into the forest.

"You too," I said, leaning down to look into the wolf's eyes. All I saw was fear and hatred. Good.

He reached down and pulled his purse out, then placed it at the boy's feet. I picked up his cudgel, tossed it into the woods, and heard a yelp. I let the wolf up, and he fled without looking back. I turned to the boy his eyes wet with tears.

"You were very brave just now," I said softly. I picked up the coin purses and counted out about fifty silver between the two. I handed it to him and patted his shoulder comfortingly.

"But sir, they hadn't taken anything from me yet," he said, holding the bag back out.

"Think of it as payment for emotional distress." I grinned and pushed his hand back. "Come on now, let's go get that food you ordered. I'm sure your sister is hungry."

We went into the inn across the street and got the food he ordered before he was tricked into going outside where those two asshats had almost robbed him. I took him back to his sister, who had begun to worry. She explained that I was a customer and that I had treated her well. The boy and girl thanked me heartily and tucked into their meal. It was good to see they were okay.

I walked away with a smile and wandered toward the smithy. I walked in to see Rowland hammering something and heard his deep voice chanting in what could only be Dwarven. I could see light channeling from the forge into his hands and hammer, but I couldn't see the product.

"He's channeling the heat of the forge to assist him in the production of your great axe," whispered the lovely carpenter behind me. I jumped a bit, and she smiled. I hadn't heard her because I was enraptured by the steady sound of the hammer shaping the metal.

"Is he enchanting it?" I asked in wonder.

"No, merely channeling," she explained. "He is pulling the heat into his work and body to feed his muscles and stamina. It allows him to keep the metal heated properly and hammer it into shape without rest. He had been looking for an excuse to use it when you came along. He had just unlocked the ability, but I've not seen it used, only heard of it being done."

I nodded in appreciation and kept my eyes on him. He kept chanting and hammering.

"It looks like he underestimated the time it might take," she said after about ten minutes. "Why don't you go look around. A great weapon is wonderful, but having a more compact alternative never hurts."

She was right. I hadn't thought about all the books and games I had played with characters that had strong weapons who are brought low by the inability to use them in tight spaces.

I went to look over some of the swords. The craftsmanship was flawless, of course. Rowland didn't seem like the type to allow shoddy work to be seen, let alone sold here.

I looked over the varying sizes of swords, and nothing caught my eye. I walked over the table with a myriad of small blades and daggers. I found a long dagger about the size of my forearm and almost as wide. It felt light in my hands, and the balance seemed great. The hilt of the dagger was a little lighter than the blade, and while I was no expert, I imagined that it would help if it was thrown.

Great Dagger
+3 to attacks
Works well as a projectile by a practiced hand

Weight: 5lbs
Made by Master Smith Rowland in Sunrise Village.

This dagger alone was already better than my Beginner's Axe. I wondered how much stronger my great axe would be, in comparison. I brought the weapon up to the counter, then sat down on the floor near the entryway to the forge area. The ringing of metal against metal was softer now but no less fervent. I closed my eyes for what seemed like a moment and drifted off.

I awoke to a tap on my forehead by the carpenter—man, I really should learn her name. She motioned for me to follow her, and I got up and stretched. I was a little stiff, but my new body eased back into a feeling of normalcy rather quickly. *I could get used to this*, I thought.

We moved to the forge area, and the heat seemed to be a living thing. It was fierce even though I could see the fires had died down significantly since I had last seen them. The dull glow from the forge and shuttered light from the windows gave off enough light that my dark vision didn't activate, but I could still see. There was the forge in the center of the room and about fifteen feet of space to the walls on each side. The walls were lined with shelves of metal ingots and tools. At the back of the room, there looked to be bins for dark wood, coke, and coal with a quenching barrel in a sand pit in a far corner of the room.

Rowland stood to the side with his hands on his hips and a smile on his Dwarven face.

"Come see, lad," he said, motioning to the table beside him. On it there was what could only be his latest work under a heavy sheet obscuring it from view.

"I'm thinking that ye'll like it," he said with pride. He lifted the sheet, and all I could do was grin.

The blade itself was a thing of deadly beauty, about a foot and a half from top to bottom on the bladed portion and tapered into the base of the head. Sharpened properly, not razor sharp like most say because it would make the blade brittle and break easily. On the other side of the head, a bladed pick came out. It looked like the pick portion of a pickaxe, but instead of four squared sides, the bottom portion had an edge to slash with, kind of like a scythe.

I moved from the blade to the handle and was in just as much awe—dark wood almost red in hue with strips of ridged metal between dark leather grips. A small rounded pommel with a slight point to the bottom completed the piece.

"Let me explain," Rowland said excitedly. "The haft of the axe has an attached metal core to give it stability, and the Blood Tree heartwood panels are tapped into gaps around the metal core to soften the vibration ye might feel. Secured the head to them. From there, the wood is glued together and sanded down, then bound together further by the leather grips and the metal guard. At the bottom, ye'll notice a piece that looks almost like the pommel of a sword. The head of a great axe is the beauty of the weapon, but in good hands, the haft and end can be just as deadly. Should you decide to brain an opponent with that, well, ye will find out yerself."

He chuckled to himself and took the weapon in his hands. All said and done, the weapon was almost up to my chest when resting on the ground. Rowland turned and walked out a door I hadn't noticed into a fenced in backyard.

Once there, I could truly see the splendor of the weapon. It was beautiful. The wood was blood red, and the black grips made it look formidable, to say the least.

"Tiny, you go ahead and explain yer portion of the weapon." The Dwarf smiled at the Carpenter behind me.

"Sarah, Rowland. Call me Sarah," she said as if she had explained it hundreds of times. She walked over to stand beside the Dwarf and pointed to the wood.

"Blood Tree wood itself is rare in these parts, but luckily, I came into a small grove of the trees a few months back," she explained. "The wood is fickle and difficult to work with in general; heartwood is almost impossible unless you have the skills that I do. You got lucky. The wood is hard, like rock, and very resistant to cutting and slashing. It will make an excellent handle, and also, thank you for giving me an excuse to test my own skills. I leveled up while working that wood today."

I congratulated her, and she muttered something about getting back to work, then stormed off.

"Ah, that poor lass," Rowland sighed and stared after the woman.

"You know," I started. "When you said 'goofy looking', I expected someone the complete opposite of Sarah."

"Aye, she is goofy looking," he said confused. "She has not one bit of a Dwarven lady's charm no matter how hard I tried when I was raising her. Did me best, I truly did, but she just kept growing taller and skinnier by the year. She's scrawny and couldn't tip the barrel of mead if she tried. Poor lass. Picked her own name, though! Said to me, she said, 'Da am no' Scrawny Arms, lass, Tiny, or even girl. I am Sarah. That's me.'"

He sighed at the memory. "Right proud of her I was. Weird name, but she's stubborn as a mule. Gets that from me, I'm guessin'."

I couldn't stop laughing long enough to breathe right, and I'm pretty sure I may have offended my new friend by the confusion on his face.

"By human standards," I gasped trying to catch my breath, "she is considered beautiful, or at least I think of her that way."

"Are ye daft, lad?" he asked cautiously. "Be ye teasing me now?"

I shook my head, smiling, and the brawny blacksmith's eyes lit up. Then he bolted my way. He picked me up and crushed me as he danced around in circles whooping in joy. I had to duck and weave my head to keep from being impaled or cut by my own axe.

"Glorious Radiance!" he called. "Me girl is a beauty! Hahahahaha!"

We both laughed when he put me back on my feet. He handed me my weapon, and as soon as I touched it, the information screen popped up.

Blood Great Axe
+5 to attacks
Perfectly balanced to deal death and destruction.
Weight: 30lbs
Made by Master Smith Rowland and Journeyman Carpenter Sarah in Sunrise Village.

"It's beautiful, Rowland." I admired the weapon in my hand. "Thank you."

He stepped back and indicated that I should give it a whirl. He had a block of wood ready, and I stepped up to chop it in half. I lifted the great axe and could feel the weight of it; it didn't bother me much, but I knew increasing my strength and constitution would help to keep me from getting too tired mid-battle.

The wood block didn't stand a chance. The head of the monstrous axe whistled through the air, and the wood flew apart. Rowland grinned at my glee and asked if I wanted another go.

He had more wood that needed chopping. I thanked him and begged off of that. We walked back inside, and he laid the axe gently on the counter.

"How much do I owe you for all this?" I asked, pointing to the great axe and dagger. I held up a hand to stop him before he started. "A fair price. You worked hard on these, and I take care of my friends."

He thought for a moment, pulled out an abacus, and started to flick the little, multicolored beads back and forth. When he finally stopped, he looked at me with a shy look, and it looked like he didn't want to say.

"Tell me what I owe, Rowland," I said calmly.

"With everything entered in, materials and labor, it'll run ye about five gold. I'll split that with the lass, and since she leveled, she won't charge as much. Now, if ye don't ha–"

"Done," I said and reached into my inventory for the required amount. I pulled out an extra gold piece and put the five on the table. He stared at the money for a moment, then reached for it slowly. I grabbed his wrist and turned his palm over to give him the extra gold piece.

"You took care of me today," I said softly. "I appreciate that. You didn't have to do what you did. You are an honorable and great craftsman. Thank you, brother."

He smacked the gold onto the table with a smile and rushed into the back. He came back out with a sheath for my dagger. It was sturdy, brown leather. Simple. I liked it.

"When does yer questing begin?" he asked with a big grin shining through his beard.

"We leave tomorrow for the castle ruins."

"Good. If yer staying with ol' Sir at his Tavern, I'll be by later with a gift of me own."

"I'll see you in a bit then, Rowland."

I left the smithy after putting my great axe and dagger into my inventory. I walked down to Sarah's shop and walked in. I heard sawing and called out to the woman. She popped around the corner with a scowl until she saw me, and then her scowl turned into a look of confusion.

"I came to give you something," I said. I'd already pulled two gold pieces from my funds. All said and done, today had put me down to four hundred ninety gold, ninety silver, and two copper. A lot better than I thought. I knew I still had my armor tomorrow to get, but that would be then. This was important.

"My da' will have taken my share of the fee when you paid 'im," she tried to explain, but I held up a hand.

"Where I come from, you give extra when you particularly like a product and you feel it's worth more than what the seller says." I strode over and held out my closed fist with the coins inside.

She slowly held her own hand out beneath mine. I dropped the two coins into hers, and she gasped.

"I also believe in equal pay for equal work," I said with a smile. "Leveling up is good and all, but if you told the truth about that wood, it was hard on you, too. Rowland has the other two gold for you. Thank you for your hard work."

She was still staring at the gold and nodding as I left. I made my way back through the square and waved at the little girl and her brother. They were safe, good. I walked leisurely back to the tavern and headed in. The others were still out, I supposed.

Sir Dillon had opened the tavern once more as a way of wishing us all well, so some of the locals were there lounging and drinking, telling tales of their adventures in the forest, fish they caught and their daily lives. It was good to hear that they didn't have the constant fear of being enslaved by some galactic asshole on their hearts. These were good folk. I wanted them to stay that way.

My friends came back a little later. They all sported fresh clothes, and their gear was tucked away for tomorrow. Tonight was all about relaxation and being together with the community.

There was a raucous roar outside the tavern, and I stood to get a better view from my spot at the back of the room. The door burst open, and all I saw was a barrel weaving through tables and people.

"Where's the traveler who thought me girl was a beauty?!" shouted Rowland.

"Rowland!" I yelled back and shot over to him. My friends visibly relaxed and started to smile. They had probably expected a brawl.

We clasped hands and patted shoulders. He patted his barrel and lifted it onto the bar.

"Willem, my friend, if you would do the honors?" The blacksmith handed the knight bartender a tap, and the man smiled. He nodded, tapped the barrel, and poured a couple mugs. Then he poured some more. And more. Not one patron was without a mug of the Dwarven brew.

Rowland raised his hand and began to speak. He thanked the community for their unity and perseverance. He praised the farmers and craftsmen for their hard work and sweat. Then he turned to the Gods for their continued blessings even as they battled for their people's freedom.

At last, he turned to my friends and me.

"To our hope, do we raise our mugs and drink our fill," he said as his voice took on a more sing-song quality. "To fight through good and through ill. They come to stand as sword and shield and heed our hopes, results they yield! Drink! Be merry! And get those bastards!"

Everyone drank, well, except Yohsuke; he never did care for drinking. He waited until the Wolf Beast-kin next to him wasn't paying attention then poured his mug into hers with a smile.

Everyone drank and had a great time. Rowland kept calling me his brother and feeding me more of his home-brewed mead. He called it Forge Mead because the hops he used were heated in his forge and added a little of the wood used to heat the concoction to give it flavor. It was sweet with strawberries brushed to a pulp and fermented but had an earthy undertone on hops. I couldn't quite put my finger on all the different tastes. So, in true Dwarven fashion, I drank until I couldn't stand. Then drank some more. It was a great time.

Chapter Six

I woke up feeling rough and thirsty. A pitcher of water and some roots were on my nightstand. I drank a good portion of the water and dumped the rest on my head over the basin on my desk to help wash the night's sweat from my fur. I picked up the roots and walked to the commons where the party and some of the locals were eating.

"Chew those roots, and it will help to ease the hangover," said Sir Dillon.

I did as he bid and was surprised to feel the pain and fuzziness ease a bit more.

We all ate, and those who needed to return for other items left to do so. I wandered over to the armorers and wasn't surprised to see Kynin and Farrin waiting for me. The lady bear smiled, and her brother dipped his head and motioned toward the back room.

The back room was well lit with large windows. The walls were lined with shelves kind of like Rowland's but they were loaded with leather, oils, and all sorts of leather working tools. In the back corner was a work table and a manikin to model the armor.

The manikin sported some fine leather armor. Black leather with some fur trim near the chest and arms. It was beautiful. As I came closer, I noticed that there was a carving in the chest. It was a bear's head, but not just any bear—this had to be Marin.

I wanted to touch it. I wanted to run my fingers over the likeness of the bear who fought me with such honor and passion, but out of respect for Farrin, I waited.

"Touch it," the bear-man said at last. "It's your's. May she protect you as she protected her queen."

I nodded and stepped forward until I could do just that. The soft fur contrasted well with the sturdiness of the leather.

Marin's Black Leathers
+3 to Defense.
Marin gave her all in life as she will for you in death.
Made by Apprentice Tanner Farrin of Sunrise Village.

I smiled at the description. It seemed fitting for someone like her. Funny how fighting with someone full throttle makes you feel like you know them better than anyone.

Farrin had left already. According to Kynin, he hadn't slept or eaten so that he could make this armor as his final respects to his friend. When I asked the price, she just shook her furry head. Finally, I bought a belt and some bracers. Both only provided +1 Defense each. It wasn't much, but I wasn't planning on taking the brunt of the damage either. The belt and bracers only ran me fifty silver together.

I put the belt on and stowed the chest piece and bracers in my inventory. I thanked Kynin, and she wished me luck on our hunt.

I returned to the tavern and found my group ready to go. They all wore their gear. Yohsuke sported some thick, blood-red, padded armor with a flowing skirt. Normally, I'd tease him about the skirt, but the man had won my respect long ago, so I left it alone. Bokaj and Balmur both wore some nice leather armor similar to mine, but Bokaj's was brown and Balmer's was a mottled grey that looked like gravel. They had no fur, but I could see that they had their normal clothes on beneath so they would be set. They also had black padded pants with what looked like leather pads sewn in for added protection. An interesting concept that I was a little upset I didn't think of.

Our tank wore a chainmail shirt and a helmet with horns, like some kind of cartoon Viking. It was pretty neat. He also had leather pants on with metal greaves around his calves and metal plates covering his quads. It looked odd, but he assured me it would be effective. Most of us decided to travel with our weapons in our inventories since they were either heavy or unwieldy after long periods, like my great axe or Jaken's shield. Yohsuke and Balmur wore their weapons since they were light and easily stowed.

I put my great dagger onto my belt in the sheath. It was a weight to get used to, but it was fine after an hour of walking. I lead the way, having been there before. The forest around us felt a little less alive than what I had come to know with Dinnia and Sharo. Maybe it was because there were three more people and not one of them a Druid or attached to nature the way I was.

We didn't run into any trouble on the way there; all was suspiciously quiet. Last time I had been this close to the ruins, I had been farming the Insane Wolves in the area. Maybe they didn't respawn like a normal game does? If so, that would be a blessing. I'd hate to have to get into a fight so close when we had no clue what to expect at the ruins.

A little further in, the greens and browns of the forest proper began to thin out and the walls of the castle came into view. The walls stood just how I had seen them last. Nothing had changed.

"How do we want to do this, gents?" I asked in a low voice. I wasn't sure what was inside, but if they had senses like mine, I didn't want them to know we were close by.

Bokaj looked around and must have found what he was looking for because he scrambled up the tree next to us. He must have gone up to get a better view; can't believe I didn't think of that.

He dropped back down a few minutes later.

"Okay," he said softly. "I saw a couple groups of mobs walking around. It looked like they were on some kind of patrol. Wolves, it looked like. They are too far to make out their levels. Each group had about three Wolves."

I'd fought more, and from the looks of it, so had these guys.

What worried me was that before, the Wolves were mindless killing machines bent on destruction. These ones seemed to have some other purpose. Shit.

"Someone could be controlling them," Yohsuke echoed my own thoughts. "It happens often enough that I wouldn't be surprised to see some kind of kennel master or controller type nearby making them do the patrols."

We nodded and proceeded to plan our entrance. Our Ranger had only seen one real entrance, so that was our way in. We didn't have the luxury of trying to be sexy about it. We get in; they get dead. Simple but hopefully effective.

"Hold up," Yohsuke ordered softly. "Before we march in there, what can everybody do? Like, I know some of the basic shit, but what can we all do that may help?"

I filled them all in on the few spells I had: Regrowth, Filgus' Flaming Blade, Frozen Dagger and whatnot. Jaken had a couple of small healing spells and a hate generating ability that attracted the attention of hostile creatures near him, and Bokaj had a couple of bow abilities tied to being a Ranger. Balmur had a really interesting one where he could move quickly from one area to the next but didn't want to give too many specifics because where's the fun in that? Yoh finished it off by telling us about a spell he had called Astral Bolt and his main weapon which was a type of mana blade.

We worked our way slowly up the hill toward a downed section of wall. When we got to the entryway, Jaken took the lead. I was right behind him, Yohsuke behind me, and Bokaj at the rear. Balmur, being a Rogue, was planning to use us as the distraction he needed to do the most damage to any controllers we found, if there was one.

The outer wall was a barren area; we must have just missed the last patrol. There was a forty foot gap between the outer wall and the inner wall. Piles of stone, brick, and vegetation were scattered here and there. We decided to walk to our right and go counterclockwise to the next entrance. We tried to sneak as stealthily as possible. Yohsuke and Bokaj were quick and stealthy already, so we decided that they would trail behind Jaken and I from about ten to fifteen feet. That way, if we were spotted, they would have a chance to flank our attackers.

Jaken and I had just reached cover a few minutes later when the first patrol had turned the corner. They moved at a trot, and I could see that the three Insane Wolves were level 6. They came our way and didn't look to be aware of our presence yet.

"Quietly," I whispered to Jaken. He smiled and equipped his sword and shield. I pulled out my great axe just as they passed us.

The Wolf in the rear saw us and growled, causing the others to stop and whirl on the spot. Jaken raised his shield just as two of them leapt at him. One hit the shield squarely and bounced off with ten percent of its health gone from hitting it so hard. The other got knocked off course by an arrow in its back. Tmont charged into the fray joined by Yohsuke.

Yoh had pulled out the base of what looked like a katana from his inventory, and a dark surge of astral burst from it. The blade was the color of the night sky with specks of white scattered throughout it. I didn't have time to look much longer as the Wolf that bounced off Jaken's shield was standing back up. I hefted my great axe and charged in.

I brought my axe down on the Insane Wolf as soon as I was in range and cleaved the poor bastard in two. Then turned to see the walking pincushion the Wolf behind me had been turned into, courtesy of Bokaj. Tmont slapped it with her left claw then her right, and the beast was dead. Yohsuke had already finished his and tucked his sword away. We all smiled at each other and got ready for the next patrol.

We looted the corpses of the Wolves, only getting a few coppers each, but hey, it's money, baby. Bokaj collected what arrows from the Wolf that he could. Out of the eight he had fired, six had come out usable. It was good that he could collect some of the used ones. He had plenty from the way he made it sound, so I let it be.

"Nice axe, dude," Yohsuke fist bumped me as we moved away from the battle scene. We didn't want to let the other patrol know that something was amiss before we could spring a trap on them.

"Thanks, man," I said back. "What the hell kind of weapon was that?! Was that your mana blade?"

"Astral Blade," he corrected mildly. "Takes half my mana to summon it and that mana doesn't recover until the blade is dismissed, but that doesn't matter much considering my stats and the spells I have at my disposal. It's pretty sweet, man."

I nodded. I was pretty stoked to see what else my friends could do. It was one thing to hear about it but another completely to witness firsthand. We set up at a pile of rubble just around the bend. This time, we had our tank closer to the rear, while the three of us waited for him to draw their attention. Jaken stood there in the open once the Wolves were in sight. Once they saw him, all bets were off. They charged straight for him. He set his feet wide and brought his shield up to take their weight, but only one actually made it past our death trap.

Yohsuke pushed his astral sword out and cut the leg off one, and I finished it off quickly. Tmont tackled another as her master put an arrow into the Insane Wolf's exposed stomach. The last Wolf let momentum carry it over our trap, just to be speared by Jaken's longsword. It looked like it was still alive but fading fast due to a bleeding debuff. A little blood drop symbol appeared beside its health bar, and the bar was shrinking quickly. He tugged on the blade the same time he smacked the beast with his shield and dropped it to the ground dead.

I had to say, I was thoroughly impressed with how smoothly things were going. We were getting some nice experience so far, although since we had decided to make a party, it was distributed evenly. Instead of getting what I would for killing a level 6, I was getting a little more than the amount of experience I would for killing a level 1 Insane Wolf, but if this was anything like dungeons in any of the games I'd played, there would be more enemies and experience with them.

We moved on cautiously; just because Bokaj had only seen two patrols didn't mean that was all there was to the place.

Once we hit the entrance to the inner courtyard, we were stopped by Balmur, who seemingly stepped out of the shadows of a building to our right. It wasn't very tall, about fifteen to twenty feet, but it looked sturdy.

"Good news... and bad news," he said simply. "Good news, we were right about the Wolves being controlled. Bad news, he's strong and definitely not alone."

He had us follow him slowly and quietly for about five minutes to where Balmur saw the problem. In the center of the courtyard near the gates to the castle proper, we saw a pack of twenty, not just Insane Wolves, but Undead Loyal Hounds, too.

The Hounds laid at the guy's feet like some kind of brown and white, mangy puppies, and the Wolves milled about restlessly. Whenever an Insane Wolf got too close to the Hounds, they would growl and snap at each other. There were four Hounds and sixteen Wolves. The guy—the Undead Kennel Master—was level 11, but the Wolves and Hounds were only level 6.

The Undead Kennel Master looked like a better put together zombie from the movies: messed up brown hair, sallow skin drawn tight over his bones with age, and kept together by something evil. He wore brown breeches and a moldy, white shirt. He was barefoot and had a sword sheathed at his side.

There wasn't much in the courtyard really, but I did see what looked like an old training tower. Maybe when the guard or army would run formations, the brass would climb up to watch and make corrections? Who knows, but it could be useful. Maybe we could drop it on him? It looked tall enough.

Jaken motioned for us to back off and go back to the shadows where we met Balmur.

"We need to plan this right," he sighed. "I can take a beating and heal well, but that will be bad news all around with him in there. My guess is that those Hounds will be his guards and the Wolves will attack anything that isn't them. Any ideas?"

We all considered the predicament for a moment, and then I smiled.

"Yeah, ever heard of a fastball special?"

After a ten-minute planning session, we had a solid enough plan of attack. Bokaj was going to get on the roof where we were planning and see how close he could get to the giant mob before having to stop or risk pulling some hate. The rest of us would be down below in the pit fighting directly. Bokaj nodded once and bolted up the side of the building with ease. His panther partner would be coming with us.

We waited ten minutes to give our Ranger time to get into position, then sent Tmont in to raise hell. The Wolves did exactly what we thought they would and gave chase. The black cat shot to the training tower and bounded up it easily. Her job was to sell it to those Wolves that she would be within their grasp soon so they would be on her like white on rice.

With a hiss and snarl from T, the obvious mini-boss's Hounds had bolted upright and were standing between him and the Wolves.

Good, all according to plan so far.

The fun part came next. Now, in my fox form, I only weighed a good ten pounds or so. Jaken lifted me up and threw me straight at the Kennel Master with everything he had from about sixty feet away. I shot like a cannonball right at him while he was looking at the Wolves and barking orders in some kind of undead groan. The deadly thing about cannonballs is their velocity and density. See, when it hits, all that compact energy was going through whatever was in front of it—unless it was sturdy enough to stop the ball. That's what I had thought anyway.

As soon as I was a few feet away from the Kennel Master, I shapeshifted into my panther form and hit him in the chest with a solid three-hundred-pound-panther-push kick. My panther form had grown as my level increased, making it heavier. Thankfully.

The bastard rocketed a good fifteen feet back and smacked into the dilapidated wall behind him next to the doors to get inside. His health went down a good fifteen percent, and while I wanted to celebrate my successful use of tactics, the

Hounds were chomping wildly at my beautiful tail. A few of the Wolves had noticed what had happened and decided that the other panther wasn't worth the wait. I began my own deadly game of tag as the Hounds began chasing me. I would smack one in the head then run, smack another then run, smack and run. I had taken a few bites and was down to about seventy-five percent HP myself, but I was good so far.

I looked over just in time to see two arrows sprout from the Undead Kennel Master's chest, and Balmur stepped out of the shadows behind him with his dual hand axes ready. He surged forward, and I saw him slice into the boss's legs, then his back. But the damage didn't stop there, oh no, because at the end of his combo, Balmur sank his axes into the exposed back in front of him, and there was a burst of black fire the same color as his hair and beard.

The Hounds broke from their game with me and bolted to their master to try and help, but his health was well below thirty-five percent after Balmur and Bokaj were finished. It was still falling because of a burn debuff from the flame. By the time the Kennel Master hit the ground on one knee, Bokaj had put two more arrows into his chest. A purple bolt flew past my left flank and hit the boss. I turned to see Yohsuke striding away from a pile of dead Wolves with an upraised hand pointed in my direction.

I shifted back to my bipedal fox form and went to help finish off the Hounds. Too late, I noticed with the Kennel Master's influence gone, the Insane Wolves' blood lust had returned with a vengeance, and they had turned on the Hounds as well. A pile six deep was currently killing one of the Hounds, and its friend was harrying the ones closer to the edge of the frenzy.

Tmont dropped on the two Wolves left beneath her, and Jaken was there to assist. He slashed with his sword, and a red aura began to cover him. All the creatures within thirty feet of him stopped what they were doing and rushed him. I pulled out my great axe and set to work. There were only five Wolves in that thirty feet, but it was still rough going. I plowed down one after three good hits, then shot another with an ice dagger. The Wolf was too busy trying to get to Jaken through its friends to care that it had taken a knife to the side.

Yohsuke and Balmur dispatched the two Hounds closest to them, then joined us. A minute later, we all advanced on the feeding frenzy. I used Lightning Bolt to zap the nearest Wolf, and it whipped around to try and get to me. Yohsuke shot it with an astral bolt; then we laid into it together. He stabbed while I chopped. Jaken saw that we were getting roughed up and threw a heal our way. I felt a refreshing warmth and saw a golden glow encompass my skin, then noted that my health bar was full from seventy percent. Yohsuke looked to be healed about the same. He had sustained less damage—but it never hurts to be at full HP.

Another five minutes and the courtyard was clear. We looted the corpses, and I went through my notifications. After that battle, I had managed to rake in ten silver from all the Wolves after the split loot and another ten from the Kennel Master. The boss of the courtyard also had a rusty sword that no one picked up and a key. We let Balmur take the key since he was the sneak amongst us, then moved to the shade of the castle wall near the door to recover our spent mana.

"There's no telling what comes next," I said. "It could be anything. So let's try to be fluid in here, and don't get separated."

Everyone nodded, and after we finished resting, I did a final check of my stat screen to check how close I was to leveling.

Pretty damn close actually. I think a few more mobs and I'll hit level 9.

It took Jaken and I both to be able to open the door far enough for us to get in. There were holes in the ceiling here and there letting the midday sun shine through. The entryway was grand, or at least it would have been if the place wasn't in a state of decay. The place was clean-ish. There was no dust, no dirt on the carpets. The room was barren of any kind of loving touch. A burnt and charred painting hung from a pillar in the center of the grand stair. It looked like a family but was too destroyed to really give much more than that impression. To the right and left of the staircase, tables lined the walls with trinkets and candelabras still polished and neat. Two doors, one on each side of the stairs, led to other rooms. A quick hand count showed that the right hallway was where we would begin our search of the place.

We crept around the staircase and through the door. The hallway was a little dark, but thanks to a light spell that Balmur had decided to pick up as a distraction, the others could see well enough. We walked slowly down the hall to the next room. It looked like it was the kennel area, likely where the Kennel Master would have been found when he was alive. After searching for a few minutes and turning up nothing for our efforts, we made our way back to the previous room, then down the left doorway.

This door led to a kitchen area with staff still inside—and undead. The Head Chef, who ironically had no head, worked in the back of the room over a cauldron. His head watched over his stirring from a shelf behind him looking over the kitchens.

The place actually smelled like they were preparing some kind of disgusting food. I gagged, fighting the bile rising in my stomach for a moment. Racks of moldy bread were scattered between tables, and the oven in the corner was still hot, as if even in their in death they had to cook.

I was so fixated on the creep in the back that I failed to see three of the Chef's Help that came at us with butcher knives. One held a rolling pin, which would have been funny had he not tried to bash my skull in with it.

The level 7 chef and his posse of level 6s didn't pose too much of a threat. Although, one did manage to damage Balmur with the rolling pin as he dodged a knife to the throat. We killed one of the help and it granted me thirty EXP.

We took care of the room and deemed that there was nothing worth collecting in here either. The chef gave me thirty-five EXP after he died though, so that was nice. We searched for secret doors, cellar entrances, and whatnot to no avail.

I healed Balmur with Regrowth, and we moved back to the central room. Once we came to the top of the stairs, we decided to go left this time. There was a set of glass doors, broken and weathered from the years and animals, that led to a set of stairs and a larger courtyard with a throne in the center of the overgrown grass and vegetation. The place looked abandoned, but we would check it out when we got to it.

To our left, we found a series of halls and rooms. The hallways looked like they were once well lit and lavish in decorations but had fallen to disrepair. The floors and small side tables decorating the sides of the hall still appeared to be clean and well managed. There were four doors along this hallway and one set of double doors at the end. The first door to our left opened as we approached and out stepped an Undead Butler level 8. He was dressed smartly in what looked like tattered black slacks and a black doublet.

It looked up, saw us, then lifted its hand, and a blast of cold shot our direction.

"Caster!" someone shouted redundantly.

Jaken took the blast to his shield, but even without a direct hit, it sucked fifteen percent of his life away. He glowed red briefly like he had before, and the door on the other side opened and out poured two Zombie Maids level 7.

He set his feet, and they were on him instantly. I cast Regrowth on Jaken and brought my great dagger to bear on the Butler Mage from behind. Balmur shoved past me and set to work, getting the more obvious flanking damage so I let him do his job. The thing's health dropped quickly between my one stab and Balmur's dozen accompanied by arrows courtesy of Bokaj.

Yohsuke decided to go after one of the Maids to Jaken's right flank, so I went for the other. By the time I got there, they had managed a few swipes at him with knives I hadn't seen them carrying. I came in quickly, and rather than risk doing so from a distance, I put my hand up to my opponent's head and cast Lightning Bolt. Her health dropped by fifty percent, and I got a notification saying it was a critical hit. I swiped it away quickly and pressed my advantage. She was stunned now, and between my stabs and Jaken's slashes, she fell to the floor dead... again. I turned to see the Butler and the other Maid had been dispatched already. Not too much loot-wise, but I wouldn't complain about the thirty EXP from each of them.

The rooms didn't have much. A few silvers here and there—and the two rooms after that had fuck all—so we decided to go into the next available area.

We finally reached the double doors at the end of the hall. Thinking it would be a shit show inside, we piled up on each side with Jaken in the middle to grab whatever could be waiting. Yohsuke stood opposite me at the door on the right with Balmur behind him, and I had Bokaj behind me with an arrow nocked and waiting. On a three count, we opened the door.

The doors opened to a grand ballroom with tables lined up like a banquet would be held at any moment. Pearly pillars of stone climbed to the ceiling with its starry blackness. The grand windows in this room seemed to be well-preserved glass murals that depicted scenes of knights fighting great Dragons with glowing swords and hunters felling bucks with impossibly huge horns.

We began to shuffle into the room in awe of the tremendous amount of attention to detail each window held.

They were so beautiful, and I couldn't stop staring. I couldn't bear the thought of having to look away, or I might miss something interesting—which was probably why I took a sudden twenty-five percent hit to my HP.

"Archer!" Yohsuke called, turning to fire an Astral Bolt, his version of my Frozen Dagger. The projectile hit the skeletal archer on the head and knocked it from its perch behind us about sixty feet up. Between the spell and the fall damage, the thing was dead... Well, dead-er, at least. I didn't get to see its level, so I guessed it must have been on the lower end. I'd have to check the EXP notifications later to see.

More archers were posted along the walls, again about sixty feet up, and they began to fire at us. Those of us who were close by hid behind Jaken with his shield. Yohsuke and Bokaj hid behind a pillar to our left and began to return fire. It seemed like easy pickings for these damned Skeletons at the moment while we were pinned down.

Balmur disappeared under a table behind us. I wasn't sure if he was hiding or trying to stealth to a better vantage point, but he could handle himself.

"Hey, can you walk us to the table over here to our right?" I pointed to the desired location. "It might provide better cover."

Jaken had been taking minor damage from shots going under his shield or over top. He wasn't looking too good; though the shots weren't critical, they were numerous.

"On three." A fresh wave of arrows rushed our way, and he snarled, "THREE!"

Keeping his shield up, we moved to the table, and I lifted it over us and in front of his shield. It wasn't perfect, and it was unwieldy as hell, but it was a quick fix until we got our problem solved. I handed it to Jaken, who took it by the only post in it at the center and watched as he sat it down carefully. I cast Regrowth on him, and he nodded in appreciation. Tmont grumbled behind me, probably pissed she couldn't be more help.

I heard a clatter of bone and looked out to see Balmur on the platform to my right where a skeletal archer had been. He whipped out a small throwing hatchet and sent it spinning across the way into the head of another archer about to take a potshot at our friends behind the pillar. Then the the cloaked figure stepped back and dissolved into shadow—emerging behind the Skeleton to his right on the next platform.

Oh, I would be asking about that shit. That must have been the ability he was talking about! But while he was up there, he was a sitting duck if the other archers realized what was going on.

"Hey, Yoh!" I shouted to grab my friend's attention. "Care to raise some hell?!"

"I thought you'd never ask, puto!" He grinned savagely. "What's the plan?"

"Back to back old west style, baby." I laughed and saw the idea take hold. "Sling some spells with me. Bokaj, care to provide some cover?"

"Oh. You know it, broham." He just laughed and started to fire faster as my brother came to join me.

"Count of three, you come over here, Yoh," I looked up at the current stock of fuckers firing at us. "One," I looked back to my friend, "twooo... three!"

Yohsuke booked it from his position of cover with Bokaj providing cover for him, and I caught him as he slid behind the table.

"Jaken, move your bacon," I commanded. "We have a Rogue to cover, bro."

"Y'all are crazy. I like that about you guys." The man picked up the table easily and started to walk forward slowly.

"Sling 'em if you got 'em!" I cast one icy blade after another into the archers coming into view as Bokaj provided cover fire from behind. I spent five MP per casting, but there was no cool down for it, so I could fling them accurately until I ran out of mana.

As we moved further in, we had to stop and rest to recover some mana We only worked until we got down to the fifty percent mark on MP. Tmont laid down and harrumphed loudly, still kind of pissy she hadn't killed anything. Yohsuke recovered his a lot quicker than I did thanks to his high wisdom stat. Good man, he knew his way around his caster limitations well. Balmur disappeared from his hunt up above and reappeared under a table beside us to rest. After about ten minutes of rest, we were ready to go again.

While we fought through the hail of arrows, my mind wandered a bit. The hall was huge, at least the size of two football fields, making me think that whoever owned the place must have partied hard—the rich greedy bastard. Then again, I could be wrong. Being in a fight with boney assholes raining pointy death on you and your friends seemed to have that effect. Kind of like the fog of war, but—you know—sharp and somehow shittier.

After another rest, we made it to the end. There was a throne with one final Skeleton there. It hadn't seemed to notice us yet, or maybe it just didn't care, who knows. I was at about half mana, and Yoh was well on his way to being fully recovered. We had collected Balmur and Bokaj on our scamper to the throne. The Rogue had gone back after the hellish rain stopped to collect his throwing hatchet.

"I only have this one so far," he grumbled as we all chuckled.

"What do you guys think?" Bokaj asked after a moment. "Boss fight?"

"Seems like it, although he should have aggro'd us already since we defeated all his goons," Jaken observed.

"How are you on arrows bud?" I wondered. "You laid down a lot of hate."

"I am so good on arrows, man," Bokaj said. "I bought out the fletcher and the armory. It only cost me around ten gold. Not bad, I'd say."

"Damn, bro," I said in awe. That had to be a hell of a lot of arrows.

"What say you fire one of those arrows into mister important up there on his throne?" Jaken pointed.

"Happy to oblige, kind sir!" Bokaj went to pull an arrow out of his quiver at his hip, but I stopped him. I wasn't topped off on mana, and I didn't want to go in half cocked to fight this guy. After a few minutes, I nodded to him, and he grinned again.

Bokaj nocked an arrow and took aim. He released, and the arrow sailed off to connect to the chin of the lone Skeleton on the throne.

I don't know why, but the knot that had been forming in my stomach the entire time we had been fighting our way through a hail of arrows tightened. A sense of unease that I hadn't felt when we entered the ruins clung to my mind, and I couldn't shake it.

The ground shook slightly, and the rattle of bone seemed to sound hundreds of times louder than the fall of the Skeleton in front of us. I looked around, and the bones of the fallen skeletal archers that we had destroyed were rolling and careening toward us.

"Incoming!" I shouted. Jaken flipped the table, and the party grouped behind it swiftly. The bones flew so fast that the ones hitting the top of the table shattered and chipped away at the wood on contact.

"Fuuuuuuuuuuuuuuuu," we all yelled, in unison.

Since coming here, this was one of the craziest things I had seen, and I could turn into animals and throw lightning at will. *AND I HAD A TAIL! SHIT.*

The bones piled into a group, then began to swirl around like a tornado of death.

Bones collected and melded together, fused into great limbs and the body of a beast. As the head finished, we all came to the realization that this was probably going to be hard.

Really hard.

There before us, in all its twenty-five-foot glory, stood a Bone Dragon level 18. Even with half its health gone, this was going to be stupidly hard. I could only assume that it was only at half health because we had gone through and killed all the enemies used to finish it.

"Spread out!" shouted Bokaj. He unleashed hell on the beast's head and moved to the pillar to his left. The Dragon's health bar barely budged, and it swung its massive head toward the assault. It roared and shot its head forward trying to snap at the Ranger. It missed; no surprise there with his high dexterity, but still, this was about to suck.

An inhuman bellow resonated from Jaken, who had stepped in front of me, arms wide and crouched slightly. Spittle flying from his mouth and a red aura encompassing his body, he roared at the beast before him in challenge.

"Come and get me, you boney bastard!" The Dragon began to stomp his way, and Jaken began the delicate dance of a tank to position the asshole's face away from the party. Naturally, a good tank would keep his healer in line of sight; that way they could heal, buff, and assist the tank in staying alive. He did not do this. As soon as the damned thing went to take a bite, he dove out of the way and away from the assistant healer—me.

Yousuke and I both brought our hands up and cast a spell apiece. He sent an Astral Bolt sailing into the Dragon's back, and I sent Lightning Bolt careening into its chin. Neither of our spells seemed to do much; they brought the creature's health down about as much as four arrows from Bokaj. Must be some resistance to piercing damage and magic. *Which meant it would have some resistance to slashing damage as well*, I groaned in my head.

"This is going to take too much," I shouted. "Anyone have any ideas?"

"Yeah," came Balmur's voice from behind me. He was almost too sneaky. I flinched and tried to glance in his direction.

His eyes were on the surrounding walls and ceiling.

"What's up, man?"

"We're thinking too small," he explained. "Look at the way the room is set up. The columns, the ceiling—think Nintendo. Let me and Jaken run distraction. You get Yoh and Bokaj to start damaging columns to drop on him. Go."

He nodded at me, then sprinted to Jaken's side to slap at the Dragon's chin with his twin axes. The Dragon roared again and tried to bite the Dwarf but only ended up tossing Jaken with its head.

"Yohsuke, Bokaj!" I shouted to get their attention. "Go for the closest column to him and try to drop it on him!"

Both immediately started firing what they could at the column in front of the beast. It didn't look like we were making any progress, but our tank unknowingly helped by tossing Balmur out of the way when the Dragon speared its head forward. Boney fangs sank into the column, and the monster pulled mightily. I used several Ice Knives on the ceiling above it as he pulled, and the bricks gave way.

The portion of the ceiling held up by the column crashed down loudly onto the Bone Dragon's back, and I heard splintering. The beast's health dropped significantly; it looked to be a little below forty percent, and the ceiling in the area was a little unstable.

Maybe we could continue dropping the ceiling on him?

I didn't get to try it out right away as a bone tail came rocketing my way. I sailed a good bit before hitting the ground and rolling to a stop twenty-five feet later. I was at about a quarter of my health. I groaned and cast Regrowth on myself. My health started to go back up slowly. I sat up and surveyed what was going on.

Jaken was panting and looked a little tired. I could see he had lost health and was healing himself as he went. The others were trying to run distraction duty. Bokaj was steadily releasing arrows at the damaged ceiling, trying to drop more bricks onto the boss. It was working, albeit slowly.

Much too slowly for us to survive this, so I decided to try something. "Run from him!"

I took my Beginner's Axe and equipped it, then sprinted up the main aisle at the Dragon and swung at the damaged column by its left forepaw with all my might. Yohsuke had been trying to get it to crumple with his magic, but the damn Dragon kept buffeting him with ghostly gusts of wind. The base of the column was cracked and about half strength I guessed—*I hoped.*

The axe shattered on impact, splintering the column, and the crushing weight of the ceiling finished my job for me. The ceiling above the Dragon began to cave in as I continued my mad dash across the aisle under the Dragon's gaping maw.

The falling debris fell onto the beast, almost all at once, and the weight of the stones caved the floor under the pile of bones. The floor kept going, quaking and trembling, threatening to give way for another few seconds. One portion of the floor had begun to give up the ghost as I passed over, and I almost fell—to what could have easily been—my death. The Bone Dragon's health was almost completely gone now, and we decided to do the safe thing and try to rain down hellfire from above. Yohsuke and myself fired Astral Bolt after Frozen Dagger until it no longer moved. The notification screen that erupted into my face was one I wasn't expecting to see.

At least not so soon.

QUEST COMPLETED: JUST LIKE NEW – You have completed Queen Kyra's request to cleanse the ruins that Dinnia showed you. Reward: 2,000 EXP, status (to be decided by the

Queen) amongst her people for you and those who assist in the quest.

CONGRATULATIONS!

Level Up! Level 11. You have 15 unspent attribute points.

I considered the notifications that I had been ignoring and saw that the Dragon had given one thousand EXP when it passed. It was ten levels higher than me, so I could see why it would. Then the two thousand EXP from the quest pushed most of us up a few levels. Jaken, Balmur, and I were at level 11, and Bokaj and Yoshuke were at level 12. I had a good bit of EXP toward my next level already.

"That was the boss?" Yohsuke asked incredulously. "We still have the rest of the place to explore!"

"Well, that doesn't mean we might not run into something else, right?" I said with a chuckle. "Besides, we have one of the major tenants of our gaming philosophy to observe."

Yohsuke smiled and looked at the rest of the group. "We get all the loot."

Chapter Seven

We spent a few minutes recovering from our fight, healing, and discussing how things went. We all agreed that the idea to use the environment was a stroke of genius, and Balmur was promised a major good time with lots of booze in gratitude.

After we rested, we decided to check out the area across the hole in the floor near the throne the Dragon had come to life in front of. We were about to just fastball special me back over when Balmur stepped out of the shadows on the other side behind the throne.

"How the hell does he do that?!" I cried.

"It's an ability he learned before coming back," said Bokaj. "Shadow Step is like using the shadows as a doorway. It has a certain range that I don't remember right now, but it's legit. You should ask him about it. He likes to explain his abilities."

"There's a doorway over here!" called Balmur.

"Toss me, bud," I said before shifting to my fox form in front of Jaken.

The Paladin picked me up once more with ease and threw me through the air like a baseball. I noted some serious difference in his strength, and I was a bit worried about my landing. I easily cleared the gap in the floor, and luckily, Balmur caught me.

He and I went into the room he had found after he checked for traps. He found one in the floor—a spring-loaded one with barbed spears that would come through the top of the doorway. He dismantled the trap easily enough, and we were in.

The room was only six square feet and fit the two of us comfortably with our bounty. There was a large chest in the center of the wall at the end of the room, and shelves lined the side walls. Items were sparse on the shelves but looked interesting. One was a simple gold necklace with a pearl in it that gave a +1 to charisma. Another was a ring of protection that added +2 to defense. The last was a pair of gloves that increased the wearer's ability to perform sleights of hand. I tossed those at Balmur right there. After that, we opened the chest, and our inner greedy gamers came raging to life.

There was gold, silver, and an even more precious metal—platinum. I had to physically wipe the drool off my face. We put the whole chest into my inventory, since my strength was the highest of the two of us. We didn't want to sit there and count the money away from the group without protection. The whole chest disappeared, and I felt a slight shift in my physical weight. It wasn't unbearable, but I knew I wouldn't be the group's pack mule. Not for long anyway.

We walked back outside, raised our hands, and gave a thumbs up.

"LOOTED!" I shouted. The group gave a cheer, and I tried to pick my way across the hole on my own by walking along the left wall in fox form. It took some time—about ten minutes of slow treading—and a couple close calls, but I eventually made it over.

I took the chest out of my inventory, and we spent a couple minutes counting, stacking—bickering like school girls—and finally finished the tally and voting process on the money and items. We would divide the fifty platinum and one hundred gold as evenly as possible. The silver and copper, we would donate to the village.

Bokaj, our charismatic friend, got the charisma necklace, and our squishiest member, Yohsuke, took the ring. Everyone agreed Balmur was the right choice to get the gloves.

We decided to go loot the body of the Bone Dragon last. We hadn't seen anything we had killed here disappear until someone looted it, so we weren't worried about it. We still had the upper portion of the opposite wing to look into.

We packed up and marched back the way we came. The arrows littering the ground told our story. I wondered if they would just disappear or if they would stay. Oh well. While we walked back, I fiddled with my unspent points. I had fifteen to play with, so I thought about what I had used the most of recently. Strength and magic. That blow took a good chunk of my health which bothered me. I thought over things for a moment and decided to up my stats like so: strength five points, dexterity three points, constitution two points, and intelligence the final five points. I figured hitting harder with my spells and strength would equal out my slightly slower mana regeneration. I also had four points for my weapon proficiency.

I opened my weapons tab and opened up the Great Axe Proficiency. A tree grew from it—kind of like a perk tree from some of the games I played back home. They were weapon skills. There were three to choose from so far, and I had four points to play with. One from not having enough to level up my Great Axe Proficiency before we left, and three from leveling up three times.

Wind Scythe – Throw your great axe into the enemy accurately up to 30 feet. One additional foot per 5 strength (max 35ft). 15 – 30 base damage. Cool down: 1 minute.

Cleave – Boosts damage of the next attack by 100%. Cool down: 3 minutes.

Devil's Hammer – Slam the butt, or a blunt portion, of your axe into the enemy. 50% chance to stun target for 30 seconds. Cool down: 2 minutes.

All of these skills were amazing, and I would have each of them, especially since this was only the beginning of the tree from the looks of it. I chose Cleave because duh, damage boosts are the stuff.

Wind Scythe would be something that could be a game changer for me. With that, I might be able to take an enemy out right away from a distance, then engage however else the situation dictated. Devil's Hammer was a must, too—who didn't want to ring someone's bell hard enough to stun them? I really had no reason *not* to take them all, so I had a point left over for later use.

We returned to the center of the place without incident, then crossed over to the wing on the right. The wing was empty—no Butlers or Maids unlike the other wing. This wing was also only two rooms. Well, two doors at least.

Balmur had to pick the lock of the first door, which took him more time than he was comfortable with. Inside, it looked like some kind of study and office combo. There was a dark desk with stamps and moldy papers on it. The shelves behind it were lined with books and pamphlets. I checked, but nothing jumped out a me. Most of the books just crumbled to dust after I touched them. The back wall hosted several large windows that opened to the courtyard we had seen earlier. The view was much the same.

We turned up some money in the desk but nothing too great—about three silver. We walked through an adjoining door off to left side of the room opposite the desk. Balmur was the first into the room, and the first out of it. A lightning burst shot into his chest and flung him into the rest of us. His health shot down until it was throbbing red, and the front of his armor was singed and smoking.

"Owwwww..." the poor bastard groaned. I cast Regrowth, and Jaken cast another spell that brought our friend's health up a good way.

"I'll go first," Jaken said and brandished his shield.

The tank stepped forward and nothing happened—no lightning burst, no traps, nothing. Balmur grumbled about him not saying something sooner, but that's what he got for not checking for traps.

We carefully filed into the room, and it was a good thing we hadn't barged in again. I could see something on the floor in front of the group. It looked like a rune tinted in a dark blue color with solid lines that shimmered the way the air does over concrete when the sun is out. The circle spanned three feet and was mere inches from Jaken's toe.

"I would wager that there is our problem right there," I said and pointed to my find. "Looks like a rune trap."

The group wasn't unfamiliar with this concept. In more than a couple of the games we all played, runic magic was pretty popular to have as an aspect for magic in general. One of the spells in these games allowed the user to pick a spot to place a rune. That spot was then trapped; if someone stepped into the rune, they received damage. Sometimes the runes had elemental damage attached to them that was more powerful than some spells. If I were to guess, I would say this was either another lightning rune or an ice one.

I took out a copper coin and tossed it into the circle. The coin plunked down near the center and nothing happened.

"Looks like it might be activated by proximity to a body," I mused aloud. "I'd say that we should experiment, but screw that. Anyone see any more?"

My friends shook their heads, and I chuckled. Good. I doubted that would be the last of the defenses in this room, especially if this was the room I thought it was. A large, four-poster bed dominated one wall; plush pillows and furs covered the entirety. A well-preserved man laid in the bed. He had long, brown hair and the beginnings of a beard on his face. He looked serene with his eyes closed, a slight nose and chiseled jaw. He would definitely be considered handsome for someone in his early thirties. I got the feeling this was the owner of this castle. Well, more like a fort at this point.

The room was bathed in warm light from the large windows; rays of light covered the red carpeted floors. Two large suits of ebony plate mail armor stood menacingly in the corners beside the bed on slightly raised daises. The one with the winged helmet carried a black and white greatsword, about a foot wide and five-foot-long blade. The center of the blade was as black as the armor, dark as a new moon, and the edge was pure white. The suit with the hooded cloak over the helm wielded what looked like two decent sized daggers.

"What are the chances those tin cans are enchanted to defend the guy in the bed?" Bokaj asked quietly. "Anyone else feeling like they're in one giant cliché?"

We all nodded. Things had been kind of basic since the beginning of this 'dungeon'. Don't get me wrong, we were enjoying ourselves all things considered. I had been busy doing something I loved in the week we had been here. We had become something akin to heroes to people we didn't even know, in my world and here, but I missed my kid. I had to keep reminding myself that I was doing this for him; the little, blue-eyed whirlwind didn't deserve to have his life taken from him, especially not when it's my job to protect him.

The sooner we finished this here, the sooner our world would be protected. I hoped. But just because I was in a hurry to get back to my friends and family, didn't mean I was going to do this stupidly or half-assed.

No, sir! Not this guy.

"I'd wager that those items might drop if we can take them." Balmur took the words right out of my mouth.

"Dibs on the great sword," Jaken whispered quickly. I laughed; the only other person in the group who could even wield it was me, and he knew I swung axe. Dork.

"Hey, Bokaj, you have any melee weapons?" I asked. He shook his head no.

"I was mainly worried about ensuring my bow skills were high," Bokaj explained.

"You may want to think about it, a bit more, man," I informed him. "You never know what kind of area we might be in. A bow may not always be the best thing to use in those situations, right?"

He nodded thoughtfully. "What about our resident Rogue here? He would be able to put them to use better than I could."

"True, but I'm having fun using my hand axes, and I'm not looking to change them anytime soon." He smiled. "Maybe I can start smithing and make my own. You guys do know you can take up jobs, right?"

There was a confused look that passed over the rest of us, and Balmur sighed dramatically.

"While I was looking at weapons, the blacksmith, Rowland I think, approached me to see if I was interested in learning his trade since I'm an Azer Dwarf. He says he wonders how the metal will react to me. I thought about taking him up on it. Since we don't know where to go just yet or what to do, what's the harm in learning a trade?"

I thought about it a moment. Yes, while we work on our trades, we would be potentially taking time away from our mission, it could give us experience in its own way. Not to mention, if we could make our own gear, we could potentially help each other in the long run. It depended on the kinds of jobs that were available. I'd have to ask about it later.

"Great initiative, man. So it's decided then. Bokaj, if you want those daggers for a back up, you got 'em," I said.

"Sweet!" He smiled and readied himself, flashing a glance at the daggers.

We stepped further into the room, and the suits did nothing. We all had a bit of a "huh" moment. That sure didn't last long though because the guy in the bed sat bolt upright and began to wail in an unearthly moan.

"Lich?" I shouted the question, and the rest of my party shouted back, "LICH!"

We all went to town on the poor bastard. Arrows whizzed through the air and connected with their mark but didn't seem to do too much damage. The real powerhouse seemed to be our tank who had a golden hue to his sword and shield. The creature, now green with a sickly glow and it's hair waving and moving behind it like a creature in water was trying to rise. Sure enough, the thing was a **Lich Duke Level 14**. Not too much higher than us, but it was still hitting hard.

It smacked Yohsuke away from it into one of the suits of armor, the dagger one, and he stayed there stunned for a moment. With such close quarters battle going on, I figured I'd try my close up Lightning Bolt again. I snuck up on the thing as Jaken weaved in and out of the creature's spell-enhanced swipes and Tmont batted at its floating legs.

I put my hand up to its back and cast my spell. The spell phased right through the creature and hit Jaken square in his shield. The spell zapped him and dropped his health by a good twenty percent.

"Hey!" he called out indignantly.

"Sorry!" I yelled back over the wailing of the creature. "Spell damage is no good!"

The rest of the group didn't really have to worry all that much, but Yoh and I would be hard pressed. Just as that thought crossed my mind, Yohsuke stabbed through the creature, and it screeched even louder than before.

So I was the only one then.

At fifty percent HP, the Lich released another wail that slammed us up against the walls, stunned. It lifted both hands into the air, and a sickly yellow aura coated the room, then dispersed. The ground shook slightly, and bones began to burst through the floor and walls like the room was made from them. Seconds later, a dozen level 8 Skeletal Warriors stood to attention in the room. They each carried some kind rusted sword or mace. The Lich raised its hands again to point at us, and they milled forward. They weren't the swiftest enemies, but there were twelve of them. This, I could do though.

As the stun lifted, we all stood and began to power through the enemies.

"Jaken, get that flying bastard, bud," I yelled. "We've got these guys."

He yelled then charged the Lich. He burst through the bones of one Skeleton, and it didn't stand up again. Eleven to go. I took out my great dagger and set to work, then snapped my fingers and summoned Filgus' Flaming Blade. I wasn't certain how well the elemental sword would do or if this counted as dual wielding, but I knew I would need to try and sort this out quickly. My movements seemed clunkier than normal, less agile or decisively less effective, but I chalked it up to the fact that I had nothing near Balmur's skill. Shitty as I may have felt doing it, though, it worked, and there was something to be said about life and lemons in there somewhere.

Yohsuke must have seen my sword because I heard him laugh and call me a rather rude name in a friendly manner.

He was tanking three of the Skeletal Warriors while Bokaj and Balmur laid into them. They fell shortly after. I took care of two more that had begun their way—death by magical flaming slash wounds was always fun. Half the force left.

"Yoh, go grab some Lich brother," I half shouted over my shoulder. "We've got this. We can't have him summoning more."

I didn't have time to look away from the Skeleton I had begun fighting, but I heard the bastard's growls and unearthly groans of pain and knew that Yohsuke had joined Jaken. I caught a glimpse of the Lich's HP bar—thirty percent, and it looked to be falling steadier with the two of them teaming up.

Balmur, Bokaj, and I focused on our small skeletal squad. Balmur dashed behind my back and stepped from the shadows behind the mob. Having a little more room to play with, I dissolved my Filgus' Flaming Blade and re-equipped my great axe. My first swing caught the Skeleton on the far right and knocked him into his friends. A black blur of fur and hand axes fell on him and ended his life quickly. Tmont bowled into another three on the left, and Bokaj loosed arrow after arrow into them while his familiar went ape shit.

I unleashed Cleave and slammed my axe into the head of the Skeleton I hadn't managed to hit, and it crumbled to dust. The only one left standing ended up getting snuck up on and slashed by Balmur as an arrow pierced its left eye socket. Tmont polished off the last Skeletal Warrior beneath her, and we turned to help our friends with the Lich. The Lich's health had gone down to fifteen percent since last I had checked. Balmur stepped from the shadows again and laid into the Lich opposite Jaken. Arrows sprouted from the enemy's shoulder, and his health dropped another percentage. So weapons worked, just not spells, groovy.

"Going high, baby, watch your heads!" I called to the group. "Please don't shoot me!!"

I swapped my great axe for my dagger, leapt into the air above the creature, and tried to bring it down. It came with me for a second, but I phased through it before I could get anything other than a jab into it. At less than ten percent, horrid chanting filled the air as its lips moved, and it raised its hands. The hair on the back of my neck stood on end, and everybody went into overdrive.

Jaken reached out, touching the thing's chest and shouted something. A flash of radiant light and the creature's health bar went from where it had been to nothing. A notification filled my vision telling us that we had received five hundred EXP. That one fight had put those of us at level 11 a nice portion toward our next level. When we checked the loot, we saw that the Lich had dropped a scroll and a ring.

"Ding!" Yohsuke shouted.

"What? How the hell?!" I shouted.

"I had gotten to ten the other morning. When we killed the Bone Dragon and completed the quest, I got most of the way to the next level, about three hundred short. That put me to the next level right there."

When we check the ring, it seemed odd.

Ring of the Lich
Raises the level cap of the summoned Undead of the wearer and allows it to reside on this plane for a longer period of time.

Made through cruelty and malice of the previous owner.

The ring was a black gold and held a blood red ruby in the face with runes inscribed on it.

Once we saw what the scroll did, we realized why the ring popped.

Summon Undead Familiar (spell)

Teaches the caster to summon the Undead to do their bidding.

Summoned creature has base stats that reflect the intelligence of the caster.

One time use to learn the spell forever.

"Who wants it?" Balmur asked. "I'm out because I don't have the intelligence nor the need for it. Having a pet would be cool as a distraction, but it would make sneaking hell."

"I'm good." Bokaj patted Tmont affectionately, and Jaken shook his head.

"I'll get one of my own eventually, so that leaves you, Yohsuke," I said. "You want it?"

"Do I want a minion?" he asked sarcastically, and we all laughed. "Stand back, fools."

He took the scroll and opened it. A fiery, aura-like glow migrated from the scroll to his hands, then up his arms to his head. Yohsuke's eyes slammed shut, and his head rocked back. The light faded, and the scroll fell away to ashes. He opened his eyes and held his hand out for the ring. Balmur tossed it to him, and he put it on.

He spread his hands and shouted, "Burst forth from Hell and do my bidding, worthless dead."

His ring glowed a sickly red, and the ground in the center of us burst apart as a skeletal hand then head and shoulders dragged itself from the ground. It stood taller than him by a good foot. Bleached white bones and a skull with a constant smile. The summoned creature's name was Bonzer, and he was level 7.

"Woah!" Jaken said. "Is that the chant you have to use to summon it every time?"

"Nah," Yohsuke said with a chuckle. "I just like to add a little flair to my spells, man."

We all gathered around the Skeleton and looked it over.

"I can give him equipment and play with his stats a little, too," Yohsuke said as he pulled up a screen in front of him—I assumed to distribute the Skeleton's stat points.

We canvassed the room, and just like we thought, the weapons were collectible loot. Jaken took the great sword while Bokaj nabbed the daggers. It appeared that the armor itself was purely decorative, much to Jaken's disappointment. We searched the room but found nothing else of note.

We left the room and went to the final area to look at—the courtyard. We would have sent Balmur to scout, but after the surprises we had gotten today, it didn't seem worth it. The afternoon sun shone in the sky and lit the courtyard well. We walked in, and all was peaceful. The ground was littered with more bones; seemingly, this would have been the location that the Lich would have summoned more of his minions if we had come here first. That could've been terrible. We didn't find anything here either, so we decided to go loot the Dragon's body in the kitchen.

The place was demolished. The skeletal corpse laid overtop the broken brick and mortar unmoving, and the kitchen equipment was crushed wholly. When we looted the corpse, we got a good amount of money—five hundred gold. The item the Dragon dropped was also pretty cool.

Dragon Bone Bow
+5 to attack

Can fire Dragon Fire arrow 3 + dexterity divided by 5.

This bow, formed by the bone and sinew of a corrupted Dragon, should serve as a reminder not to mess with the owner.

"Oh! This has Bokaj all over it, baby," Jaken said with a smile as soon as we all saw the weapon.

Bokaj picked it up and grinned. "Oh hell yeah, that's me."

He equipped the weapon, and it slung over his back easily. The bones looked bleached, the curved portion of the wings joined by a piece of leathery sinew acting as the string. It looked disgusting but cool as hell.

It was a sweet piece of gear. *Looks like the dungeon had taken care of my friends so far*, I thought to myself. *Wow. The rewards were stacking up.*

We decided to go ahead and head on back to Sunrise. Once we cleared the dungeon grounds, we saw another surprise waiting for us. Bears had come to the hill leading up the path entryway. Not just a couple bears, hundreds. I couldn't count them all because they were pouring out of the trees.

* * *

Jaken came to the front and roared, his enmity generating aura coating his armor, and the others readied for battle.

"Put them away, guys," I said, swatting at them. "They're friends."

I could see Kyra, the Bear Queen, lumbering my way. I activated Nature's Voice.

"My queen." I smiled and went to a knee in front of her hulking thousand pounds. She smiled and patted my shoulder.

"Rise, friend of the bears," she allowed.

To me, she sounded just fine. Her tone sweet like honey. To my friends, she must have sounded like she was about to fight because they had their weapons at the ready again.

"Seriously, if you hurt any of these bears without them attacking first, I will fuck you up," I said mildly. "I'm a Druid. I'm talking to my friends. Specifically, to the queen of all these bears."

"Good enough for me, my dude," Yohsuke said and put his Astral Sword away. He stepped up to join me but didn't kneel. I knew his reasoning—he would kneel to no one, willingly—and the queen didn't care. The others followed suit and joined us. Tmont didn't like all the attention she was getting from the bears, but she liked the queen's cub enough to romp playfully.

"You did it, my friend," the queen said softly. "We had faith, and you came through. Our people's deaths were not in vain, and we can finally mourn them properly. With the lands opened again and free of the infection that minion of War brought, we can hunt and prosper."

"All in a day's work, my Queen," I said smiling.

"Stop that," she reprimanded and pawed my chest softly. Warmth radiated throughout my being starting at that point and moving outward.

BLESSING RECEIVED!

***Blessing of the Bear Kingdom** – The bearer of this blessing is to be treated as an emissary of the Bear Kingdom.*

Given by Queen Kyra, ruler over the bears to the east and ally to Ursine peoples of the world.

"Bear kind will treat you with the utmost respect with that," she said. "If you will translate, I would speak to your friends."

She went to each one of them, and I relayed her thoughts. She thanked them all and blessed each of them in turn, including Tmont.

"Thayron, my heart, please come here for a moment," Kyra called out softly over the murmuring din of bears who had gathered.

A large, brown dire bear, easily the larger of the two, lumbered over. His bulk shook the ground a little, and his muscles shivered with each stride. Slightly larger than Marin, he towered over me in my natural form, and though I knew I was safe, I would *not* want to piss this guy off.

"My love," he greeted her sweetly in a growling bass that made my fur stand on end.

"Zekiel has the ability to take the forms of animals he interacts with. I believe the requirements were two minutes of constant touching or through fighting?" I nodded. "Would you like to receive the dire bear form?"

"I would be honored." I smiled, and then my features shifted slightly. "Though I do remember that I gained the panther form from being bitten once by Sharo."

"Sharo bit you?" Thayron puzzled aloud. "You must tell me that story sometime, maybe over a honeycomb. I would like that. It would be my honor to share my form with you, Friend Druid."

He held his great arms out as if to give me a hug, which I took at face value. One doesn't often get to hug a bear. "Ouch!" His teeth, as large as one of my clawed fingers, pierced my shoulder and neck as gently as he could probably manage it. He licked his now-bloody chops before giving me a bear-like grin. I grunted a "Thanks," before seeing my friends tense as he reared up.

"It's cool, guys. He's helping me. Chill," I said before they could take action.

I cast Regrowth on myself, and the wound closed slowly. Jaken helped by giving me a pat on the shoulder, and I felt his healing spell take root. My HP shot up to full, and I felt so much better.

I focused like I did for my panther form and found another animal waiting for me this time. I pulled the animal up and out of my skin, and my body changed in an instant. I stood and looked down at my friends, then my new body. Bulky and powerful, this felt more like my normal body—though two-and-a-half-feet taller than I was normally. My fur had retained the black pigment of my original form, but I had a tuft of fur that looked brown on my chest. My claws looked and felt razor sharp. I dropped to all fours, and my powerful muscles coiled and flexed as I took my first steps as a dire bear.

"You make a handsome bear," I heard a light voice say behind me. It was a female bear about the queen's size with the same colored fur.

"Thank you," I replied simply and warmly. I wasn't going to return the compliment because I didn't know what the bear standard of beauty was. I didn't want to be rude.

She laughed and joined the queen. "Will he be staying with us, mother?"

The queen had multiple cubs? Well then.

"No, little one," she said and nudged her lovingly, "but he and his friends are welcome whenever they should need it. Go, friends, and continue your great quest."

She stood and roared, a long bellow, and the rest of her people stood and joined her. I stood on my hind legs and roared back as loudly as I could. Spittle flew from my mouth, and out of the corner of my eye, I could see Jaken smiling and trying to copy us. He roared with delight. After the last roar was spent, the bears turned as one and began to filter back into the woods. Some of the braver ones filed up to us and bumped their heads against mine with words of encouragement and strength. One particularly playful bear stood at her full seven feet and looked Jaken right in the eye before bellowing into his face and then licking him. She scampered away at a trot as Jaken tried to get the drool off his face while sputtering.

"Haha!" I heard Bokaj chuckle. "Dude got slimed."

Our walk back to the village was uneventful, though I did note a small contingency of bears matching our pace toward the village in the fading light. Despite the growing shadows, the village was alive as it always seemed to be, but this time it was different. The villagers cheered when they saw us. The whole village must have been in the square. Tables and chairs were set up like a party was about to go down.

Our friends, Sir Willem, the bear-kin armorers, and some of the other friendlier villagers met us at the outskirts. People flooded the square and patted us, vying for our attention to tell us how grateful they were. Finally, Sir Willem stood on a table and called all to a quiet.

"Our Lady Radiance would like to congratulate her champions, Balmur, Bokaj, Jaken, Yohsuke and Zekiel," he said, and the crowd truly stopped talking now. "She implores you to rest and prepare how you will for the next leg of your journey. She and her brothers are working tirelessly to keep War out, but they will also be searching for your next target. She has left word that you are to celebrate this victory and that you did well. More aid will come to you soon."

He motioned to his left, and there was Rowland with his daughter hefting another barrel of his Forge Mead. This was going to be bad. He put it down next to several other barrels, and I knew this was going to be really bad. People brought food, and the music didn't stop until sunrise the next day. We partied and celebrated however we could. Hell, I even shifted into my bear form and decided to dance a little. Not a good idea. I almost crushed Rowland, and I'm fairly certain the lady armorer was flirting with me at some point.

We awoke the day after next, feeling refreshed and discussed what we might be able to do until we got word for our next target.

Balmur had decided to take Rowland up on his offer of training but for jewelry rather than arms and armor. Jaken had decided to try and get the Dwarf to teach him some of his techniques. Maybe he could pick up on how to make weapons.

Bokaj had decided to take to fletching and woodcraft, since he would always need arrows, and he may even be able to improve our weapons at some time.

Yohsuke hadn't decided on one yet, and to be honest, neither had I. As a caster, I could do the whole enchanting thing, sure, but that just didn't sound like something I want to pursue until I saw how the rest of the group fared.

"Cook," Yohsuke suddenly blurted. The rest of us looked at him confused.

"I want to be our cook," he said. "I like good food, and it's something different. I'm all about different."

I laughed inwardly and patted his shoulder.

"Then I'll see if I can't pick up enchanting," I said finally. "Let's get to it guys. I have a good feeling about this."

Chapter Eight

"This was a terrible idea," I muttered to myself.

It had been a week, and I had managed to learn one element to enchant with and that was fire. Which was so cool, but I kept super heating the metal and failing to *actually* enchant. When I first started, I would melt the metal completely. Now it was just warping and failing at times. I was coming along, and luckily, I wasn't costing anyone any money because I was just working on ingots.

No matter how hard I pushed myself to learn it, it didn't help that the asshole training me—Tarron Dillingsley—gave minimal instruction and was a self-proclaimed messiah to the enchanting world. He hadn't even bothered to come see how I was doing in the last two days, either. Again—he was an asshole, but I pushed him from my mind.

What I thought I ruined, Rowland just used to smith since the metal was already hot. I heated it faster than his forge, apparently. The others had all grown in their skills quickly, and though no one had leveled, it seemed that leveling up your overall level with use of the skill took quite a bit of work. It was like having a secondary class. Every twenty levels would bring your main level up, unless crafting was your primary class, in which case, that was your actual level. It was an interesting dynamic that I liked. The gods here had done some amazing work.

The crafting system was cool, but enchanting was *shit*. It didn't work like the skills I had seen in other games—other games gave you the option to give a very specific enchantment. Sometimes you had to find a blueprint for it, or there were even mini-games that allowed you to pass magic into objects. Here, you had to do something different, and I wasn't sure how the hell to do it.

I was on my thirteenth ingot that morning when the beautiful Elven Druid, Dinnia, and her partner Sharo came into the forge.

"Got a minute?" she asked. I nodded and followed her outside. She looked a little frazzled, her hair unkempt and her eyes slightly wild. Well, more so than normal.

"What's up?" I asked as I wiped my hands on my borrowed apron.

"Mother has spoken to me. She asked me to find a creature that is in trouble. It is in the mountains near where the ruins are," she explained hurriedly. "She believes that you can help me find the creature. Also, when you find it, we will know what to do with it."

I froze for a second. A quest from Mother Nature herself? Damn.

Quest Available: Nature's Way - Mother Nature has tasked you, through Dinnia, to find a creature in the Lightning Mountains. Restrictions: Two person party. Reward: Unknown, 500 EXP.

Will you accept? Yes/no?

"You've got it, Dinnia," I said, taking off the apron. "I'll let my party know, and I'll set out right now."

She nodded and turned to leave, then stopped and turned back.

"I have Sharo as my partner to watch my back in this," she said, and Sharo peered in from the outside. "You should have a friend come with you to watch your own."

I nodded, and she left. I poked my head around the corner and shouted at Jaken and Balmur to get their attention.

"Hey, I'm going on a quest to try and get on Mother Nature's good side. I don't know how long it's going to take, probably a couple days."

"Give us a minute, and we'll get the party together, man," Jaken said as he started to take his apron off.

"No need, just wanted to let you guys know. I'm going to get Yohsuke for this. I'm going to need his help," I responded. "It's a two-man party restriction. Once we get back, we will fill you all in."

"No worries, man," I jumped as Balmur spoke to my left. "We'll let Bokaj know what's up. You and Yoh are a good team and know each other too well for it not to make sense. Good luck out there, and be safe."

I shook their hands and thanked them before going to find my brother at the local inn.

Yohsuke was at the inn, learning all kinds of things from the cook in the back. He had been making meals off and on and had some seriously good food to offer. Turns out, a lot of different aspects fed into his skills. Gathering herbs was one of them. Pretty interesting stuff.

I stepped through the doorway, and the aroma of some sweet meat hit me full on. My stomach gurgled in delight, and I followed the scent through the door to the kitchen. Inside, my friend, the mighty spell sword Yohsuke, the strongest amongst our party, was seeing to a loaf of what looked like freshly-baked bread. The outside was dark brown, and I could see it was sliced a little on top, showing the pale inner breading.

"Hey, brother!" I greeted him boisterously. "What's cookin'?"

"Yo, dude." He smiled, and I could see a little flour on his left cheek and the bridge of his nose. "Check this out, man." He sliced into the bread with a practiced hand.

The slice he gave me was about an inch and a half thick, and the loaf itself was about eight inches wide. The bread was a light color inside with a dark slice of roast rolled into the center. The juices soaked into the bread, and that was where the aroma was coming from. I picked up the slice in both hands and took a bite. The bread was light and soft with just a hint of moisture from the roast. The meat was divine. It was cooked just right so that it fell apart when I chewed.

"Oh my gough," I tried to relate what was going through my head but couldn't. It was too good.

"Leveled my cooking up just this morning, man." He laughed, and pointed to his bread. "At level 5, we start to get a better idea of what a recipe might take to make. Sometimes it's just instinct, though. I take it you like it?"

I nodded, not trusting myself with words. He took off his own apron that had a Demon and said "Overlord's Kitchen" sewn expertly on the front.

"Okay," I said after I swallowed. "I'm going to demolish the fuck out of that, but first, wanna help me on a quest?"

"Dude, you already know!" He grinned. "When do we leave?"

"Now," I said before another bite. He nodded, scooped the bread onto a plate, and gave it to the cook to give to our friends. He grabbed us enough food for a few days, and we bounced out of the kitchens and headed toward the forest path that would lead us to where the ruins were.

Not wanting to wait, I cast Nature's Voice and shouted into the forest, "Hey! Do we have any large deer or elk out there?"

About a moment later, a giant buck poked his head out of large bushes to our right. His fur was light brown with red and white dappled spots on his chest. His antlers were large, at least a sixteen-point rack, and he was massive.

"You called, Druid?" he said nervously; his ears flicked

"Yes! What's your name, my friend?" I asked excitedly. He looked like he was about to bolt but seemed to think better of it since I was here.

"Melal, Druid," he said. "Can I help you?"

"Yes, I think you can," I said. I explained my quest from Mother Nature and that seemed to embolden him further. I told him that we needed to move with all haste, and that Yohsuke would need a ride. If he could manage it.

"I will do this thing for you, Friend of Bears," he said as he held his head higher. I could see I had been wrong; he had a good twenty points to his horns. He turned his head to my friend and knelt. "Climb upon my back, but do mind my antlers."

"Also, would you mind if I touched you for a couple of minutes?" Melal quirked his head at the odd question, so I explained, "I wanted to acquire your shape, so that I could try and keep up with you, but I don't want to carry my friend in case we are attacked. I'd like to try and conserve what strength I can."

He assented, coming over to stand beside me, and I put my hand on his side. At the two-minute mark, I received a notification that I had acquired the Large Stag as a shape I could take.

I relayed his request to my friend who shrugged and hopped on. The massive buck stood and Yohsuke shifted his weight so that he could get a better grip on the stag's sides with his knees.

Melal looked to me and stated, "We will break often to keep you feeling well."

I shifted into my own Stag form, a version the same size and build as Melal, but my fur was black with dappled light brown and white. My antlers were smaller as well.

We made it there in a quarter of the time we would have on foot. While traveling, I watched my position change rapidly on my internal map. Melal led the charge with great ease, and I followed closely behind. True to his word, Melal had us break often; the buck needed little other rest than to get a drink that I provided from my water supplies. Then we were back on our way. Three hours after that, we were at the base of the mountain. Yohsuke was a bit saddle sore, but I cast Regrowth on him; it seemed to ease his soreness. We both thanked the stag, and he bolted with a promise to help us again if he could.

I referenced my map, and the area highlighted in an opaque blue was a large portion of the mountain range to our right, the eastern portion of it. I guessed my former trainer and her partner were taking the west side. Sweet. We had a decent amount of ground to cover, as it seemed to radiate in a large oval. After about ten minutes of planning, we set off. Yoh and I had partied up so I could see his health bar. We walked for a few hours and stopped to eat. We followed pretty much the same routine over the next couple days. After we would move so far in a direction, the blue highlight would fall away, showing that it wasn't there, so it was hard to double back on ourselves.

We slept at night in caves if we could find them and only ran into a couple of bears, who were more than happy to share what little they had in the way of shelter and information. The information they shared must have been helpful because the area we had to look through shrank to a third of the size by our third day.

The next morning we had an easier time of things. There was a plateau that we looked around on that covered a majority of the area we had to explore. There was a large rock structure in the center of the area where the ground was littered with glass and sand. I guessed that may have been why the mountains got their name. Lightning struck the ground here so often it left the residue of the strikes on the ground and was so hot it turned the sand into glass.

It looked awesome!

The ground around us was littered with the stuff and what looked like charred bones and fur. Something was hunting around here frequently, and it seemed that it was a messy eater. Hopefully, it wasn't around still.

The large rock structure looked to be about thirty feet wide and twice as tall. As we stepped closer, we heard a harsh, high pitched, guttural language. We decided to hide behind a rocky outcropping of bone and glass just in case. The exchange lasted about thirty seconds before we heard a slap and scuffle. Then a green body was flung from the entryway.

The little, green thing stood about three feet tall and had a strangely shaped head with long pointed ears and sharp teeth. Three fingers adorned each hand, and they scrabbled at the ground. This had to be a Goblin, and Goblins always traveled in groups in the games I'd played back home. Sure enough, Goblin level 9 was what we were looking at, and about four more stepped out of the structure to start harassing the smallest one whose health was already pretty low.

"I think it's time to summon Bonzer, man. This could get fun," I said and readied myself for a fight.

Yohsuke just reached out and flipped two fingers into the air like he was motioning to someone behind us. The Skeleton stepped from the ground easily, and I saw that my friend had taken the time to gear his guy up. The Skeleton wore leather armor and sported a wooden shield and a scimitar. He even had an eyepatch.

"Nice, man," I whispered.

"He can tank," Yohsuke advised. "You and I can wreak havoc. Just let him get the hate first."

I nodded, and the Skeleton went to work. It shrieked a wordless, soundless cry and charged the Goblins who, to their credit, only freaked out a little bit. After getting their shit together, though, they started to wail on the poor Skeleton. So then we went to work. Between the four standing and the one on the ground, Tiny, I chose to attack the biggest dickface there. That's just me, though.

I engaged Wind Scythe and threw my axe at the poor sod. My great axe hit him and pinned him to the stone behind him; he was hanging on with a sliver of health left. I leapt from my spot behind our makeshift barrier and flung a Frozen Dagger at Tiny. The cold blade hit the poor bastard in the neck and polished him off.

The other Goblins had noticed us now, and one decided to try and go for Yoh, who looked to be the least threatening. Yohsuke welcomed the foolish creature by feigning fear, then lashing out with a freshly released Astral Sword. The Goblin was dead before it hit the ground, its head separated from its shoulders. Two more were left, and they had managed to get the Skeleton's HP to about sixty percent in the seconds that we had been distracted.

I jogged over to my weapon that still pinned the struggling Goblin to the rock and activated Devil's Hammer. It helped me pull my weapon from the stone and bashed the Goblin on my left side in the skull with the blunt side of the axe head. It didn't damage it, but it left the Goblin stunned, so I turned my great axe and began to chop into the poor, stupid creature. It fell shortly after, and Yoh had killed his with help from Bonzer. The fight had gotten us a good amount of experience since there were only two of us. The Skeleton's level was entirely dependent on its summoner, so it gained nothing—I didn't think.

We walked into the structure slowly, just in case there was something left inside, and I let my eyes adjust to the light. The interior was musty and smelled like recent death. I looked over and saw the reason why; a large yellow and gold bird lay covering a nest. There were dozens of little Goblin bodies littered about the room. We must have gotten here just after the fight. The air was still humid, and I could smell the lingering stench of burnt flesh. The Goblin corpses still smoldered and smoked. It was probably only minutes ago with the great beast had bitten it.

As soon as I thought that, the bird's head shifted, and its eye opened to look right at me. On instinct, I activated Nature's Voice.

"You came," the soft voice wheezed. "Thank the Mother."

I went to cast Regrowth on her, but she pecked at my hand angrily.

"Do not waste your magics, Druid," she said. "I need your aid. Come, assist me in my final task."

Quest Available: A Mother's Love - The great bird before you has requested that you help her. Reward: Unknown. Will you accept? Yes/No?

"I'll help. What can I do?" I asked. She brought her wing out and pulled me close.

"You know the Lightning magics?" she asked, and I thought of my only one, then nodded.

"Good." She pushed a small lump from beneath her. "This is to be my only progeny. The others were crushed inside me before I could lay them. You and I will channel our Lightning into this egg together."

The lump, I realized, was a sapphire colored egg. It looked fragile—only about a foot and a half in size and oval in shape.

"What?" I stuttered. "But won't that kill it?"

I could hear her chuckle. "It will make her stronger than ever."

"I can only cast once every minute," I warned. She turned and shocked me with her wing.

It didn't hurt; it was more of a surprise than anything. I looked and saw that it was a buff.

Lightning Roc's Static - Disables cool downs on lightning abilities and spells. Lasts until shocked again.

And so we began. I had two hundred fifty MP to go through, so I hoped it would help. I was able to cast the spell ten times while the bird fed Lightning to the egg at a steady rate. Then I was out of mana. With twenty points in my wisdom, I regained ten MP every five seconds. As soon as I had the mana for the spell, I cast again.

Yohsuke was interested, but with the lightning playing in the air, he decided to sit nearby and watch. He had his Skeleton stand in the doorway in case more Goblins came.

It had been half an hour of this—casting, waiting, then casting again. Half an hour turned into an hour. Then two. I was pretty tired at this point, close to reaching my mental limits. The casting didn't bother me; by now I felt pretty numb to it, like I was closer to the element of lightning than before, but damn, I was tired. Felt like I could sleep forever.

After one last round, the Roc had suddenly stopped. I looked over and saw that she was dead, her last breath given to her baby. I knew what I had to do next. I sent a silent prayer to Mother Nature and sent Lightning Bolt into the egg. I put my hand up against it, and cast with both hands, something I had never done before and kept casting.

I felt a presence in the egg, and I lifted it to my chest. I cast the spell in quick succession four more times with both hands. Even though it took less than a minute to recover the needed mana, the mental strain was almost unbearable. After I gained the mana for one final casting, my reserves were completely spent, and I dropped to my knees.

"Yo, man, are you okay?" Yohsuke was next to me with his hand on my shoulder. I felt like a vortex had opened inside me, and I began to feel a warmth flow from his hand to me, his mana flow going from his into my own pool.

"Oh shit," he said slightly aghast. "You got it, brother. Take all of my mana. I'll be alright."

With his mana, I dual cast the spell another seven times before I felt the life essence inside flutter, then arc stronger than before. The shell began to crack and break. I looked down, and I saw a blue beak begin to break through. I cradled the egg in my left arm and used my right hand to help the little thing. After a few minutes, we had cleared the top portion of the shell away and there was this blue Roc chick sitting there, staring up at me.

CONGRATULATIONS!

You have completed the quests Nature's Way and A Mother's Love - You have received 500 EXP, the body of the Lightning Roc of the Lightning Mountains, understanding of the element of Lightning, and the adoration of the Roc's only chick.

Alert!

The Lightning Roc's chick has imprinted upon you. Would you like to take it as your familiar?

Yes/No?

I accepted happily. I couldn't imagine doing all that work to help this little thing live just to toss it away and let it fend for itself.

Alert!

You have accepted the Lightning Roc's chick as your familiar, would you like to name it?

Yes/No

I looked over the chick, blue feathers beginning to dry in the dark. I decided to take it outside to look at. In the light, I saw how deep blue the feathers really were. They were glorious—a royal blue and big eyes, the pale yellow of bursting lightning. I felt a presence brush up against my mind. It was warm and inviting, so I mentally tried to open myself to it.

Abilities Learned

Mental Link - There is a mental link between a Druid and their Animal Familiar. This link allows for the quick exchange of information and will. As time goes on and as the bond grows stronger, more can be shared than simple, basic thoughts.

Upon reading this and closing the notification, I felt the contentment coming from the little bird. The mind that touched mine was feminine, and as my son would have lovingly said as he tried to pet her, she was so cute. I missed him. Maybe I could have him play a part in naming her.

"How does Kayda work for you, little one?" I asked as she looked at me with her big eyes. I think she must have felt how dear the name was to me because I felt her happiness instantly. Then I felt her hunger.

She looked to the Goblins behind me, and I got a very distinct "food" vibe from her. Great. She's a predatory bird.

When I didn't react fast enough, I got a solid zap that stole five percent of my HP. Damn, that hurt. After a moment, I realized that my buff was now gone. Oh well. It had been a few minutes anyway, and I was back to full mana. Yohsuke was almost back to full himself when he came walking out to join us.

"I don't know what the hell that shit was," he said finally, "but holy fuck! Having your mana drained doesn't feel good, man. Fuck all that. How is the bird?"

I held her out to see him, and Kayda was confused. I tried to impress how I felt about him into our bond, the times that he had saved me from myself when things got hard in the Corps, how he and I had always seemed to be there for each other no matter what the odds looked like. This man was truly my family, and I needed her to know that.

She chirped at him softly and ruffled her fuzzy feathers at him in excitement. It seemed like she had forgotten about her hunger, thankfully. I passed her over to him, and she struggled to nip at his armor.

"Ah!" I heard my brother say. "Cute little fucker likes me. I shall call you Minion. Yes. Good little Minion."

She continued to chirp happily and glanced from Tiny's corpse over to the two of them. The little bird turned around and started to eye the body greedily.

"Better put her down, brother," I said, trying to prevent the shock I thought might be coming. "She seems to be hungry."

"She ain't eating that shit, man," he said and pulled up a screen. "Fuck that. She gets the finest foods."

He pulled out some food and fed it to her by hand. I could sense that it was filling to her, and she was content for now. I left them alone to see about the bodies inside. As I thought, the loot was open since the bird had passed. There wasn't much, about a gold piece worth of money all together, but one had a gem that looked really nice. I picked it up and saw that it was a topaz. Nice. Maybe Balmur could use this?

I went to the Lightning Roc and touched it reverently. She had given her life so that Kayda could live. I would never let her memory fade from the little bird's mind. Her sacrifice would never be forgotten.

I looked into her inventory to see if she had dropped anything.

I got materials from her body: *10 Lightning Roc Bones, 30 LR Feathers, 5 LR Talons, 20 Lightning Ore, 10 Lightning essence* and the last was something new.

Lightning Roc Astral Adaptor
+6 to attacks.
Lowers mana cost of mana weapons and adds Lightning elemental damage to pure mana at will.
Lightning Rocs have protected the skies above the Lightning Mountains for generations. Their weapons are rare but powerful. Use them with respect.

I walked out calling to Yohsuke, holding the weapon out as I approached. It was much the same as his current one. The handle looked to be made of bone, and there was yellow leather the color of her feathers. The cord wrapped around the handle had three small feathers dangling from it. It was beautiful.

"Duuuuuuuuuude," he whispered. I handed it to him, and he held it aloft. "YES!"

"All yours, brother."

He closed his eyes, and I saw the pure Astral leap to life as a sword. He opened his eyes and then grinned broadly.

"This changes everything."

"How so?" I asked.

"Check it out." He held the blade out in front of him and focused. The blade began to glow yellow, like he held lightning straight from the sky.

"That's tight, man!" I said in awe.

"But wait," he grinned again, "there's more!"

The blade extended from the base of the adaptor and shaped itself to look like a spear.

"Gonna get me some dragoon action going on, baby!" He laughed in a borderline evil manner.

I joined him in laughing, and we both turned just in time to see Kayda tucking into her meal of Goblin Ear. Both of us made sounds of disgust, but she looked happy.

Chapter Nine

We made it back to the village without incident within a couple of days. At the bottom of the mountain, we called to Melal who gave my friend a ride as he had before. Kayda rode on Yohsuke's arms where she snuggled in on herself and slept.

Upon our arrival, Dinnia and Sharo bolted to us from one of the connecting streets to our left on the outskirts of the village. The Druid thanked our helpful Stag and sent him on his way with a casting of Regrowth to ease his aches and tired muscles. I kind of felt like a jerk for having not thought of the idea myself. Noted.

"I see I had nothing to worry about," Dinnia said with a smile. "She probably just fell from her nest, right? But why bring her here? Where is her mother?"

I related my tale to her then—how the Goblins had come for the mother dozens strong and how she had defended her only egg valiantly. I told her about our efforts to speed this one's birthing process so that she could have a chance. That the chick, Kayda, and I were bonded, and she was my familiar.

By the time the story was finished, Sharo had slunk off in silence and Dinnia was in tears. She reached for Kayda with a pleading expression, and I let her pick the little bird up. Kayda had grown in size already; she was the size of a small adult chicken now but slightly larger.

Dinnia closed her eyes and whispered, presumably to the Mother and passed her hands all over the little creature.

"She may never grow to her full size because of the nature of her incubation," Dinnia said sadly. "She will grow. She will grow quickly. However, she might stop well before she reaches the majesty her mother held. I just don't know when that will be or how big she will get for sure."

I nodded. "At least she lives."

The Druid smiled, bright and cheerful, then hugged me.

"You did well," she said. "Thank you."

Sharo came out of the forest behind me with a small rodent, a level 1 Field Mouse and held it in his mouth to Kayda. The little bird squawked in delight and snatched the still living Field Mouse into her beak. I think she swallowed before she even finished getting the poor thing into her gullet. She cooed happily and fell asleep.

Dinnia sat her in my hands, and we continued to walk back toward the square. Yohsuke had left after ensuring that I was cool. He had some cooking to do.

The elder Druid filled me in on how a familiar worked. Basically, they were a bonded animal, so whenever one of us killed something, both would grow to an extent. I remembered my skill for bonded animals and the blessing I got put the flow of EXP going both ways at fifty percent which seemed to be well above the norm according to Dinnia. I guess even Mother Nature was trying to help the gods stack the odds in our favor. I thought our luck had been too good lately. I kept that to myself—didn't want to seem like I didn't appreciate it.

The higher level she was and the more she ate, the faster she would grow. There was also a familiar screen in my display now that allowed me to look over her stats, of which she had none, surprisingly. Dinnia assured me that upon her first level, Kayda's stats would reveal themselves and I'd be able to move her attribute points accordingly.

I looked into my inventory because I wanted to talk to her about the items I had gotten from the adult Roc, but Dinnia had no idea what any of it was.

I took the deep-sleeping Kayda up to my room and left her on my bed. There was a good chance she wouldn't notice my absence for a while, and with our bond, I could always check on her.

I went back to my place at the forge. Rowland was busy with his work, and Balmur and Jaken were gone.

"I came by to check on you the other day, but you were gone," a small, wizened voice came from behind me.

An older Gnome with grey, balding hair over storm-grey eyes on a serious and wrinkled face stared at me. Tarron Dillingsley looked unimpressed as he always did when he was around me. The man had made the same faces when he started trying to teach me how to enchant items—seemingly deciding without any effort that I was a waste of time. He walked in wearing his usual brown tights and flamboyant green blouse this time and an oak walking staff.

The white wooden staff was a lovely thing, covered in a single stripe of metal spiraling from a cap at the base to the top handle portion. The metal had runes engraved throughout it. It was his enchanted weapon, from what I could see. Where it was beautiful, he was not.

"I gather you've been out gallivanting and wasting your time killing things, like a savage?" he said in a dismissive tone. "Really, I can see that you would be frustrated with your lack of talent, but hard work pays more than doing nothing, young man."

Now, I've never been one to be disrespectful to the elderly, and I've never wanted to hit a Gnome, but this guy was asking for it. I know I shouldn't expect special treatment from everyone for what we were brought here to do, and I didn't. These people had prayed to their gods fervently to be able host us, to have them bring us here. The least he could do was appreciate my trying to learn his skill.

"I got a special quest," I said simply. Then a thought struck me. "Do you know any lightning enchantments?"

He snorted and pointed at me. "You can't even master fire, yet you want to try lightning? Sure, stubborn boy." He pulled a scroll out and tossed it at my feet. "I will supervise you electrocuting yourself, and when you do, you can find a new instructor, maybe one who's talents aren't wasted on you and this piss-poor village."

I picked up the scroll and read it. The words made no sense to me, but the knowledge surged into my mind and took hold. I could recall how to do it like I'd grown up doing it. Like breathing.

Abilities Learned!

***Lightning Enchanting** – Give accessories, weapons and gear aspects of elemental lightning.*

I reached into my mind for the embodiment of my mental energies, mana. I then thought of what lightning meant. The swift, arcing currents of energy that can fry a human with ease. The static that collects just before a strike. Searing heat that was there for mere seconds then gone. I held those thoughts in mind and reached for an ingot.

I grabbed what was closest and began to push my mana into the metal but not a steady push like I had tried with the fire. I let my mana become like the element itself, striking the metal like lightning. It etched my will into the metal, giving it the property that came to mind first. When I felt it take, I closed the flow of mana.

I checked what was in my hand and saw that it wasn't an ingot; it was a mallet. I looked over and saw that the pile of ingots was still there, but the Gnome was standing closer to me and had a cruel smirk.

"Well, let's see what havoc you've wrought on that poor instrument you've stolen from our blacksmith," he said smugly and took the tool from me.

"He didn't steal a thing, ye spineless, beardless old goat of a Gnome," growled Rowland from the doorway behind my other instructor. The blacksmith walked over and snatched the mallet from the Gnome and looked it over.

"Look over yer work, lad." He passed the object to me and then turned to glare at the Gnome.

I looked at the item and smiled.

Thunder Mallet

+1 to Smithing.

Imbued with quick-flashing heat, this hammer crashes into metal with the power of elemental lightning.

Enchanted by Apprentice Enchanter Zekiel Erebos.

"Only plus one, though?" I groaned, defeated.

"Tell him, ye old prune, afor' I do and beat ye for it." Rowland growled and stepped menacingly toward the old, surly Gnome.

"You did better than any apprentice I would have had in the city," the Gnome admitted grudgingly.

"AND?" The Dwarf was closer now, his hands flexing, and I was pretty sure I saw a vein bulging in his neck.

"And nothing!" he shouted. "He's lazy, puts in no effort, and understands nothing! He was off playing at being a hero with his worthless friend rather than perfecting the craft I was brought here to waste on him!"

My heart pounded, and my blood began to boil. I leapt to my feet and began to stalk forward. He stood his ground, and that made me angrier. I lunged as fast as my dexterity allowed and caught him by the front of his pompous blouse. I picked him up so that he was eye level with me.

"Say what you please about me," I growled—actually growled, I think my beast was starting to peak out at the little man, "but if you ever dare to speak poorly of any of my friends in my presence again, I will personally throw you to the wolves outside this village. Do we have an understanding?"

"You don't scare me, whelp," he whispered back menacingly. "You and your weak band of miscreants have no right to be here. It should have been our kind, the true people of this world, to save it. You and yours should just go back to whatever disgusting hole you crawled out from."

One second I was holding the tiny man, and the next, he was flying through the door and Rowland was howling after him in a fury. The mallet I had enchanted in his hand, he flew after the offender and hit him as Rowland kept coming.

"Ye will no longer be welcome in this forge, Tarron Dillingsley," the blacksmith roared. "Ye did what ye had to by order of the Goddess and are free to leave when ye please, but I will not suffer slander against these good folks!"

The Gnome slumped forward and stood slowly. The wall he had crashed into had no sign of damage, but the Gnome was bloodied. The hammer had hit the staff and done nothing.

"I will say and feel as I please," he cried. "Nothing you or any of the other backward hicks of this village, will ever stop that. I will leave, and I will do what I can for our world as is right!" He made to leave and winced in pain.

I hadn't noticed due to my anger, but I had a throbbing headache; all I could feel from Kayda was a burning rage. I felt her presence in my mind growing, like she was getting closer, but I didn't know how that would happen with her in our room.

I heard a small screech, like the hawks that I used to hear when I was a kid, and a blue blur sped toward me from the direction of the inn. I was wrong. I guess the little blue bird wasn't so little anymore after all. She was about the same size of a hawk, her wingspan almost forty inches. Her feathers were no longer the fuzzy mess they had been; they were sleek and looked strong. Azure lightning roiled off her body angrily as she came to a halt a foot or so away from me. She seemed confused by the scene but noticed I didn't appear hurt so she calmed down a little.

Kayda fluttered over and perched herself on my left shoulder, little blue sparks of electricity playing over her feathers like wind. She screeched angrily at the little Gnome, and I got the picture from her. She could feel what I was thinking, and she knew I was upset and that he had pissed me off. This seemed to only piss her off more, so she stretched her wings out and ruffled her feathers at him in challenge. If her wing hadn't been in front of my face almost slapping me, I may have been impressed.

"I suppose that little beast is the reason you were missing?" the Gnome asked imperiously. "A likely excuse. Probably stole it from its mother after killing her, poor thing."

"You know what?" I said at last. "I can accept that you think that I'm worthless because you feel powerless and unimportant for once. I can also accept that, in your own way, you think that you should be able to try and solve your own issues. It's commendable, really. But I'm nowhere near the evil or disgusting person you think I am. Kayda's mother and I spent hours pressing lightning into her only egg to ensure that at least one of her babies would live after a Goblin raiding party attacked. If you don't believe me? Cool, I don't give a shit. I'll find another trainer, and anyone who knows the skill will most likely know of you, right?"

The Gnome nodded. "And they would do well to remember the greatest enchanter this side of the world."

"Outstanding!" I shouted jubilantly. I startled both Tarron and Kayda. "Then they will know exactly who I mean when I tell them that the great Tarron Dillingsley half-assed his job training someone out of spite. That even he wasn't good enough to teach me."

By now I was closer to the diminutive man. I knelt so I could be a little closer to him. I needed him to feel the gravity of my words.

"You don't want to train me?" I asked softly. "Fine. I'll find someone who can, the right way, and I'll be sure to study hard so that I'm better than you. Go away, you little shit stain of a man. Your self-important presence is no longer required."

I raised a hand and dismissively cast Regrowth on the little asshole as I shooed him away.

"Yer a good man, Zeke." Rowland clapped me on the shoulder that wasn't occupied by a preening bird. "I'd have let him limp away to lick his wounds. Ye healed him and injured his pride. I'd watch for that one."

He went over to the wall where the mallet had fallen. He scooped it into his hand and walked back.

"Ye mind if I use this?" he asked.

"Of course!" I smiled and clapped him on the arm. "Least I could do for you sticking up for the party. I also had some materials I wanted to show you to see if you could do anything with them."

I showed the craftsman the goods I'd mentioned, and he said that he didn't have the skill to work these kinds of materials.

"I've got kin everywhere, and they smith better than I do, so they can help ye if ye like." He smiled. "Just let me know where ye'll be going, and I'll see to it."

I smiled back and thanked him again. Kayda was still resting on my shoulder. I could feel how tired she was through our bond and decided to go ahead and call it a night. We would go back to the inn and see about some food.

Chapter Ten

My friends were already waiting at the inn when I came in. The group was complementing our Spell Blade on his cooking, as usual. When Kayda and I sat down, the conversation came to a halt. Everyone had questions and wanted to touch her or pet her. Yohsuke was smiling quietly.

Yohsuke and I spent a bit recounting our adventure, my Grey Elf friend filling in details I missed. The bird flew over to him when he produced some food for her, and he patted her affectionately.

"When did she get bigger, man?" He motioned at her.

"A little bit ago," I said. "I left her in my room to sleep and went to practice enchanting. Tarron pissed me off and some shit went down. She came swooping in like this a few minutes after the worst of it. She looked like she was ready to shock the hell out of him."

"What did he do?" Jaken asked around a mouthful of food.

"He talked some mess about the people I care about and didn't care to do his duty for his people," I said.

I related the events to them as they had happened. Being who they are, they couldn't care less. If you didn't like them, they didn't care because you obviously didn't matter. What pissed them off was his flippant dismissal of my abilities and his unwillingness to teach.

Sure, he didn't have to do it. Free will worked like that, but he willingly came here rather than letting someone else answer the call. What a dick.

See, the way Sir Dillon had explained it was that Radiance had put together a list of what she thought might be needed for us to get our start back when she and her siblings had heard that War was gunning for their world. After they had gotten a few generals in, they acted on that and the people in this village's wish to host us. Trainers came in from all over who heard the call to act. This included crafting trainers, at least those good enough to pass on their skills well. Then they collected their champions, us, and brought them to this learning-rich environment to hopefully stand a chance. Instead of saying no, Tarron came and fucked it up. Now I would be significantly left behind as my friends continued to work on their crafts, but at least I could go and find another trainer. I hoped.

Kayda fluttered her wings at my doubt and eyed me reassuringly. I would practice what I knew so far and try to help her level as we waited for news on our next destination. I slept fitfully that night as I worried about our future.

The next morning, I woke up and went straight to the forge to practice. This time I took Kayda along. Last night, I saw that she had broken my window escaping my room, and I didn't want to irk our host with another Houdini act. She cooed happily as she rode on my shoulder. More than a few of the villagers admired her as we walked through the square. A few of the braver ones actually came to her and tried to touch her. The first few she allowed, as these ones were children. The last one, a large man with calloused hands, attempted to pick her up off my shoulder claiming that animals loved him.

Not the case for her.

Kayda zapped the man, who dropped her in his shock, and she flew to my shoulder again. The man cursed, and I asked if he was okay; he just walked away shaking.

"Hey now," I said in a heavy disapproving tone. "You can't just go around shocking people like that. He could have been seriously hurt."

I got a definitive lack of caring from her as she preened her feathers. I swept her off my shoulder and let her fly to the forge. If she couldn't play nice, I wasn't going to be her ride. This also left the people here a little safer.

I came to the forge, and Kayda was perched on the roof. She hopped down to my upheld hand, and we went inside. After a few hours of bouncing ideas off Rowland, I held a dagger and reached for my mana. This time, I kept my eyes open and concentrated on the fact that lightning causes damage, the sharp sting of it, the way it can paralyze you if struck. I pulled the mana away from my mana pool and sent the bolts of it into the blade. I realized that while before my lightning mana had been a yellow energy, it was now the same azure blue as my familiar's. *Sweet*, I thought. I lost my concentration, and the enchantment failed, charring and ruining the weapon, unfortunately.

I offered to pay for it, but the smith just informed me that he would have no such thing and that Jaken had made it for just such a purpose. He had made others as well: swords, daggers, and even a few shields. I guess I got to play with all of these, as they weren't the best in the shop. They looked really nice, though.

The next dagger I worked on, I didn't let the lightning surprise or distract me. I focused on the damage and the element could do and that only. After I brought my now azure lightning to bear on it, the enchantment took effect and I got the result I was looking for—Lightning aspected damage. The damage rating was only +1 which Rowland informed me meant an extra one percent damage added to the actual damage of the weapon. So in this case, it was +1 to attack and +1 for the element equating to two percent more damage per attack. Not too bad for a beginning weapon. He also said that an enchanted weapon almost always doubled the price of the weapon when it sold.

I spent the next couple hours enchanting. I failed at times because my concentration slipped or, as I comically found out, I ran out of mana. It was an informative time, and my level in enchanting went up by three so I was a level 4 enchanter. Pretty nice. The levels didn't seem to do all too much for me now, but I imagined that as I got used to it and raised my level, it should get easier. Not to mention the special skills and abilities that could be gained like the one I had witnessed the blacksmith use. At least, that's how it sounded from the way Rowland and my friends spoke about leveling craftsmanship.

After that, Kayda and I went into the forest. While we were there, she took wing and began to hunt and prowl. We had some luck after I had shifted into my panther form and flushed out some game. It would have made me feel bad, you know since these weren't the same crazed or infected animals I was slaying, but Kayda wasn't killing and looting them just for experience. She was eating them the way she would have if she were a wild Roc. I wasn't getting anything from these low-level creatures, the grouses and forest voles, but she was. When she was full after about twenty minutes of hunting, we left. As simple as that. I wasn't going to make her gorge herself, and I didn't want the local wildlife to take too big a hit.

We spent the rest of the day going back to working on our bond, communicating thoughts and sights, emotions and concepts. The more we worked on this, the easier it would be for her to be my eyes and ears later on.

At least I hoped.

I needed to get a flying form of my own, but when I tried to acquire her shape, it didn't seem to take. I think maybe the Roc is a little outside the realm of my abilities. I'd just get one later; hopefully we would be moving on soon. The quiet life was nice, but we needed to move on—we had a mission to complete.

Chapter Eleven

A couple more days of that routine and I was ready to go, regardless of what anyone said. My companions felt the same. I had leveled my enchanting up to level 7 at this point. My friends were in the teens since they had decent trainers, and Kayda had leveled since our hunts had begun in earnest. Level 2 looked good on her. She got three points per level and one natural one that applied on its own. Since she was my familiar, I put her points where best suited, not where they might naturally fall if she were wild. Her stats looked like this to begin with.

Name: Kayda
Race: Lightning Roc
Level: 2
Strength: 1
Dexterity: 8
Constitution: 3
Intelligence: 4
Wisdom: 1
Charisma: 5
Unspent Attribute Points: 3

She was already pretty smart and agile. Her constitution worried me, though. One good hit and she would be hurting bad. She leveled after only two days of hunting low level creatures, so if we were to go after some big game she might level faster. Then again, she needed the HP now, so I poured it all into constitution. After I did, she looked a little more robust than she had before. The sixty HP did her some good. We would worry about her other stats as she leveled.

The village was bustling as usual, people buying and selling wares. Nothing I could use, but it was nice to see.

"Yo!" I heard Yohsuke shout.

I turned to see him jogging toward me from the direction of the Inn.

"Hey, man," I greeted him. "Did we get word?"

He nodded and began to jog back the way he'd come. Kayda took off after him, and I bounded off to catch up.

We broke off from our jog as we reached the door and stepped through. The air inside the inn was comfortable as compared to the heat and humidity outside. The atmosphere here was almost homier than home? It was hard to put my finger on. Even empty, you felt welcome in this inn and tavern environment, and it was because of that welcome atmosphere that I was so much more comfortable here than most places. Sir Dillon stood before the group and smiled as we walked up.

"Good," he said. "Let's begin. We've received intelligence that Maven Rock, a city a few days West of here, has reported citizens disappearing from the lower wards. We believe this to be the work of War's minions."

"We don't have anything concrete to work with?" I asked.

"As of yet, no," the old Paladin said, "but we have people among us who can relay messages to you and one has offered to teach the magic users among you how to do so."

My brows raised in surprise. Mental Message spells were game changers in some games. If you can talk over distances, you can feed information to others freely. I had to admit, I was curious to see how that worked here.

Our host bid myself and a surprised Balmur to go the small courtyard out back.

"Why not Yohsuke and Jaken too?" I asked.

"I spoke with the person you are about to meet beforehand and informed them of your capabilities." He cleared his throat. "She believed it best that the two of you learn this spell as the others' magic isn't suited to this kind of spell."

Fair, I thought to myself and looked to Balmur. He simply shrugged, and I followed him out the back door.

Once we arrived, a kindly old lady, one I had seen tending some of the cats in the square, was sitting on a bench. The courtyard was usually a place that farmers preferred to take their drinks and food. It let them be outside under the stars and away from snooty noses who couldn't handle the scent of hard work.

The little old lady, slumped forward in age, wore a plain brown dress and her grey hair loosely plaited over her shoulders and hobbled toward us. Balmur reached her first; he gently grabbed her arm to steady her, and she reached out and touched her palm to his forehead gently. There was a mute burst of light that shone like a star even in the afternoon light, then nothing. Balmur let her go, then looked at me in confusion. The woman waved me over. I stepped forward, and she did the same to me. The same muted burst of light and I knew how to cast the spell I needed.

Abilities Learned

Mental Message – Send a message to any person you are familiar with and allow them to respond instantaneously. Cost: 25 mana.

That was cool. Wish I could have done that with enchanting. The lady was walking away by now, and I wasn't sure she would say anything to us anyway. She seemed content to keep to herself.

After she left, we walked back in, and the old Paladin was waiting for us. He had us pull out our map and indicated the area we were heading. Like before with Kayda, the area to search was rather large, but I figured we could see it from a distance once we got closer.

We decided to spend the night in town and head that way in the morning. We relinquished our bladed weapons to Rowland for maintenance, and Bokaj cared for his bow himself. Yohsuke didn't have to do anything, but from his grumbling, I could tell he was making decisions on abilities. I had gotten a couple myself but nothing I was keen to use just yet—fireball and a new ability that allowed me to charge spells. They were mana burners, and I was looking for a chance for them to be of use other than something flashy and stupid. No real reason to be stupid. *So far.* I smirked at the thought.

Rowland and some of the other villagers joined us in a rather tame goodbye party. We let them know that we would be back before we moved on past the city. Yohsuke's trainer came, an elderly Elven woman who wore her wrinkled skin with regal pride. She kept her hood up, so I couldn't make out much of her actually, other than her pointed smile and dainty fangs. My Spell Blade friend waved off my question, making me think that she didn't like talking about it.

We turned in early that night, wanting to be well rested for our travels. I had procured some items I thought we might need. I also spent some time working on my enchanting. I was leveling up a little faster now that I knew how to use my mana correctly, but I felt I was missing some kind of fundamental knowledge somewhere. Damn miserly Gnome and his dick-ish ways.

* * *

I laid down on my bed, closed my eyes, and—not for the first time since I had been to this world—dreamt of my son. His smiling face and blue eyes were beaming up at me while he ran around, encouraging me to chase him. The sky was a cloudy blue that would be described as a perfect day. We were at the park we played at a few times with a lot of houses nearby. His small, surprisingly muscular arms were waving back and forth as he sprinted away from me, screaming in joy. Peace and calm enveloped me; my muscles eased. This. I missed this.

I smiled and blinked, and his cries of joy turned to terror. He screamed. Not out of fear but genuine horror and pain, and my blood ran cold. He screamed for his daddy to come and help him. The sky blood red and the world around me aflame—I could see him in some shadow beast's claws, tears in his eyes as he begged me to come to his aid.

Rage and fury gripped my being as I started forward toward him, but the flames grasped at my limbs and held me still. I struggled harder as voices began taunting me. The shadow beast growled in delight, and I shifted into my bear form without thinking. I pulled harder and roared my fury at the world.

"CHRIS!" several voices shouted into my ear, my real name breaking through. The world shattered, and I came awake to the dawn light and my friends dangling from my arms. Jaken had his arms as far around my waist as they would go, Balmur dangled from my left arm as he hung on, and Bokaj was wrapped around my swinging right arm. Yohsuke was on my shoulders, punching me in the head.

I shifted back, and we all went down into a pile with a series of grunts and curses.

"What the hell, man?" Balmur asked. "What happened?"

I explained the nightmare to them, and everyone seemed to understand. The room was a wreck. When I shifted, I had broken the bed, and my furniture was clawed and gouged. The rest of our party had piled into the room thinking we were under attack. I just took ten gold out and pushed it into Sir Dillon's hand. He understood and tried to give it back to me, but I shook my head and left the room. The dread had gripped my soul, and I needed to be alone at that moment.

I walked outside, and Kayda perched on my shoulder. I gently brushed her off, and she flew into the sky. My friends tried to follow me outside, but Sir Dillon stopped them, "Let him be, boys. Let him be."

I walked into the forest and began sprinting to try and get my still restless body under control. It felt good to actually run, and in this body, I moved faster than I ever had before. After five minutes at a dead sprint, springing over obstacles and dodging trees, I felt better. I found a log to sit on and just sat there in silence. Warmth dripped into the fur on my face, and I realized that it wasn't sweat but tears. That nightmare, like so many before it, had been so real. The threat, fueled by my anxiety, was never real.

But now that there *was* one that could do that? Fuck. *FUCK.* My slightly heaving chest began to spasm as I let the tears flow until they were gone. I had lost track of how long I sat there with Kayda cooing softly from a tree nearby, but eventually, I picked up movement larger than the native wildlife. I looked up, and Sir Dillon came out of the tree line with a soft expression on his face.

"I know your fears, Zekiel," he said simply. Rather than fire back that he didn't or that he couldn't possibly understand, I shut my mouth and let him speak.

"When I was young, before the call to serve the Lady, I had a son." He sat next to me and stared into the partially wood-covered sky above us. "He was a beautiful lad, auburn hair, stubborn streak a league wide, and the brown eyes of his ma. He would come out and play in this very forest on his own and did not heed the warning of his parents, but back then we didn't have to worry about the crazed beasts that you and yours slew. Still, like any good father, I worried. I let the boy make mistakes but guided him and taught him as well as I could."

He picked up a stick in front of him and looked at it for a moment before I had to ask, "Did something happen to him out here?"

"Nay," he sighed. "It happened after the call to serve Her Light came to me in a dream. By this time, he was on the cusp of manhood and I was a Paladin already. He had thoughts to join the order himself. It was then that tragedy struck. He was in the area of that first battle with the dark forces of War, and one of the Generals slated him for being on his way away from the fighting. Your fears are well-founded ones. If you do not stop them here—they will go to your world and slaughter your son as they did mine, but here, you have a chance that they do not. You can make a stand."

He clapped me on the shoulder and made me look him in the eyes. "You can protect your son, where I did not protect mine. Do not let him become a victim. I will help you and yours however I can, I swear it, but you cannot let this destroy you. Use it."

He clenched his fist in front of him, the leather of his gloves creaking a bit, and held it before me. I nodded and bumped it back. Jaken must have taught him that.

"Thank you, Sir Dillon," I said and stood up.

"Aye." He clapped me on the back. "While we walk to the tavern, will you tell me of your son?"

I nodded and we began a slow walk back to the village, stories about my son and his adventurous nature renewing my spirit to fight for him.

During breakfast, we got our final briefing from Sir Willem.

"Maven Rock is a few days away by horse," he explained. "Between our village and your destination is a swamp area that spans the forest exit to the west, then the plains. I'm going to venture a guess that none of you have mounts?"

We all looked at each other and shook our heads.

"Well, I hope you're okay on money because they cost a pretty penny." He sighed and told us to go to the stables on the outskirts of town to the south—a portion of town I hadn't been to yet, to be honest.

"Good luck, my friends," the older Paladin said and shook each of our hands.

We left for the stables. A few of the villagers stopped to wish us luck, but it was a solemn walk otherwise. The stables were what one might expect—a home tacked on to what looked like an open barn. The stalls each held horses of various colors and sizes. The owner of the village stable turned out to be a Dwarf by the name of Swelles. He looked like he could have been Rowland's twin, but he had silver hair and a bushier beard.

"Ho there!" he greeted us kindly. "Be ye seeking mounts?"

I smiled at how direct he was. "Why yes, sir, we are."

"I can get ye mounts." He nodded sagely. "Don't ye be afeared. Hopin' ye have the funds for it, though. It stops most from trying to get a mount worthy of them. Horses like the ones ye see behind me will boost speed by a quarter but can only be rented. Once ye travel so far, they get tired and spooked easier, but they're a reasonable price. Only cost ye about twenty gold a day and any time ye dismount after the final day, the horse will take off for the nearest stable. If the beast is killed or hurt, you have to pay another fee as well."

"That sounds rough, considering what it is we have ahead of us," Jaken said.

"Aye, that it does, but most people don't travel much these days," he said simply. "Royalty, nobles, and the well-off can afford to buy their own mounts or steeds to do what they like. Or even breed their own. Even adventurers who go to the dungeons and questing can save up for a horse of their own. Two hundred gold per steed. Most hold out and stay near their current location until they can afford it, some never can. It depends."

I whistled softly. We could afford that easily, and I would be perfectly fine after. I wasn't tracking the others' funds, but I'm sure they should be fine too.

"Now, afore ye decide," he held his hands up quickly, "there be options, so hear Ol' Swelles out, now."

He reached into his pocket and pulled out a whistle. It looked to be carved from stone, a slender tube about the size of his pinky. He blew on it, and a second later, a large goat with a saddle bolted toward him from behind our backs. The goat was a solid, stocky thing with great horns and intelligent eyes. His shaggy, brown fur rustled in the breeze as his caller patted him.

"This be a soul bound mount," he explained. "They be sturdier and at ye beck and call. They be expensive but worth it. They don't have the rental fee, and if they get hurt, they just disappear until ye summon them again. They don't fight, but they be faster—one hundred percent faster than your speed walking—and need only half the rest and feed as a normal mount. Be ye interested?"

"Yes!" blurted Bokaj. "How much are we talking about here?"

"Four hundred fifty Gold," the Dwarf said apprehensively.

We all whistled. That was steep, even with our good luck and funds from the gods.

Bokaj stepped forward with an appraising look on his face. "Well, that's a bit steep for us, especially since we don't have *that* much coin. We spent a good deal getting ready for the ruins we cleared out. Now we're on our way to fight the next minion of War. Is there any way you could drop it down a bit? Maybe say, half?"

The Dwarf looked shocked. "That lot was ye?" Bokaj and the rest of us nodded. "I canna do half. Four hundred?"

Bokaj winced visibly. "How about two seventy-five?"

The Dwarf bit his lip and shook his head before holding up a hand. "I canna go that low either. These were difficult to procure."

"I guess we will have to walk then, guys." Bokaj looked over his shoulder and winked slyly.

"Hold fast, sir Elf." Swelles put both his hands up in front of him. "I canna go that low, but how 'bout three hundred fifty gold and an agreement that when ye come back, ye buy me a round and tell me a tale?"

"Sold." Bokaj dug into his pockets. "Do you take platinum?"

The Dwarf's eyes grew large, and he nodded three times. My friend dug out and counted thirty-five platinum coins and handed them over. Swelles looked at the coin and then at Bokaj and then sprinted inside quickly. Just before it seemed like we had been fleeced, he bolted out with a handful of items.

He pocketed all but one and gave it to his customer. It was a simple piece of wood roughly the same size as the Dwarf's whistle.

"Now, hold it afore ye and focus on it," he coached. Bokaj did as he was told. "Now, touch it with your mana."

Bokaj continued to focus as his hand lowered toward his crotch before saying, "Mana."

"Dude, what a time for a joke about your junk." Balmur laughed. The poor stable master looked concerned, but we weren't going to explain the joke if he didn't get it.

Once more, Bokaj focused, and a dull blue glow emanated from his hand, and he opened it to show a whistle like Swelles's but made of ice.

"Woooaaah." I heard Jaken whisper.

"Blow it, lad," encouraged the Dwarf. The guy was walking into these now.

No one went for the easy jab but watched captivated as the Elf used the whistle. There was no noise from the whistle at all. Maybe it was broken?

A second later, a large, white polar bear with claws and teeth made of pure ice appeared in front of Bokaj in a burst of arctic wind and snow. The mount was about the same size as some of the bears we had seen after clearing the dungeon. It was surely big enough to ride. It turned to the Ranger and sat in front of him, swatting playfully.

The rest of us were sold instantly. We all forked over the platinum to get our mounts and attuned to our whistles.

Balmur's mount was a chameleon the size of a horse that appeared inches from its owner's face as it released its camouflage. This was awesome because then they could scout ahead; if the thing could stealth the way Balmur could, he would be able to move faster. Its eyes roamed every which way, and it slithered it's tongue out in affection at Balmur.

Jaken's was a pure white stallion with armor that came charging into existence from our left, appearing gradually. He reached out and stroked the horse's glorious mane, and he laughed when it snuffled at him and tried to shy into him.

Yohsuke called to his, and I was pretty sure that Swelles crapped his pants. The nightmarish creature burst from the ground and flame rolled out from the area. It stood proudly, wings flared, front hooves clawing at the ground with flames burning the grass. Claws gouged the earth at its flank, and its beaked jaws screeched in defiance. It looked like a bone griffin with wisps of purple flame emanating from it. Holy shit.

My own whistle turned into crystal in the shape of a lightning bolt. I blew into the whistle and heard the crash of thunder. I looked around and saw that no one seemed to have heard what I did, so I waited for it to come eagerly. Black lightning flashed and hit the ground in front of me, tossing me back three feet. Where the bolt had touched the earth, a gate opened, and a myth stepped through.

The beast reared and kicked its fore hooves out before standing still, surveying me with regal eyes. Black skin covered its muscled body head to hoof with gold streaks of lightning that almost seemed to move as it stood there. He shook his head, flinging his white mane about, and regarded our surroundings before looking back at me. I didn't realize until then that the beast had horns sprouting from his forehead above his eyes that curved gracefully back toward his mane.

I stayed where I was and cast Nature's Voice.

"Hello," I started. He looked at me in surprise, poking his head slightly forward more.

"It speaks?" it asked in surprise. "How do you speak Kirin? And why am I here?"

"I speak the languages of all beasts," I said simply. "As for the why of you being summoned here, it's because I need a worthy mount. I don't know how the process works, but if you would be so kind as to let me ride you, I would appreciate it."

"Ride me?" he asked incredulously. "I don't even know what you are, let alone if you are worthy to treat me as transport. How do you think to prove yourself to me? Prove your worthiness to an heir to the lightning."

I stood and dusted myself off. "What do you think, Kayda?" She came to me from her perch in the tree nearby and landed on my shoulder.

Show, she replied simply through our link.

The Kirin looked at her with obvious curiosity and came closer. Kayda ruffled her feathers at him, and her constant static loosened a bit. It zapped his nose as he got too close, but he didn't seem to mind at all. He snorted and sneezed, but that was all.

"I will show you my own lightning then," I said. "If you'll stand back?"

"No lightning you could ever conjure would harm me, thing," he said dismissively. "Hit me with your strongest bolt directly. Let us see what you can do."

I just smiled and nodded. I turned to my now-mounted friends and gave them a thumb up. They nodded and watched.

Luckily, one of the new abilities I had gained as a Druid was Charge Spell.

Charge Spell – Doubles the damage output and mana cost of the next spell cast per every 5 seconds held. Restrictions: Maximum hold time is 20 seconds. Will raise enmity generated by the caster and attract enemies or hostile foes' attention. If casting is interrupted, spell backlash will harm and stun the caster for the period held.

While it was risky, I could do a lot of damage on a sneak attack if I was well hidden or away from my target. Otherwise, I'd be a sitting duck with a duck season sign strapped to his ass.

I triggered the ability and held onto my Lightning Bolt spell. My clenched fist began to spark as lightning sought to escape my grasp, but I clenched harder and focused. After five seconds, I felt a pulse. Five seconds later, I felt two. Then three. Then one long one, and I unleashed hell on the Kirin before me.

The lightning blast shot into the beast's chest, and he reared up. I thought I had done more damage than I intended, but all I heard was a grunt. Then he disappeared. I tried to use the whistle, but it wouldn't work.

"That be a drawback, lad," the stable master explained. "If the mount is attacked without a rider, it returns home. Ye can summon him again in a couple of hours."

Did I just get played, I asked myself.

"Can our mounts hold another person?" Jaken asked.

"No," the Dwarf said. "They can carry their owner, but that be it without the movement being severely decreasing."

"What about a small animal?" asked Yohsuke after a second.

"Oh?" The stout man thought for a moment. "I suppose he could try it. I can't say that I know outright."

Jaken smiled and took off on his charger at full speed, then looped back around to stand before me. I shifted and leapt my foxy self into his arms, and he took off again. There wasn't a noticeable decrease in speed, so we decided to give this a try for a while. Although I hated to admit it, this was much faster than we had moved with Melal—and we had been booking it.

We set out west from the stables. The ride was so boring through that first bit of forest that I fell asleep. The guys let me nap for a few hours. Then it was time to summon my mount again.

I cast my speaking spell and blew the whistle once more. There was no flash of lightning this time; the Kirin just stepped into being at a brisk trot.

"My name is Zekiel Erebos," I introduced myself. "My friends and I vanquished one of the lesser minions of War plaguing this region, and we ride for the next. Will you render us aid as a friend, or need I find another mount who will stand ready?"

His eyes went a bit wide as he listened to my spiel, but he stayed quiet a moment after I finished.

"I asked our elders about you," he said quietly. "They felt the stirrings of the Gods and their plight but didn't know what to make of it. Then the Mother of All proclaimed a Lightning Roc was lost to us, one of so few left, but one of her clutch lived on because of a Druid and his friend."

He stepped forward with his left hoof forward and bowed his head a bit.

"You have our thanks, Zekiel Erebos." He stood up once more, his head held high. "I will carry you so long as you will have me. The Lightning is your friend, as are the Kirin."

"Thank you," I said, slightly taken aback. "What do I call you? Do Kirin name each other?"

He snorted. "Do you think us savages? My mother named me well, I am called—" and as he said his name, it sounded like electricity.

I looked at him in confusion, but he seemed to understand.

"You may call me as you like, Zekiel Erebos," he allowed.

"My friends call me Zeke," I said. I stepped up to him and tapped his shoulder. "I will call you Thor."

"Is this a name to be proud of?" the Kirin asked uncertainly.

"Where I come from, he is the god of thunder," I informed him. "He is a mighty warrior and revered by all in many fashions."

I swear, the Kirin grinned, and I got an eyeful of his sharp, shark-like teeth. Oh fuck, I was supposed to go near him?

"That name will do," he said proudly. "Come, we must make haste then."

And so we went. My mount was willing to work with me. We didn't always need to talk, and he was understanding since I had only ever ridden a horse once in both lives. It wasn't pretty. Did I mention I had a tail now? Because that thing was a nuisance. One: it ached on top of being saddle sore, and two: it tickled Thor. His laughter was entertaining, but eventually, he started to get sore from laughing.

After I face palmed hard enough to actually do damage, I shifted into my human form. I looked down at my hands and saw that my skin was the same color as my fur. I didn't have a mirror to check my other features, but it would do.

"Better?" I asked smugly. Thor nodded and kept a running.

That night, we spent the evening under the stars, opting to keep our tents in reserve for later on when cover was less likely. Our mounts had been dismissed, and we sat around a small fire with our cook tending to some food we had brought along.

"I've been meaning to ask, man," Yoh started. "What is that sword spell you have?"

"Oh, that's Filgus' Flaming Blade," I said and summoned it for him to see. I felt the pull of mana, and a burst of flame shot from my fist. The blade of roiling fire took a solid form about the same size as a short sword. I discovered after some experiments that the length of the sword could be changed from long sword to short sword and vice versa.

"That's tight, dude," he said as he turned to look closer at it. "How much mana does it cost? How long does it last?" I filled him in on the stats of the spell and the considerations to take into account. It disappeared if dropped or let go and only lasted ten minutes.

"I only really took it because I lost my weapon once at an earlier stage and wanted to have a weapon as a backup that I could rely on until I'm re-armed. The elemental damage it does is nice, though."

"Yeah, bro, Astral Blade is legit, but the unaspected damage was getting to be an issue in my mind because it's just flat damage." He stirred the pot in front of him absently. "We got really lucky that we found that Astral Adaptor that we did. I wonder if there are others."

"I wouldn't doubt it, man. The gods can't interfere too much, but we've been incredibly lucky so far. Makes me think that they're helping how they can," Jaken interjected.

"We have Mother Nature with us, as well," I said, turning my eyes to the sky and smiling.

"What?" Bokaj asked. "That's not a thing, right? Is it?"

"Yeah, she's the one who gave me my Druidic powers," I said as a breeze blew gently through the camp. "She's also the one who gave me the quest to find Kayda."

At the mention of her name, the bird ruffled her feathers and picked at the Level 3 Vole that she had killed while helping our cook and Ranger find dinner. She was doing well enough in her own hunting here lately that I didn't have to worry too much anymore. She still had a little attitude problem with people touching her, but she was okay with the party.

I had worried about her and Tmont; the panther had been absent the whole ride, but that was because when her master was mounted, she took on a passenger size. That size was that of a kitten, weighing a negligible amount as to not interfere with the speed of the mount. Since she could fly, Kayda didn't need a travel size. The cat had wisely abstained from screwing with the bird, mainly because she had something against being shocked, I guess. Who knew.

"But she's a real entity?" Balmur asked.

"Yup!" I laughed at their looks. "I don't think she's as powerful as the gods, but she's up there, and as far as I know, she's looking out for us."

"Thanks, Mama!" Jaken said laughing. A swathe of leaves dumped down on him, and we all laughed.

The food was ready a short while later, and we ate before bed. We kept a guard for watch. The Elvish members of the party volunteered to take watch considering that they only needed four hours in a meditative state to get a full rest.

In the morning, we ate a light meal and mounted up again. By midday the next day, a bog was visible in the distance. We stopped to camp near a big tree along our route. Big was an understatement—the tree was huge; the bark was reddish brown and rough to the touch. We enjoyed our meal as the sun was setting, and as the golden rays of sunlight died, an entity separated itself from the tree.

Tmont was the first to notice it, and a growl let us all know something was going on. We stood and watched as our guest stepped into our camp, just out of the light of the fire. It appeared to be a man but covered in bark, leaves, and moss. It raised its hands to show it was unarmed and meant no harm.

It stepped into the light, and its moniker appeared.

Great Tree Dryad level 25.

If this thing meant us harm, we were in for a seriously heavy battle.

The Dryad began to speak to us in Druidic, its voice like wind moaning through the limbs of a tree.

"Have care, travelers," it began. As it spoke, I translated. "Beyond the edge of this tree is the Nightmare Bog. There have been multiple excursions by Lizardmen into the forest as of late. They have migrated here, but we know not why. They cut and burn our trees, kill our people, and flee back to the Bog. They are many, and they fall under the control of their chieftain, a mighty warrior who has slain many attempting to take the mantle."

We nodded, appreciating the warning.

"Will you assist us in culling some of their brood?" it asked, and a notification popped up.

QUEST ALERT!

Does a Lizardman Shit in the Forest? - Lizardmen have been raiding the forest line and killing the Dryads while pillaging the wood and herbs they use to heal the land and keep the Bog monsters away. Will you assist them in culling the number of Lizardmen? Requirement: kill at least 15 Lizardmen. Reward: 20 Exp per Lizardman vanquished.

Will you accept? Yes/No?

"I'm in," I said. "It gives us an opportunity to farm and hopefully level up a bit. The stronger we are, the more likely we are to succeed in our main quest, right?"

The group agreed, and the Dryad was so happy that he told us to let him stand guard over our camp.

That next morning, we decided on our course of action. Why screw around and beat up on the raiding parties when we could go right at the big bad?

Chapter Twelve

That wasn't the plan at all. That would be reckless and stupid—right up our alley normally, I know—so we did the opposite. We went looking for the raid parties. Numbering at about eight Lizardmen each, they were going to be a little rough but hopefully manageable. The Dryad warned us that the Lizardmen would be around our level, so finding them and being crafty would pay dividends in the end I hoped.

We ate a hearty breakfast and spent a little while telling each other about our latest capabilities. Bokaj could speak to animals now, the same as me; he also had a healing spell and a spell that conjured a barrage of arrows.

Balmur got a spell called Languages that allowed him to understand any language as far as he knew of. He got Magic Shot and a spell that allowed him to climb any surface that wasn't greased.

Jaken got another enmity ability that drew in a creature of his choice and kept that creature attacking him until one of them was dead. So either Jaken and the rest of us whooped that ass, or he was hurting. Then he got another healing spell that gave a regenerative buff and improved regen out of combat.

Yohsuke gained the ability to dual wield his weapons and an area of effect—AoE as we would typically call it—spell called Star Burst that sounded interesting. He could lob a magical attack that went off like a grenade. He also got a buff that upped his defense.

I took a spell called Nature's Hidden Path that let me move from one tree to another up to five hundred feet away in any direction and another that allowed me to summon a large sphere of water to trap my enemies.

After some discussion of a semblance of a plan of attack in certain situations, we set out to see who—or what—we could hunt down.

With the Bog being as treacherous as it was, we couldn't use our mounts, so the going was slow. Luckily, Bokaj made the trip at least a little easier by finding better paths through the quagmire. The scent of decay and death coated us as we walked further in. Trees littered the area still, but they looked to be in a more decayed and deadened state. You could smell the rot and grossness easily. Another unfortunate side effect of being a Kitsune was that my nose didn't die when I was around a scent for too long. I kept getting those same disgusting whiffs of yuck.

Great.

After a circuit of the area to the south of us, about two hours of travel, we found a raiding party sleeping in a small copse of trees. They either must have thought themselves the baddest in the area, or they had a lookout somewhere. Bokaj held up six fingers and mouthed that two weren't there. Maybe it was a small party? Maybe two had wandered off to scout or were hidden? Either way, we had our work cut out for us. Each one was level 13. If these were an indicator as to what they could afford to have roaming, the harder enemies were likely near the chieftain. That's what I would do, consolidate my power base and send the weakest out to roam and pillage to get stronger.

When I got to thinking about what I would do, I started thinking about our predicament. Almost any normal person would probably be freaking out right now.

Here I am, stuck in this world that is based around a favorite pastime of mine, for gods know how long, and the fate of our world hinges on the safety of this one. Sounds pretty mind breaking to me—any sane or reasonable person might have a hard time coping, or at least it would be an issue if I hadn't been so used to having to adapt quickly and keep myself focused on the mission—it could have me fucked up, too.

Sure, there were fun times to be had here, but we all had reasons to go back home: loved ones, children, family, friends, and so much more that we could call upon to help us fight for what we believed in. Whether they knew it or not, they were counting on us to step up here. They couldn't afford for us to let the situation cripple us in fear. Through all of our fantasy-ridden adventures together, you could probably say that the whole group had been conditioned for this while we played our games, constantly questing to save some new world from countless enemies and monsters.

How was this really any different?

I'm certain that my friends all felt the same, but we would need to have that talk later. It was time to get stronger now.

The Lizardmen were what you might expect, although they resembled alligators in the faces. Huge maws hung open in sleep, showing rows of sharp teeth. The creatures all had muscular builds and carried primitively made spears in their hands while sleeping. The heads of the spears looked to be some kind of black stone, probably obsidian.

We backed up to a safer distance away and tried to plot our attack. Bokaj had the better idea, so we went with his. He would climb the tree we used as cover and look at the area, then give us a better idea of the best approach. After climbing back down, he let us know that the waters near the islet they were using looked to be deep and dangerous. Probably why they felt they could sleep there without much fear.

Knowing that, we decided to test our new spells. Balmur would stealth and walk where Bokaj told him using the Mental Message spell. Slowly—in increments of a few feet—our Rogue moved forward, dodging sinkholes and deep water with the guidance or our Ranger. It took about half an hour for Balmur to get into position from the one hundred feet away that we had been. He stopped just outside the circle of trees and back another ten feet to the rear of them, facing toward us.

It was time to bring out the big guns. I'd only used this ability once, but this was the perfect opportunity to use it to full advantage. I activated my charge spell and held on to Fireball.

Fireball – The caster shoots a beam of red fire at a target of his choosing and once struck, erupts in a 20 ft sphere of flame. Deals 100 damage at the focus point and 10 less for every other creature hit for a minimum of 50 damage. Cost: 100 mana. Cool down: 5 minutes.

The spell's area of effect wouldn't change, but it would increase the damage. That mana expenditure made it a hellish drain, though. Oh well. This would help us kill them quickly, I hoped.

After five seconds, I felt the first pulse of mana, then the second and unleashed the spell at the center of the group. Unfortunately, not one of the sleeping bastards had the common courtesy to make my job easier by sleeping closer together but oh well. The resulting detonation was devastating. A crater formed where my beam hit, and it was one hell of a wake up call. The flames bit into each of the Lizardmen and drained their health to about seventy percent each. They were up and agitated.

They started to call out to each other, and I had no doubt the boom from the blast might cause more to come investigate. We needed to try and make quick work of them here. Bokaj focused his fire on the slowest Lizardman to the right side, with Yohsuke joining him. For this fight, Jaken had to be closer to them to use his enmity collecting abilities, so he just tried to line himself up and make noise so they might throw their spears at him.

Balmur did what he did best and royally dismantled the one who was calling to the others the loudest. He hit hard and fast, and the guy went down quickly. Bokaj and Yoh had moved on to the next one, and two were on the way toward us. The fuckers were walking on top of the water like it was solid earth. Shit!

Jaken was ready for them, and as soon as they were in range, he began to glow red and shouted wordlessly at them. The two Lizardmen turned on him and started to sprint forward. Balmur began to fight the last one in earnest, weaving and dodging as the Lizardman jabbed at him with his spear. One of the attacks landed and grazed the top of his thigh as he whirled to try and dodge. He grunted and unloaded on the poor bastard. I threw a Frozen Dagger at the creature to distract him for a moment then turned toward the two on Jaken.

One had managed to get past the great sword he was now wielding and stabbed him in the stomach. I cast Regrowth on Jaken and brought my great axe to bare on the offending Lizardman. I was a good ten feet away, so I activated Cleave and used Wind Scythe to throw my axe at the scaly thing.

It hit with a meaty thud and chopped off a good fifteen percent of its life, dropping it to a little over half. I leapt to the side as it threw its spear in retaliation but got grazed myself. It knocked off about ten percent of my own HP. They hit hard. Jaken used my distraction to chop down with his sword, cleaving through the injured creature and dealing critical damage that killed it.

He took another stab for it and was starting to look a little rough. He glowed golden for a second, and I watched as his HP climbed back up above sixty percent. I yanked my axe out of the dead creature and tore into the next one. By the time all the creatures were dead, those of us at level 11 were more than a quarter of the way to the next level. We rested up and healed ourselves while we could. Once we got the chance, we moved on, heading further south at a decent pace.

We didn't make it too far when we stumbled upon another patrol heading our way. They had seen us already and were sprinting at us. These ones weren't walking on water so far. That must have been a spell from a shaman maybe? Did they have shamans?

They must have had some type of shamans.

I readied my great axe and activated my Cleave and Wind Scythe combo, throwing the beastly axe at the center Lizardman. There were eight this time. We were in for one hell of a fight. Kayda took wing and zapped the one I had hit. He went down hard and stayed there with a lightning shaped mark next to his HP bar.

Paralyzed? Yes!

I didn't look into it too much at the moment. I was bum rushed by two more of the downed Lizardman's buddies and shape shifted into my bear form. I roared at them and slapped the one on my right with my massive paw and sent him sprawling to the ground. I took my left paw and drove my claws up into the soft under chin of the creature attacking me. The claws pierced flesh slightly, and it sent him off balance into the Rogue waiting behind him.

I turned back to the paralyzed enemy before me and dropped on him with a fury. Tooth and claw stole his HP swiftly. He never got to stand again. I turned about to see that Jaken was, once more, the focus of attention and that Yoh had summoned his skeletal pirate Bonzer to assist us. Two more of the Lizardmen had died, and three were engaging with our tank.

Jaken had switched to his sword and shield for this one, and he seemed to be lasting a little longer but not by much. I lumbered into the three focused on him and received a jab at my flank while passing too close to one of the enemies. It hurt, taking about fifteen percent of my HP away. I was still looking good, but that would suck with another few hits. I asked Kayda to stun another one, but she couldn't. That skill was on cool down, I guess.

Soon, she thought at me.

I bear hugged the closest one and turned with him in my paws, meaning to throw him down. As soon as I had completed the turn, Bokaj sent three arrows into the scaly beast and took him down to fifty percent. I pushed him down, feeling another slice go across my back; this one dropped my health by twenty-five percent.

Then came the Feral Rage. I turned on the offending bastard and grabbed him by his jaw when he hissed at me in defiance. He tried to bite me, and I thrust my claws into his mouth and then thrust my right paw and his bottom jaw down. A sickening pop came, and the jaw hung loose. I thrust my right paw into the injured Lizardman's throat and lifted while lowering my body weight. The poor humanoid tried to scream, but I just threw him and roared at the opponents around me.

There were only five now; the one I had thrown made a most excellent battering ram as it careened into two of its friends. I fell on those two, stomping and growling, using my claws to tear out their throats and just generally make a mess of them. Of the last two left, one had fallen.

Yohsuke joined my rampage. His skin glowing—changing before my eyes and becoming red and rough—he grew small, demon-like horns from his forehead and fought beside me. The enemies rallied and attempted to flee, but Balmur and

Bokaj kept them from going far. The rage left slowly, as it had the first time. I shifted and helped heal myself and everyone who had been hurt. I guess there had been a ninth enemy because Tmont came strutting back to us with something else's blood on her fur. Awesome.

"Hey, man, what gives on the new look?" I asked Yohsuke as we started to loot the bodies.

"Infernal Body," he said. "It's the self buff I was talking about earlier that increases defense by an additional fifteen percent plus your armor. Lasts thirty minutes and only costs fifty mana. Cool down is the same as the duration, though, so if it were to be dispelled, I could be in trouble."

He grinned and said, "If I was a little bitch!" We both laughed pretty hard at that.

"What the hell was up with you, though?" he asked.

"Feral Rage," I explained. "If I'm dealt more than twenty percent of my HP in damage in a single attack while in animal form, I fall into a murderous rage. Halves the damage I take and increases damage dealt by half. Cool down is an hour. I'm going to have to see if there's an update to it, though."

"Holy shit, man," he awed in a low tone. "You fucked them up. That shit was brutal. And why is that?"

"Because I lose control of myself to my anger. I attack the enemy, sure, but I'm not sure if that's going to affect party play or not. If I attack one of you guys... I don't know what might happen."

"You won't attack one of us, man," he said, his voice dripping with surety, and he clapped me on the back, "cause I'll fuck you up if you come at me incorrectly, son."

We laughed at his stupid joke and bumped fists. We looted the corpses—there wasn't all that much on the bodies; they ran slick—but the obsidian tips off the spears were cool, so Bokaj collected the them.

We spent the rest of the day finding and destroying patrols. Once we had traveled a good distance away from where we had previously camped, we moved into the forest line to camp again. Another Dryad offered us refuge near her tree in support of our quest, which let us know we might be going in the right direction. At least, in my mind it did. We slept and then hunted again the next day for some food. Our travels took us a little further into the forest line where we found some wild boars.

We killed two of them and made our breakfast before moving back out into the boggy lands. Yohsuke cured some of the meat from our kills so we didn't have to kill as much and take away from our grinding time too much either. Grinding being the thing most gamers either love or hate, it's the process of killing monsters or enemies with the sole purpose of getting stronger in mind.

Usually, that whole process was a mind-numbing pain for me. I hated having to grind in some games. Here, with it being real? I saw the necessity of it—hell, I even welcomed it.

Jaken, Bokaj, and I had leveled up once and were well on our way to leveling up again. Kayda had also leveled up three times. Kind of like adding water to a large pool with a group of friends. Not just the person who puts the most amount of water in, gets to swim, everyone gets to. In this case, as long as she was providing some damage and doing what she could with her paralyzingly ability, she got a portion of the experience. The experience per kill and fifty percent extra from my kills seemed to be doing her some real good.

Sure, it made my leveling a little slower, but she was worth it. The little badass flew over my shoulder. She had grown again; now she was a little bigger than an adult eagle. The feathers on the sides of her head had started to turn a sort of teal-green and lengthened to stand out like little horns reaching back toward her back. It was so cute and mildly terrifying. She had almost as much of a reaction from our enemies as our Bokaj's house cat did. They about crapped themselves when Tmont pounced at them, and they would try to duck when Kayda flew by.

    I could have smacked myself right then. What if we had gotten into a fight? She could have died, and it would have been on me. I checked her stats out and looked to see if I could glean any more information. Her wisdom seemed to be attached to her ability cool downs, so she could use her lightning attacks more often with more wisdom it seemed. Although, lately, it looked attractive to have her be able to physically attack some things while her cool downs were active. I had nine points to play with here, so I decided to try and figure out what would work best.

    Obviously, she needed more HP, no brainer there—four points into Constitution. A little extra muscle wouldn't hurt, either—three points into Strength. Finally, I put two points into Wisdom to hopefully help with her cool downs. Her three natural points had gone one into Strength and two into Dexterity, leaving her status page looking pretty nice.

Name: Kayda
Race: Lightning Roc
Level: 5
Strength: 4
Dexterity: 10
Constitution: 10
Intelligence: 4
Wisdom: 3
Charisma: 5

Unspent Attribute Points: 0

I had to say, the increases in strength seemed to have beefed her up a little. She looked healthier overall, and I was excited to see how she would do in battle.

As for my own stats, I felt I needed to change up. See, we had our physical damage dealers: Balmur, Bokaj, and Tmont—plus Yohsuke who attacked with his spell sword. Yohsuke could also act as a caster to a lesser degree, but only because his ranged spells seemed to be a little less powerful than his sword. I did well in the damage area so far, but I had been focusing on my own physical damage output. I nodded to myself and opted to drop three points into Intelligence and two points into Wisdom. Time to start slinging spells a bit more seriously.

After heading south for about another hour, we had almost decided to take another direction when Bokaj and Tmont spotted a cave off to the west a bit. We had been approaching a mountain range—maybe a continuation of the range that I had explored to get Kayda. We headed toward the cave's entrance and discovered something that none of us were expecting.

Snoring off in the corner was a humanoid-shaped sleeping bag. Bokaj nocked an arrow, while Tmont and Balmur dropped into stealth and crept closer. I nodded to Yohsuke, and he held a hand up to cast if needed. My darkvision activated after a moment in the darkness of the cave, and the pitch black became grey. I could see almost as if in twilight.

"Hey!" I shouted. The snoring stopped, and the person shot up into the open, into a battle stance.

If I were in Bokaj's position, I'd have shot him up. Luckily, I wasn't, so the poor guy didn't get an arrow in his chest. Yet. Although, I did almost throw a Frozen Dagger.

The black skinned Elf turned his golden, reptilian eyes onto all of the people he could see and smiled, baring sharpened teeth at us.

"You guys got here quickly," the figure's voice sounded familiar.

His sharp features seemed to come into focus a bit more because Balmer had dropped his stealth and cast light. It took me a second to adjust to it. Tears streamed from my eyes as I closed them to reduce the strain. I was going to have a chat with him about using light spells like that unannounced.

"How did you know we were coming?" Jaken's voice held a note of cautionary suspicion.

His shield was out but his sword was away. I had no doubt if this got ugly, he would be able to draw it. There wasn't much room in here with all of us, but there was an opening to the rear of the cave, yawning like the mouth of a great beast.

"The Monks at the monastery told me you guys would have finished your training and received word on the next location of one of War's agents," he explained as he bent over and started to clear up his makeshift bed. "They told me to head north to see if I could find you guys and bring you back."

"For what, Aaron?" Yohsuke asked. I looked at my best friend and saw that he had relaxed and started smiling.

"Hey, Erik," the other said with a wolfish grin. "Glad to see you made it, buddy."

"Aaron?!" I asked softly in realization. I bolted to the man and pulled him into a bear hug while laughing.

This was the first time we had ever met in the flesh. It sucked that it was here, but damned if I wasn't excited that my friend was okay.

"What're you doing here, man?" I asked, holding him at arm's length. "And what the hell are you?"

Looking at him up close, I could see that while his skin was indeed the same deep black as my fur, he had a dusting of scales on his cheeks that ran down his neck and grew into full body scales. They looked tough enough to withstand damage. His hands had finer scales, and his nails jutted out like claws. All he was wearing was a simple pair of cloth pants that were tied loosely with a sash and a pair of leather-soled slippers.

"I'm a Dragon Elf Monk. Here, check it." He pressed a couple of buttons on his status screen, and I could see his stats.

Name: James Bautista
Race: Dragon Elf (Black)
Level: 12
Strength: 18
Dexterity: 40
Constitution: 31
Intelligence: 20
Wisdom: 25
Charisma: 8
Unspent Attribute Points: 0

"Wow," Yohsuke whispered. "You have the same amount of Dexterity as me, and I'm a level higher."

"That was because of the training at the monastery," James—as his new name would be—explained. "Their training was grueling, but as time went on, my stats increased. I would go out into the training grounds cultivating the skills they thought necessary and fight every day to get to where I am now. I heard you guys got to do some awesome stuff. Wanna talk about it over breakfast?"

We all sat down and introduced our new characters, going over the things that had happened to us and our quest so far. While the others were explaining our most recent adventures, I started thinking about the kind of training that might help increase my own stats: weightlifting, maybe reading books, or trying to work out how to use magic? Maybe in the next city we could figure some of it out.

"Well, you guys ready for another dungeon?" James stood and stretched himself a bit.

"Another of War's minions?" I asked.

"Nope, this one is natural," he explained. "The elders at the monastery told me it was here and that it would be a good idea to try and go through it. They said something about War's minions not being the only evils in this world."

"I'm up for it," Jaken said. "Better to grind it out while we can and be stronger, right?"

"Yeah," agreed Balmur. "Where are we going?"

James pointed toward the rear of the cave. "Right there."

"Wait, you were sleeping there, with the entrance to a dungeon not ten feet away?" Bokaj asked incredulously.

"Nothing had come out the day before, so I figured it was safe." He stowed his things in his inventory, and we started into the opening. "Besides, it's right here and with everything out there being so close to our level, shouldn't we use this opportunity to get a little stronger and keep the area a little safer?"

We walked for the entrance with Yohsuke and I both shaking our heads. This was our friend alright—he was the only one to use that kind of logic that we knew of. Goofball.

Chapter Thirteen

We walked for maybe ten minutes before we found a group of Goblins, only three, but they had us all surprised. They were all level 14 and seemed to have a class and simple weapons without armor. We had two Goblin Rogues and one Goblin Fighter.

The alcove they were in was tiny; if not for Balmur leading us, we might have missed it and they could've been behind us. He signaled that we should stop and back up until we had a plan. They were sleeping, with the Fighter "watching" the door, propped up on what looked like a little anvil. His version of watching were a pair of eyes painted on the backs of his eyelids so he could sleep, too. Clever. Too bad today just wasn't his day. The room they occupied was five-foot square, and the guard sat in the entryway.

There was no light spell cast here for this one, since almost all of us had some version of Darkvision. I don't know why the Rogue had cast it earlier; maybe he just thought it was a good idea at the time. Balmur had his Dwarven Rock Vision, an ability that allowed him to see clearly underground. Well, I guess we weren't technically underground then were we? Hell, if I knew, but it seemed to be working.

We had Balmur go in first, using the shadows to his advantage and shadow stepping into position over the sleeping body of the Rogue on the left. He held both his hand axes out and at the ready when he nodded to Bokaj, who had a bead on the sleeping forms with two arrows nocked. James slid around the Goblin on guard and took a position over the other, and we were about set.

Jaken stepped in front of me, and Yoh stood off to the side, watching for any others who may try to ruin our fun.

Fireball was out of the question—too many friendlies and too much noise. That also took out Lightning Bolt because it was too bright and would blind us, so I cast and held the only other spell I could—Frozen Dagger. The held spell only cost twenty mana, and with our tank standing in front of me, the light the spell gave off was blocked. After the fourth pulse, Jaken stepped aside at a hiss from me, and I unleashed the frozen projectile at the green thing. Balmur and James struck swiftly. Then Bokaj released his arrows. The Goblins weren't all dead; after that, it took another couple hits from the two party members inside to kill the Rogues. The Goblin Fighter took minor damage, only about fifteen percent, but had a status I hadn't seen before. It looked like ice cubes, and the Fighter moved very slowly.

"Nice frozen debuff, man," Jaken whispered to me and set to work attacking the Goblin before the status effect fizzled out. Once their targets were eliminated, Bokaj, Balmur, and James turned to the Fighter and helped finish him off.

So, with the spell a little stronger, I could cause detrimental effects as well. I'd have to save that for a rainy day.

CONGRATULATIONS!

Your experimentation with spells and abilities has increased your intelligence by 1. Further experimentation and implementation may yield more damage, detrimental effects, or upgraded spells. Good luck, traveler!

WELL THEN, I screamed in my mind.

I looked, and sure enough, my intelligence had gone up one. Oh, I was going to play alright. I chuckled, and we looted the corpses and found some garbage. I did take the small metal daggers the two Rogues had so I could practice enchanting on actual weapons that I didn't care about. We got a couple silver pieces and gave them to Yohsuke to hold until we could divide it up later.

We headed on down the tunnel, putting the alcove and entrance behind us. After a ten-minute walk, we found a larger room, about twenty feet around with two different tunnels leading in opposite directions. I saw two Goblin Rogues of the same level as the ones we had defeated standing outside the right-side tunnel. Balmur walked into the room first and still hadn't noticed the two Goblins. They were watching him intently and drew their weapons.

I wasn't about to let him walk into this trap, so I cast Frozen Dagger at the one to the left of the entrance. It dodged it easily. The best part was that it alerted the rest of the group to something being wrong, and they were all alert now.

"Two Goblin Rogues by the right entrance, same level as before," I said before shifting into panther form and bolting at them.

I swiped at the one who had dodged my spell attack. It dodged again and cut my arm, taking twenty HP with it. With it having done damage, the Goblin's stealth dropped, and it became visible. I shouldn't have rushed them because as soon as his friend was visible, the other Goblin stabbed me in the back and dropped me to half health. I dropped to the ground instantly, and Feral Rage kicked in hard.

"Fuck!" Yohsuke shouted, the need for silence abandoned. "Get away from him. He's gone feral. Jaken, get those heals flowing."

"On it!" Jaken reached, out and golden light wrapped around me.

I whirled on the Goblin behind me and whipped my right paw out to catch it's stupid, grinning head. The green creature bounced off the wall with a fractured skull next to its

HP bar. It didn't get up. The red of my vision set in fully, and I leapt onto it, taking it into my jaws and shaking my head furiously while trying to beat it to death with my paws. The Goblin behind me stabbed me, trying to help its friend, and I turned to get to it. Something black was in my way, and I batted it aside to get to my prey. I heard cursing and saw golden light out of the corner of my eye, but the Goblin was trying to sprint away from me. Further enraged, I bounded off the wall to my right, smacking the gold-light, metal thing beside it with my shoulder. I caught the Goblin and pushed it down with my left paw. I went to bite it, but the Goblin in my mouth got in the way. I spit it out and lunged, digging into the soft underbelly of the creature beneath me. I bathed in its screams, music to my ears. It raised its weapon to try and strike me, but I hissed at it and batted the metal aside. I buried my teeth in its face, biting down as hard as I could and tore it back. The blood trickled out of the wound, and the foe was vanquished.

 My vision was still red, and I lifted my nose to the air and breathed in deeply. To the right, where the Goblins who had stabbed me came from was a scent that wafted up my nose. I crouched and slunk forward as quietly as possible. The room at the end of the tunnel was small, but there was another Goblin Shaman holding a book. I crouched and pounced, landing on the creature and knocking the air out of its body. It began to glow, but a purplish bolt of dark light slapped it in the side of the head and went quiet and still.

 It still had HP so I bit into the back of its neck and twisted, with a sickening crack resounding off the walls. The red in my vision began to ebb, and the bloodlust left me. Yohsuke stepped into the room and approached me cautiously. Once I shifted to my fox-man form, he relaxed a bit.

 "What's wrong?" I asked softly.

"You got James pretty good when you pushed him out of the way," he explained. "You knocked Jaken out when you wall ran at the other one. To be honest, I thought it was badass, but if the rooms are small like this, the whole party is going to be in trouble if you go feral like that too often."

I looked at the little room and noted another tunnel at the back.

"I've got an idea on how to mitigate that," I said. "Let's go check on the others."

We went back and talked it out. There were no hard feelings over what happened; it was just dangerous.

"Awesome," Jaken said, rubbing the back of his head, "but dangerous."

"Sorry, man."

"No worries, brother." He laughed and held his fist out to bump knuckles.

"This split is going to be an issue," Yohsuke stated. "No matter where we go, there's going to be the risk that there is something at our back. What do you guys think we should do?"

"Maybe we split up for a bit?" Bokaj suggested. "I mean, we have two people who can act as tanks. Balmur and I are used to working together, and with Jaken taking the hate and Tmont to try and sniff out the stealthy Rogues, we could do pretty well. The way you all made it seem earlier, James, Zeke, and you are thick as thieves so you guys know how to function as a team."

"Yeah, we do," I agreed but shook my head. "Every table top game I've ever played has punished people for splitting the party in some way, shape or form. If you all want to do this, I'll take it, but we have to have a system in place."

"We contact each other every couple hours at most via Mental Message to update each other on things," Balmur suggested, "and if there's something that is too crazy for us to tackle alone, we call for backup and sit on it until the other team arrives. If there isn't a response to a Mental Message, the other group comes running."

"Sounds good to me," Yohsuke grunted and looked to James and I.

The idea was sound enough that I couldn't complain too much. James nodded, and Balmur and Jaken gave a thumbs up.

Jaken, Balmur, and Bokaj would go to the left, and we would go right, with Balmur and I communicating to each other through our Mental Message spells.

"Now, let's get this loot, eat, and then we can get this show on the road." Bokaj rubbed his hands together excitedly.

We had looted the bodies, then rested, and ate a small lunch. Yohsuke, James, and I had gone back to the room I had cleared while I was enraged and looted that Goblin. The book it had was a tome that none of us could read, bound in leather and inked in what was probably blood. Yohsuke stowed it for later, thinking we could find someone to read it and tell us what it was.

We moved on shortly after. James had pocketed my portion of the gold because I wouldn't take it as part of trying to say sorry. He just shrugged, and we moved on. I led us on, since I could see the stealthier Rogues with my True Sight. It was an ability that let me see invisible things, creatures, or objects and the true nature of shape changers. I hadn't had a need for it before, especially since no one ever tried to hide anything with magic that I could think of in Sunrise.

I didn't see any creatures as we moved, so we pressed on. After our first check in with the other group, we got to a mushroom covered area. The chamber was large, more like a field than a cave. I guess you could call it a cavern. Maybe the Goblins cultivated these for food?

"Hey, some of these are edible," Yoh said while he picked at a patch. He took some and added them to his inventory.

"Since we're here, and this looks like a good food source, there has to be some Goblins nearby," James said as he looked around. "Maybe let the others know that we found this place, Zeke?"

I nodded and cast the spell, "*Hey guys, we found a mushroom cavern. No sign of anything bad yet, but we thought we should let you know what was up. Be safe.*"

"*You got it man,*" Balmur responded. "*Let us know if you need us.*"

We found a group of about twelve level 4 Goblin Pickers after a little walking. They wore nothing but loincloths and were currently snacking on their latest harvest, having a lunch of their own. We couldn't leave them behind us in case one of them saw us and tried to attack us unaware, nor could we let them go and risk them telling their master and bringing the whole dungeon down on us. We had to get rid of them. It was a a slaughter.

I'm not proud of what we did, but it was a necessary evil. I just hoped that at the end of this, the truth about their ties to these "evils" in the land became apparent because no matter how vicious these little things had been on the mountain and here so far, I couldn't get their frightened visages off my conscience.

Through my memories of the event, Kayda recalled that it was a raiding party of Goblins who had stolen her real mother from her and had no issues snapping up the little green creatures. She was a brutal monster at that point right then. I wasn't proud of her actions, but I wasn't going to deny her the sense of justice she could try and take for herself.

Chapter Fourteen

We had come across another room where I saw hidden enemies, and the others only saw one Goblin Ranger level 15. I had forgotten about one of my natural Kitsune abilities—Fox Fire.

Fox Fire – Caster summons and controls faerie fire, able to shape it into any form desired. This spell lines hidden creatures and objects in flames that do not cause damage but reveal location. Range: 60 ft. Duration: 10 minutes. Cool down: 10 minutes.

I thought about the spell I wanted to cast and willed it to spark on one Goblin Rogue who immediately began to freak out and run toward his other stealthy friend. The clueless Goblin was promptly tackled, and the faerie fire spread to him. Both lost their shit and began to try and roll around on the floor. The flames didn't die out, but the Ranger nocked an arrow while trying to figure out what was going on. It began to shout at the other two in a high-pitched and clearly irritated voice.

Yohsuke nodded at me, and we both sent a spell at the Ranger. My Frozen Dagger caught him in the shoulder, while Yoh's Astral Bolt hit him right in the temple, doing critical damage. The Ranger's HP dropped to seventy-five. It shook its head and sent an arrow flying right at Yoh, but a black, clawed hand snatched the arrow out of the air and whipped it at the Goblins still rolling around on the ground. It hit one, doing minor damage, but it brought the thing closer to a frenzy because it hadn't felt pain before with the flames. Now it did, and it freaked out more. The other Goblin who was rolling around stopped abruptly, stood, and then kicked his friend before pointing at us. He motioned to the flames and spat on the ground, then began to advance toward us with his injured friend in tow.

"I've got the Ranger," James said and closed the distance between them. The Rogues made to follow, but Yohsuke sent another Astral Bolt flying that smacked the lead Goblin right between the eyes. Its eyes crossed for a second, and then it was wobbling right at us.

Changing his weapon from Astral Sword to Astral Spear, Yoh drove the bladed tip at the green creature, but it sidestepped and tripped.

"He's confused!" Yoh shouted, and we both fell on him quickly, my friend's blade stabbing swiftly, joined by my great dagger. The Goblin's HP drained, and it lay still after a few seconds.

I turned just in time to watch as the cowardly Rogue tried to sneak attack James, who weaved in and out of the way of arrows sailing at him. Just as the Goblin behind him was set to strike, James rolled out of the way. The arrow meant for him struck his would-be assailant in the left eye, leaving the Rogue with only a sliver of HP left. It lay panting in pain on the ground. Kayda dove out of nowhere and pushed the arrow deeper—the Goblin died, and Kayda began to feed on her fallen foe.

I got a notification that Kayda had leveled up again.

"Fuck, that bird is brutal, dude." Yoh laughed as he jogged over to join James against the Ranger.

I walked behind it and cast Frozen Dagger, which it seemed to dodge as if by instinct. James spun, grabbing the icy projectile and stabbed it into the neck of his opponent, bringing the Ranger to its knees. Yohsuke slashed with his sword and cut the thing's head clean off.

We looted the bodies, then sat down for a moment.

"What the hell was up with you guys?!" I asked. "James is out here catching arrows and spells and shit. Yoh, you're a fucking lucky dickhead. What's going on?"

"Monks get an ability to catch projectiles within reach, but there's a cool down, about ten seconds," James explained. "So, I can catch one, maybe two at a later level, but anything more during that cool down I either dodge or get turned into a pincushion."

We both looked to our other friend and he smiled. "I unlocked something called Spell Sniper. I got it back when I caught that one Goblin earlier, but I was saving it for a time we needed it."

He took a moment to fill us in, and I had to admit, I was more than a little jealous. Spell Sniper allowed a caster to increase the accuracy and strength of his spells. This one added a couple of neat effects, like confusion and stun at a certain percentage chance. It was a passive ability, something that was always there that boosted abilities or spells. He hadn't gotten the chance to truly try it out until just a few minutes ago, and even then he had been weary of it.

"I didn't want to go too trigger happy because there's a chance that I could hit you guys, and it would hurt a lot," he continued.

I couldn't blame him for that. I was still jealous, though.

They were common in a lot of games—passive abilities like this one—but this was my first time seeing it here in Brindolla. I'd have to ask about it from people who knew more in this world, but, typically, a passive ability like Spell Sniper added a little extra something to your skill set. A mage, for example, could use a lot of fire-type spells and earn an ability that caused him to do more damage to creatures, cause burn damage over time, or lower mana cost of a specific kind of magic. All of those were awesome, and it was really lucky that Yoh was the one to have gotten Spell Sniper.

I spent the rest of Kayda's stat points. Her intelligence had naturally increased by one, probably due to her distributing retribution to all the Goblins she could in cruel—but brilliant—ways. I put another point into Strength and two into Wisdom.

We rested a bit longer, long enough for my Fox Fire spell to cool down, then moved on. I checked in with the others, who were doing well, and then we moved on.

The next fight we got into was an all-out brawl. There were three Goblin Fighters level 14 walking toward the room we had just left. We looked at them, they looked at us, and no one moved for a second. Then all hell broke loose as the lead Fighter took the initiative and charged us. He went for the target with no weapons — James.

James laughed as he push kicked the Goblin in the chest into the one behind him. The Fighter left standing went straight at Yohsuke. What was I, chopped liver? I growled at the little bastard and stabbed it in the back with my great dagger. It was wearing hodgepodge, rusted metal armor too, so I cast Lightning Bolt after I pulled the blade back out. Hey, I may be stupid, but I'm not that bad. The lightning struck the metal backplate of its armor, and the little thing shook violently. Yoh took the opening to drive his Astral Blade into the creature's exposed ribs and cast an Astral Bolt point blank into its head. The Goblin dropped—its head a smoldering ruin—and we moved onto the next opponent.

This Fighter was assisting his friend in fighting James. Both worked well together, probably used to fighting as a team. One went high as the other came low, then mid-strike swing and a jab from the partner. If James hadn't had high Dexterity, he would have been skewered a few times. It was bad enough that the Monk had lost thirty percent of his HP and the Goblins were near full.

Yohsuke summoned Bonzer behind the Goblins, and the Skeleton went to work on the Goblin with the least health.

"James," I said over the grunting and fresh clash of metal. "You go with the Skeleton. Yoh and I have this one."

I turned to Yoh and nodded so he would take the lead. After he and the Goblin had begun to weave their deadly dance, I took in my surroundings. The tunnel was actually fairly large at twelve feet wide and ten high. I had just enough room for my great axe in here, but it would be close.

I equipped my great axe and activated my one stop combo, Cleave and Wind Scythe. I threw the axe at the Goblin as soon as it was clear of my friend. It hit his armor and knocked him five feet back. The armor mitigated some of the damage, but the attack had dropped him to less than half of his health. He tried to pick my axe up to use it against us but could only drag it behind him. Another idea occurred to me.

"I'm going to trip the little bastard up," I explained to Yohsuke. "Don't hit me."

He nodded at me, trusting me to do what I said but still confused. I shapeshifted into my fox form and bolted between the Goblin's legs. He dropped the haft of my axe and tried to grab me, but I was too quick for him. From that first miss, I bounded around the thing's feet and distracted it until Yoh stabbed it in the head with his Astral Spear.

"Call off the Skeleton. I've got this," James called out with a grunt. "You guys rest."

Yohsuke and I sat down off to the side of the tunnel. Bonzer kept a lookout since he had nothing better to do and Yoh didn't want to dismiss him just yet. James was down to fifty percent HP, and I was about to cast Regrowth on him when his body flashed with golden energy just beneath the skin and his health bar was at full again.

"Woah!" I whispered to Yohsuke so we didn't distract our friend. "You see that?"

"Yeah, man," he said back. "Looks like Monk is a pretty badass class."

James disengaged from the fight for a second with a back handspring, then lunged forward swiftly and thrust his palm out. More golden light surrounded his outstretched hand, and on impact, the thud from the Goblin being thrown violently away into the wall behind him made the two of us cringe. He closed with his enemy before it could stand and dispatched it with an axe kick. It was a beautiful, brutal strike.

"Nice going, man," Yoh said. "What was all that?"

"My Ki," explained James. "Ki is the force inside all living beings. I can manipulate my own, and with the understanding of how to do that comes the ability to use it on myself and others. That last strike was a Ki Strike. It costs about ten Ki per strike, adds magic to my attacks, and depending on where I strike, it will stun, knock a target prone, or push them back fifteen feet. The other thing was a self-heal that the class uses called Healing Aura. It uses half of my Ki, so I'm going to need to meditate real quick."

"That's pretty freaking sweet, man," I said with a whistle. "How do you like punching things?"

"It's pretty relaxing. I get a good work out, but I can use weapons like staves, nunchaku, short swords, and some other simple weapons. Most of my skills lay with unarmed combat so I may stick to that unless something comes along."

We waited while James meditated. He sat up against the wall, legs crossed, and his body seemed to relax slowly. Once he was completely relaxed and still, he stayed that way for a little bit. While he was doing that, Yohsuke and I spent our time leveling up. One point to Intelligence and four to Wisdom. Then I picked my next spell.

Heal – Heals the target or caster for 100 HP instantly. Cost: 100 MP. Range: 60 Feet. Cool down: 5 seconds.

Kayda leveled up again. At level 7 now, her natural point, the one that went into the most used stat between levels, went into Constitution, so I threw two more into that and one into Wisdom. I checked and saw that a couple levels ago she could have a spell of her own. The spells were limited because of her elemental alignment, but I could see potential there with a couple. The first I picked was her own Lightning Bolt. That should help us out. I could've kicked myself, but with how busy we'd been lately, there just didn't seem to be time to check.

I took a moment to check on the other group. They had met some resistance but otherwise seemed fine. They were going to push a bit further then call it a night.

Moments later, James stood up and stretched.

"You guys ready to move?"

We nodded and got up to loot our kills. The drops from these guys were okay; the swords would help like the other weapons, so I took them. The money we split evenly this time because James threatened to punch me if I tried to baby him anymore. I didn't want to be on the receiving end of that knuckle cannon of his so, I graciously agreed.

Further down the tunnel we came to a room with an altar and three hooded Goblin Acolytes level 15 huddled closely together before it. A section of the room was partitioned away with a thick material and incense was burning heavily behind it. It stung my nose something fierce, but I got out a rag from my old clothes and tied it over my mouth and snout like a bandit. It helped a little. There were torches on the walls, but they didn't smoke or sputter like normal flames, and they didn't screw with our dark vision.

The group decided it was too risky to stay and plot in easy sight of this doorway and went back down the tunnel to talk out a plan.

"What are you guys thinking?" I asked.

"I'm guessing those are casters," said James. "Most likely some kind of Black Mage type."

"Yeah, gotta go in and get 'em quick before they lay down a good amount of damage," said Yoh.

"Well, I have a crowd control spell, but it's expensive mana-wise," I offered, "but if it works, Kayda and I could fry them really fast. I'd be spent on mana and have to fight close quarters after. Water Grave, if you remember?"

"I could throw Black Snow down or Star Burst as well," Yohsuke grumbled, his eyes closed in thought. "It's expensive, too but worth it if we can do as much damage as possible to them before we have to go in. What're we looking at dimension-wise for this spell?"

I explained my spell, Water Grave, as a ten foot by ten foot globe of water that holds anything it touches in and slowly drowns it, unless they can manage to get out. I hadn't tried it before, but I figured it could help. Pair that with a charged Lightning Bolt from myself and Kayda's own spell, and we could do some serious damage—provided the laws of science held on this planet.

We discussed our options quietly and decided on a plan. After that, Yohsuke cast his Infernal Body spell, and we waited while his mana recovered.

A quick mental conversation with Kayda later, and our attack was set to begin. The first bit went off well; the sphere sucked in all three Goblins no problem. Yohsuke's Star Burst blew up and did a little less damage than we had thought, about ten percent apiece, but it was something. The force from the spell rippled and forced one of the Goblins close to the edge of the sphere, where it continued to struggle to get free. I guess some Goblins can't swim? I finished charging my spell, and Kayda cast her own the same time I did. The effect was exactly what I had hoped it would be. The water magnified the lightning damage threefold, and two of the Goblins inside were dead and crispy.

Unfortunately, the third Goblin who had been pushed back was able to escape the full force of the blasted lightning as it slipped out and fell against the altar. It screeched in a high pitched, guttural language and produced a knife. Before any of us thought to move, the little green creature leapt onto the altar and slit his own throat. His HP fell to zero, but a burst of flame claimed the falling body, producing a charred-looking creature with small horns, small wings like an over large bat, and glowing red eyes.

It pointed at us; a red beam shot toward us and exploded like a Fireball, knocking Yohsuke and I back. Luckily, James had ducked out of the room and was spared. My health had dipped by thirty percent and Yoh's about a quarter.

"Gonna need Bonzer on this one, buddy," I said. "I think is going to be rough."

The Lesser Demon level 18 looked at us and grinned. A small, nasally voice spoke in my mind, *"Yes, it will be."*

"Great," I said as I rolled my eyes. "Telepathy. Oh goody."

"You'll die first, disrespectful worm."

"Your mother."

It shrieked and hurtled my way, quickly closing the distance between us. James seemed to just be there, planting his foot into the side of the enraged Demon's head and shooting it into one of the magical torches. The spell from the torch didn't do much to it at all.

"Might be magic resistant," James said before I could.

I brandished my great axe and got ready. I had fifty mana left, and it was going up slowly but surely. Bonzer stepped into view; the Skeleton was level 8 now. His gear remained the same, pirate-style getup as before. His jaw lowered in a wordless cry, and the Skeleton charged the little Demon. The Demon met him head on and began to smack its attacker swiftly, attacking three times for every one of the Skeleton's attacks. The kick from my friend had done only about five percent of its HP so we stood a chance if we did this right.

Yohsuke had come up behind the creature, his Astral Blade slashing forward, while another, smaller Astral Dagger came across the opposite direction. He slashed, weaved and bounced out of range, and slashed more until the little Demon turned to attack him.

I took the opportunity to activate Cleave and Wind Scythe before launching my weapon end over end at the little asshole. The blade only nicked its back a little but shaved off its right wing entirely, leaving a bloody gash. The greater axe embedded itself into the altar. James was right there, his hand glowing green for a moment before he stabbed his clawed fingers into the wound. The flesh around it began to sizzle and pop like bacon and fried eggs. Faster and faster, James stabbed with his hands until his arms were a blur of black and green.

The Demon's HP was at fifteen percent when it began to intone something and a tear began to appear over the altar. I could see tiny insect swarms over a plane of red fire and sickly yellow gasses. They began to crawl this way, and I began to panic. Screw bugs.

"Shut him up!" I cried.

I leapt over my friends and began to tug at my axe. The swarm was closer now, and I could see that the insects were two feet long with leech-like maws, salivating acid. Oh hell no. I pulled harder, but the axe was stuck. I activated Devil's Hammer, and that got it out, but I wasn't going to make it in time to stun the little monster.

Suddenly, the Demon grunted and fell silent. The portal shut as one of the insects leapt toward it, trying to get to me. I looked back, and James had his glowing fist shoved into the Demon's mouth. His HP had gone down a bit—he was at sixty-five percent—but he seemed okay with it.

"We can make a deal, yes?" the nasal voice begged but none of us listened. This time, I took pleasure in ending the little thing while it was helpless.

Chapter Fifteen

We were hurting. We all sat down after checking behind the curtain and James had seen nothing but a small chest waiting. We grabbed a snack, and I took the chance to send a Mental Message and check on Balmur and the rest of the crew.

"Hey!" Balmur's voice spoke into my head. *"How are you guys managing?"*

"Good, man. We just cleared a mini-boss room, I think," I responded with my own spell. *"I think we're going to call it a night. We got fucked up bad, but we made it. No need to come get us. The loot is good, too. How are you all doing?"*

"Good. Had our own shit to handle for a minute there, but we got through. You guys be safe. If anything happens, I'll give a shout."

"Same here, brother. Be safe, and whoever gets up first messages the other. Night"

I relayed the message to my friends, and we all relaxed. It had been nice to have such a good fight, but none of us expected that Demon. What the hell was going on with these guys? Goblins summoning Demons?

After we were healed and recovered, we looted the bodies. The Goblins gave us some gold, and one gave a ceremonial knife. The Demon dropped a scroll, a ring, and a large, blood-red ruby that hadn't been cut yet.

"A one-time use item," James said. "Summons the defeated Demon to do the summoners bidding for five minutes. Anyone want to take the helm on that?"

"I will." Yohsuke held out his hand to take the spell. He took it and looked it over. "I have an idea about that book."

I picked up the ring to look over its stats.

Band of Inferno

Increases fire damage, +10 to attacks with flames.

Infernal fires bend to your will, strengthening the flames of your castings.

A gift from a careless, stupid human.

That looked nice. I checked with the others and asked the others if they wanted it; they looked at me as if I were stupid, so I put the ring on. I felt the ring heat up until it felt almost uncomfortable, then it stopped.

Yohsuke summoned the Imp, Betzits, into the material plane before us.

"Thank you for summon–" the Lesser Demon began, but was cut off.

"Quiet, minion," he ordered. "You can speak and read almost any language, right?"

The Lesser Demon looked furious but nodded slowly.

"Good." The Elf produced the book. "You will read this, honestly and out loud, to us in our language. Go"

He regarded his temporary master with open disgust but complied. The book, which was only a few pages, was a log of things that the Goblins had been collecting, ingredients and incantations in order to summon a Greater Demon at their leader's order. It didn't explain why, just that those were the orders and that all priests and shamans were to consider ways to gather the right things needed.

"That is all, master," the small Demon said finally. We had used about four minutes.

"Good, any of the spells they gathered look like they will work?"

"No, though they are close to a breakthrough it seems."

"Okay, good. You guys have any questions?"

We shook our heads.

"Okay, Betzits," Yoh looked back at the Demon with glee, "kill yourself and donate the experience to us."

"Master, no–"

"Do as I command, minion."

The Demon screamed its rage loudly as infernal flame swept over his body, and he died again. We received the experience; it was less than we had gotten the first time, but it was something we needed desperately.

"Brutal," I commented. James nodded, and we both smiled–this was the Overlord, a portion of our friend's personality that peeked out occasionally. Erik usually liked to joke that he would rule the world, and that we would be his vassals. This was him stepping into that role and embracing it.

"Let's rest for the night then," I suggested, and we did. They let me sleep through the night, taking turns standing vigil.

After I woke up, I Mental Messaged Balmur, who let us know that they were good and that the night was easy. I informed him that we would be moving on, and he said that they would do the same.

We had a quick bite, then moved on. We fought our way through a few more waves of Rogues and Fighters, stopping for a short, ten-minute rest and to check in with the others, then headed on. We gathered more trash loot, but I left some of the heavier items behind, hoping for better gear later. The morning was looking good so far.

* * *

Eventually, we made our way into a larger chamber with a throne–more like a poorly crafted chair on a mound of rocks, but I'm sure the Goblin King felt important in it.

The head Goblin was a mean looking thing—larger than his kin by at least a foot and broader and fatter than his subjects—but he held a scepter in his hand and had a crown on his head. His sausage fingers clutched the scepter, and it had a couple shiny rings on that looked to not fit too well.

Smaller Goblins ran around, bringing it food and performing little dances for his amusement. Occasionally, he would lash out and smack one with the back of his hand and scream loudly. I saw one Goblin in the corner step out of a puddle to bring him a pitcher. Most of the others in the room were extremely low level compared to him.

"What an asshole," James whispered. "Level 18. Think we got this?"

"It would be rough even if he was alone," I said quietly. "He has at least a dozen level 8 Goblins in there with him, and who knows how many in the area."

"I don't like it either," said Yoh. "Look at those guys, though. They're terrified, man. We go in there blasting, chances are high that they bolt."

I thought about it some more and couldn't find the fault in that logic, so we went back to a small cubby in the rock where we could come up with something.

"We need to let the others in on what's going on," James advised first.

"Good shit, man." Yohsuke fist bumped him.

"Balmur, we've got a boss over here. Level 18 with a bunch of other level 8 Goblins serving him. They look scared shitless of him. You guy think you're close?"

"We came upon a few assholes but nothing too extensive. Some kind of storage—they've got rancid meat in here. Might be close. Think you guys can hack it until we get there? Or can you wait?"

"Let me ask."

"They think they may be close," I relayed. "Think we can hold out until they get here? Or do we want to risk it and see what can be done?"

"It's risky, even with Bonzer. There's a lot of them." Yohsuke scratched his head. "Although, I know we're some bad motherfuckers, I think we should wait."

"Yeah, I agree." James nodded. "Let's wait it out, and then we go stacked deep and ready to roll."

I relayed our message to the others and Balmur said that they would hurry. After half an hour of waiting idly, we weren't expecting the five level 8 Goblins that came wandering into our cubby and caught us by surprise.

We bolted to our feet, and all of them tried to flee back toward the King's room. Kayda swooped down and latched onto one of the Goblin's head and began to peck at his eyes. Yohsuke caught one in the spine with an Astral Blade strike that caused it to fall paralyzed and went for another one. James caught one, and I was able to cast an Frozen Dagger at another, but it didn't stop the fifth one who made it into the room and started screaming at the head Goblin. A couple of strikes, and the four we were able to get were dead.

"Looks like we're going in hot, now," I growled, then cast Mental Message, *"Beat feet here, guys. We've been spotted. Can't talk."*

We rounded the corner, and they were still listening to the screaming Goblin and weren't paying attention to us. Looked like the new ring I got would play a large role in what we were about to do. I also went ahead and got a few mana potions ready.

I charged Fireball for five seconds, then unleashed it into the room. At the same time Yoh cast Black Snow and then Star

Burst right after. The Fireball collided with the King's chest and burst out, smacking into a couple of the lesser Goblins around him. The fire, which had been orange and normal before, now looked a little more red and black. That must be the power up from the ring. I downed four of my MP potions and brought myself back up from sixty-five MP after Mental Message and a charged Fireball to two hundred sixty-five MP.

The black cloud that appeared over the now smoldering Goblin King unleashed a large gust of air. Then specks of darkness began to fall down onto the large Goblin. He screeched just before the Star Burst exploded and shot him backward into his people. The thing had so little health now, about forty percent, that we felt confident in our ability to take him out.

The Goblin King raised his scepter, and a black aura surrounded his body. The Goblins around him began to shrivel and cry out. Their bodies became lifeless, and the King stood once more, his HP full.

There were now half the number of Goblins left, and they were clamoring to get out, pulling each other down to get away from their leader to no avail. The King tapped his crown with his scepter, and a red aura shot straight out of it and into the bodies of his remaining subjects. Their bodies crumbled to dust before our eyes, and his body began to grow. His muscles enlarged and thickened. The now-seven-foot-tall Goblin cried out in a deeper voice, and we all got ready for a knock-down, drag-out boss battle.

James was just to the left of the large creature before I could blink. He kicked it in the knee with a Ki empowered strike. The knee buckled a bit, but the King shrugged it off and swiped at the Monk with his scepter in a backhanded swing. The scepter connected with James's chest and sent him flying back ten feet. His health had dropped a fourth, and it took him a second to get his legs beneath him. He seemed dazed, and that made him an easy target. The King had begun to bear down on him while he had the chance when a blast from Yohsuke took him directly in the head. The Astral Bolt knocked the creature forward, and it stumbled over the kneeling figure before it.

I activated Cleave and then Wind Scythe and sent the axe flying. The attack hit the creature and took ten percent of its health. It was at eight-five percent now, and it seemed angry, yelling loud enough that those of us too close had to cover our ears. More level 8 Goblins streamed in from an entryway off to our left that we hadn't noticed before. They saw him, then saw us and went on the offensive right away. The newcomers were across the room from us, a good twenty five feet away, when the black aura rippled out again and sucked them dry. The King's HP was full once more, and we weren't looking all that great.

I was sitting at full health, and my mana was nearing full, while Yohsuke had full health with almost no mana left after casting his spells and his sword activated. Poor James's seventy percent health wasn't reassuring with the way the King was truly hating on him after tripping over him. The Goblin King recovered and started for James once more, raising his scepter like a club.

James recovered enough to stand, and just before the attack landed, I trundled in on all fours in my Dire Bear form. I roared in defiance at the Goblin King and slapped half-heartedly at the scepter raised above his head. The green bastard swung it at my paw, and I shot my head forward and dug my fangs into the creature's left shoulder. It screamed, and I saw that Yoh had chosen that time to go for his hamstrings. The Goblin King sunk to one knee under my bulk and the damage to his muscles before he screamed again. Once again, three more low level Goblins entered the room.

"Kill them!" Yoh shouted. "We can't let him heal again!"

James and Yoh bolted for the new Goblins and set about killing them. The aura started to rise off the King's skin, and I tore into him. I still had my teeth in his shoulder, so I set my jaw and sliced into his exposed chest with my clawed paws. I cut him back down to eighty-five percent including the damage from my friend before the aura shot past me. The King finally managed to slap me with the scepter and dropped me by ten percent. The hit was enough to dislodge my teeth from his shoulder, and I saw his health only go up by five percent. My friends were coming back when the King swung at me full force and cracked me in the ribs on my right side. My health dropped by thirty-five percent, and I entered Feral Rage hard.

I roared at the stupid thing and unleashed hell. I swiped with my left and right paws. When he lifted his ringed hands up to defend itself, I tore into his ribs, and when he dropped them, I tried to bite his stupid head. The King cried out for further aid, a larger group of Goblins answered this time, but the group was met by the two with me.

I was too focused on the reason for my pain. My HP was at half now and dropping slowly. My right side was tight, and I had a broken bone icon and a blood drop next to my HP bar. Oh well. I growled in frustration and focused on the bastard again because the sooner he died, the better.

My friends managed to kill a few of the Goblins but not enough. This time, instead of the black aura, the red aura swept across them, and they ground into dust. The Goblin's muscles thickened once more, and it swung a ham fist at me that I ducked, but his other hand that held the scepter connected and sent me reeling back. My health bar throbbed crimson at ten percent. I began to feel sluggish and lethargic. I fell onto my backside and watched as the Goblin King whooped in victory.

The scepter began to fall, and I almost accepted that I was about to die.

A subject that, surprisingly, none of us had thought of before as deeply as maybe we should have. A hell of a way to go out—this. On my ass in front of a pissant Goblin jacked up on steroids. The scepter dropped and with it, my heart. The great thing collided with the ground, and the Goblin King sat on his ass.

Kayda had swooped down and zapped the monstrous Goblin right on his chest and screeched at him. I had lost sight of her in the fray and then in my frenzy. Luckily for me, she hadn't done the same. Then came the real cavalry. My rage was gone now; losing my ability to fight had distracted me enough that it had fallen away.

Golden light bathed my body, and my health shot up by one hundred HP and seemed to be regenerating a lot faster than normal. I looked and saw a slight boosted regen next to my HP bar, and the broken bone and blood drop debuff were gone. I turned to see Jaken standing next to me.

"Could you not die?" He smiled and offered me a hand up. "I kind of like having you around, man."

I smiled and noticed that the rest of my friends had come to our rescue. My HP looked good, so I rejoined the fight. With the party back together, taking the green asshole down was a lot easier. The ranged attackers laid waste to the Goblins the King summoned, while the close-quarters attackers kept him busy. After a few minutes, the King fell to Balmur's hand axes, and the party had cleared the dungeon. At least, so far as we were aware of.

The King didn't drop the scepter or the crown, but we got some cash and a few of his rings: a Ring of Storage that allowed someone to cast one spell into the ring to be used by anyone, a Ring of the Ram that threw pure force out to damage an enemy and send them flying, and a Ring of Regeneration that healed five HP per second for a minute at will—that we gave right to Jaken. The storage ring went to Yohsuke, and the ram ring went to Bokaj.

We looted the room as well, gathering coin and even some raw materials that had both Jaken and Balmur almost drooling. Twenty five pounds of mithral ore, one hundred pounds of iron ore, five sapphires, three diamonds, ten opals, one hundred twenty-five platinum, and one hundred gold.

All of us had leveled up. Bokaj leveled up to 15 as well since he had been so close to leveling up again in the first place. Tmont leveled up twice, and Kayda leveled up three times amazingly. I threw the points I could into Intelligence and Constitution—five points in Intelligence and four into Constitution. Her natural points went to Wisdom this time, all three of them. She also had the chance to learn another spell—Lightning Ball. It sent out a small ball of lightning that attached to an enemy and electrocuted them every few seconds. It only lasted for thirty seconds, but it seemed interesting.

A pretty good haul, I thought.

We cleared the room, and I wanted to check the offshoot room I hadn't seen before, but that was the way that my friends had come. We decided to go back out through our direction, since theirs was still swarmed by large bats that were crazy hard to kill. I supplied that it would be good experience, but they warned me that the fighting took place over a chasm that they had no idea how deep it went. The only reason they had made it before was because there had been a Goblin raiding party trying to clear the bats when they arrived. The Goblins fought both enemies, and the bats focused on the Goblins until they were gone. Didn't mean they hadn't fought their fair share, though.

The bats struck quickly and used their echolocation to their advantage; it was horrible. Their equivalent to the Demon fight we had was nightmarish. They had to fight a larger bat with the body of a man, almost like a vampire. The only thing that had saved them was Bokaj's Ice ability and Balmur's Shadow Step. When the creature had been about to finish Jaken off, the Ranger froze its leg, and Balmur had Shadow Stepped and leapt onto its back, driving a stalagmite next to the Paladin right up into its heart.

On their way to the King's throne room, they hadn't had to fight as many enemies due to them all running here. That was how they had actually found us. Damn good thing they had, too, or I'd be dead.

We made it out of the dungeon without incident. That night we would camp in the forest line, back far enough that we didn't really have any worries about running into any raiding parties, but it was better to be careful. There was still a few hours of daylight left, so I approached Balmur about a thought I had while we were in the dungeon.

"Hey, brother, you got a minute?"

"Yeah, what's up?"

"How good are you at making rings?"

"Good enough, I think. What did you have in mind?"

I explained my idea. It was simple, at least from my perspective. I wanted him to create some heavy rings for Kayda to wear or carry while she flies. If it worked, she would gain points in Strength and Dexterity. He took some measurements from her with a string that had some markings on it. I explained how I was also thinking that we might be able to do the same for ourselves, but from the way James had spoken about it, the training took some time.

"I'll look into it, man. That seems like a pretty awesome idea. You want to let me run with it?"

"Knock yourself out, man. Thanks."

We spent the rest of the mid-morning journey swapping stories about our time in the dungeon and showing each other some of the abilities we had in our arsenal now. It was a great time.

Balmur showed me his new ring. It was a Blink Ring. It allowed him to use the spell Blink up to three times a day. Blink was kind of like an all-purpose teleport up to sixty feet. It didn't require mana to power or shadows to step through. I had to admit, that seemed pretty damned overpowered.

During a break, Balmur took some ore out of his inventory and had me heat it the way I had when we worked together in the forge. I obliged, and he sat a small anvil on the ground. It was ten inches tall and wide with a horn to bend metal on.

I held the now heated handful of metal out, and the Fire Dwarf pointed to the anvil. I set it down, and he beat the imperfections out of the metal with a small mallet. We repeated the process twice. Then I reheated it and sat it on a dish he set on the anvil. As soon as I did, he snatched out a tool and used it to carve away a portion that he thought was appropriate. Then he rolled the heated metal around on the anvil while tapping on it with his mallet. After a minute, he had me heat it again, then tapped away some more. After a half an hour, the piece began to take shape.

The piece was thick, and from the looks of it, was meant more for function than fashion. Eventually, it began to look like a thick bracelet of grey metal. The thought dawned on me that this wouldn't fit my familiar, but I let the man work in piece. I provided heat when he needed it, and he kept shaping.

After an hour and a half and another piece of metal, he was done. The finished products, cooled by a jug of oil he had been carrying in his inventory, looked just like I had envisioned. I held them out in my hands and looked at them. They weighed about five pounds apiece. The metal was sturdy and held in place by a clasp.

The weighted rings fit perfectly over a piece of cloth bandage wrapped around Kayda's legs. She complained that it was heavy but soon realized what I had in mind for her. When I reasoned that she would be able to kill many more Goblins if she was stronger and faster, she took flight. It was awkward, but she soon got used to the weight.

After our rest had finished, we traveled back into the forest for a bit more safety than the cold uncertainty of the underground. It was a great deal easier going back out of the dungeon without having to worry *too much* about running into more Goblins. The trip back was uneventful, and we made it to the forest line just after night had fallen.

We all went to sleep a little easier that night.

Chapter Sixteen

"ATTAAAAAAAAACK!" Yohsuke shouted, and a second later, a resounding boom shattered our slumber.

I jolted upright, still half asleep, trying to figure out what was going on. Level 13 Lizardmen were swarming in—at least a dozen of them, and they were moving swiftly towards us.

Bokaj and James were the fastest to react since they were only in a sleep-like trance with Jaken right behind. Bokaj usually entered his trance with his bow in hand anyway, so he bolted into a tree using Nature's Hidden Path, an ability we both now shared, and used the second spell I'd never actually seen him use—Barrage.

A blast of a hundred arrows rent the air and streaked toward the invaders—and me since I was still in the area. Jaken stepped in front of me with his shield raised, protecting me from the arrows. Balmur stepped through the shadows, and the other Elves were nimble enough to avoid the worst of the attack.

"You guys better get in on this. Try and get them close together, I'm gonna use my big attack but I need the time to down some mana potions!" the Ranger shouted to us.

"You heard the man!" Jaken yelled, spittle flying from his mouth. "Come on, you little bastards!"

"Get'em, Bonzer," Yohsuke ordered, and the Skeleton lumbered into the fray.

With the party's tank and the Skeleton fighting back to back, the rest of us fought the crowd from the outside. Bonzer wouldn't last long, but we hoped to have a few of them finished before they tried Jaken all at once. The eight enemies who had taken the brunt of the damage were at seventy percent, so we tried to whittle them down first.

I brought my great axe out and started to hack at the Lizardmen in front of me. The damage dealers split up the group of enemies kind of like a pie. Yoh and I took the ones on Bonzer, and James and Balmur went for the ones attacking Jaken. Each of us had a section that we stuck to, and Kayda was raining lighting from above and clawing at their heads. The three directly in front of me were at sixty percent each when we got the call to clear the immediate area.

"Get to the trees!" ordered Bokaj. "Jaken, get as low as you can and put your shield toward the sound of my voice!"

Our Paladin roared, and red aura surrounded him, forcing the enemies there to focus on him again, then did as he was told.

The arrows rained down on the area for forty feet around the tank in a circle. It was quite literally raining arrows, and it didn't stop for three seconds. I barely got away, taking an arrow through my left foot that disappeared as soon as I pulled it out and cast Regrowth on myself.

I couldn't see Jaken to cast a heal on him, but his health was barely going back up now. The Lizardmen looked rough, but the scaly pincushions they had been reduced to were still there standing. One of the Lizardmen on Balmur's side was dead, and then another on Yohsuke's side fell. We went back to work, and Bokaj rained death from above. Within a couple more minutes, the last of our invaders had fallen. Bokaj, Jaken, James, and I leveled once more. Tmont had been asleep in a tree and hadn't even bothered to wake up, lazy thing.

We decided to move on for the night. No point in staying here. I had gotten roughly six hours of sleep anyway, so that was a blessing. Balmur grumbled a little, but killing things and leveling up had helped calm him a bit. We looted the bodies and got some coin out of it and even one necklace that wasn't anything special but just looked cool, so Bokaj held onto that.

We decided to set our new staging area up a little further north and east than we were currently, back toward the direction we had come from originally. While we waited for our personal chef to cook breakfast, all of us decided to practice our jobs. I took out some of the weapons I had collected from the Goblins and began enchanting them.

My results were pretty good actually; of the almost two dozen I had, all but two held an enchantment. The other two? Well, let's say that those smoldering holes in the ground had always been there, shall we?

The enchantments I had gotten were pretty interesting. Lightning Damage was the one I was the most excited about. It was only +1, but still, it was a step in the right direction. The others I wasn't sure about. On top of the four lightning Damage knives, I got Blur which made weapons fly faster–ten of those and four of Stun. Last but not least, four Magnetized, which attracted the weapon to armor a little better, like little homing missiles. I imagine that it wouldn't do too well at plus one, but still, pretty cool. All of these would probably go really well for our Rogue, so I asked Balmur what he thought.

"Hmm..." He held the weapons for a moment each. "The Damage would be almost negligible. However, with the status effects, it could be worthwhile, especially if you were to level those skills up. Have you tried more than one enchantment on one piece?"

"Yeah, the metal these knives were made from isn't very conducive to magic. They take a spell or enchantment, sure, but they resist it. If I had better materials, better metal, and some gems, I might be able to do more. I need to level my skill up, though, so I'm not too worried about materials just yet."

"Sweet, man. You mind if I play with these? Maybe they could help in our coming battles?"

"Brother, nothing would make me more proud." I patted his shoulder.

"Hey, man, you wanna try on some of these?" Bokaj had wandered over and held out a fist full of arrows. The heads were tipped with iron, a little more conducive to my magic than the odd knives—bronze?—I had been working with.

"Sure." I shrugged and sat with them. This was the first time I think that the Ranger had gotten to see me work, so I let him watch me.

I focused on the arrow itself and brought my lightning infused mana into it, thinking of the speed of lightning flashing in a storm. The arrow disintegrated. All that was left was the head, so I picked up another. This time, I focused completely on the tip of the projectile. I held the same thought in my mind's eye and let my mana flow and arc into the iron in front of me.

Arcing Iron Arrow

+1 Lightning Damage, +1 Arc

An arrow imbued with the power of lightning. When loosed upon the enemy, this arrow will release an arc of electricity to the closest metallic object.

"Okay. That's pretty fucking cool." I showed him my work and let him hold the arrow.

"Dude, that's fucking sweet."

"Wanna see what it does?"

"What will we shoot it at?"

I stood and walked across the camp to stand well away from the rest of the party and took out my great dagger.

"Shit dude, we don't know what the hell this thing does. Wouldn't it be better to..." he never even finished the sentence. He nocked, drew, and loosed in one fluid motion. It was fast enough that I hadn't caught it with my response for him to just woman up and do it.

"Fuuuuuuuuuuuu–" I seized as the arrow-turned-lightning bolt struck me in the chest, and I plopped to the ground.

Once I could move again, I sat up and got to witness the show that was my familiar chasing Bokaj around, her electrified feathers giving off static. I tugged on our bond and told her to relax.

She screeched and flew at me, landing on my shoulder. She actually had to straddle my head with a clawed foot on each shoulder to fit now. She settled her feathers before glaring at Bokaj still smiling across the clearing.

"So what happened?" I asked. I wasn't mad. My health had taken a hit, about ten percent. The mana cost had been much steeper for that arrow as well at fifty MP.

"It zapped the hell out of you, added five percent more damage than my average shot, and when it hit you, electricity hit your weapon, adding a little more damage. Can you make more? Once it's released, it eats the arrow."

I nodded and sat back down. I made six more for him over the next few minutes, draining my mana completely. Then spent roughly two minutes resting to recover my mana. I repeated this process until breakfast—I went through a lot of arrows—some burst into flame, others the metal warped—but I managed to make about thirty of them. By the time I had finished, my enchanting had leaped to level 11—four higher than I had been.

We ate our meal in relative silence; the mushrooms had been sautéed with some nice, salted fish that we had in our chef's inventory. I wasn't one for fish or mushrooms back home, but here? We ate what we had, and Yoh was a damned fine cook, so I stuffed my food hole. It was better than the chow when I was in the field. Not to mention—we didn't want the food to go to waste.

We entered into the bog again, and Bokaj whipped out his next surprise, Watery Path. None of us had to wade through the boggy grossness so we made great time, treating the mud and water as if it were grass.

We didn't run into any more patrols as we traveled north once more. We did run into a few Bog Crocodiles, but they were only level 10 and left us alone, so we returned the favor. Although, Yoh did say something about boots at one point.

By the time we needed to set up camp for the night, we had returned to the tree the first Dryad had come out at. We spoke to him briefly and filled him in on our exploits. He took heart in knowing that a nest of Goblins had been wiped from this plane, especially if they had been attempting contact with Demons. The Dryad was also excited to hear that we were decimating the Lizardman ranks. We accepted his offer of protection so that we could sleep in peace once more.

The following morning we awoke to something rather odd.

Bokaj was gone.

Like, straight up gone. There were signs of a struggle outside the camp's circle, well away from our camp. He had probably come out to do some business, and a group of Lizardmen had captured him and taken him hostage. Tmont was beside herself, hissing and spitting at anything that moved. She chomped on my tail, and when I went to swat at her, she hissed and growled at me before sitting down.

She must have something to say, I reasoned and cast Nature's Voice.

"What's up, T?"

"I have Master's scent. You all will follow me, or I will do more than simply bite your tail."

"Let us all eat first, and then we will move out."

"We go now!" she spat at me and turned to leave.

"We go after we eat and gather our strength. If he's in trouble, we are better off doing so without hunger gnawing at us. You too."

The Dryad provided us with berries and some mushrooms to speed our departure. We left shortly after, following the cat's nose northwest.

Going was slower without Bokaj's spell, but we managed. It was dusk, and after a few patrols had been slaughtered mercilessly, by the time we found what we were looking for—the Lizardman village. The area was disgusting. There were bones of animals killed hanging from lines surrounding the place. The homes and buildings were a mix of tents, thatched overhangs, and mud-covered huts. Fire pits dotted the outskirts of the village, while a large bonfire marked the center. There, the largest hut was situated, and it seemed to have a large congregation of Lizardmen milling about making noises and celebrating something.

"Gah, if only we could understand what they're saying," Yoh said.

"They're celebrating finding a mate for their chieftain," came Balmur's soft voice.

"How the hell do you know that?!" I whispered quietly.

"Spell. Shhh."

He dropped into stealth and crept forward, followed by Tmont who looked like she was fading into stealth as well.

The rest of us waited patiently. Half an hour later, Balmur came back alone.

"We found him. T wouldn't leave him. He had her stealth and hide. I don't think he's in as much danger as we thought."

"What? Fucker was kidnapped. How is he not in trouble?" James said incredulously.

"Come on, better to let him explain," Balmur said as he gestured for us to follow him.

Balmur led us through an offshoot path through some open buildings until we were back behind the Chieftain's tent. There was an opening there that we filed through, and I had to admit, it looked great—furs on the floor, which was wooden, and there were colored sashes and what look like tapestries hung up. A makeshift bed of furs was piled in the corner to the back off to our right. There in a pile of furs, wearing a loincloth and a crown of crocodile teeth, was Bokaj, our mighty Ranger.

"Hey, guys!" He stood, and all of us made a pointed effort to avert our eyes to anywhere but him.

"What happened, dude?"

"Well, I went to use the little Elf's room, and I got snatched up by these guys. They brought me back here to sacrifice me or something, but the chieftain took me as her own right after she saw me."

"Her own?" I asked.

"Yeah!" He laughed and took a sip of a mug off to his right on a table. "She speaks decent common, and she's treated me nicely."

"I had hoped King would like," came a deep, feminine voice from the front of the tent. "Who be, our guestsss?"

There in the doorway, silhouetted against the fire, was what could only be the chieftain. She stood taller than the male Lizardmen and had feminine features and finer scales, almost like our Dragon Elf companion. She wore a loincloth as well and several layers of beads and bits of precious stones about her neck that lowered and covered her... assets. Her facial features were attractive, odd, but attractive and distinctly humanoid. Thick pouty lips, a small nose, and high cheekbones. Her eyes were unsettling; they were a pale green that seemed to glow eerily with a reptilian slit in the center.

"These are my friends." Bokaj waved to us as he walked closer to her. "They're cool."

"Cool? What isss thisss?" She frowned in confusion, and her dainty teeth flashed in the light. All of them were razor sharp and probably the reason she protracted her 's' sounds so much. "It means that they are okay. They're friends."

"Ah." She smiled, and it was both endearing and creepy at the same time. "Welcome then, friendsss of King. What you do here?"

"Uhm," I muttered, uncertain as to what to say. Do we tell her we were sent here to cull her people's' numbers?

"We were sent here to try and make your people see that going into the forest is dangerous," replied Yohsuke before anyone else could say anything.

"It jussst wood," the chieftain said as she pet Bokaj's arm absently, like he was some kind of pet. "How it dangerousss? My people ssstrong. Take what they want and need."

"It hurts the forest," Yoh pressed. "The Dryads are dying because their trees are being cut down and the bog spreads. The Dryads asked us to come stop you. We have been, and we will complete our quest."

He shifted his stance, obviously ready to fight, and this is one of those times where I thought to myself, *If this fucker gets us killed, I'm gonna kill him.* I love Yohsuke; he is my brother. I would fight through Hell with a toothbrush beside him if he asked, but goddamn, can he be stubborn. I chuckled.

"You fight all outssside, tiny Elf?" She laughed, and it sounded like a hiss and a hiccup. "You die. Sssorry, King, but they all die."

"What if we competed against your best warriors?" I asked as last ditch chance to get out of this alive.

"You cannot hope to win, and you kill my people," she said, dismissing it outright. "You all die."

"Let them try," said Bokaj putting his hand on her hip. He leaned forward and whispered something in her ear that I'm pretty sure no one else wanted to hear and that I would not pass on.

The chieftain's eyes widened, and she smiled fully. She clapped her hands and stepped outside, motioning for us to follow. In full view of her people, she began to speak; Balmur translated for us.

"These are the monsters stalking our lands." She pointed to us. It was weird hearing her hiss and spit to her people and having our friend tell us what she was saying. "They wish to compete with our best in order to leave here unmolested. Our warriors will split them, and we shall dine on their flesh tomorrow evening!"

She appointed five competitions. One each of strength, accuracy, magic, speed, and battle—all of which would take place the following morning.

The chieftain had us all taken to a building close to her own and put guards there to watch us. She even attempted to make us comfortable by having furs and food brought to us. Yohsuke looked the food over, deemed it something we could eat, and took the first bite. He closed his eyes and listed off ingredients that had been used to make it. I was impressed. We all took turns sleeping that night; the others kept a watch, as no one completely trusted the Lizardmen around us.

Bokaj went with the chieftain, no doubt paying for our chance at freedom.

* * *

We began at dawn. Bokaj, limping but happy, led us to the competition grounds.

The grounds themselves were actually very stable and dry. There were little weeded roots, and the setups were good too, probably so we couldn't bitch about it being rigged. The islet itself was more than one hundred feet square and looked to be a training ground.

The first competition was for accuracy, and Balmur was the one who volunteered for that. The object of the match was to see who could get the most of ten weapons into a target at sixty feet. The Lizardman competing against Balmur was a lanky thing who wore a leather belt with knives on it. He looked competent, and I should have been worried to be honest; we had no clue what we were getting into here, but we had to hope we had some luck going on out there.

Two targets were set up at exactly sixty feet on posts with red and white circles painted on. The bullseye itself just a straight black circle. A small Lizardchild walked over to stand between the contestants and raised her palm, then dropped it, signaling for the start of the contest.

Arms blurred and knives sailed. Balmur's arms swung in concert, each one tossing a blade end over end into his target. After each had thrown their weapons, Yohsuke stepped forward with the chieftain and looked over the targets. Balmur's opponent had eight in the red circle around the bullseye and two in it. Balmur had six in the bullseye and four on the lines. Balmur collected his blades while we celebrated.

The Lizardman who had been his opponent bared his teeth and stepped forward, raising a clawed hand. I readied my great dagger, and Yoh pulled out his Astral Adapter. The creature hissed something at Balmur, who nodded and held his hand out. The two shook and walked away from each other.

"What did he say?" I asked.

"That he hopes eating me will raise his accuracy."

The next competition was the strength competition. Of course, Jaken stepped into the arena. The standard was a log toss; whoever threw the thing the farthest would win. The log weighed two hundred twenty pounds, was thick, and about five feet long.

A body-builder-looking Lizardman, seven feet tall and easily more than three hundred pounds, stepped forward. His large muscles bulged as he picked his log up and tossed it nine feet. Jaken stepped up to his—his armor would have gotten in the way so it had been taken off—and squatted down. He gripped the base of the log, took a deep breath, and heaved with all his might. Veins bulged in his arms, and I could hear the wood of the log splinter a bit in his grip as it lifted and sailed into the air— only to land nine feet away. The Lizardman was beside himself, and he challenged Jaken to personal combat, to which the chieftain said no outright. The battle would come later. Then we would die.

Right.

The competition couldn't be a draw, according to the chieftain. So we had to come up with another way to settle it. Another log toss? Nah, fuck that. They got to choose that shit.

"Hey, Jaken, you remember how to play mercy?" I asked slyly.

He grinned, and then we began the process of explaining it to the chieftain. Well, Bokaj did. He was the sweet talker in the group with his higher charisma score.

"The rules are very simple," he assured her. "All the competitors do is interlock fingers like Zekiel and James are doing."

We demonstrated slowly, our palms pressed together and our fingers interlocked with both hands.

"Someone says go, and then you try to push or squeeze the other person's hands into a painful position that will make them give up. The person who says mercy or stop or something to that effect wins."

James clenched his fingers together and pushed forward with his hands quickly.

I feigned pain and said, "Mercy!" to signal that he had won.

The Lizard Chief considered this, and she addressed her chosen competitor to see what he thought. He seemed to understand the premise, but he did have her ask some questions.

"You can bite, kick, knee?" she asked on his behalf. We shook our heads and pointed to our hands.

"It's just the hands. You can do almost anything you like with the hands, but no other body part is involved," Jaken explained. "Also, you can't let go. If you let go, it means you lost."

The tall Lizardman considered this and nodded his consent.

Jaken and his opponent squared up to each other, and Jaken held his hands out with his fingers to the sky. The Lizardman pushed his large fingers through the other creature's and clasped them loosely. He looked uncomfortable with the contact but otherwise just glared at Jaken.

The chieftain looked at her warrior, then Jaken, and announced loudly, "Begin!"

Jaken and the Lizardman's fingers tightened, and bones popped. Both men grunted in pain, but neither looked to want to stop. The Lizardman pushed his hands forward, and Jaken let his wrists give way slightly. The Lizardman gritted his teeth and attempted to press his perceived advantage, but Jaken just smiled.

Jaken twisted his hands out, tucked his elbows tight to his body, then pushed his hands forward with his knuckles facing the ground. The Lizardman grunted harder and tried to save himself from the move, but Jaken began to physically lift his opponent off his feet. I looked and saw that blood was dripping from his hand—the Lizardman's claws had dug into his skin.

Sweat began to bead on Jaken's brow as he clenched his fists.

"Thisss isss good?" the chieftain asked Bokaj pointing to what was happening.

"He's only using his hands and strength," he answered honestly. "According to the rules that you agreed to, it's fine."

She didn't look pleased but remained silent. Jaken groaned, more blood dripping from his hands. His opponent began to smile and then whipped his arms out to the side to mirror what Jaken had done. He lifted our friend off his feet into the air and began to kind of juggle him in his grip. He was shimmying Jaken. Jaken's grip loosened, and he eventually let go because he couldn't hang on anymore.

The Lizardman raised his bloody claws into the air and bellowed to his clansmen. He lifted his fingers to his maw and dragged his tongue across the blood-stained claws while looking at Jaken.

"It's cool, man," I said with a pat on his back. He glowed golden for a second, and I watched the skin on the back of his hands begin to mend and knit back together.

Next came the magic portion to the competition. Contestants would each attack a level 10 Bog Crocodile of their own that had been tied and hung from poles. Whoever finished their target first won. The angry creatures struggled futilely by snapping jaws, hissing, and spitting vehemently. The Village Shaman level 16 came forward; his scaled skin hung in wrinkles, but his yellowed eyes were sharp and bright. He scuttled slowly to his indicated spot next to Yohsuke.

Once the signal was given, Yoh cast his first spell, an Astral Bolt. The black bolt sailed straight into the Crocodile's eye, gouging it out in a burst of visceral gore. Then he threw a Star Burst that, by some miraculous chance, landed in the now furiously struggling creature's injured eye. The spell released and spattered grey matter all over the surroundings. The shaman hadn't even finished his first spell and, due to his distraction by the burst of pure mana his opponent cast, dropped in agony from spell recoil.

Jaken cast a healing spell on him with a wave of his hand, and the anguished look spawning on his face stopped. The Lizardman fell into a restful state. A healer from the Lizardmen came to inspect him, then nodded to the chieftain.

The speed contest was a no brainer. Our Monk pulled out all the stops, testing his speed against the same Lizardman who had thrown against Balmur. The course was short—three laps around the little island we were on. It wasn't that much of a run—more of a sprint, really—and we all thought James had this easily. Turns out the scaled bastard was a lot faster on his feet than he was throwing knives because he actually won the race, even though it was really by a nose. Seriously. The bastard ran, and when it looked like he was going to lose, he stuck his damn neck out to gain the last few inches.

We patted James on the back, trying to let him know it was okay. He just shrugged it off and stared at his former opponent angrily.

Finally, it was time for the battle portion. The circle in the center of the isle took up a good amount of space, no one eager to be too close to the contestants. I entered the ring as the last person in our party who could compete, and a new Lizardman entered opposite me, his level at 16. He wasn't as big as Jaken's opponent nor slight of build like the one who had gone against Balmur and James. He was well muscled and looked strong. Competent. He entered the ring unarmed and squared himself up to me. The chieftain explained the rules.

"Thisss fight will be to the death," she explained to all gathered around us. "You use what weapon you have at your disposssal, no magic, and no familiarsss."

The Lizardman looked at the weapon I had at my belt— my great dagger—and smirked. He hissed at the crowd, who did their hissing laugh, and someone tossed a spear into the ring for him to use. He picked it up and showed it to me, to which I shrugged and equipped my great axe. His eyes went a little wide, and he bared his sharp fangs at me. I smiled back and motioned to Balmur and the chieftain. While Balmur stepped over to me, I planted my axe in the ground by its head and stepped up to the Lizardman with purpose. The chieftain joined us.

"Will you translate for me, my lady?" I asked, and she nodded, clearly puzzled. "Balmur, you just be sure the message gets across." He nodded, and I looked back to my opponent.

"Where I come from, to some of the greatest warriors, it is the ultimate honor to die in battle. The gods will smile upon us this day, and the victor, tell tales of the fallen one's glories. May you fight well and know that I harbor you no ill will. May your death take you to your promised land or me to mine."

I waited for the chieftain to finish relaying what I had said, and Balmur confirmed she had gotten the gist of it across. I held my hand out to shake his hand and waited. The Lizardman looked at me quizzically, then nodded once before grasping my forearm firmly. He spoke, and Balmur translated.

"I will honor you with a good death and send you to your gods so that I may feed my people. It is my hope that your spirit will carry with it great power and nourish our bodies and spirits well. Fight with honor, die in glory."

My grip tightened at his words, and I smiled again before letting his forearm go. I stepped back to my weapon and patted my friend's shoulder. I had neglected for a while to put points into my weapon skills, so I had done it the night before, tinkering and applying my points where I thought best. I had some new abilities to use, and I was excited to get started. I had upped my proficiency with great axes to the second level and it gave a three percent increase to damage, and I'd also gotten two more skills with the two points I had left.

Charge – Allows the user to close the distance to an opponent of up to thirty feet away. Cool down: 30 seconds

Feather Axe – Lowers the weight of the weapon used by two thirds. (Current weapon weight 30lbs; will now be 10lbs) Duration: 10 minutes. Restriction: Weapon must be a great axe. Cool Down: 15 minutes.

The chieftain looked to her fighter, who nodded, then to me. I grinned savagely as I plucked my great axe from the ground. I nodded to show I was ready, and then she dropped her hand to signal a start.

I activated Feather Axe, then Charge, and the fight began in earnest. I swung my axe a lot faster than even I was expecting, and it left me off balance. Instead of the metal head hitting my target, the haft near it did. The Lizardman used that small strike and the opening it left to maneuver quickly and took a stab at my exposed right flank. I used the momentum of my swing to dive into a forward shoulder roll and got out of the way. He just barely missed me, and I felt the wind near my tail. Popping up onto my feet, I sprang as high forward as I could and activated Devil's Hammer. The attack connected but didn't take, and he used the opportunity to slash with his spear. My health dropped ten percent, and I growled in anger. I took a step back and took a breath. I swung my great axe a few times to get used to the weight and then refocused on my opponent.

    He was craftier than the average enemy and good with his spear. He was quick, too, able to dodge my attacks easily enough. An idea began to form in my mind, and I decided to go with it. I choked up on the haft with my right hand and lowered my left like I would for a more controlled, wider swing and strode forward with purpose.

    A few feet out, he jabbed at my chest with the spear, but I knocked it out of the way and began to swing in an exaggerated diagonal chopping motion. He did what I thought he would and dodged to my right. Instead of committing to the attack with the axe, I spun and bashed my left fist into the side of his head, then stabbed the spike of the axe into his thigh. His health dropped fifteen percent, and he was forced to take a knee. Next, I put a new spin on an old trick and activated Cleave before leaping into the air a good six feet. I used Wind Scythe, and the axe nailed the Lizardman on the back of his neck and whistled through, decapitating him. The axe continued its downward travel and sliced through his bent leg and thunked dirt, blood seeping from the wounds. The body thudded against the haft of my axe and slid to the side on to the ground.

I landed next to my axe and pried it from the ground. The force of the throw must have been increased due to how light the weapon had been. That would mean a new combo if I played this right. I would definitely be playing with a few ideas that popped into mind at that second.

The crowd around me began to hiss and snarl—a few even wept—but I ignored them. I put my axe into my inventory and bent down to gently lay my opponent's head on his chest, then lifted his lifeless body into my arms. I walked slowly up to the chieftain who had a look of controlled anger on her reptilian face.

"Where may I take his body, so that it can be prepared for whatever your last rites are?" I asked softly.

"We eat dead, if we can, to pressserve ssspirit and ssstrength of fallen."

"Then where should I take him?"

"To big fire." She led the way to the bonfire we had seen in their village's center.

Once we arrived, two Lizardmen took the body away reverently. Once they had gone, the chieftain stepped forward and cast a spell to light the fire. It burst to life, and she said something to her villagers. Promptly, a dozen armed guards stepped forward and grabbed Jaken and James.

My party wasn't having any of that, so we all brought our weapons out ready to fight. Kayda took to the air, and lightning began to arc from her feathers.

"What the hell do you think you're doing?" Bokaj shouted. He was now standing in front of the chieftain with his bow drawn and trained on the guard with a spear to Jaken's throat.

"We take thossse who did not win and eat flesh," she explained as if it made total sense. "We agreed thisss."

"No, we said that the winners went free," Bokaj retorted.

"And they are. They won, they go." She pointed at my two captured friends. "They no win, they ssstay."

"We won three of the five competitions," Bokaj persisted. "Our group won. Let them go."

"Not what wasss sssaid." She smiled sweetly, her fangs looking deadlier. "They die. They pay for all your sssinsss."

"Look, you saw what we are capable of," I said, trying to be the voice of reason, "and that was limited by the rules you put forth. Do you really want to see what we can do without rules? What kind of magics my friends and I can perform? Not to mention, one of our stronger team members, who didn't even take part."

"King?" She laughed her hissing laugh and pointed at him. "He no fight. He isss mine."

"If you hurt my friends, I'll kill you myself." Bokaj had an arrow nocked and pointed at her instantly. Tmont stood in front of him protectively. "They are that important to me."

"You dare threaten me?" she cried incredulously. "I ssshould have you killed, too!"

"Bring it, bitch," he said softly. The arrow he had drawn began to glow white hot, then burst into flame. "Let them go, now, and all this stops. No more of your people need to die. Leave the forest alone, and we will leave you alone. I give my word."

The chieftain seemed to think about it for a moment, then sighed. She raised her hand to her guards and signaled to let our friends go.

"We can be friends, chieftain," I offered. This was beginning to sound like an awkward break up. "Just leave the forest alone, and we never need to turn our attentions on you for ill again."

"We need wood from foressst. We need meat from foresst. What will we do without?"

"Maybe if you can spark some trade between yourself and the Dryads, they will help give you wood and meat?" offered Balmur.

She agreed to at least try and foster a deal but not until the next day. That night, after the body was appropriately prepared, everyone ate a piece of the Lizardman. I had battled in his memory.

They offered some of the meat to us, as a way to share in their tradition of passing on strength. Bokaj, Jaken, and Balmur looked a little green under the gills at the idea of eating someone else, even though it was cooked well. Yohsuke, James, and I just did what Marines do best—eat weird shit in country. The meat was tender and a little fishy, but otherwise, it was bearable. Balmur interpreted for us when the shaman said that it was a great insult to refuse the sacrifice of the fallen, and knowing it could result in what we had just been able to narrowly avoid, the others choked back the offering.

The morning after, we all gathered and went to the Dryads. There was some tense bargaining, but Bokaj eventually got the two to reach an agreement—the Lizardmen would hunt the animals that harmed the trees for meat and bring fresh manure and other nutritious foliage from the swamps for the trees. In return, the Dryads would give them wood.

That ended with us completing our quest by turning it in. We had killed forty Lizardmen altogether which gave us eight hundred EXP a piece. We even got a reward from a secret quest.

Unite Two Peoples – You've brought two formerly hostile people together, where before they wanted to kill each other. Isn't life weird? Reward: 200 EXP and +2 to Charisma.

That put all of us up a good way toward leveling up. At level 15, we needed a good deal more experience to level. Two thirds of the way there, though, was not bad at all.

We took our leave of the two groups, bidding them farewell and almost having to sneak our Ranger away due to a distraught chieftain.

We went south out of the bog lands, toward the monastery where James had received his training. When asked what they had for us that was so important, he simply replied with, "Information." So on we went into the mountainous region.

We traveled by foot, as the land would be too tricky for a mount to traverse, and got there early the second morning.

The monastery was built into the mountainside. The halls that were visible from a distance looked like catacombs, but the place was well lit and had a large valley floor where there were huts and small buildings throughout. A section of the valley was walled off, which James explained was the Monks' training grounds with enemies coming from an underground source of mana that streamed them out every new dawn. It wasn't a dungeon, per the Monks' telling, but a blessing from their deity, a place they could channel their monastic abilities safely and learn to combat the darkness.

We made it to the bottom of the valley floor and halfway into the village when we began to attract the locals. Monks and villagers under their protection flocked to us. They were curious at first but then began to recognize the Monk in our party and celebrated his return.

Some of the children began to dance amongst us asking to see what we could do. A few of the more fleet-footed teens among them sprinted off toward the monastery. By the time we arrived, it seemed like the whole village was there.

A bald, elderly looking Halfling greeted us at the archway. The Elder Monk wore simple, light robes colored orange without sleeves with a red sash across his left shoulder hanging down to his right hip. His feet had simple, black slippers covering them, and the brightest thing about him was his smile. It was so cheerful. He looked at James through storm-grey eyes, like he would a son. James knelt in front of the three-foot-tall Monk and bowed his head.

"Elder Leo," he said softly. "I brought them home to hear out the Grand Elder, as you asked."

"Yes you did, and you returned stronger," he observed. His voice was even and deep—not what one might expect from someone his size. "Come."

He walked us through the archway and back into the entry off to our right. We washed up after our travels and changed into some new clothes that we had brought along. I had to admit, I was beginning to smell gross. Some of the Monks inside offered to wash them for us, saying it would be an honor to help us, which we allowed although awkwardly.

Once we were all cleaned and ready, Elder Leo took us out into the courtyard again and up the main steps toward a dome-like structure that we hadn't been able to see from the distance. Inside, incense burned, not cloying the air but clearing it. I inhaled and felt cleansed, as if the air were healthier in here. Even though smoke was everywhere, it was better for me.

There were dozens of Monks meditating; the ones closest to the front of the room sat directly on the floor. The dozens behind them on cushions that looked so soft that they could be clouds. Toward the rear, where we walked in, Monks were floating at various heights—some a few inches off the ground, others up to two feet. All different races, all different creeds humming to the same mantra, all together working toward enlightenment—or whatever it was they sought here.

Elder Leo motioned for silence as we walked toward the front of the room by way of a side aisle. Once we got to the front, the small man leading the mantra opened his eyes but didn't stop intoning his words. He smiled at us, and his bright blue eyes sparkled at us. He motioned for Leo to take his place. Leo bowed and began to intone the same words of the mantra and traded places with the younger man. Now that he stood, I could see him better.

He wore the same colored robes as Leo with a purple sash rather than the red one. His arms looked well-muscled and toned. He motioned for us to follow him and cheerfully stepped off to a room on our right. We followed the bald Monk into the room, and he closed the door. He motioned to a tea pot and some cups on the table and sat down expectantly.

James filled him in on what we did before coming, and the young Monk listened intently. He sipped his tea quietly and pondered what he was hearing. Once James finished, he motioned to us and waited expectantly. Yohsuke was the one who offered to tell the tale of our progression in this world.

He listened well, gasped a little when he heard about our time fighting the Bone Dragon and the Lizardman village in James's portion of the tale. It was almost unsettling.

He took it all in and, for a few minutes, just sat and sipped his tea in contemplation.

"Sounds like all of you have endured a great deal." His voice was light and youthful. "I'm glad that you made it safely to our monastery."

He stood and bowed to each of us in turn. None of us knelt the way James had, but a couple of us stood and returned the greeting while others nodded.

"I am Grand Elder Hiteno, leader of the Monastery of the Rising Sun. I was told of your coming and asked to fill in some of the gaps in your education about this world. Will you require rest before we get started? It's rather late now."

We looked to the sky and saw that was an accurate statement. The sun had passed over the valley and was now setting in the western sky. We looked to each other, and it didn't look like anyone was tired now, so we opted to stay.

"Then here is what I know. Our gods learned of the threat to our world, and by extension, our neighbors, your world, more than a millennium past. Once they learned of our fate, they sought aid. Ours is a land rife and rich with magic and wonder. Your world? Not so much, but—you had the imagination to create glimpses into worlds that work similar to ours." He smiled and clapped. A younger Monk came, and he asked him to bring food before returning to us.

"The gods took the magic they had here and molded it to mirror what they had seen of your attempts at what we had. The result is what we have today—Brindolla, our land. For centuries, I have been blessed with glimpses of what the gods saw in your world, and it is fascinating. Weapons that bark fire and metal, beasts that carry you to and fro made of metal. Simply amazing. Mind boggling and terrifying. With our magics and might, here, we might forestall War and his minions, but your world would fall as so many others like it—all technologically advanced but no magic to bring forth and stop him."

The Gnome looked sad for a moment, then refocused on his words and went on. I was still trying to wrap my head around the fact that he had said he'd been watching my world for *centuries*, but he continued; I had to shake my head to follow along.

Page | 257

"Bringing you here, people from different walks of life but who have all worked together to accomplish great things in your 'games' is our only hope, and unfortunately, your world's as well. Now, time here moves differently than your world. Dozens of years could pass here, and in your world, merely an hour would go by. Maybe less time, maybe a bit more, but that is what we have gathered. When we asked you here, our worlds were closest to the veil that separates them, so it was easiest to get you here. Being truthful, we aren't sure what will happen if you were to die here. Our Gods have the might to bring you back, but with them so distracted with keeping War out, it could be a while—if at all. You may wake up in your own bed at home, thinking this a strange dream, or you may get to meet your own gods."

I wasn't sure if anyone noticed, but I could feel my stomach sinking and the blood draining from my face.

Wow.

We could die for real here. The thought crossed my mind... but fuck. My son could be fatherless. Jaken's daughter, too. Yohsuke's wife a widow. Bokaj and his family, James and his fiancé, and Balmur and his true love.
For fucks sake, man.

This was a bit too real at the moment. I looked at my friends—men I had fought and triumphed with. Risked life and limb—unknowingly—for.

Could we do this? Did we have the right to even try?

"It was unfair of the gods to do so without giving you the whole picture before you agreed. That is why they dote on you so. We here who know of you, have sworn to help you how we can. As you are now, we don't know that you could take the next minion of War's. The one you seek to find has a hold on that entire region now, not just a piece of the city. It had been half asleep before; only its presence had brought about lunacy and strife, causing some to turn against their fellows quicker. Now that it is awake, the whole area belongs to it, though for now, we have it contained to the city. It doesn't want to bring the power of the gods against it.

You will need to be stronger and better equipped to handle this threat. We have many here who will seek to aid you. Then we will send you to others still. We will help to strengthen your bodies and minds while you are here. Then we will send you to the Dwarves to arm yourselves, though we have not the influence there to truly be of more aid."

We all nodded and were about to leave when suddenly, "Hold up."

Jaken stood and peered down at the little Monk. With the height difference, most normal people might be intimidated, but not this Gnome. He just smile serenely.

"Yes?"

"You mean to tell me that we can die here? I might never see my daughter again?"

"Unfortunately, it is all too possible of a reality."

"But we have a chance to beat this guy? Make him move on? What?"

"It is my hope, and I merely echo the Gods in their wisdom, that if we defeat the minions and Generals of War who are here, he will be unable to break through the combined powers of the Gods, that he will be held at a standstill and will be stopped."

"What's to stop him from just moving on and coming back?"

"Pride," the Gnome admitted. "Lady Radiance and her siblings watched as he took world after world after world. Never once did he let one not fall before moving. Never once did he pass over. He seeks to claim all life. Everywhere. His pride is what will stop him."

"So we have to ice this fool here and now, so that you guys don't fall first."

"If it is possible, yes. But he is a cosmic entity, and I don't know that anyone but the gods could do so."

From the time we had first gotten here to now, we had been going almost balls to the wall the entire time. The little downtime we had was spent either traveling, eating, focusing on improving ourselves, or sleeping. This was the first chance we had truly had to let this actually sink in. I looked around the table, and the faces I saw were bleak, slightly pale, and contemplative.

"Fuck that," Yohsuke said softly. We all looked over and a look of steely resolve passed over his face. "Fuck that. We will take him out, or I will myself."

"I'm not going to make you guys come," he said looking at all of us in turn. "Jake, Evan, hell even Jaken—I don't know you guys as well as I wish I had on Earth. You guys are fucking awesome, but I'm not going to sit here and let this asshole threaten the people I care about. Aaron, Chris—you guys are my brothers, and as awesome as I am, I can't do it all by myself. You guys in?"

"You know I am," James said with a smile.

"Ask me again, and I'll beat your ass," I said. I still had doubts, and I'd be lying if I said I wasn't afraid. But I wasn't about to take this lying down. I'd dealt with a lot of shit in my life—a lot of pain, confusion, and bullshit. Who better to fight beside than my brothers, especially when my boy and my loved ones were on the line.

But still, even with them fighting beside me, was I up to this? Could I hack this? Sure, I had joined the military—I'd even been ready to take a life if I had to in order to defend my loved ones, but this, so far from home? So far, things had been easy enough. Terrifying and brutal at times, yeah, but still, we were able to come out on top. But now? Now we were facing stronger enemies. More cunning and they weren't going to hold back because we were outsiders. It was all a little much to take in. Luckily, I had a little reprieve from the darkness in my head.

"Hell yeah, homies." Jaken grinned and slapped us all on the back. "That's what I'm sayin'."

"I'm in," Balmur said simply. There was a lot going on in that man's mind, but he kept himself well.

Bokaj looked at all of us, grinned, then patted Tmont. "Hell yeah, I'm in, broskies."

"I'm glad to hear that you are all fighters." The Gnome smiled.

"Are you really that old?" Jaken asked, and all of us couldn't help but laugh.

Chapter Seventeen

"AGAIN!" barked my trainer. I swung my now weighted great axe for what seemed like the thousandth time that morning in a series of chops, hacking motions, and double handed twists.

It had been three days of doing this training. The muscles in my arms, shoulders, back, core, and legs screamed in agony. By the end of this round, my strength rose another point. That was four points total. Then after this, we went on a run, one mile with one hundred pounds attached to my body.

See, the Monks had these ingenious little weights that wrapped around a limb, kind of like the ones I'd had made for Kayda. These weighed thirty pounds on each of my legs. A twenty pound vest was strapped over my chest, and ten pound weights went around each wrist. My dexterity had gone up four points as well. This was the final day of this portion of the training, and I was honestly looking forward to it. Jaken was right there with me. His load distribution was similar, but his weights were heavier at two hundred pounds. His strength had gone up by three, but the Monks had been drilling him to increase his dexterity, so that went up six points.

Balmur had been undergoing similar training but more specialized. He was throwing weighted knives as fast and accurately as possible for hours at a time. Then when he was out of knives, he had to endure walking over hot coals, hotter than even his resistance to fire would halve while being bombarded with blunt arrows. The poor Dwarf went to sleep with healing salves on his bruises, nightly. His dexterity raised by three points, his constitution by three, and his strength by two.

Kayda had grown quite a bit with her training. Her weights had been increased; they now weighed eight pounds apiece rather than five. Her strength had gone up on the flight here by one point. Then during the three days of hellish training, her strength and dexterity had gone up by another four in each. They fired the same blunt-tipped arrows at her as they did Balmur, the poor dear. She weaved in and out, carrying items with her claws, then eventually a bucket filled with a little sand. She was growing stronger and larger by the day. She was now bigger than any bird I had ever seen in my own world. They were feeding us a lot to keep us in top form but her most of all. Must be bird people.

After the end of the third day training our physical traits, we switched to train our mental ones. Jaken was taken somewhere to learn meditation and to help him gain some wisdom, and I was taken to train my magic and see if I couldn't raise my intelligence stat.

The training actually wasn't what I thought it might be. As soon as I came into the room, I was told to sit and crack a book. I read theorems on different types of magic by people whose names were completely foreign to me. Much like the gift of the common tongue that the party had been blessed with, we also had the ability to read and write in the languages we could speak.

The book I was currently reading, *Flitwing's Feast for the Magically Curious Mind* by Syllius Flitwing, spoke about the histories of magic and how the Gods eventually gave the people the ability to copy their divine feats, thinking about how the people might be better suited to their environment if they had the powers to fight back the monstrous hordes that had populated the planet at the time. You know, because creating just one thing that might be seen as inferior didn't sit well with some of them. Beasts like Dragons, Leviathans in the seas, the great birds in the skies, Goblins, Kobolds, warrior races such as the Orcs, the trickster races such as the Sylphs, and the other Fae creatures wandering the realms.

As I learned more about the history, I realized that this didn't seem much like the games I was used to playing but one that I had always admired watching others play and wanted to play myself, one of the first tabletop role playing games to ever grace our world. Which led me to wonder when the ability to cast spells had changed from a certain number of spells per day to the use of mana and why?

I mean, I wouldn't complain. I was slinging spells, shapeshifting into animals, and swinging a big ol' axe like a beast. I was not going to look the gift horse in the mouth, but my curious mind almost always gets me into trouble.

The more I poured over the tome, the more I realized that they didn't actually know when the change had occurred. Hell, it may never have needed to if the well of mana inside the individual had always been there; it may have been easier to define their spell casting ability that way. The pages did tell me that the stats given to each person are different and that they grow. Also each spell caster can claim different types of spells, and certain spells can be learned regardless of class. So, as a Druid, I could learn a spell cast by Warlocks and Wizards, so long as I could understand the concepts and had the ability.

"Take, if you will, the simple Dimensional Sleeve spell," the book stated. "Commonly used by those with a knack for magic and sleight of hand. The caster takes an object into his hand and, with a flourish, pockets it into a small dimension in his sleeve. This spell allows for objects of up to five pounds to be stored there until needed, at which point the caster need only think of the item and pull it from his sleeve. Trivial, but wonderful for children and drunkards."

There was an example of how to create such a dimension in a sleeve, taking mana into your hand, then holding it in the sleeve and filling it, seeing a small tear in the space between sleeve and wrist, and putting the object in it, like a bag or a small sack on the wrist. I tried it several times; nothing happened. I wondered if Balmur might be able to teach me the spell himself, if he knew it. I'd ask later.

After that, it was all just theory on how magic continues to evolve and change. Purely conjecture and opinion. No other real spells or practical application.

Next, I flipped through a book on elemental magics. Food had been brought in sometime during my reading, and much like my previous life, I had ignored my body while I read. I ate while I studied, and the book on the elements had to be my favorite by far. There was no title and was very small, but it was so descriptive. It described how pure mana was turned into aspected mana for spells. The passage at the end of the book was fascinating. It read:

"The mind naturally accesses information on elemental processes without the need for conscious thought. As a magus grows older and experiences the world, he is exposed to nature and the elements in their natural state. All magus will their mana to change into the appropriate form when casting a spell. Reaching for the heat necessary to lob a fireball. The soothing cool of water, the chill of ice, and the void of dark, all are elements known to us, but further understanding is necessary to truly evolve as a magus."

The Monk who had been taking care of me for the most part of the day was sitting off to the side, meditating quietly. When I turned to him, he smiled and looked at me quizzically. His older human features had softened in age, and he was slightly stooped forward. He wore the same brown robe as the other non-elder Monks, plain and unadorned with a sash.

"Is there anything more?" I asked.

"No," he said simply. He stood and took the books away. "Stay. Think over what you learned. Think of what you don't yet know."

He shuffled out the door quietly and left me sitting there in the room. What I don't yet know? Well, I didn't really *know* anything. Sure I had learned a little more than I had before but nothing to rave about. Nothing to make me think I knew anything more than your moderately trained wizard or sorcerer. If anything, I knew less.

CONGRATULATIONS!

You have gained an important piece of wisdom this day, that you know nothing, but fret not, that is where some of the greatest in their fields begin. It's a step in the right direction! +2 to Wisdom, +1 to Intelligence.

I was looking over the new additions to my stats when I heard the door open. Elder Leo came in, the same serene smile on his face. I took a knee out of respect, and he chuckled. Putting a hand on my shoulder, he ushered me out the door and down the hall to a quiet courtyard.

The courtyard was small, only forty feet square, less than an eighth of what we had been using to practice our martial skills. There were some small trees, flowers, and shrubs outlining it. A small waterfall dominated a corner of it off to my right. Elder Leo stood in the center of the courtyard and smiled at me again.

"Welcome to my garden," he said. "I bring people here so rarely because no one lets me teach anymore."

"Not that I'm ungrateful, but why are they now?"

"I may have put my foot down a bit too enthusiastically." He chuckled at the thought, and I worried for whoever argued with him.

"Much like your Druidic magics, my own are drawn toward nature and the elements," he said, his voice taking on a kindly instructor's cadence. He indicated that I step back, and I did so.

"For generations after I reached the peak of my abilities in the monastic arts, I wandered and honed my skills while learning all that I could about the world around me. Nature, the Great Mother, smiled upon me and blessed me with visions and dreams of ways to harness the elements that she held in her loving embrace and use them in my own way. I have shown your friend my way, but I seek to impart upon you the knowledge you need to further your understanding of nature and the elements."

He sat where he stood and motioned for me to join him. I sat in front of him, and he smiled as he closed his eyes. I did the same, and we sat there for a moment. He coached me for a few minutes on how to empty my mind of useless thoughts and worries.

Meditation to a Monk isn't simply making themselves devoid of thought and emotion; it's letting go of what doesn't matter. Emotion not tied to the focus is let go. Thoughts and worries outside the focus are let go. Meditation doesn't empty you, it just fills you with the focus you need to find on a specific subject. Some turn this on to themselves, some turn it on an outside problem. This was kind of both for me.

Elder Leo told me to focus on my attachment to nature and to envision an element to start with. My mind began to scream lightning, but I already had a pretty good understanding of that element. This time, I focused on fire and told him what I had chosen.

"Ah, fire," he intoned softly. "Destructive, burning heat. Eats greedily all that it can, but that is not all. Fire provides light, warmth, ways to heat and cook food, and removes impurities from water and metal. Fire takes, and fire gives. Let the element of flames, the avatar of fire, wash over your mind. Envision a flame in your mind's eye and ponder it. How can this element be used? How can you make it your own?"

In my mind, I saw it. First, an ember, glowing and kindling into something greater, a small flame. I thought hard and long about what fire had done in my life. Here and at home. Making my food on a grill, watching my friend use it to burn our enemies. The heat it provides at night in the center of our camp. The more I thought, the more I let the heat and light build in my mind's eye. Soon, the small flame had become a pyre, blazing and swirling. It consumed my focus and was all I had become.

I see you, Druid. I see the blaze of your mind, the heat of your heart and the burning of your passion. You who would burn your enemies and provide light to your friends and those in need. I recognize you, as you are, little flame. Burn brighter with my blessing.

I opened my eyes when I heard the voice in my head and looked into my now hot right hand. There in my palm was an orange flame no bigger than a small stone. As soon as I looked at it, the flame fell into my palm, and searing pain flashed in my mind. Where the flame had been, a flame shaped, orange tattoo now decorated it an inch wide and long. There was no pain, no inhibited movement, nothing.

"Oh, my," whispered Elder Leo. "Come, let us move on to the next element. Begin the process again, this time with another element. Not water."

"Wind."

"Air," he corrected gently. "The air we breathe, the life of all. The breeze that cools and blows through the trees, lifts the wings of the birds in the skies, and transfers the seeds of the flowers and pollen. Air, the destroyer, the winds that rip across the plains, stealing the breath from those in its wake. Bringer of the storms and rains. Ruthless and unstopping as a tornado. Wild and untamed for all time. How would you seek to tame this and make it your own?"

I thought on it. I had always thought that wind was the element, but that wasn't the case; it was air. What I subconsciously filled my lungs with. What kept me living and breathing. The times as a boy when I had been playing outside with a breeze to keep me from dying of heat stroke, or when I used to read outside and a gust of air would make life hell by turning the pages. I remembered seeing little dirt devils while I was serving back home—the examples of tornadoes and hurricanes. As before, a small, cool wind came into being inside my mind's eye. I could see it lifting and flowing clearly. As I thought about the air more and more, it began to whip around in a frenzy, getting stronger and faster until it too stood in a spiraling column of blue light.

Never will you tame me, Druid. You cannot be as free as I, but I have seen you. I have seen into you and noted that you try. That you, too, are relentless in pursuit of your tasks and journey. I have seen the storm you bring, and it tickles my interest to see what you will do. Will you be a breath of fresh air to the land, or will you smash all before you? Time will tell. Take my blessing, and show me something worthwhile.

Once more, I felt a stirring, this time in my left palm. I looked, and a burst of air swirled in my hand; faster and faster it swirled, then pushed down into my hand. A chill dominated it, then nothing. A blue, swirl-like tattoo sat in my palm, a match to the one on my right.

"Next, water," encouraged the Elder.

I cleared my mind; it took longer this time, but I did it.

"Water, life giver. All creatures need it to live. It cools and soothes, provides transport to ships. Gives life to crops and livestock for food. It aids in cleansing and purifying, but there is also darkness to water. It carves paths through the land and in the oceans. It holds dark secrets, sinks ships, and drowns those foolish enough to attempt to challenge its strength. It freezes and kills the land for a season. Tidal waves wash away entire villages in its fury. Rains flood entire valleys and kill all. Water is powerful, unforgiving, and necessary. How can you bend the tide to your will?"

I had begun to see a puddle at the beginning of his speech. I knew water well. Not only did it give life and reside in every living being, but it also filled the majority of my body. Our bodies. It ran through our veins, but it was so much more than just that. I had lived near it for years in my own world, flown over it, listened to the waves beat the shoreline. I knew what water was capable of. Tides eating away at cliff sides until they took the ground into the briny ocean. Rivers flooding and destroying property. Sucking people into the depths, never to be seen again. The water, to me, had been a terrifying thing. I had a healthy respect for large bodies of water—I could swim—but I never swam in the ocean, not because I wasn't confident in my ability but because of what I couldn't see lurking in it. The water grew into a great ocean, spanning inside my mind—endless and deep.

Ah, fear. Usually all who think of my form are filled with calm and serenity, but you, Druid, know that my calm form belies my strength and depth. I have seen you, felt your need to be there for those you love. Water shifts and takes many shapes and forms, filling up what can be taken. I would fill you with my blessing so that you may fill this land and quench it before it burns. Go, take this boon.

Water formed in my left hand and spilled out. It flowed and sank into my palm once more, forming a green river around the wind mark that actually looked pretty damn cool.

"And finally, earth," I said.

"Yes."

I closed my mind and let the thoughts and emotions fall away. This time, I focused on the element before Elder Leo even said anything.

A small hill of loose earth formed in my mind's eye. Earth—solid, timeless, and powerful. It provided food from its soil, allowed the trees to grow, and hid the burrowing animals. Time immemorial has seen it become a home to man in the form of caves, brick, stone. Its immenseness alone crushes rock to the point that it makes diamonds. Home to the Dwarves. Home to metal. Giver. Taker. Great plates beneath its solid skin shift and crash together causing great quakes that can split the ground and swallow whole civilizations up in mere moments. The more I thought, the bigger the hill in my mind became until finally, it was a mountain, great and heavy.

Dirt and stones appeared in my palm, growing into a wall bordering the flame on my right hand in a circle.

Tiny Druid, I feel your footsteps on my back. I feel the strength you have in your bones, the solidness of your soul. Though you know fear, your path does not waiver. You stand firm for your friends and for what you believe in. You would shield strangers from sin and suffering. I like you. I will make you as a diamond to those around you. Take my strength and use it.

The wall hardened, and I felt it quake under some immense, crushing pressure. The wall didn't give but became a diamond border that slammed into my palm under the pressure.

"Excellent," Leo said. "That is enough for today. You have done exceedingly well. The Lady chose well."

I hadn't noticed, but the sky was now dark, and I was sore and hungry. I thanked Elder Leo, and he smiled at me. He informed me to come here in the morning, and we would do more.

I had some notifications to look through, but my grumbling stomach ensured that I would just look at them later. I found a meal in the monastery dining hall. I had a quick bite that filled me up, then went to the room that I shared with Balmur and Jaken.

The two of them had already passed out, and Kayda was asleep in her nest of blankets next to my bed. She was too big to sleep on the bed with me now. Before I fell asleep, I took a look at my notifications.

Congratulations!

You have received the blessing of multiple Primordial Elements! Each blessing individually grants the recipient a boon of the primordial's choice!

Fire: Flame Hand – Caster can wreath his hands in flames, doing added fire damage to all attacks, magical and physical. Duration: 3 minutes. Cool down: 5 minutes.

Since the Flame Primordial liked your spirit, he has seen fit to bless you with the Force Flame passive ability which gives a small damage boost to any fire spell cast by you. Wasn't that nice?

Air: Levitate – Caster can levitate at will for 5 minutes. Cool down: 10 minutes.

Water: Ice Storm – *Caster calls down a column of ice shards on a 40 foot by 60 foot cylinder. Cool down: 1 hour.*

Earth: Diamond Body – *Caster covers his body in diamond-like skin that halves all damage. Duration: 3 minutes. Cool down: 10 minutes.*

You hold a special place in the... whatever counts as the Earth Primordial's heart. She has seen fit to bless you with 3 points bonus to your Strength and the ability Diamond Claws.

Diamond Claws – a passive ability that permanently makes your natural claws hard as diamond, though not nearly as pretty.

I had to admit, I was feeling a little overwhelmed. All of these new abilities and the faith of what was probably as close to the Gods themselves saying they liked me. Except for Air, that guy seemed like a dick. I fell asleep after saying a quiet thank you to the Primordials.

Chapter Eighteen

I ducked into the garden that Elder Leo asked me to come back to after eating. When I arrived, I noticed that I was alone, so I sat and meditated while I waited.

I thought about what might be coming with this training and just relaxed. After a I had steadied my mind and gotten through the worrying, I stood up and began to play with the new skills I had. Diamond Claws was awesome. There wasn't anything around to toy with and try them on, but I took a rock on the ground and scratched it. Where before it might have hurt my nail, the rock stood no chance. I carved a smiley face into it with a satisfied grin.

"May I keep that?" said Elder Leo from behind me to my left. The small man was standing over where I was crouched, looking over my shoulder at my work.

"Uh, sure." I handed it to him, and he took it with a boyish grin.

"Thank you," he said, gazing at it. He slipped it into a pouch attached to his robe belt and motioned to the center of the garden, and we walked over.

"Yesterday, we focused on what the elements were and what they were capable of," he began. "Today, we look into how you will make their power your own. In my way, I transferred the power of the desired element into my limbs, so that I could strike my foes. You have different abilities and thus need to come up with your own way. This is what you will meditate upon today, but first, a demonstration. Sit, please."

I sat a few feet away and watched. Elder Leo moved, swaying and striking rhythmically to a tempo of his own design. His feet kicked out, and gusts of wind cut the air behind each foot. He punched with his right fist, and a gout of flame belched from his fist. Then he struck with his left, and his hand became encased in stone. He jumped into the air, double his own height, and axe kicked the ground, and a burst of ice crashed into the ground where his foot landed. His movements were so fluid and graceful that it was difficult not to be drawn in. Once he finished moving, he bowed and smiled.

"Were you a Monk, I would have taught you that happily, but you chose a different path. Find your way, young Druid."

He sat across from me and began to meditate once more. I did the same and began to wonder how I could incorporate these blessings into my own fighting style. I could attempt to use my understanding of these elements to enchant my gear. That was an idea, but it was only one aspect. I had more to offer than just my enchanting skills. I could maybe make elemental weapons, like have my axe do increased damage by trying to surround it with a given element, say fire. But would that damage it? Would ice make the metal brittle? Shit.

An idea dawned on me. I thought about it for a moment, and it seemed possible. Combining an ability with a spell had increased the damage, right? What if I combined my elemental blessing or understanding and used it to shape shift? There were elementals, beings made up of a given natural element made living through magic. I had seen them often enough in games back home, and I had seen a spell in my choices upon leveling up that would let me summon one.

I thought about an element—water—and focused on it the way I would to shift into one of my other forms. I cast the spell, and it took effect. A flash of muted blue and the familiar drain of mana, and then I looked down to see water encompassing my being. My body was vaguely man shaped but completely made of swirling water. I could walk, and the ground beneath me was wet, the way it might have been after a light misting.

I gurgled in glee and noted that I couldn't communicate at all. Elder Leo leapt up and laughed with me.

"You did it!" he shouted. "You found your way!"

He reached out and touched me. I could feel his fingertips touch my elbow, and water engulfed his hand. It didn't hurt. His hand was drenched but neither of us cared.

Congratulations!

You have discovered a variant of Druidic Shapeshifting! Ability unlocked!

Elemental Form – Caster takes the form of an elemental of choice. Cost: 150 Mana. Duration: 5 minutes. Cool Down: 15 Minutes.

Currently Unlocked forms: Water, Fire, Air, Earth.

Congratulations!

That was some clever thinking! Since you're so smart, let's have your stats reflect that, shall we?

+4 to Intelligence.

Interesting. Currently unlocked forms? Meaning that I may be able to combine some or make my own at some point. I would worry about that later. I dropped the form and looked at Elder Leo who was still bouncing on his feet.

"What do we do now?" I asked.

"Well, I don't know," he admitted as he stopped bouncing. "I wasn't expecting you to do it so quickly, but now that you have it, we can go to the training grounds and see what you can do. We can let you play."

"There's a fifteen minute cool down on this ability so, it'll be a bit before I can use it again."

"That's fine. Let's go."

We took our time going to the Proving Grounds, as my companions and I had begun calling them. He asked me about the process I had used to come up with the idea, and I explained the thought that had struck me. I also told him about some of the games that I had played before coming to this world that had allowed similar things.

"Amazing," he said in awe. "Truly incredible. This world of yours is amazing and terrifying."

I couldn't fault his beliefs because I had times that I had felt the same way. At times, I felt my world was improving and heading in the right direction. Other times, I felt that we were failing ourselves. It was terrible at times. Humans could be great scions of change when they wanted to. The problem was that they didn't always want to; hell, some outright wanted things to go back in time, when some freely oppressed others. I hated that about humanity.

I broke from my thoughts once we got there and looked at the great gate guarded by two Monks. They were levels 19 and 20. They smiled at me, then knelt to Elder Leo. They had seen me sweating and cursing on more than one occasion because of the training. I shook their hands as we passed through and went to find something for me to beat on.

The monsters in the Proving Grounds were pretty nice, actually. The ones closest to the gate were lower level and didn't attack unless provoked. As you went further in, they got stronger and more aggressive, all the way until the mouth of the cave where they came out. No one went in there; it was decided long ago that the monastery would leave the place be so that new monsters would come forth to replace the ones they destroyed.

We picked a middling level for me to start with, a couple of level 8 Snakes the size of large dogs. Think Great Dane. They were sunbathing but eyeballing me something fierce.

"I am looking forward to seeing what you are capable of," Leo said as he plopped onto the ground.

I activated the spell after focusing on the desired element, and my body became living flame, roughly the same shape as my water form. I stepped toward the two Snakes and punched at the closest one. The snake took thirty percent damage outright, then became burned, a little flame symbol appearing beneath its health bar. It attacked me, not understanding that my whole body was made of fire. It hurt itself and only dealt around three percent damage to me. Hardly noticeable, but it was good to know that I could take damage in elemental form. I smashed both hands into the small creature and then finished it off with a kick.

The other Snake tried to slither away, but I grabbed its tail and pulled it back, damaging it slightly. I thought about it really quick and willed the fire in my arm to stream from my hand. It worked, but I felt the drain on my mana instantly. The flame rocketed into the snake and fried it. The stream of flame from my hand had eaten thirty mana altogether.

I took a moment to step away from any potentially hostile enemies and look at my spells as a Fire Elemental. After looking for a moment, I saw that each form had a spell list.

FIRE

Fire Stream – Casts a blast of fire from a hand up to 5 feet. Cost: 30 mana.

Flame Burst – A radial blast of fire that can push enemies back. Range: 15 feet. Cost: 75 mana. Cool Down: 1 minute.

Enhanced Fireball – Cast 25-foot sphere, deals more damage than the original spell. Cost: 100 mana. Cool Down: 2 minutes.

AIR

Wind Blades – Caster uses limbs to create projectile wind to damage enemies. Range: 60 feet. Cost: 30 mana.

Tornado – Caster creates a whirlwind that sucks in enemies up to 25 feet away. Range: 60 feet. Cost: 100 mana. Cool Down: 3 minutes.

Chain Lightning – Caster sends a bolt of lighting into a target, then the nearest target. Range: 120 feet. Cost: 150 mana. Cool Down: 3 minutes.

Ability – Can fly as movement.

WATER

Water Whip – Caster creates a whip composed of water. Duration: Until dropped. Range: 10 feet. Cost: 30 mana. Cool Down: 1 minute.

Gentle Rain – Caster creates a rain cloud that when rain touches an ally, heals them, and when it touches an enemy, harms them. Maximum HP restored: 30%. Duration: 30 seconds. Range: 60 foot radius. Cost: 200 mana. Cool Down: 3 minutes.

Drain – Caster siphons water and HP from one target it touches using it to restore 25% HP instantly. Range: Touch. Cost: 50% mana. Cool Down: 5 minutes.

Ability – Can move freely on and in water. Water adds power to spells and size to elemental form.

EARTH

Stone Spike – Caster flings sharp stone projectiles at will. Range: 60 feet. Cost: 10 mana.

Shell – Caster creates a protective barrier of stone around a target. Duration: Dropped by caster, or receives 250 damage. Range: 90 feet. Cost: 100 mana. Cool Down: 1 minute.

Iron Maiden – Wraps target in a spiked, metal tomb. Duration: dropped at will, target dies, or sustains 500 damage. Range: 10 feet. Cost: 50% mana. Cool Down: 5 minutes.

***Ability** – Can travel through earth, dirt, and stone at will at greater speed.*

A lot of these spells were beyond amazing. Holy hells.

"What did you discover?" Elder Leo asked.

"A lot of spells that are going to keep my mana well lowered," I joked.

"Can I see one?"

I nodded and went to the next set of Snakes. My mana had since recovered from the shapeshifting and the spell usage, so I opted for my strongest fire spell and took aim. I released the Enhanced Fireball directly at the two Snakes about sixty feet away. The spell detonated, and a wave of heat burst into being. The Snakes were engulfed and burnt to a crisp. I didn't see the black flames of my infernal ring, so I didn't think it counted when I was in this form. Oh well. It was powerful as hell anyway.

I dropped elemental and sighed. It was nice to be in my own skin. Of course, those were just as much "me" as my current form.

"That was incredible!" shouted a new voice.

I turned to see a younger-looking Monk, probably around ten to twelve years old, sprinting our way. He leapt over a Snake that lunged at him and snatched it up by its neck. He snapped his fingers closed tightly, and the struggling reptile stilled.

"Ah!" exclaimed Elder Leo. "Samkin, how is our youngest?"

The boy skidded to a halt and bowed on his hands and knees, the strangled Snake still clasped tightly. "Elder."

"Samkin, enough," chided the Elder Monk. "Talk to me!"

"I'm well, Elder Leo," the boy said from his bow. "My studies go well, and I'm growing as best I can. Please, forgive my outburst."

"It's okay," I said before the Elder could reply. He looked a bit sullen that the boy wouldn't talk to him normally.

"I'm Zekiel," I said as I picked the boy up by his robe. "Who's 'Samkin?'"

"I'm Samkin!" he said as his feet kicked to try and get back to the ground. "Put me down, please! The Elder is watching!"

"He doesn't care, right?"

"Not at all!" the grinning Monk replied.

"You know, I thought the same thing about my attack, but I think I might be missing something. Any advice?"

I dropped the boy, and he landed back in his bow.

"See, where I come from, when an Elder tells you to do something, you obey," I observed aloud. "And here I am asking for help? I must have asked wrong."

"Elder Leo is right there. He's so much better than me."

"That's true," I admitted, "but I asked you. See, the Elder is already impressive. He's seen so much and done so much more, but you, you see without the benefit of age or wisdom. He would tell me what he thinks I want to hear. I know you won't, so answer my question. Is there anything you think I could do differently?"

He seemed to think about it for a moment, then said something. I could hear it, but that wasn't what was needed.

"Hmmm. I can't take advice when someone mumbles and can't even look at me."

The boy groaned, then stood up. He looked to me, then to Elder Leo and at me again.

"If you struck your opponent with a fist before you released your flames, you might do more damage."

"Brilliant!" Elder Leo clapped. The boy looked ready to bolt, but I stopped him.

I knelt in front of him and blocked Elder Leo from his sight. "Do you think so?"

He nodded and smiled. "A strike—with flames up close—could really hurt, or I think it would if it was me."

"Sound judgement," I admitted. "Think you can show me a good strike tomorrow? Maybe I can show you my other forms while I'm at it?"

"Really?!" He almost smacked me when his arms shot up, the Snake swinging up as well.

"Yeah! How about it? Wanna trade? You teach me how to throw a decent punch, and I show you what I can do with my magic?"

"Okay!" He smiled at me and looked happy. His little bald head was bobbing as he nodded.

"I look forward to it."

"Bye!" the boy said and waved at me, then realized Leo was still there and fell into a bow. "Goodbye, Elder Leo."

"Train well, Samkin."

Once the younger Monk was gone, Leo looked at me funny.

"What?"

"You were purposely trying to get him to open up, weren't you?"

"Yes, I was." We had turned to head back, so I was watching the creatures around us.

"Why?"

"He seemed to need it. You had given him leave to be himself, but he wasn't giving it up. Sometimes someone has to help children be children. Monk or not."

The Elder stopped in his tracks and looked at me for a moment. "How do you know this?"

"I had to grow up way too fast. I was a lot like him when I was his age. Threw myself into my schooling and books. I took things too seriously, too often. I needed help lightening up, and I wanted the same for him. No big deal."

"It is to me," he said softly.

"Oh?"

"I found him and brought him back when his family had been taken by surprise by bandits on the highway. He was but a babe, and watching him grow from the shadows has been hard. He knows the tale. That's why he tries so hard, I think. I just want him to have a good life. At least what we can give him here. He's so strong. Smart. The cleverest young disciple we have here, and he's only getting better."

I smiled. "Glad I picked him to teach me then!"

The Elder laughed, and we continued on our way. As far as Leo was concerned, my training here was completed. It was time to rest and let my friends catch up to me for once.

Chapter Nineteen

I spent the next morning with Samkin, and I had to admit I was surprised by his level of skill.

He hit so hard that there wasn't much here that could give him a run for his money. We had enjoyed breakfast with Elder Leo, to the Halfling's pleasure, and the lad seemed to be opening up. I could honestly say that I hoped my own son would grow up to be as strong and disciplined as Samkin. Of course, he was already well on his way—not to brag, of course.

"Okay," he said, pulling me from my thoughts. "Your turn!"

I chuckled. I really didn't have to worry much. The kid seemed more like my boy the longer I was around him.

"I did promise, didn't I?"

"You did," Elder Leo said with mock seriousness in his tone.

"Very well then." I closed my eyes and shifted into my fox form. The boy exclaimed and bent down to look me in the eyes. I shifted back and whispered to him that when I shifted again, he had to throw me at Elder Leo.

I shifted back to fox, and Samkin threw me at the Halfling. Once I was just above the confused Monk, I shifted into my bear form and landed on him with a "humph." I chuckled as a bear, which sounded like a growl, when I felt two tiny hands in my stomach lift me. I looked down and saw Elder Leo picking me up with ease and started to panic.

"Oh come now, Mr. Druid," the Elder chuckled. "Afraid? Good!"

He tossed me back at the boy with a grunt, and I flew faster than I could control. I turned into a fox and hit Samkin in the chest, bowling him over. We tumbled to the ground while the Halfling howled with laughter. I shifted back after rolling away from the poor kid. We both started laughing, too. It was to be our final day at the monastery, and we would be moving tomorrow morning.

My time with little Samkin gave me hope that I could see my son again someday. Before I could fall into depression over it, the Elder came over to me and slapped my shoulder.

"I haven't had that much fun in years, my boy," he said with a grin. "Thank you. To you and your friends."

"My pleasure, Elder Leo."

"Leo, young Druid. Just Leo."

"Then call me Zeke. It's my true name, and I would have you know me for me."

"Zeke," he said, seeming to weigh the word. "Very well then, Zeke it is. I should gladly call you friend."

I smiled and held out my hand for a fist bump. When he looked at me in confusion, I chuckled. I took his right hand and made a fist, then held it out again.

"Where I'm from, friends do this as a sign of friendship," I explained. "It's called a fist bump."

I tapped my fist against his gently, then smiled at his look of wonder. I turned to Samkin and held my fist out. The boy bumped my fist enthusiastically and bounced on his toes.

"Friends," I announced.

The rest of the afternoon we spent discussing my world, some of the things that were there and some of our customs, like enjoying sporting events and fighting for entertainment. I was surprised to learn that this world had arenas in a lot of major cities, where people fought to settle disputes, for glory, and for money. Sounded eerily similar to my home.

That morning, we all woke up and joined the Elder for breakfast. He told us that we had a guide coming and that they would take us to the Dwarven underground city of Djurnforge. The guide was to arrive at almost any time so we spent some time going over everyone's training. My friends had all gained a decent amount of strength and dexterity; even Yohsuke had gained four points in strength from the training. All in all, the training had paid off.

A commotion erupted at the gate as a Dwarf came strutting through. His skin wasn't pale like you might expect from someone who lived underground but a tan with red cheeks. His beard was black, and his hair tied into a topknot on top of his head. He was a short, stocky man who sported a double-headed war axe strapped to his back. His coal-black eyes glimpsed Elder Leo, and he barked a laugh at the shorter man.

"Leo, ye git!" he huffed and marched up to him. The Dwarf put his hands on both the Halfling's shoulders.

"Brawnwynn!" The Monk smiled in greeting and did the same with his hands. The two looked at each other a moment in a brotherly way, then whipped their heads forward, head-butting each other. The crack that followed made the party cringe a bit, but the two came away laughing.

"Gentlemen, this is your guide, my old friend Brawnwynn," said Leo. The Dwarf seemed to notice Balmur first and sprinted at him with a gleeful shout that none of us had expected.

"Cousin!" the Dwarf greeted him. "How be the fires treatin' yeh?"

The stout warrior was prepared to butt heads with Balmur and our friend was ready. They grasped shoulders and cracked their skulls together. Both came away a little shaken but grinning.

"Oh, cousin, ye been keeping with 'the Way.' Good." He patted his shoulder and looked to the rest of us.

"Ah! Elves!" Brawnwynn waddled over to Bokaj and Yohsuke. "How be ye lads? Good, eh? Glad ta hear it, I am. Oh, a Grey Elf? Lad, yeh be in good company with me, I swears. Not a harm will come tah ye."

He looked to me next and squinted a bit. "Sylph?"

"Kitsune," I answered simply.

"Keep yer thieving paws to yeself, and we be a'right," he growled. My hackles raised slightly.

"Brawny!" Leo shouted and smacked the Dwarf upside his head. "These are my friends! They are on a most honorable mission. Zekiel would no sooner steal from your people than I would. They have my blessing to be among you and your kith and kin. Treat them as you do me."

"Even the bastard Orc over there? That's right, I seed ye. Think ye can take me? Tusk mouth?!" The Dwarf growled and stepped forward menacingly. "I sees ye wearin' piss-poor armor like that, starin' at me with yer beady, filthy eyes. Ugly. Even iffin ye got some Elf in ye. Sooner kiss an ass's ass than look at ye."

He spat on the ground in contempt while Jaken just glowered at him coolly.

I'd heard enough and stepped forward, putting myself between the aggressor and my friend. I shifted shape and put my bear muzzle right in front of his face, then roared for all I was worth. Flecks of spit and foam flew from my jaws, and my heated breath blew his beard back a bit. He reached for his weapon, and I shifted back before equipping my own great axe.

"Bring it," I growled. "I'll take you."

"I'm inclined to let him, Brawnwynn," Elder Leo barked angrily.

"It's cool, gents," Jaken said as he stepped forward, his hands at his sides facing out to show he was unarmed. "Look, Brawnwynn, Dwarves hate any kind of Orc, right?" The Dwarf nodded his head. "I thought so. How about this, you respect combat, right? That's a part of the Way?"

The Dwarf looked a little taken aback but nodded slightly.

"Then you and I will fight, unarmed and unarmored. If I lose, you don't have to take me with you, and I will stay away from you and yours. First to half health, deal?"

"Aye, we have an accord." He spit on his hand and held it out expectantly. Jaken did the same and clasped the Dwarf's meaty hand.

They took a few minute to take their armor off and lay down their arms, only wearing cloth pants and boots. They circled each other in a makeshift arena of Monks and villagers. The Dwarf was a level higher than Jaken at level 16, so it stood to reason that the fight might actually be pretty even sided.

Elder Leo deemed that he would officiate and signaled a beginning to the bout. The Dwarf wasted no time and lunged at Jaken. He deepened his stance, and as soon as the Dwarf got to him, leapt over him in a somersault. Brawnwynn dove to try and knock his opponent over and landed on his face.

Jaken landed three feet away and stood calmly while Brawnwynn collected himself. His opponent did the same thing, sprinting at him to try and tackle his legs from beneath him. Jaken shifted his legs into a wider jumping stance once more as the Dwarf tried to dive into the taller man's legs. Jaken acted as if he was going to jump, and the Dwarf pulled up short. Using the feigned leap to slow his opponent's momentum, Jaken whipped his knee into the Dwarf's head. The damage done was minimal—

the Dwarf's powerful neck saw to that—but the damage was done to the nose because it looked bloodied.

"First blood is mine," said the Paladin.

"The last shall be yers on the ground," growled the surly Brawnwynn. He was done trying to tackle his opponent and now walked calmly to the center.

"Come," he said.

"You aren't pretty enough," Jaken said haughtily. The crowd chuckled, and more than a few of the Monks blushed.

To my surprise, Brawnwynn actually laughed at the lewd joke. He grinned and stalked toward my friend. From there, it turned into a knockdown, drag-out brawl. Jaken's strength and dexterity were challenged and there were a few close calls, but in the end, Jaken won with a decisive blow. He took a giant step forward to lower his center of gravity, then snagged Brawnwynn in a headlock that made him pass out after a couple minutes.

The crowd clapped and cheered, and Jaken did something no one expected—he offered Brawnwynn a hand up. The Dwarf nodded and clasped the outstretched hand. A golden light enveloped the two, and both of their HP bars began to fill up.

"Ye won, Orc blood, fair and square," the Dwarf announced. "Ye be within yer rights ta ask a boon. If it be in me power, I will grant it."

The Fae-Orc seemed to think a moment then grinned. "I want you to look at me like you would a brother and close friend, like Elder Leo."

"PREPOSTEROUS!" shouted the Dwarf. He stomped about the circle throwing his hands into the air and muttering unintelligibly, "Orc wants... bloody laughing stock... children think? Friend my hairy arse... Mother was a goat..."

He grumbled and paced for a moment longer until Leo stepped out to his friend saying, "Brawnwynn, you haven't lost your Way, have you?"

The Dwarf stood still as stone for a moment, then lowered his head in shame. He turned to his friend and sniffled, "Aye, I almos' did. Thank ye, Leo."

He regarded Jaken, and then he shook his head. He took his ax from the ground and stepped toward our friend, and I took my own axe back in hand, just in case.

"Hold out your palm, Orc," he said.

Jaken obliged, and the Dwarf slit a gash in the proffered palm, then did the same to his own. He dropped the weapon, clasped his bloodied palm to Jaken's, and began to speak.

"Weak blood with no home, through plains and forests ye did roam. Cleansed with the blood of the stone under the mountain, now called yer own. Kith and kin ye now be, me to ye and ye to me. Welcome now, newborn son of Clan Mugfist!"

Shocked awe had settled over the crowd as the Dwarf finished his prayer.

"If you know of the Way, follow it, and ye will be accepted as that of Dwarf blood. Our honor is yers and yers is our own. Do the clan proud. Yer me brother now, but friendship will come after a while."

The crowd went ballistic and surged toward the two men. They clapped each on the shoulder and back and wished them well.

"He did everything as planned," said Leo mildly from beside me. I jumped a bit because he hadn't been there before.

"You planned this?"

"Had no choice, really." He shrugged. "We had no idea what you would be when you came here. An Orc was an eventuality, and this was what I had cooked up in case it came to pass. That's why I picked Brawnwynn as the guide. His clan takes in the misfits and those without a clan. Orc blood might be a first, but the Way is stricter than some might think. The Mugfist Clan is an honorable sort. I think you will like them, though they will be weary of you for your Sylvan ancestry."

"Would it be better for me to go with them as a human?"

"No!" he blurted. "They would see that as a lie, and they would never trust you. Be yourself, and mind your manners, at least while you're with them. Who knows, they may even like you."

Chapter Twenty

A few hours later, we were all walking through a tunnel we hadn't noticed to the right of the entrance to the valley. Kayda cried out and landed near me—now too big to land comfortably on my shoulder—where she thrust her head into my stomach. While we were down below the earth, she and Tmont would stay here and train some more with Leo taking care of them. We were bonded, and she understood that where I was going was necessary. Didn't mean we liked it or that T wasn't pissed.

The rest of the party filed by and gave her pats and caresses. Tmont licked the bird's cheek and then pounced on Bokaj to lick his face. It was a sad sight, but temporary, we hoped.

The bird nuzzled me affectionately, then tore off in flight toward the training grounds.

"Come now, Tmont," called Elder Leo. "The sooner they go, the sooner they return."

The panther growled at the little man but rubbed against him as she walked by. She hissed at me and sat down. Guessing that she wanted to talk, I activated Nature's Voice.

"Yes?"

"Take care of my master. Sometimes he has to be swatted in the middle of the night to keep him on his toes, and if anything happens to him, I will do more than simply nip your tail."

I nodded and patted her head. She purred briefly then padded off toward the monastery. After a nod from Leo, we were off.

The walk to the city was uneventful, albeit confusing as hell. There were false passages and drop offs to be avoided, but the guide seemed to be drawn to the city without fail. We rested rarely but still needed to stop to sleep since the city was more than a day away.

We rose early and ate what we had on hand, then moved on. We continued into what felt like the early afternoon when we came upon a large, solid metal door. It was easily fifteen feet tall and almost as wide with an almost silvery-blue color that seemed to swirl in places. Large runes were carved into the metal, and it was both intimidating and beautiful.

"Oi, ye milksops in there!" shouted Brawnwynn. "Open tha' door right now, or I will whack ye good, I swear on me great-great-great grand-uncle Fenick Mugfist!"

"Hold yer horses, ye daft bastid!" greeted an equally surly but more muffled voice.

A smaller door, about a third the size of the main door, opened on the right side, and out came a burly form that looked almost identical to our guide, but he had red hair and a fiery beard.

"What's with this mix-matched lot, Mugfist?" the guard questioned.

"Fresh lot of customers for the forges Ironnose," he said offhandedly. "Told to bring 'em from the monastery, so I did. Gonna let us through or try to court one of 'em?"

"Yer ugly gob?" barked the guard after laughing. "Get ye gone afore I smash yer noggin, boy."

We filed by, but the guard growled and shouted at Brawnwynn, "Lad, the Seven Hells is wrong with ye? IRONNOSES TO ME! WE HAVE AN ORC!"

Two more guards came out with hand axes at the ready and surrounded Jaken. To his credit, he didn't so much as flinch.

"Ye dare bring our most hated enemy here to the cit–" the guard began but got cut off when Brawnwynn decked him with the meanest right hook I've seen in quite some time.

"Any of ye lot touch this one, ye'll pay," he growled. "He follows the Way, surely as ye do and won the right to be counted amongst the numbers of the Mugfist Clan. Raise yer ax to him, raise it to me clan. Ye'll incite war."

"How did he defeat ye?" asked one of the other guards as he helped the first to his feet.

"Honorable combat under the sight of the Mountain," Brawnwynn said proudly as he stood to his full height.

"Aye?" the first said while rubbing his jaw. "Ye lost?"

The Dwarf nodded, silently with his fists still raised.

"Stand down then, lads. He's safe," the guard said. The other two shook their heads and chuckled as they walked back through the door.

"What's yer name, uh..." the Dwarf looked at a loss for words for a moment.

"Jaken."

"Well met, Jaken." The Dwarf thought a moment, then held out a hand which our friend shook once. "May want to get the clan sigil put on yer armor or a necklace. Might help keep folk from reacting how we did. Brawnwynn, me apologies, lad. I'll let the rest of the clan know what was seen and the situation. Hopefully, we can keep things from getting too out of hand."

"Aye, all's well then. A pint when next we meet for yer achin' jaw?"

"Aye, lad, that'll do."

"The hammer falls."

"And rises again."

We went through the gate, just after getting Jaken an extra cloak to put over his Orcish features. We didn't want to have to fight the whole bloody city, did we?

The walkways were as wide as normal roads on the surface. Dwarves of all shapes and similar sizes walked here and there. Some greeted each other and spoke in friendly tones, mostly in Dwarvish, so all but one of us was at a disadvantage there, but it was nice. There were poles with enchanted lights on them that glowed a pale white, like the light of day, that lit the area surprisingly well. I said as much to Brawnwynn, and he just laughed.

"We aren't savages, fox. We don't need light, but those down here who do appreciate our efforts on their behalf. The white light signifies daylight hours. When it is 'night', the stones in the lamps turn pale red. Keeps us all on a schedule o' sorts."

That was actually really interesting to find out. "What else can you tell us about the city?"

"Everything," he said with a shrug. "What do ye wanna know?"

"What will we be doing today?" asked Yohsuke.

"Today, we go to the clan to see about beginning our bargaining with the forging clans. We can take inventory of what ye brought with ye, materials and the sort, and that will help us figure out who can work with ye the best. Here we are. This be our quarters here. We can take the time to teach ye more of our culture later if ye like."

"I would love to learn more about your culture, thank you," I said, and Balmur nodded his head in agreement.

Seemed like the best bet to go with to me. We would have to sit down later and discuss it in greater detail to see what could be learned. Learning more about a group of people like the Dwarves may help us better assimilate into society.

There was a gate before us that opened into a wide yard of packed earth. Dwarves with battle axes trained there, grunting and yelling battle cries. Most of them had black hair like Brawnwynn, but a few of them had red beards, blond, a couple brown.

"Well look it here!" shouted one of them. "If ever I saw a sorrier Dwarf, it'd be Brawnwynn and his merry band. Ho there!"

"Shut yer gullet, you lot. Swing yer ax before I ring yer necks and show ye how a real Dwarf swings it!" They all laughed heartily and got back to their training. The buildings, like the people, were stoutly built and sturdy, made wholly of stone and artful but functional masonry. There were more than a dozen buildings with similar training grounds in front of them.

"Wow, that's a lot of buildings," Balmur observed. "What's the purpose of the Mugfist Clan?"

"We drink and get all the prettiest lasses," shouted Brawnwynn, to which every Dwarf in earshot shouted something to the effect of an affirmative, "but, to be serious, we are the warriors of the clans—the army, so to say. We prepare for war and send teams into the tunnels to clean out the vermin that come in. We are also to guard the city from the denizens of the Great Below."

"You guys have a... what was it? 'Great Below' here?" I asked, stopping mid stride. "Shit, of course they do, there are Drow Elves and Dark Dwarves. Deep Gnomes."

"What're ye mumblin', fox?"

"Nothing important," I said. "Do they venture this far up often?"

"Not for a while they haven't and never for long," the Dwarf growled proudly. "They don't last long when we bear down on 'em."

"I'm sure they don't." Balmur laughed.

My adrenaline spiked a bit as I went over what I knew about the information presented from previous knowledge. The places below the surface were rough places from all the books and games that I had ever read concerning them. Everything that mentioned it made the place out to be a den of the most evil, vile, and cunning villains to plague that world. Doesn't mean they were the only ones, but still. I didn't want to fuck with them. Not if I didn't have to.

We went into a larger building toward the center of the compound; it had to be where the big wigs hung out because it made the most sense. All those bodies between them and any potential threats. It's what I would do.

We were left in a large receiving room for about half an hour. A pretty Dwarf woman brought us some ale and water. Her rosy cheeks had dimples, and her chocolate brown eyes shone with mirth and laughter. She said her name was Roslyn and that if we needed anything to shout and she'd come a scootin'.

Brawnwynn came back in, followed by someone who looked like an older version of him, though broader in the chest and shoulders, and his beard was long and plated with metal beads to keep it neat. He had stern eyes and a scar that bisected his milky left eye.

He scanned the group of us until his eye fell on Jaken. He motioned with his hand for the Fae-Orc to stand before him. Our friend stepped in front of him and looked down at him with a blank face. I heard several breaths other than my own catch slightly. My hand fell to my side, and I saw Yohsuke's drop to the hilt of his weapon at the same time.

"Jaken?" the older Dwarf asked softly. His deep voice sounded like two stones grinding against each other. It was impressive.

"Yes, sir," the Paladin answered.

The smaller man reached over and grabbed a sturdy chair from the wall to his right side and stepped onto it so he could look the taller man in the eye. He considered him for a moment, lifted the taller man's beefy arms like he was some kind of show animal, then pulled him into a headlock.

"Was it like this Brawny-boy?"

"Aye."

"Good with an ax? No, well that be unfortunate. Good on you, Jaken!" The Dwarf laughed as he let the other man go. "Welcome to the clan, son."

All of us let out the breath that we had been holding. Yohsuke let his astral blade dispel and put up his adaptor. I hadn't even seen him summon the blade. Must have been pretty worried.

"Friends of the clan!" the Dwarf greeted all of us. His smile was unabashed and infectious. "Cousin!"

The burly man hopped off the chair and did the seemingly traditional headbutt with Balmur.

He shook all of our hands in turn.

"Fox?" he questioned as he stopped at me.

"Yes, sir," I said.

"Friend of the clan," he corrected. "What is your name?"

"Zekiel, sir," I said, "and yours?"

"Blast my manners," he said as he waved his hand in front of his furiously. "I am Farnik, leader of the Mugfist Clan."

"Father, yer so much more than simply our leader," Brawnwynn said in exasperation. "This is Farnik the Brave. He led our army himself against the largest invasion force the Drow Elves sent forth in four hundred years.

"He slew three Driders, Drow Elves with the lower body of giant spiders, who were guarding a Priestess of the Spider Queen. Then he brought the priestess low, too. All. On. His. Own."

"You exaggerate, boy," growled Farnik.

"I saw it all, you forget."

I had to admit, I was thoroughly impressed. These were creatures that I was familiar with from the games I had played and the lore I knew. Looking around, I might have to explain some of it to my friends.

"It's late, and a feast has been prepared in your honor. We would have you join us and tell us of your glories. Please?" asked Farnik, a little hopeful.

"I'm down," Bokaj said.

"Sweet, I'm in," agreed Jaken.

The rest of us opted to join in, and we spent the night recounting our adventures for the clan. Much to the delight of the party, with Farnik's blessing, Jaken was treated just like any other Dwarf. Soon after the food was gone came the heavier ales and meads, hearty laughter, and song.

It was a good night.

* * *

The following morning we brought a detailed list of the materials we had with us to the dining hall and enjoyed a rowdy breakfast with the Dwarves. These guys went ham on breakfast. There wasn't an empty plate, and the food didn't last long so we had to eat quickly. More than a few of the Dwarves started conversations with Balmur about the smithing in the fire plane and wondered how he was at arms. The Rogue told them his class and preferences, and they nodded in respect to his choice. A few saying that he at least used axes.

From our host's perspective, the materials we had were of decent enough quality and he sent out messengers to two clans close to the forges.

"Why not just have us go to them?" I asked.

"Because there are hundreds of smiths here in Djurnforge," Farnik said. "To visit all of them would take months, maybe years if they decide to bluster at you and try to con you into letting them do the job. This way, we already know the capabilities of the smith you need, and we have narrowed it down to a couple of the clans in good standing with us who might help you, especially with materials as rare as your Lightning materials."

I had forgotten about those until this morning when we inventoried our stuff. We still had all the lightning materials, twenty five pounds of mithral, one hundred pounds of iron ore, and assorted gems.

"With those things in mind, the two we sent for will be a good fit, I should think. They may even compete for the contract to make your weapons and armor. Though that may not happen. Representatives will get here, sooner or later. While we wait, please Jaken, go visit your new family. Zekiel, stay with me a moment, please."

Yohsuke made to stay with me, but I nodded at him to let him know it was cool. I knew he would stand outside the door.

"My son told me what he said to you in passing," the Dwarf began. "I would apologize on his behalf. I won't say, however, that his thoughts were wrong. Now, afore you get offended, hear me out."

I nodded, leaning back in my seat. The chairs were made of heavy wood, but they were built for the stout warriors and not someone almost double their height, so the wood dug into my back. It felt like a comforting sort of pain, though, loosened my muscles a bit. Kept me from getting angry.

"We've had times in the past where the fair folk, Sylphs like yourself, have stolen and tricked our kind. It's left bad blood between our two races. Some here may wish to see harm come to you—if not your body, your purse."

I nodded. I had expected that something like this could happen eventually, but that didn't ease my unrest.

"I will personally see to it that you receive fair treatment."

"Why?"

"You are a guest here with my clan," he said as if it was the most obvious thing in the universe.

"Is there a way for me to prove myself like Jaken did?"

"Are you familiar with the Way, lad?"

"No," I said after a moment, "I can't say that I am."

"Be you against religion?" he asked with a suspicious glint in his eye.

I shook my head. I'd had a strong raising in religion when I was in my world as a child. I had grown away from it, but I didn't hate all religion itself. I just didn't appreciate blind bigotry and the use of religion to justify horrible treatment of others. I had met too many people and seen too many examples of monsters hiding behind holy claims to be overly accepting.

"Yet, your friends know the Way, and you do not?!" Farnik looked horrified, like I had slaughtered his child before his very eyes.

"Roslyn!" he shouted. A stout, pretty lady we had seen before poked her head in. "The strongest ceremonial mead we have. Get the Clan Elders, too. Gather them outside in the training grounds out back, and you shout to every able-bodied warrior that is here. Go!"

The girl sped off to accomplish her task.

"Come, lad, time to learn the Way."

Outside, a long table with hundreds of mugs filled with golden liquid resting on it was set up in the center of the giant yard. Wizened Elder Dwarves, beards gone grey with time, stood near the table as Farnik ushered me through the doorway. The warriors, a rowdy and boisterous bunch the entire time I was with them, were quiet, and their eyes were on the table and us.

"Brothers of the stone that makes the world. Today we gather to show another the Way for the first time. Join me in calling to the Mountain."

"Let us hear his deeds!" they shouted in unison.

Farnik looked to me and gestured to the gathered. "Tell them, lad, tell them all of your greatest accomplishments."

I took a deep breath and began; I spoke as loudly and firmly as I could. I told them of my arduous training to join an elite fighting force, which was true, but in my own world. They didn't need to know that last bit, though. I told them of Mother Nature's blessing and acceptance of me as one of her chosen. Of our party's defeat of the Bone Dragon at the ruined fort that was infecting the forests. My friendship with the Queen of the Bears and all of her subjects as a result of clearing said fort. How Yohsuke and I slew the survivors of a Goblin raiding party to protect the Lightning Roc until we could hatch her final chick and how I took that chick into my care when her mother succumbed to her grievous wounds. I told them about our fight with the Lizardmen and their Chieftain, then the Goblin Dungeon where we fought a Demon, though it had been small, and finally, of killing the Goblin King.

I told Farnik that I was finished, and he raised his arm in a gesture foreign to me. His fingers were clenched except the finger next to his pinky, and his thumb was out at an odd angle.

Those gathered raised their voices in unison, "Father of the stone, rock to the light and maker of home, open to us now that we might find our Way."

The warriors filed by as they sang a song of passing. From the darkened void of nothingness, then heat from the fires of their God's love for them. How he forged each Dwarf in his image, shaping them with his hammer, the strength of his arm, and the sweat of his brow. Each took a mug into his or her hands and filed away, still singing.

After the forging and trial of the anvil came the quenching. Where their God poured sweet mead onto their bodies and into their mouths, that their veins might fill with life, and once they were quenched, they were cleansed by the blood of the Mountain, the dirt of his vein covered them from head to toe and strengthened their arms and hearts.

Their song reached a fervent pitch, chaotic and seething, when a clear note rang out in the tumultuous sea of noise. That clarity was the Way. The beginning was dark and hard, but on the Way, the Dwarves could walk to the Mountain. The more they fought in the name of honor and protecting their kin and the weak, the louder the call of the Way became. More voices joined with the one of the Way, and it became easier to follow.

When they drank the mead of the brewers, the sweet sound of the Way helped them remember their fallen and gave rhythm to their feet so that they might march forward in unison. They created a better path together. More voices joined the calling of the Way.

As the song came to a crescendo, I learned that the Way wasn't just a path to their God but a path to what it meant to be a good person. That those who find the Way can find friends and family on the path who will help them stay strong. That all are equal along the Way.

Finally, the voices faded and Farnik called to them, "The hammer falls, brothers and sisters!"

"And rises again!" they returned.

"The forge was hot."

"The mead was cold."

"The Mountain made us."

"Dwarves the Bold."

Farnik raised his mug, then turned to me. "Zekiel, Kitsune, we have brought you here to show you the Way. Brothers and sisters, would you walk with this man?"

"Aye!"

"If he stumbles, will you catch him?"

"Aye!"

"And when he goes to the Mountain, will you sing the songs of his glories and raise a mug to his name?"

"Aye!"

"Zekiel, be you ready and willing to walk the Way with us, your brothers and sisters? Would you take ours as your clan and use the strength of your arm to protect the weak and those in need? Will you walk with us as our brother?"

Chills jolted down my spine, and the skin on my body was covered in goosebumps—but I was unafraid. "I will walk the Way with you, brothers and sisters. I will take your clan as my own and lift my arm to protect those I can. I will walk with you, if you will have me."

"You have heard his words, you have heard his deeds." The leader of the clan looked over his people. "He has been vouched for by one who we all call friend, Elder Leo. How do ye judge him? Be he worthy?"

There was a moment of silence so deep that my ears buzzed from it. The Dwarves closest to me began to stomp their right foot to a beat that I didn't recognize. Within a moment, the whole of those gathered were caught up in it.

Thump. Thump. Thump.

Like the beating of a heart. My heart or theirs? I couldn't tell anymore because my heart had begun to synchronize with it.

I fell into the rhythm of it. The Dwarves before me, stoic, strong, and hearty, stomped in time with my pulse. It didn't quicken; it didn't leap. It was steady and strong.

"You have your answer, lad." Farnik smiled with tears in his eyes. "They give you the Heart of the Mountain. They approve."

He lifted his mug, and every Dwarf joined him.

"The Way is long and winding!"

"But never are we alone!"

"MUGFIST!" roared Farnik. The whole clan echoed his shout and everyone drank.

The liquid inside was the sweetest, best tasting alcohol I had tasted on this world or my own. I felt the goosebumps fade as the euphoric sensation of the alcohol began to set in, but I didn't feel the usual effects of drinking but a sense of clarity.

I felt *welcomed*.

I felt close to the Mountain, closer to anything I ever had, other than my son. I had found the Way.

Or it had found me.

Chapter Twenty-One

After the Dwarves had swarmed around to congratulate me on finding the Way, we received word that the representatives from the other clans were here.

The first we met with was the representative from the Stone Hammer Clan, a young Dwarf whose name I didn't catch. He said that the true representative was on the way, and he was here mainly to see that he didn't appear rude showing up unannounced.

At his request, we waited about ten minutes before the "true" representative arrived. The door opened, and in shuffled an older looking Dwarf, his hair and beard gone white with age. His brown eyes still sparkled with life, and he clasped Farnik's wrist. The Mugfist leader went to speak, but the other Dwarf stopped him with a raised palm. He came to the rest of us; the party had since gathered and waited together. He greeted us each in turn, his soft voice pleasant and kindly.

He stopped before me, and a smile almost split his face.

"Hello, sir," I greeted him and held out my hand.

"Hello, young Kitsune." He gripped my wrist and gripped hard. Holy fuck that hurt. "A pleasure to make yer acquaintance. All of ye."

"Grandmaster Granda," Farnik started, "had I known you would be here, I would've had some mead ready for you. Please let me–"

"I'll nay let ye do that, lad," the elder Dwarf said. "I felt the Heartbeat of the Mountain earlier this day and could nay pass up the chance to come see the results meself!"

"Oh," said Farnik. "Well that'd be Zekiel here. He took the first step along the Way this very day."

"I welcome ye then, my child," the white haired Dwarf said and patted my shoulder.

"Thank you, sir."

"That will nay do," he said, taking a stern tone. "Call me Granda. All the children do."

"Okay then, Granda." He said it like, Gran-Da, like grandad without the d. It was both cute and weird all at once.

"Be ye a smith, boy?" The Dwarf looked hopeful.

"No, Granda, I'm an enchanter," I said, and his face fell, "but my friends Jaken and Balmur are smiths, if you would like someone to train?"

He looked back at the Fae-Orc and smiled. "Would ye like to train yer smithing, lad?"

"I would. My name is Jaken, Granda," my friend said.

"And yerself?" He looked to Balmur.

"I'm Balmur, Granda. If you deal in accessories, jewelry and the such?" he asked hopefully.

"Nay, we do not. My clan deals in arms and armor," he said and rubbed his hands together. "Jaken be welcome to come and train. Sorry, Balmur, I be thinkin' you'll have someone under the Mountain capable of givin' lessons. Let me see these materials, then."

We took out our materials and sat them on the table. He picked up each item after pulling out a monocle. He appraised each item in a business-like manner and set each item down gently as not to damage it.

"High quality," he muttered. "I would love to work with some of this, and o' course, our stock of materials will be open for purchase and perusal. With our clans both having long standing friendships, I see no reason not to give ye a discount, and o' course, with an apprentice to teach and pass on my trade, I'll be doubly pleased."

Farnik clapped his hands together. "Very well then, thank you!"

"May I ask yer preferred weapons?"

We all spoke up, and the Dwarf took down some of the weapon types. Our only armored individual who would need any kind of smithing was already going to be working with Granda, so he would get his measurements later.

"Ye say ye call yourself a Rogue, but ye use hand axes?" the Dwarf asked Balmur. "Oh, ye slash 'em from behind? Right, I've been waitin' to work on a new project, and I'm hoping ye won't be opposed to letting me try some new things for ye? I'll waive the price of labor, of course, and all ye have to pay for is materials. I'll sit with ye once we finish and explain my meaning."

He looked to me and squinted his eyes. "Zekiel, lad, ye say ye sport a great axe, aye? Okay, that I will make meself, as well. I can use some of that ore ye collected from the Lightning Roc, if you'll allow me? Elemental ore can be tricky and difficult to find. With yer say, could I show some techniques to my other students while I work with it? Maybe let some of the senior smiths help me? Ye're okay with that?" I nodded eagerly. " Good, thank ye, lad."

"Would you be able to do anything about an Adaptor?" Yohsuke asked.

"I would nay, lad," Granda said. "We of the Stone Hammer Clan tend to steer clear of magics. No offense to those who use 'em, but we believe, as a clan, that solid metal is what gets the job done. Spells are all well and good, but a good blade doesn't need a spell to make it better to us."

"So you don't like enchanting?" I asked.

"It's nay that we don't, we just don't see the point. If you get the blade we make, and ye want to spell it, by all means, spend yer coin, but we will nay do that for ye. Our work is our pride, our weapons our contribution to our kith and kin in their trek along the Way. A good axe in battle can save yer life, if nay the lives of others. We stand firmly behind that."

"I can respect that." I nodded.

The hard work that they believed in? There's nothing better.

"Good. Alright, on the morrow we begin our work," said the white-haired Dwarf. "Jaken, I'll send a runner for ye in the morn'. He'll know what to expect, so ye and yer's shouldn' need to clobber him, but if he gives ye lip, smack 'em good. Ye're clan to our friends, an' we do nay need trouble. Aye?"

"Aye," we all said and watched him hobble out of the room with the younger Dwarf trailing behind.

"That was fortunate," began Farnik. "He's one of the best smiths under the Mountain. You couldn't have asked for a better Dwarf to do the job or to apprentice under."

"Would ye be ready for the next one, Da?" Roslyn asked. Her father motioned her in, and she came in with what I could only imagine was a thin Dwarf. He had toned arms and a studious look about him. His glasses, made of light material and thick glass, made his eyes look almost comically large.

"You're the representative from the Light Hand Clan?" asked Farnik.

"I am," he said in a very proper voice. "My name is Garen, and my clan specializes in enchanted accessories such as rings, necklaces and earrings."

"We could definitely use some of those," Bokaj said. "You enchant them yourselves?"

"We do," affirmed the representative. "We, to the discomfort of our brethren, have an affinity for magic that is not common amongst Dwarves. We charge a fair price, and I also hear tell that there is someone amongst your group who fancies himself a budding artisan?"

Balmur raised his hand, and the diminutive Dwarf sighed in relief. "I will be able to take you on as an apprentice in that time, if you would like?" Balmur nodded with a shit-eating grin on his face. "Good. I'm glad to help, cousin."

"Would you be willing to have me apprentice with you?" I asked.

"No," blurted the representative. "I would not."

"Would someone else?" asked Farnik. "He follows the Way now. My clan claims him. He is now kin."

"I can check with the clan, but the odds are slim that anyone will want to."

"Can I ask why?" I asked, suspecting the answer.

"You aren't a Dwarf," he said as if explained everything, and I was daft for asking.

"Ask your clan, boy," growled Farnik. "Afore I do something you might regret."

The Dwarf gulped audibly, whispered a spell, and closed his eyes for a moment. He gasped, his eyes shot open, and he nodded fervently.

"YES, MA'AM!" he shouted out loud.

"I take it you got your answer?" Farnik barked at the other Dwarf. "Spit it out then."

"Our clan leader, Shellica has offered to train you," he said, his forehead slightly perspiring. "The cost will be what she deems is worth her time. You and the Azer Dwarf will be collected tomorrow morning. Goodbye."

And with that, he fled.

The following morning, way earlier than was strictly necessary, a runner from the Light Hand Clan came to get Balmur and I. We were walked further into the city where the air seemed to heat slightly step by step until the heat grew to a very high level, like being outside in the desert sun. It was hotter than anything I had ever experienced, and I wasn't comfortable in the slightest. The downside to wearing a fur coat, except that I couldn't take this one off without appearing like I was trying to hide what I was.

Squat homes and buildings surrounded us; some with storefronts and stalls outside with vendors calling out their wares in Dwarvish.

Eventually, we reached a building off to the right of what seemed like the hawkers' main thoroughfare. It had a wide berth, and the grounds outside were almost like the ones at the compound of the Mugfist Clan. The gate swung open at a touch from the runner, and we followed him inside. The building was made of metal that I hadn't seen before and had runes like the gate to the city that we had passed through initially.

I walked in, expecting to be greeted by sweltering heat due to the metal building, but it was actually pleasantly cool. Not to the point where you would be uncomfortably cool, more like a warm autumn day.

"Ah, there you are!" said Garen, the thin Dwarf we had been speaking to yesterday. "If you will follow me. Balmur, we can see where you're at and how much we have to work with." He waved dismissively at me. "You, stay here."

"Okay."

I waited for about five minutes before another thin Dwarf bounced in. She had grey hair, and when she looked at me, her bright green eyes flashed. She looked visibly older than some of the other Dwarves I had seen, almost the elderly smith Granda's age but with none of the seeming physical ailments.

"Zekiel?" she asked. Her voice was strong but quiet, like a stern grandmother.

"Yes, ma'am."

"Good lad!" she cackled. "You know manners already. Your ma did you well."

"Sure thing, ma'am." I smiled. I had been raised well, despite the circumstances. "Would you be Lady Shellica?"

"Aye," she smiled, and a few of her teeth were missing, "and you will be learning all I can cram into that head of yours."

"Thank you."

"You say that now." She turned around and bounced away with me following closely.

The building was a series of rooms and workshops that looked like cells with doors, the largest of which that I had seen was my now-master's room. It wasn't by much. Each room had a small forge that seemed to run on nothing at all. I saw no wood, no fuel, or even actual flames, but I could see the mirage-like waves of heat rolling out of it. Dwarves tinkered and tapped at their creations with precision I doubt I could have mustered on my most focused day. It was so interesting that as I watched a female artisan work on an intricate neck piece, I almost lost Shellica.

She had taken us to a storeroom filled with items and pulled pieces from the shelves after a cursory glance at each. When she felt she had enough, we returned to her workshop room, and she shut the door.

"Here," she said as she tossed something to me. It was a simple gold ring, no adornments, definitely nothing special. "Enchant that with your strongest enchantment."

I shrugged and closed my eyes, thinking about the ring. I reached for my magic and began the process of feeding the enchantment in my mind into the ring. When I was finished, I admired my work.

Gold Ring of Lightning Damage

Adds +1 lightning damage to all attacks made by the wearer.

Ring forged by Filgus of the Light Hand Clan and enchanted by Zekiel Erebos.

She snatched the ring out of my hand and observed it, then threw it on her work table.

"That would be decent for the first time, yet that's all you can manage, yes?" she asked as she peered at me. "You aren't holding back, are you?" I shook my head dejectedly. "That was highly inefficient enchanting. You didn't do any of it correctly. It's a wonder that anything you make gets any kind of enchantment and not fried."

My face fell a bit, and she must have seen. "Now you know why I said, 'you say that now.' I am harsh but fair. Who the hells taught you?"

"Tarron Dillingsley, ma'am."

"Who?" she asked, and I repeated the name. "Never heard of her. They didn't teach you to engrave the item? Either by hand or with magic?"

I told her the story about how he had taught me next to nothing, then bailed on me because his pride was hurt. I left out the bit about us being brought here from another world because, well, that would sound crazy, and we didn't know who could be trusted around here.

"You say he carried a cane? Was it engraved or did it have runes?" I described it to her and noted it did have runes. "Then he didn't teach you on purpose. How strong is your enchanting skill?"

"Level 11, ma'am."

"All on your own? And with almost no skill to speak of!" She clapped her hands in delight. "Oh, lad, there's hope for you yet! Pay attention."

She held out a ring of her own, and I saw that it was identical to the one I had worked with.

"Listen and observe."

She held the ring out and focused on it. "When you enchant without engraving, you leave no path for the magic to follow and thus must saturate the item with magic to a greater, less efficient extent. More magic is always better, most would think, but you would be wrong. The spell itself and the engraving you use are everything. Now, there is no specific way to engrave. Some prefer to use tools if they have the skill for it. Some can use magic to do it. Some can use sheer will alone to perform the greatest enchantments, although that is rare, and I have seen it only once. An engraving gives a path to the magic and compresses it, giving the spell you have in mind form, shape, and strength.

To do so with magic, the way I am, takes about the same mana as simply using the spell and saturating the item in it. If you have the time, which you will while you are with me, you will prepare your items with engravings beforehand. Attend the ring."

As I watched, lines began to develop in the ring. Small at first but increasing in length, and they became more and more bold. They looked to be forks of lightning arcing from clouds to the center of the ring, then to the other side in a mirror image. The engraving finished, and she shut her eyes and focused. The ring began to glow with a muted light in her palm for a moment. Once she was finished, she handed the ring to me, and I shouted in alarm.

Ring of the Storm

All spells with lightning element cast by the wearer cost 25% less mana.

Ring forged by Filgus of the Light Hand Clan and enchanted by Grandmaster Shellica of the Light Hand Clan.

"That's with no preparation and poor quality materials," she said. "No, you can't have it. Give it here. You have to let go, boy."

I grudgingly let go, and she tossed the ring into her forge.

"Fuck!" I shouted as I leapt to try and get to it. She tripped me, and the heat melted the item quickly.

"That was entertaining. Now we start your training."

I spent the next two hours showing her I was absolute shit at engraving with tools. She enquired about my mana pool, and I told her that I had three hundred ninety MP. She nodded her head and told me that I could do it with magic, but it would be some time before I could magically engrave and enchant at the same time.

"Does the engraving matter to the spell?" I asked suddenly, the thought striking me. Most of my enchantments has been successful due to instinct. If that was the case, I was screwed if I messed up that part.

"The act of engraving is what is important to the enchantment," she began. "The engraving itself, as far as how it looks, doesn't necessarily matter, although having a ring with a fire enchantment engraved with water symbols might be confusing. There is a theory that if an enchantment is given over to an engraved item with an odd engraving, it might weaken the spell. I've never taken the time to actually study it in depth, but I would suggest that you try to keep the engraving in line with what you want for the spell. At least for now."

That made sense, surprisingly. My last 'tutor' had hardly given the effort to explain anything like that.

Asshole.

"I want you to take this ring and engrave it," she said and handed me a ring made from copper. "Copper is a good starting metal. Takes less mana to actually engrave than other metals. Think of a spell you would like to try, and then use pure mana to engrave the metal in a suitable manner. Take your time, and *do not enchant it yet.*"

The only thing I could really think of was the ring she had just wasted, so I started there. I reached for my mana, then brought it through my fingertips and into the ring. I tried to get control of the flow of it, since I was just used to letting the magic go on its own. It was a little difficult, but I was able to manage it. I thought of my magical energies spinning, like a diamond engraving tool that I had seen back in my own life. I always did love watching videos of people making things, even though I never had the talent myself.

I never was all that artistically talented. Don't judge me.

The mana I envisioned spun and touched the metal, carving into it slowly before fizzling out, my concentration broken by my joy at success. I sighed, then began again, working in the same groove I had made before, then expanding. I figured something simple would suffice, at least at first, to test the waters. The going was slow, but I managed to copy her design at least for the bottom half of the ring. It took my mana running dry three times and a throbbing headache—but it was done.

Shellica looked over my work with a critical eye, grunting, and a few "tsk" sounds could be made out before she handed it back.

"Your lines are shoddy, the depth of the engraving varies, and overall, your mana control is sloppy," she said, finally smiling at me, "at best."

"Then why the hell are you smiling at me?!" I cried with my hands in the air.

"Because that can be worked on!" she cackled. "Do you know how many of my clan struggle at that until they give up and go to using real tools?" She looked me in the eyes, then smiled. "ALL OF THEM!"

She rushed around the room grabbing more items, setting them down, then finally grabbing what she wanted to find. "AHA!"

She sat a crystal in front of me, then tapped it, "This is what you will be working with. Fill it with your mana, then take it out again. The crystal is an extension of your mind, your body, and your mana. Do it now."

I picked up the crystal and tried to look into it. I'd read books where people had done the same thing to work on their magics, and I was having some serious trust issues here. I couldn't believe that this was an actual thing that people could do.

"It's hollow. Stop being a pussy and do it," she shouted, her old voice commanding.

I reached for my mana again and tried to push it into the crystal. The crystal lit up a gentle blue, then turned red and shocked me. I dropped it, and the Dwarven lady guffawed so hard she fell on her ass.

"I can't... haha, believe—hahaha—you fell for that!" She struggled to breath for a moment, then got to her feet.

My cheeks burned so hot, I was surprised my fur didn't burst into flame. I stood and brushed my lap off then turned to leave.

"Where—hic—do you think, you're going, boy?" she panted. She was standing now and had laughed herself into having a hiccup fit.

"I won't be made a fool of for wanting to learn," I fumed and kept walking.

The door in front of me was locked tight, and I turned to see a smile on the Dwarven woman's face.

"Ease your mind, boy," she cooed. "There is a way, but an old woman has to have her fun, you know?"

I growled at her and clenched my jaw. I really wanted to do the crystal thing! My inner nerd was raging so hard right at that second, I was worried I might swing at her.

"Come here." She held her hands out and motioned me to her.

I counted to ten, then twenty before I finally stepped forward toward her stupid fucking face. I stopped in front of her, and she made me kneel down in front of her. I did as she motioned and knelt down. At this height, I was still a little taller than her as she stood, but she could reach.

"Do you know what I am, Zekiel?" she asked softly.

"Clan leader?"

"And?"

"Crazy?"

She cackled and kissed my cheek.

"I like you, boy." She beamed at me. "I'm a high priestess of the Mountain. I know who you and your party are, the same as he does. I knew you were coming, and I—and my clan—will aid you how we can. With that in mind, the Mountain, Fainne, in his wisdom, has asked I grant you a boon. This is my gift to you, a little extra kick in your reserves."

I felt a warmth as she completed her last sentence. The sensation started at my temples, then pushed inward, growing warmer and warmer. As the sensation traveled slowly down my body, the feeling turned from calming to uncomfortable—then to straight up painful.

I grunted in pain and felt the heat rip through my body, the same way my mana felt when I called to it but in reverse.

Heat filled my entire being, dripping through my veins like molten lead. It hit my mana pool, and out of the corner of my eye, I saw my mana bar dropping rapidly. Once it hit zero, my health started to drop as well, albeit slower than my mana.

    I didn't try to man up and bear the pain, I screamed. I roared so loudly my throat felt like it should have been bleeding—then nothing.

Chapter Twenty-Two

I. Was. Nothing.

There was nothingness about me, black as far as I could see.

"Welcome, tiny Druid," greeted a voice behind me. I "turned" to look, and there was a Dwarf made of pure mithral. His beard was gold, and his eyes cut from emerald. He was bald and had a small smile peeking through his beard.

"This gift," he started, "is not a gift I give normally. My children don't take well to magic, something about how I made the Dwarves in the beginning made them less drawn to the magics of the world, but some do. These ones I grant the boon of more mana and a Molten Core. I can't give you the Molten Core because it would interfere with your elemental magics, so you will have to do without."

"Then what was all that heat?!" I gasped at him, then gasped at my outburst. "Sorry."

"Baaahahahaha," the God laughed and clapped a hand on his knee. "I like you, tiny Druid. Don't apologize for that. That was the Forging—you've been told the story of my making my people. I made only a select few with mana pools, and in order to do so, I had to forge their mana pools inside them. What you experienced was a minor version of the process that takes the mana pool in a Dwarf and deepens it. With this, you'll be able to hold more mana. That was actually little Shellica's idea. My gift to you is to deepen your understanding of engraving. I can't increase your levels in enchanting, not really my thing, but I can do this."

He hadn't moved, but somehow, he was closer, and his great hand cupped the top of my head. Much like when I learned a new spell, knowledge seeped into my brain, and I knew that engraving was something I could easily do now. Before, my hand wouldn't let me. Not for lack of trying—I had been attempting to draw my whole life, and to be honest? I'm absolute shit.

No, no. Don't feel bad for me. Everyone has their gifts. Drawing and things that involved relating the beautiful bounty in my mind to paper by hand was always doomed to be crap.

So I couldn't engrave by hand, but magically? I could definitely do that.

"I hope that this will assist you," he grunted and patted my shoulder. "You will do well to have your friends with you along the Way. Work hard, fight well, and drink with friends. Goodbye, tiny Druid. I've been away from my post long enough, and the others call to me."

He pushed me back, and I felt that I was falling. The black nothingness around me turned grey, then lightened further.

"... boy..." said an older voice. "BOY."

I grunted and sniffed before jolting upright. I sat there and looked about with bleary eyes. The room was the exact same as it had been when whatever happened had happened.

"Finally back, eh?" The old coot chuckled at me. "Thought you had gone to the Mountain."

"I did," I said and rubbed my aching head. "He's a really nice guy."

"So he came to you, did he?"

"He sure did, let me in on some trade secrets, too."

I stood up slowly, then walked to the desk and sat down on a stool there. It was a bit short for me, but standing made me a little woozy. I picked up a ring, again the same kind we had been playing with, and thought of a design I wanted to press into it. That's right, *press*. I pictured the image and reached for my mana.

My mana didn't feel any different to me, not at first, but I did notice that the pool to take from was larger. Significantly larger. I looked at my mana bar and saw that I now had four hundred forty mana rather than the three hundred ninety I had before.

"Thank you," I whispered to Shellica, careful not to let my concentration slip.

I held the ring up at eye level and closed myself off to my surroundings. I brought my mana to my fingertips, and it began to weave itself into a net-like pattern that narrowed at the bottom of each loop. As it finished weaving, I slipped the net over the ring and began to pull the mana so that it would sit against the metal and heat it, then pulled the mana tight like a noose. The pure magic I had woven heated where it touched and laid the design I wanted. When I finished, I had next to no mana, but the design was perfect.

Shellica looked it over while I rested and let my reserves recover. I was drenched in sweat and starving, but that level of control was something that even I felt was unreal. It totally wasn't me—it was divine.

Using it felt like cheating, and I hated to do it, but the longer I was here, the more I realized there was more at stake than my gamer pride. Sometime, at some point, I was going to have to make a hard decision—be willing to cut the corners and take the cheats where I could to protect what I held dearest, and even if I hated myself, I would do it and live with it because I had to.

My mana had recovered fully as I had fallen into my own mental ramblings and moral conundrums. There would be more time later before I went to sleep, just like in my own world. At least that never changed.

I cleared my mind and began to focus my will and intent before I reached for the mana. Once I touched the astral substance, it turned into molten liquid, and I brought it through my body and into the engraving. The mana flowed evenly and slowly, seeping into the design as it ate away at my mana reserves. I kept my focus and continued to pour my mana in until I was spent. I had filled the engraving enough to power the spell, but a nagging feeling kept telling me not to stop.

I examined the ring, saw the stats, and was thoroughly impressed with myself. +2 to flame attacks was the highest I had done so far.

The old Dwarf reached out expectantly, and I let her have my work. I was proud of the work I'd done and puffed my chest up, just a little, so that she could tell me how well I did.

"Terrible." She turned and tossed it into the furnace. There was an actual physical pain in my chest that told me my worst fear in that moment was true. She had to be a sadist.

I roared and rushed toward her. I didn't know what I was going to do, but it would be violent. She cackled at me and held her hand up, her bracelet sparkled, and then a shield burst from it and stopped my fist cold. It may have actually broken a bone in my hand. I roared again, in pain this time, and scowled at her.

"What did I tell you about using too much mana?" she asked. "Typical beginner, needs to put all the mana they can into the enchantment. Thinks it could have been stronger with more. Bull-headed fool! It's the engraving that matters and the perfect amount of mana. That could have been doubled if you had used the right amount!"

"How do you even know what the right amount is?!" I cried in exasperation.

"Me?" She pointed to herself. "Instinct." I groaned. "You? Well, you will learn not to oversaturate it. How much mana did you use to power that?"

Thinking back, I had blown my entire pool of mana—four hundred forty MP into that one tiny ring. Now I understood why it was wrong. The thoughts in my mind must have shown on my face because my teacher chuckled.

"So you see now," she began. "You oversaturated it. That one small ring, and you used up all your mana. On a much larger item? I could see the need, but a ring? No. Again."

And that's how I spent my time with her. For days, she showed me the appropriate amounts of mana to use on certain items, design ideas to engrave that would strengthen certain types of spells, and she helped me redo some of my earlier works. I didn't necessarily learn all that much that was new from her than that. She didn't teach me any new kinds of enchantments, just theories and advice where she thought it was needed. Which, in her mind, was every time I did any-damned-thing.

Despite her previously seeming insanity, I could see her brilliance. It didn't make her any less nuts, but hey—we all have our quirks, right?

Chapter Twenty-Three

By the end of the week, our weapons and gear that we had requested were finished. I had raised my enchanting to level 26, which actually gave me a full character level once I hit level 20 with the crafting skill. I even put my intelligence at forty-five points and added two points to wisdom and constitution each—putting me at thirty-four and twenty-seven respectively.

I was now considered a Layman Enchanter. My enchanting skills and spells were much stronger than before, and now I didn't over saturate my items. It was a nice feeling.

"So you think you're rid of me, do you?" the old hag, as I had endearingly begun to call Shellica, said. "There's still the not-so-small matter of payment."

I sighed and turned around, "Wasn't my suffering payment enough, you old crone?"

She cackled in delight at my blatant disrespect. The third time I had gone completely ape shit and tried to attack her, I had called her everything—including the kitchen sink. She had burst into tears, she had laughed so hard. Through gasping breaths, she had said it was refreshing and to keep it coming.

"Think of that as merely the head on the mead, my little screw up," she purred. "No, my payment is that you will tell all who ask who trained you and my clan's name. Next, you will not lose your Way. You must always help kin in need, lest he turned against the Way and his kin. Finally, hold still."

She stepped closer to me and plucked some of the fur growing on my arm, not a couple hairs but a patch. I growled at the pain and bared my teeth at her.

"A memento for an old lady." She smiled and patted my shoulder. "I'll miss having you around, lad."

"Like a hole in the head," I half joked. Truth was, I liked her a little. She pushed me to better myself and didn't coddle me too much. It was nice.

She waved me away. "Goodbye, shitty little fox."

"Later, damn stump granny." I smiled at her and walked back to the clan's hall. Her clansmen looked at me in both open horror and mild respect as I left. They were terrified of her—rightfully so—but seeing someone talk to her that way was new to them. I think some of them liked it a little.

I was so spent the last week that I had no idea what was going on with any of my friends. I was excited to see how their own apprenticeships had panned out.

When I arrived to the hall, lunch was set at the dining table: great racks of ham and bread with cold cheeses to be used to make sandwiches and lunch mead, as we had begun calling it. These guys ran on alcohol, I swore it, and they would too. My friends were gathered around the table with some of the Dwarves they'd begun to associate with.

"Hey, guys!" I greeted them as I walked over. They all greeted me, and we started to catch up with each other.

Yoh had been bored out of his mind, so he'd begun exploring the city, trying to find a place to learn some new recipes. Turns out that a clan down the way owned a restaurant that they let him begin working in it. He spent a week with the head chef there, cooking like a mad man. He was well on his way to journeyman with his cooking skill, only about two or three levels away.

The same could be said for both Balmur and Jaken, both of whom leveled their skills up to almost journeyman level. James didn't have any crafting abilities, so he had spent most of his time just hanging out with our hosts and beating on the troops when he got bored. More than a few of the Mugfist Clan members gave him a wide berth when he came onto the sparring field.

"It was some bullshit, man," Bokaj had said at last. "I searched this whole damn city for wood—haha laugh it up, man—all they had were bits for pommels and shit. I couldn't do anything. I've been so bored. I actually got an instrument, though, so you know, that was cool."

The instrument in question looked suspiciously like a guitar, which I'd seen him play before back home, and he was pretty fucking amazing.

We all spent some time together, speaking about our training and how much the others had grown to respect their crafts. I told the group about my time with Shellica, and they all couldn't believe she was the way I said, so Farnik had to back me up on it. We spoke well into the evening, and all went to bed around the same time. We would get our things in the morning, then set out to get on with our mission.

We all woke up and had breakfast with Granda. The old Dwarf chewed his bacon and eggs enthusiastically, as if he was just as excited for us to get our items as we were. Once we had all eaten our fill, we went to the receiving room where we had first met the old Dwarf and waited as he began to show us what he had made.

The first thing he pulled the cloth back from was a new sword and shield for Jaken. The sword was beautiful and deadly with a long, thick, double-sided blade, forged from what I now knew was mithral. The shield was beautiful as well. Thin but stronger than the shield he had used before. It had his Goddess's crest on it, a golden ball of light. When he picked both up, he commented on how light they felt. The armor had the same motif and design on it. It too was made of mithral and weighed significantly less than he was used to.

Next, Granda pulled the cloth back on a matching pair of the strangest looking weapons I think I had ever seen. They had the head of a hand axe and the haft as well, but at the bottom, each curved down into a thick dagger. The metal was a dark color that looked slightly like gun metal, but I wasn't sure what to make of it.

"Wow," breathed Balmur. He picked them up almost reverently.

"I told ye I had an idea I wanted to try." Granda chuckled. "They be made of a light alloy, mithral and ebon iron. Rare metal, that, but I wanted to see if it would take, and it did. Oh it did."

"What are they called?" I asked without thinking.

"Well, I haven't named 'em." He shrugged. "Any suggestions?"

"Mountain Fangs," Balmur whispered.

"Oh, lad," said Granda. "Ye be well along the Way. Mountain Fangs it is."

Unfortunately, Granda's clan specialized in metal armor, so Balmur and the rest of us who thrived without it were shit out of luck. The weapons were cool as hell, though.

Next, Granda pulled back the cloth, and there was a matching pair of daggers made from the same alloy as Balmur's Mountain Fangs and a set of what looked like black metal brass knuckles attached to gloves.

"I know that Monks pride themselves on unarmed combat, but I thought that a little extra '*umph*,' might be called for, eh?"

"Thanks." James tried them on and flicked out a strike, testing the weight and feel. "I'll get used to them."

"Now, I know they aren't your weapon of choice, but I can't make a metal bow for ye, lad. Me apologies."

"It's cool, Granda, I'm just happy you thought of me." Bokaj took the daggers and their sheaths and started to attach them to his belt manually.

Finally, Granda pulled back the cloth above my weapon. The axe was like something I could have never even dreamed of. The metal was golden hued and black in some places. The head of the axe was as large as my blood axe but had a curvature to it like a lightning bolt. The feathers that had been part of the loot from the Lightning Roc had been worked into the blade, sharpened and fanned out like a wing. The metallic feathers formed a serrated edge. The rear of the axe's blade came to a protruding head like a large hammer. The haft of the axe was made of the same combination of black and gold metals. It was captivating and feral, an odd combination of words—I know, trust me—but that's how it felt to look at it.

"I been making weapons going nigh on a century," Granda said. "I love this craft more than anything, other than me wife, of course, and some good mead. Nevertheless! This, this was a fun project. The metals we used to make this ate up the supply of ore you gave me, me apologies, but the ebon iron will work well and compliment the elemental damage of the lightning ore you gave me. We're calling the alloy it makes shadow lightning. The feathers there are harder than the blade itself, so they will cut well. I'm proud of all of these works of mine. Thank you for your patronage."

I didn't even want to touch it because I knew as soon as I did, I wouldn't be able to pay attention to anything else around me.

"What do you ask in payment for this gear, Granda?" Farnik asked.

"Well, take into account the cost of labor, fuel," the old Dwarf grumbled and figured with his fingers. "Taking into account that you provided a large portion of the materials we used, allowed us to take one of your own for a small apprenticeship, and let me have my way with the creation. Top notch work that was by the way, Jaken lad. Also, the clan discount knocks a bit off too. I'd figure around one hundred gold for Jaken's gear. Now, that does come with full plate leggings and bracers lad, so that's a damned fine deal there."

"Done." Jaken pulled the coinage out of his trouser pocket and gave it to the Dwarf without a second thought.

Next, Balmur paid fifty gold, Bokaj thirty, and the same for James. My own took more than a little bit of thought. I ended up happily shelling out one hundred of my own gold for the weapon. That was after I had let them use and keep the materials they hadn't used. Damn, the axe had better be worth it.

"Will it take an enchantment?" I asked. "Not that I don't love your work, but we need every available edge we can get."

"I know ye meant no disrespect lad." He nodded and closed his eyes in thought. "Aye. Each of these weapons and the armor will take enchantments. The metals we used are highly absorbent to magic, though yer axe may be a little temperamental with it. Ye'd better ask the enchanter outside on that part. He might be able to examine it for you."

"Thank you, Granda."

"Give 'em hell out there, lads!" He grinned and shook all of our hands before leaving.

Garen entered next with a medium sized chest which he sat on the table gently, and a cloaked figure strode in behind him. The grey cloth hid everything from sight, and I couldn't make out who it was. Although, my nose was telling me I knew the scent. I really needed to get a hang of my heightened senses.

"Here are the items each of you requested, made to the best of our abilities."

The Dwarf pulled out four small drawers from the chest and handed one to each of my friends.

He clasped his hands in front of his thin body and waited while his customers looked over their things.

Farnik cleared his throat loudly, "Ahem, I assume you have Zekiel's items as well?"

"We received no orders from him," Garen sniffed. "Clearly he thinks he can do better on his own."

"That's bullshit, and you know it, Garen," I growled at him, stepping forward.

"No, it isn't," he snapped back. "You were so busy wasting our clan head's time and hard-made items that you didn't put any requests forward. It's too late now, you animal."

"YOU WILL NOT SPEAK SO TO A FRIEND OF THE MUGFIST CLAN!" Farnik roared, rocketing out of his seat so fast the heavy chair clattered to the floor.

"I do have to agree with Farnik, Garen—you overstep," spoke the cloaked figure. Hands cleared the sleeves and pulled back the hood. Shellica stood there with a grim look on her face. I thought I had scented death and insanity.

"Matron," Garen yelped and fell to his knees before her. Everyone else was surprised to see her, too. Then I remembered my True Sight skill, and it made sense that I could see her and no one else could.

"Please, I can explain!" he began to plead, looking up at her beseechingly. "The rest of th–"

"No." She stared at him with an intensity that I had seen before. In our week together, the only time she had looked at me in that same way was the hardest day I had lived here so far. His face fell, and I almost felt sorry for the little bastard.

"Your racist remarks are not lost on me, Garen," she growled. "You had better go back to the hall. You and I have much to discuss. And Garen? Yes, look up at me now, lad—it will not be pleasant."

"Yes, matron." He stood and shuffled out of the room.

"My apologies, Farnik. My clan has sullied your hospitality," she said with a nod to our host.

Farnik looked like he had seen a ghost and just waved it away. "N-no problem, Shellica."

"Nonsense," the female Dwarf countered. "As is the custom, I will have a dozen barrels of my finest mead brought to your clan within the hour."

Farnik just nodded and fumbled with his chair a bit before falling into it.

"Lad, I took it upon myself to make your items. I made one for the rest of you, as well." She pulled something out of her pocket, a bag no larger than a sack someone would use to carry their lunch, and began pulling things out.

The first was a set of five earrings, all of them made of jet black metal with a single obsidian stone piece dangling from a thick link of blackened chain. It looked very ominous.

"Earrings of Telepathy," she explained. "They will allow you to mentally communicate with each other up to a mile apart. It works by will, so don't worry, your thoughts are your own."

She tossed me a simple mithril ring with a clear gem set into it. It was a Ring of Storage that functioned just like the one Yoh had. The next was a bracelet made from rough onyx. When I slipped it on, it shrunk so that it fit my furred wrist perfectly.

"An Elemental Bracelet," explained the crazy old bat. "It halves the damage of magical attacks with elemental affinities and stores the magics in the bracelet to be used by you."

"How?"

"You'll decide." She shrugged. "You can add the magic to a spell that you cast or to a weapon attack, a punch, a fart, who cares. Should I take it back?" Her eyes narrowed dangerously.

"No!" I blurted and pulled it close to my body. I liked how that sounded; being able to turn my enemies' magic against them was always a good idea. Halving elemental damage? Sign me the hell up for that.

"Good lad." She patted the table. There next to her hand was a thick band of dark-colored material with a large, black stone that seemed to suck up the very light from the area around it.

I lifted it up, and she cackled. "Proud of this one, I am. That's a Shade Realm Collar. Only one I ever made, and I don't be wanting to make another. It will let you store one willing creature of your choice safely for as long as you like. When you want the creature to come out, simply summon them with your will."

"How..." I started to say, but she held up a hand.

"You mentioned a creature called Kayda and how much you wish she could have been here." She smiled in a matronly way. "I thought that this might help a bit."

"Thank you."

"Right. Oh my!" she exclaimed as she looked at my great axe still on the table. She hefted it with no visible strain and looked it over intently. "Oh yes, yes, this will do quite nicely for a weapon this lovely."

She closed her eyes and began to hum to herself. Her mana flowed from her fingers, a bright yellow light that etched lightning down the haft of the weapon, the bolts arcing out and touching each other in matching patterns, spiraling down the haft. It looked like touching it would shock anyone. As she finished, she sat the weapon down and smiled at me.

"No charge at all. You paid my price, and my son disrespected you and the Mugfist Clan. For that, none of you have to pay for the earrings."

I went to touch the weapon in front of me, but Farnik stopped me.

"The first time you touch it, you have to name it," he said gravely. "It's a tradition with weapons so well done. Granda outdid himself on this one."

I thought of what I might call the weapon and picked it up.

"Storm Caller."

Storm Caller

+8 to attacks, +5 to lightning damage

Weight: 30 Lbs

Returning weapon – weapon will return to the owner's hand at will in the most direct route possible.

Weapon forged by Grandmaster Smith Granda of the Stone Hammer Clan and enchanted by Grandmaster Shellica of the Light Hand Clan.

"Can we go test these out?" I asked.

"I'd be offended if you didn't." Farnik laughed.

We all went into the training yard, and a few of the Dwarves were training there with their axes. Training dummies were erected in front of a wall for us, and we decided to test our new weapons that way.

Balmur threw his, and they arced right into the dummy with his typical accuracy. The two Mountain Fangs blurred out of existence and came to rest back in their places on his new belt. Bokaj threw his new daggers at the same dummy, and they sailed nicely. He actually had to go and get them, but they worked. That was all that mattered.

I lifted my new weapon and activated Wind Scythe, sending Storm Caller spinning at the dummy before me. It was surprisingly light for how brutal of a weapon it looked to be. The great axe connected and, with a muted zapping sound, set the straw inside on fire, and the head lodged in the wall behind it. I was about to run forward to collect it when I remembered the enchantment. I thought of holding the weapon again, and it turned into a bright lightning bolt and streaked back into my hand. The electricity didn't burn or hurt in the slightest. As soon as my grip was secured, the bolt reverted into my axe.

"That's fucking sweet, bro," Yoh said, walking forward. "Lemme see it. I want to try something."

I tossed him my axe, and he caught it, although he stumbled a bit. Must not have had as much invested in strength as I did.

"Now, see if you can summon it."

I performed the same mental exercise, and the axe turned into the same golden bolt as before. My friend shouted and let go of the weapon. It came back to my hand once again.

"Damn, that shit hurt, man," he said as he shook his hands. "Not too much damage, but it's something."

I cast Regrowth on him as thanks, and he nodded my way.

"Travel well, lad, and don't let anything out there get the drop on you."

"Thanks, you psychotic old bat."

She beamed at me proudly, and I smiled back. She thumped my arm and turned to walk away, lifting her hood up as she went.

"Ah, the witch is gone." Farnik sighed after a few seconds.

I laughed hard enough that my sides hurt. He knew how hard of a taskmaster she was and how insane she could be. I couldn't imagine his dealings with her were fun.

Chapter Twenty-Four

Brawnwynn led us back to the surface after we said our goodbyes to the clan. We slept underground that night, and when we came out of the cave the next day, well dawn, I couldn't have been happier.

I called out to Kayda through our bond and felt her joy. She felt a bit different, too, but I couldn't quite place it. We began our trek to the monastery, traveling into the valley, when a screeching cry echoed off the walls. I looked up, rewarding myself with a view of the sun like the idiot I could be. I shielded my eyes quickly and tried to find the source of the noise.

"No fucking way, man!" Yoh shouted. He pointed to my left, and I looked to find a shadow careening toward me. Meathook talons outstretched toward me, and I yelped, shifting without thought into my fox form. The claws collided with the ground and tore up the soil around me.

Kayda had found me.

"Bird!!" I shouted as I finished shifting back. She stood taller now, at least four and a half feet, and her wingspan was massive. Her sleek feathers were well groomed and fuller than before. She looked stronger, more sure of herself, too. I knelt and wrapped my arms around her in a hug. She ruffled her feathers and craned her neck about my shoulder trying to return my affection.

Yoh and the rest of the party of the party gathered around us to give her playful pats.

"I gotta find, T," Bokaj said as he started to sprint toward the monastery. He was moving pretty quickly.

Fly? Kayda's mind touched mine, and I knew what she wanted. I shifted into my fox form, and she gingerly took me in her claws before she took to the sky. I was simultaneously exhilarated and terrified. The ground and my friends shrank and began to swim beneath us. I was used to flying—hell, I had ridden the air currents in helicopters for years. I had no problem flying.

But I didn't have a gunner's belt up here, and all that came between me and certain death was my companion.

You're safe. Baby, my pilot assured me teasingly. She did lower her altitude a bit, though, which I mentally thanked her for. I could see my pale friend still running beneath us; he'd made it halfway to the monastery when we saw a black shape blur toward him from the shadows.

Kitty! Kayda squawked loudly. I squeaked a fox laugh. I had to admit, it was a weird sensation laughing as an animal.

Lower, love. Let's watch this closer.

I immediately regretted that because the telltale dip and weightlessness of a dive pushed my stomach up then toward my tail a heartbeat later. We dove low enough to see Tmont spring onto Bokaj's back and pull him to the ground. They wrestled and played for a minute before we landed beside them.

Tmont eyed me for a moment, then came over to me and bumped her head against mine gently. I thought she was thanking me for bringing her master back safe, so I bumped her head with my own.

I shifted back, and we waited for the rest of the group to arrive. Brawnwynn had left the group to go home, and the others made the walk shortly after saying goodbye.

We spent the afternoon with Leo. We all took turns telling him about our time with the Dwarves, and when I told him about Shellica, he shuddered a bit. He knew. Poor little fella.

We left the following morning, freshly supplied and rested. We turned our sights toward our original target—the city. The walk there was uneventful; the mountains gave way to plains and hills. From there, we rode our mounts. Thor was happy to get to stretch his legs and hear about what had happened to us since when he'd seen us last.

Within the next three days, we had Maven Rock in sight. We could see lights in the night. By the fourth day, we were close enough to actually see the wall. It was a large work of bricks as long as I was tall. It stood fifty feet tall and spanned the entire city. A monstrous stone monolith rose into the sky from the center of the city. Had to be the rock the place was named after. We decided to camp for the night and head in tomorrow.

I was feeling restless—we all were—so I took first watch with Jaken.

We talked about how much we missed our kids. His little girl Luna was supposed to have her first birthday party soon. With the theoretical time dilation between our worlds, he could make it back in time. I had to admit, I was proud of him. He loved that little girl so much that it was almost like a disease. It was contagious. Made you want to love her too. We joked about the time I was changing her diaper, and she peed on my arms.

Good times.

Fog had begun to roll in, and by the time our shift was over, it was pretty thick. We hadn't had a fire because we wanted to have some say in who knew our position. Didn't want to attract any unsavory folks, did we? I did Kayda the favor and put her into the collar around my neck. Her form began to blur and turn into shadow, then filtered into the gem. The fog was dry but chilling, and I shifted into my panther form, hoping I could see better and stay a little warmer. It worked a bit; the dull grey around me cleared a little, and the fur warmed me more than my own but not as much as I hoped. I huddled under my blanket and napped a bit after Bokaj took over. Tmont leaned against him, watching his back.

"So we get in and speak to some witnesses about what has been taking the citizenry," I outlined while we ate a light breakfast the next morning. "From there, we scour the place for signs of War's minion as quickly as possible to try and help these guys out. These are people being taken, so it's gonna get rough fast—we ready for that?"

"If they're anything like the Wolves, Skeletons, and whatnot that we fought before—they aren't human anymore." Jaken shrugged. "Maybe we'll get lucky, and the minion will be as easy as the last one but with people in the same state as those animals? Fuck man."

The understanding of that hit us pretty hard, so we packed up in silence and began to close in on the city. The light fog couldn't hide the city's outline from us, so it wasn't like we could get lost. After walking a couple hours, we made it within a hundred yards of the gate to the city.

A large crowd gathered at the gate and stood in near silence. As we walked closer, the crowd parted. There, in the center of the gate, stood a sharply dressed man with a goatee, perfectly coiffed blond hair, and dark eyes. He was of medium height, slight build, and wore what looked like a tuxedo. He had a small child in front of him with a hand resting on his shoulder. The child looked to be around four or five years old.

"Ah, the guests of honor!" he exclaimed amicably. His voice was like that of a practiced showman. "Do come closer, please. I would hate to have to yell at you the entire time we entreat."

We looked at each other but obliged, Jaken taking the lead. With him stepping in front of me, I could see the people around us; they looked terrified.

We stopped a good ten feet away, easy speaking distance.

"I expected nothing less of assassins." The man grinned at us.

"Who are you?" Jaken asked.

"Oh, do forgive me!" He corrected himself in mock disappointment, "Where are my manners. My actual title is Blight, General of his Eminence War, may he conquer all the stars in the sky. You may, however, call me... Rowan, or at least, the host you see before you used to be called that. I have come to speak with you personally. See, it was most impressive that you took care of my minion to the east. Most impressive, indeed, and I assumed you came here expecting to find another? I think you will find that your information was somewhat skewed. As a General, I have an offer."

Jaken gripped his sword and settled into an easy fighting stance.

"Ah-ah," Rowan warned, his hand tightening on the child in front of him. The little boy whimpered a bit but didn't scream. "Wouldn't want anyone here to suffer needlessly, would we?"

"Jaken, ease down, bud. Let him talk," I advised my friend. There was no play to be had here. My friends could snipe this guy easily, but if we started swinging blades and slinging spells, people would be caught in the crossfire.

"One of you seems to see sense." He eased up on the kid but didn't let go. "Where was I? Ah, my offer. Leave me and my brothers alone to do our work, and we will spare your own planet." One of us gasped, but I couldn't tell who. I know I looked surprised. "Yes, don't look so surprised. I know all about you. Why you were brought here, what you intend to do. That you may even stand a chance at defeating me, laughable as that is. Do you actually believe that? Sorry, I mean no insult, just truth."

"Why would we ever believe what you say?" Yohsuke asked. He had his left hand on his astral adaptor and his right hand ready to cast.

"Because I have the authority to make such a promise," he said as if it were the most obvious thing in the universe. "Really think about it. Given time, I could take you back to your world, and you could be with your families again, your other friends—safe, sound, sane, and with the knowledge that we will leave you be. All you have to do is stand down. My brothers and sister will awaken in their own time, much like I did, and we will bring order to this chaotic, disgusting planet. That doesn't sound so bad, does it?"

So, the other Generals were still asleep? *You guys believe this guy?* I asked through our earrings.

Fuck no, answered Yohsuke and Bokaj at the same time.

He's full of shit, man. They're coming for all of us, Balmur said angrily.

"Let us think about it for a second?" I asked as if I actually believed him.

"Take your time, please. I know you will see the wisdom of this deal." He smiled like an indulgent father.

Bokaj, Balmur, you guys ready if this goes tits up?

Yup! I have an arrow nocked with his name on it, broskie.

I can shadow step, too, maybe nab the kid while he's distracted.

Solid plans, stand by. Jaken, bud, keep it cool and conversational. We need him to think he has control.

Okay, man. This guy sucks. I can feel the evil from here. Bokaj, let me know when to move, and I'll clear your line of fire.

Got you, fam.

"You can get us home?" Yohsuke said after a moment. "Back to my wife?"

"I can," Rowan said smoothly. "Given a little time to look into the spells they used to get you here, I could."

"I'm about it guys. I miss my wife. Don't you guys miss your kids?"

"Yeah," I said. "He's all I've got, man. I don't really like it here. Too many people look at me funny, and I miss pizza."

We started to walk forward a bit, Yohsuke just behind and to my right, trying to obstruct his view of my stealthier friends.

"You see reason," he said as he lifted his free arm.

NOW! Bokaj shouted into our minds.

The rest of us stepped to the side, and a flaming arrow shot straight toward his right eye. Balmur stepped out of the shadows and waited for the arrow to connect with its target.

But it never did. The arrow stopped mid-flight—a foot away from the General—and clattered onto the stony ground.

"As I said, woefully unprepared," he said with a sigh. "Oh well. So much for doing this the easy way."

The boy in front of him cried out in pain, and blood began to seep from his eyes like tears. Just as the first drop of crimson hit the ground beneath his feet, his head exploded, spattering all of us in gore.

"Begone." He raised his hand, covered in blood and vibrant crimson magic, in a flippant dismissive wave. I heard a *pop* like a cork being popped, and my sight went black.

Warning!
You are now leaving this realm of existence. Goodbye.

Chapter Twenty-Five

I tried to take a breath and scream; no sound escaped, and no air came in. My insides felt crushed, and the pressure around me threatened to pull me apart as if I was being sucked through a giant straw.

Bits of grey and white flecked into my vision and began to speed past my sight.

Nothing.

Sometime later, I woke up, vomited, and tried to get my bearings. The first thing I noticed was that the waist-high grass was purple and green as it swayed in the breeze. Second, I noted that my friends were in their own respective positions, sitting up groggily.

"The fuck happened?" Jaken groaned. I heard retching off to my right and saw Balmur stand, just taller than the grass around him.

"We got our asses handed to us, and that kid paid the price for it," I growled.

I could see him, his brown eyes pleading, begging for help, his sandy brown hair, fair skin, and freckles stained crimson by bloody tears. My eyes stung with unshed tears, and my cheeks began to burn.

"Don't let it get you, man," Yohsuke said softly from behind my right shoulder. "He died—that's on us—but it's that fucker's fault. He's gonna pay, and the price will be his life."

I didn't trust my voice at that moment, so I just nodded.

We were all standing, bloody and gross. I summoned Kayda and had her fly above us and scout for water. She found a lake off to the rear of us, about half a mile away, so we started walking. The grass around us swayed on, at times seemingly moving out of the way. The lake was serene. The water was calm and crystal clear, trees behind it about thirty feet or so back. A perfect spot from some kind of fantasy novel or movie.

Once we came to the water, we knelt to clean ourselves up. As soon as I was about to dip my hands into the water, a cold spout hit me right on the tip of my muzzle.

"That's not yours!" a small voice squeaked at me. I looked and saw a little blue head bobbing in the water before me. It looked like a little person, but the head was like that of a dolls. The eyes were a deep blue, and its lips were set in a scowl.

"Forgive me," I said. My friends had met similar opposition.

"What did it say?" Jaken asked.

"That the water isn't our's," I responded. "Wait, you can't understand them?"

Everyone but Balmur shook their heads. I looked back at the indignant blue creature and sat on the ground.

"I'm Zekiel," I said warmly. "These are my friends, and we're a bit lost. Could you tell me where we are?"

The blue creature put his hands out of the water, pulled himself out as if it were solid ground, and sat atop it. He regarded me critically for a moment, then shrugged and must have decided I meant no harm.

"This is Harmasker's End," he said, motioning to the side we were on. "Nasty place to be, if you ask me. What are you doing here?"

"We don't know. A bad man sent us here."

"Oh? How did he send you? Was there blood of the innocent involved?" the little creature asked, jumping to his feet.

I nodded, and he hung his head. "I was afraid of that. You have been banished here, to Faerie."

"What's Faerie?" asked Balmur. I hadn't heard him come over. I repeated his question when our little friend just stared confused. I made the guess he didn't speak the common tongue.

"Faerie is the plane of the Fae. All Sylvan, Fae and Elves began here before crossing to Prime a millennia ago."

"I see. Is there a way for us to get back?" I asked. As I was speaking to the creature in Sylvan, Balmur translated to the others.

"I dunno." The Fairy shook his head, crossing his arms.

"Do you know someone who might?"

He thought a bit and brightened up. "Yes!"

"Can you take us to them?"

"No."

"Can you tell us where they are?"

He nodded.

"Okay, where?"

"What will you do for me?" The Fairy looked at me expectantly.

"What?"

"Everything has a price here in Faerie. If you want information, you pay for it."

"Okay, I'll bite. What do you want?" I rolled my eyes.

"A certain beast has been drinking our water but is too large for us to stop on our own. If you can either kill it or scare it off, I will tell you where to get the information you seek."

"What kind of creature is it?" Bulmar asked.

"A Fel-Hog. Huge beastie. The lot of you together might be able to get it, though."

"Okay. Is there water around here where we can clean up?" I motioned to the blood and dried gore on my person, and the little man rolled his eyes dramatically.

He asked, "None of you have magic?"

I had a headache after the epic facepalm moment. I spent the mana to summon my Water Sphere. We all reached into it and pulled water out of it to clean our faces and gear. We got what we could from our shirts, those of us without armor, but I just opted to burn my clothes. Blood was all over them, and I needed to feel clean again.

I pulled another set of clean clothes from my inventory, a dark blue shirt and a pair of simple, black trousers, and put them on after I was clean. The little people had gone except our little friend. While the others continued cleaning themselves, I went in for more information. Like a direction of travel.

He pointed and said, "It's that way, north and into the forest. I don't know where it holes up, but you'll recognize it when you see it. And do mind the trees."

"Okay. I'm sorry, but you never told me your name."

"Names have power, Zekiel." He emphasized my name. "You haven't earned the right to call me by anything yet. Prove yourself with this, and I might be inclined to give you a name."

Quest Alert

Hog Wild – This tiny Fae has asked you to either kill or drive off a Fel-Hog who has been drinking their Lake's water if you can.

Isn't that wild?

Reward – Information and ??? EXP.

Unknown experience? That was odd, but oh well, it had to be done, so let it be done.

We finished cleaning ourselves and our gear while we laid out a basic plan. We had options on this kind of quest, and avoiding bloodshed after what we just witnessed was on all of our minds. So I would attempt to speak with our target while the others followed at an easy distance. If things went well, the beast would leave. If things went to hell, well, I could at least count on my friends to get there to save my bacon. Hopefully.

After a few minutes of walking, Bokaj caught the trail that we would need to follow to find the Hog. Broken twigs and branches brought attention to the hoof-made grooves in the ground where the animal made multiple trips a day to get fresh water. We followed the path for about ten or fifteen minutes or so while keeping the tracks in sight and eventually came to a large entanglement of trees that seemed to form a den. The roots formed a gaping entryway that seemed dark at first, but as I watched, the light seemed to filter into it a little.

I nodded to my friends and stepped forward until I was about halfway between my friends and the entrance. I activated Nature's Voice and shouted, "Hello?"

Nothing for a moment, then a rustle off to my right. I turned and crouched a bit, ready to spring out of the way. A bush began to shift and rise as a pig-like snout cleared the ground and snuffed. The bush continued to rise, and soon, a large, four-foot-tall swine that had to weigh hundreds of pounds was staring at me with brown eyes. Brown tusks, thick and powerful, jutted out from its mouth that looked like small trees that had just begun to sprout. Green moss grew on its sides and forehead over skin pitted with stones and bark. The creature looked like it was meant to live in a forest. Made of the forest itself.

It looked strong, and I noticed that I couldn't see a level attached to it. Come to think of it, I hadn't seen one for the little Fae either. Weird.

"Hi," I said as I tried to force myself to relax.

"You speak to me?" she asked. Her voice was distinctly light and feminine for such a large, porcine figure.

"Yes, we came to ask you a favor. I know you don't know me, but just hear me out."

"Okay."

That was easy. "The Fae who guard the lake you go to say that you are bothering them. They want me to hurt you. Yes, hurt you, to make you leave. I don't want to hurt you. Could you move on? Maybe find somewhere else to get water?"

"I like here, though," she said as she raised her head. "Places to hide. Food. Water for all, not just little folk." She snuffed the air a bit. "Bring friends?"

"Yes. They're back there. We didn't know if you would be mad about me trying to get you to leave, so they stayed back a bit to give us space to talk."

"Friends nice. No friends here. Lost here." She was sad. I could feel it.

An idea hit me, and I wanted to go over it with my friends really quick.

"Do you want to meet my friends?"

She stilled and eyed me for a minute. "Not hurt?"

"We won't hurt you. I give you my word."

As soon as I made the promise, a weight settled on my chest for a moment, and a notification screen popped into sight.

ALERT!

You have made a promise here in the realm of the Fae. One's word is their bond, and if broken, can have disastrous effects.

Choose your words carefully here, young friend.

One of the Gods must have been looking out for me on that one. Holy shit. I tried not to break my word once given, but this was just insane.

"Come on out, guys. She's cool." I turned my head to call back to them. "No weapons."

Everyone came forward slowly, and she regarded everyone for a moment, then stepped forward slowly. She stopped at each of us and snuffed at our chests. Learning our scents, she admitted when I asked her.

"I'm thinking we take her back to the lake and try to talk things out with the little protectors. I thought of something they said, and I think I can make it work."

"Have her act as a guardian or something?" Balmur suggested, completing my thought.

"Bingo."

"I like it," Jaken said. He reached out slowly and patted the pig on the head with his gauntleted hand.

I asked the pig what she thought, and she agreed, pleased at the concept of having a home and friends.

We made our way back to the lake, the pig—I needed a name for her, but somehow, Bacon and Babe just didn't seem cool—led us to it. She and I spoke for a bit; I had to re-up my spell, but it was a good chat. Gave us time to plan.

She cleared the tree line before we did, and I heard the little folk begin shouting out commands to battle stations. I sprung forward with my hands raised. "STOP!"

A dozen bows lowered slightly, but I felt two stings on my left palm that almost dropped me to my knees. I looked, and there were two toothpick-sized arrows sticking out of my palm. A third of my health was gone from two tiny arrows. Fuck me, if they had all fired at once, I would have been a dead man. I pulled the arrows out, a couple more points of health off, and healed myself. My magic felt denser than normal, but that could wait to be investigated.

"Why is it here?!" screeched the same little Fae that had given me the quest. "You mean to kill us all and take our lake? NEVER! SCOUNDRELS!"

"SILENCE!" I roared as little voices began to raise in alarm again. "No one needs to die. I bring you a proposal."

The little negotiator leapt onto the water and raised his own bow, arrow nocked and aimed loosely in my direction. He stayed quiet and nodded to me to speak.

"She's lost. Alone and afraid. You all said that you couldn't dissuade her from drinking of your lake. What if she were to help defend it in times of need? Like another guardian. All you would have to do is share your water with her, and she would happily be your ally. What do you say? Can you do it?"

"No," he said flatly. "We asked you to get rid of her because we didn't want to share our water, not for you to make bargains and deals. Get rid of it."

"No," I said just as flatly.

"You don't want your information? Fine. Stay banished."

"Okay. I keep my word. I and none of my friends will harm her, so if she decides to decimate your ranks and take the lake, so be it. Later." I waved and turned away to walk back into the forest. I hoped my plan would work. If only Bokaj could speak for us; his Charisma was the shit.

That's when I heard the snuff and angered oinks of my newest friend. I heard her ripping at the ground beneath her hoofed feet. She let out a screech and charged at the lake. Once I was safely behind the trees, I turned and watched it unfold. True to what I had said, she didn't feel a single thing as the little projectiles bounced off her hard skin. She lowered her head and brought it to the side, sending a group of little people flying out of the water.

"Aim for her eyes!" shouted one. I waited long enough.

I popped back out into the open, off to the side so as not to take an errant arrow, and once more made my presence known, "Enough!"

The little ones stopped again but didn't lower their bows. "You are a betrayer!"

"No, I'm not. We agreed to exchange services. If—and you said if—I could get her to go away or kill her, you would give me information. I didn't want to kill her, so I didn't. I also didn't drive her away from the only place she knows when she could have bettered your defense of this lake which is what you really seemed to need. I tried to give you that, and she was willing to be a part of the team, but you attacked her. You attacked *me*. Now I'm not quite certain you ever meant for us to come back for the information."

He huffed and stomped his little foot. A drop of water plopped up and onto the top of it, and if the situation wasn't as tense as it was, I might have laughed at the ridiculousness of it all. Somehow, I think that might really have pissed him off, so I kept my bearings.

"I just wanted it gone!"

"Here's a question: what is so important about this lake?" I asked finally. I had to admit I was curious.

"I can't tell you." He crossed his arms. "It's a secret."

"Tell you what, if you can give me a satisfactory answer—one that I can't refute at all—then I will take the Hog and my friends and leave you in peace. The only reason you would see us again is if we just happened to get lost, and, to sweeten the deal, I won't divulge it to anyone else. How does that sound?"

"Your word?" he asked slyly.

I sighed. The little shit—though I couldn't blame him—knew the laws here better than I.

"I swear it." The familiar weight settled on my chest as it had last time.

"Good." He stepped off the water and onto land.

He stepped closer to me, so he wouldn't have to shout the secret—I thought, anyway—and the big animal by my side huffed threateningly.

"It's okay, dear," I cooed. I patted her solid side and waited.

"This water is sacred to my tribe. Drinking it or bathing in it allows the creature who partakes to live longer. It grants strength and recovery. It's what keeps my tribe strong and healthy. If we don't care for it and use it wisely, it's gone. We protect it to protect ourselves. That's why this beast is so strong. She's drank the water. Bathed in it."

"But doesn't that mean she also has a reason to want to protect it? Think about it—you would have an almost unstoppable protector to fight beside you to keep creatures from getting to the water long enough for you to defeat them. All she wants is friendship and a little water. Some place to belong."

He seemed to mull it over a bit. "What you say makes sense, and as captain of the Lake Guard, I can approve it. She just drinks so much!"

"Do you have spell casters? Does it rain here?"

He shook his head. "Our casters reside with our queen, and rain is rare."

"Do you have a large basin?" I looked around, but the little creature just shook his head. "No. I'll see if I can't do something. Give me a little bit."

I racked my brain for a little while. In some of the stories I had heard as a kid, in all the books I read and games I had played, there were objects that made water. Drinkable water. What if I tried it myself?

"Hey, guys, I'll need some stones about fist size or larger. Find at least ten. I don't know how many I might need."

They set to their part, and I set about mine.

I walked away from the lake, about forty feet, and began to draw a large circle with my great dagger. I'd need to do some maintenance on it later but no biggie. Once the circle was about two feet in diameter, I shifted into my bear form and began to carefully dig it out until it formed a bowl a foot deep at the center. While I did that, the rocks piled up behind me. I shifted back and used my diamond claw ability to carefully cut the rocks down into flat and rectangular or square shapes. After that was done, I pressed them into the ground inside the hole I made, snuggly against each other, kind of like tiles on a floor.

"We have any metal that we don't need? Copper or something?"

The guys checked their inventories and produced a couple pounds of iron that we collected after fighting the Goblin King.

I heated the metal much the same way as I had when I first tried enchanting and used the now-melting iron to seal the cracks between the makeshift tiles. I inspected my work and had both Jaken and Balmur look it over. They found a couple of places that looked like they could reinforce, so I had them guide me while I fixed them.

Once the corrections were made, I used more melted iron to make a small circle on the bottom of the bowl. It was about the size of a fifty-cent piece, and to finish the piece, I embedded a cut sapphire that Balmur provided from his inventory into it so that it laid flush. I spent the mana to summon some Ice Knives to fill the bowl.

While I let the metal cool, I tried to devise an engraving and spell that would make a self-refilling water bowl. Once I thought I had it, I realized I would need one final ingredient.

"Can you give me a drop of the lake water?" I asked the tiny Fae. "I need it to complete this enchantment. You can carry the droplet yourself if you have to, but you'll have to wait until I tell you."

"It will keep her from drinking from our lake all the time?" he asked skeptically.

"If it works, she will only need to drink from the lake itself if the effects aren't permanent. Are they permanent?"

"Sadly, no. They last a few years or so, dependent on the amount of water used."

"Okay, So, you might have to add a drop to it every couple weeks or a month. I'd say bi-monthly just to be safe."

He mulled it over and acquiesced. He brought out a tiny vial and dipped it into the lake. He brought the droplet back and stood silently next to me, eyeing my work with obvious curiosity.

I sat down and cleared my mind, then thought of the engraving. I summoned my mana and went to work. The engraving began at the edge of the basin. Water marks, three symmetrical flowing lines one over the other, sealed the water in so that it would rise to that level and stop. Then a whirling watery spiral worked its way to the base of the structure where it met the heart of the enchantment, the sapphire. On it, I engraved an infinity symbol with a drop of water forming at the center of it. It was there that I had the Fae Commander pour his vial. A single drop of lake water met my mana just as I had almost stopped. I felt the spell swell with power, and water began to rise from the gem. Once it met the seal, it stopped, just as planned. My enchanting leveled up to 27 as well.

"Magnificent," he breathed. He stuck his hand into the water and pulled it out. "It's potable. That's all that matters."

"I'm going to try it out now." I motioned for my hog friend to come over and introduced her to my creation.

She lapped the water up greedily, and once it was almost gone, the basin filled to the seal once more.

"She has all the water she could need," I said. "She won't drain your lake, so will you take her as a protector?"

"We will now. Thank you." He smiled.

The little shit.

Quest completed!

Hog Wild – You went above and beyond to keep your word to both parties. You're alright, kid.

Reward – Information and 1,000 EXP.

"The place you seek is in the north. A village is there, filled with your people. They may be able to give you more information on how to return to the Prime."

"Thank you. Treat your new friend well."

He looked at me in surprise and nodded. "And you want nothing in return for your creation?"

"You have nothing that you can give me but your name, and to be honest, I don't want it if you aren't willing to give it."

"You are an odd creature," he observed suspiciously, "but things must be exchanged here. Good will is hardly ever truly good will, and I will not have you return here to collect some unknown ransom from me because I am indebted to you. Stay here."

He went out onto the water, then came back with something in his hand. "Who among you is the best tracker?"

All of us pointed to Bokaj, who stepped forward with Tmont slinking just behind.

The little creature bid him to kneel, and he stepped forward and threw water in his eyes.

"What the– oh," Bokaj said. "Oh, that's cool as fuck."

"What is it?" Balmur asked.

"It's a map that he just added to my sight. Kinda like our usual ones but this one works specifically for here. I can't read shit on it, but I can tell where we are and where we need to go."

"Sweet, works for me." I looked at the Fae and smiled. "Fair trade."

"Good. Please leave," he said.

The ungrateful little shit.

We patted our big pig friend who was busy greedily drinking from the water basin, but she seemed content.

According to Bokaj, we weren't too far from the village. Maybe more than a few hours depending on our pace, so we decided to try and cover as much ground as we could.

I called Kayda back to me and put her into my collar. There was no telling what hunted in these skies, and I wasn't going to risk her. Hell, there wasn't even a chance for us to use our mounts here just for the simple fact that the whistles didn't seem to be working. Looked like we would be hoofing it.

Near as we could tell, it would have been around noon to mid-afternoon on Prime, so we weren't all that tired physically, just emotionally drained.

Chapter Twenty-Six

We walked for a few hours in relative silence; none of us were really in the mood to eat so we just drove on further. We walked until we had to stop to rest, rested, and had some water, then took up on foot again. After about six hours of walking at a good pace, we reached the marker on the map, but we didn't see anything among these huge trees.

I'm not talking normal sized trees. These were the kind you could drive a car through. Gigantic. As I followed them up toward the sky, I noticed what it was we were searching for. The village.

A series of rope bridges leading to branches grown into homes and pathways high above us. I could see thick rope ladders and pulley systems that had buckets leading to the ground. It was like something straight out of a fantasy book that I had back home.

"Can I help you?" a light voice asked from behind us in Sylvan.

I turned, and there was a Kitsune, her long, chestnut colored fur muted in the dull light under the great trees. She wore leather dyed green and brown like the scenery around us; it fit her well, and I had the feeling she could move swiftly in it as it looked. She was as at home in it as her own skin. She didn't appear to have any weapons on her that I could see. Strange.

"Uhm, please?" I asked. I couldn't smell or hear anything off, so she was legit. "We are new here, and we were looking for information on how to get back home."

"Where is home for you, then?" she asked, her head tilted slightly to the side, like she had heard something we couldn't.

"Prime," I said, hoping that would peak her interest enough to help us.

A look of horror passed over her face, and she looked around wildly before coming toward us. "Go that way, behind you, up into that large bucket to your right behind the fern."

"No. Not until you tell us what has you freaked out. We just met you," I told her matter-of-factly.

"GO! If they don't know you're here by now, they will soon. I'll tell you everything. You have my word!"

A binding contract right there. I relayed her words to my friends, and we beat feet to the bucket she was talking about. As soon as we began to move, the world around us came alive. Archers and stealthier Rogues had moved, and we could finally see them. Dozens of warriors had us surrounded that whole time, and if we had been enemies, we would've all died. Fuck, I hated this place already.

"What's going on?" Balmur asked. The rest of the group looked ready to draw their weapons if needed.

I asked her for him, and she just held a hand out for silence and motioned us to follow her into the bucket. Once we were all inside, she touched the tree and blew on it in a quick puff of air. The bucket began to rise swiftly like a jungle elevator. As we rose into the air, I could see more of the structures in the branches, and it was more of a city than a village. It must have been a long time since the lake Fae had been here. The structures were made entirely of wood, and the figures in the crowds going around them were made of different creatures: Kitsune, Elves, Dryads like the one we had seen before coming across James, and all other manner of strange creatures.

"Where are we?" I asked.

"This is Terra's Escape," she said. Her eyes roamed the horizon line. "Our village isn't a village anymore but a small city.

We like our privacy and newcomers don't just happen by like you all. Who told you of us?"

"The little lake peoples."

"Ugh, Lake Pixies," she grumbled in disgust. I had to admit I felt the same.

Once we got to the right branch, she turned, and I noticed her tail. Then another came into view. And another. She had three tails, all of them as bushy and beautiful as mine. I was dumbfounded. She saw me staring and growled a little. She motioned for us to get out of the bucket and follow her.

We followed her through the crowds, easily keeping up with her because people were staring and moved out of the way when they saw her coming.

We entered a hut with a couple guards posted at the door. They saluted her with a fist over their heart then stared stoically forward.

The hut was sparse with actual furniture, but plants were everywhere: a bed that looked to be made of interwoven vines that grew from the ceiling, a table made from a branch that grew up and laid almost flat at a ninety-degree angle, and the chair was made of wood but not grown. Our guide turned and mumbled something to her hut, and the tree beneath us shivered. Wooden bumps rose up, and she motioned for us to sit.

"Forgive me, I did not mean to be inhospitable," she began. "Your arrival here was both unexpected and dangerous for all of us here. I am Farin F'arine, High Druidess of Terra's Escape and speaker for the forest you are now in."

"How is our arrival dangerous to you?" I asked. "Also, do you speak the common Prime tongue?"

"I don't, no." She shook her head. "Although, your Azer friend seems to understand me just fine?" Balmur just smiled at her without comment. "There, he smiled. As to the danger, your arrival could spell a visit from the hunt."

"What hunt? Why?"

"The Wild Hunt. Surely you have heard of it. You're Fae. Did your parents never teach you of your ancestry? The plane from which you came?"

"I never knew my parents." Not technically a lie. This avatar had been created specifically for me. "But I have heard legends and myths in passing from texts and storytellers."

"If you did not know your parents, then how do you speak our tongue?" she asked, and I think I could see the curiosity behind her deep brown eyes. "And what did you hear about them?"

"A gift from a goddess, that they protect the realm from Demons and evil. A horde of creatures that hunt in a pack for things that don't belong?" I said to her.

"The last bit is correct, but they are the evil, not the protectors. They hunt for sport, killing creatures who are banished here, who don't belong. You and your friends have been put into great danger, and being here draws the hunt. If they haven't gotten your scent by now, they will soon. Why did you come?"

"We were looking for information to get us back to the Prime plane."

"The only creatures strong enough to get you back are the queens—the Seelie and the Unseelie."

"Wait, who is the leader of the Seelie Court? They're the good Fae. They would help us."

"Where did you ever get such an idea?" She actually balked and rolled her eyes at me. "The leader of the Seelie Fae has the Hunt out looking for things that don't belong. She's the reason you're going to die, just for her entertainment, and the

Unseelie Queen? She's insane. She might just kill you for breathing. You're in trouble. We all are. You need to leave. Now."

"Can't you help us?" Balmur asked, and I relayed his request.

"If you will leave, I will do what I can. Is there a magic user among you who favors nature?"

I stepped forward. "I'm a Druid, like yourself."

"Excellent, lean forward." I bent at the waist, and she put her right hand on my head. "This will hurt."

"Wha–?" Then my entire being was pain. Searing, blinding light swept through my mind, and I felt something in me shatter as my knees buckled.

For the second time this day, all was darkness.

I awoke to see the Druidess above me frowning. "I did not know that would happen. Are you well?"

I grunted and raised myself up onto my elbows; my brain throbbed a bit, and my backside ached as well. I could see that I had some notifications to sort through, but my sudden cottonmouth was a little more pressing.

"Could use a drink." She bustled off to grab something from outside.

I opened my notifications quickly and looked through them.

CONGRATULATIONS!

The following racial trait has been unlocked for you.

Nine Tails Bloodline – As a Kitsune grows in strength, their blood may awaken to the power of their ancestors who sported multiple tails. Each tail signaled growth of abilities, statistics, or other unknown traits. The results and gifts will vary from individual to individual.

You have gained one extra tail for a total of two (2) tails.

Please choose one spell from current or previous spells that you did not pick. The spell will become permanently learned by you.

CONGRATULATIONS!

You have been bestowed Druidic knowledge specific to the realm of the Fae.

Fae Heart – Grants a measure of favor and control over nature in the Fae Realm, such as the forests and animals.

Fae Shape – Fae Druids naturally tap into the ability to take the form of their realm's animals and beasts. This ability has been passed on to you. It works the same way as normal Shapeshifting, but you can turn into Fae creatures now, too.

By the time I had read these through the second time, Farin had returned with a wooden cup of water. I drank it down and thanked her.

I chose my spell, Mass Regrowth. It was basically just an AoE heal that I had passed up originally because of the steep cost of mana, one-fifty MP a pop. I had wanted Heal at the time. This would help take pressure off our Paladin a bit, I hoped. Besides, I had other tricks up my sleeve now too after my last level.

"Thank you." I heard a groan, and Bokaj was getting up off the ground. She must have given him something too as a Ranger.

"You may not live long enough to repay me, so I ask you this—leave. Now. So that my people aren't slaughtered while they search for you."

"Done," I said. "Can you tell us where to go to get to the Unseelie Court?"

"Keep traveling north until the cold surrounds you. There, they will find you. Go."

I nodded to her, and then we all piled out the door. I reached back and felt my rump—boom! Two tails. Oh yeah.

"Tails lookin' ass," Yohsuke muttered at me. "Think you can fly?"

We had neared the edge of the branch near the bucket we had used to get up in the first place, and I saw that there was a branch below us about ten feet down. If this didn't work, I'd land there. For now? Time to play.

"Only one way to find out." I smiled at him and stepped off.

I dropped and activated my Nature's Hidden Path spell. I felt the wood on my leg. Then I was inside the tree as if it were an elevator you might see in a cartoon. I willed myself to the bottom of the tree where the bucket would land and stepped out to wait.

My friends came down in the bucket moments later. Yohsuke was smiling at me, and then I felt a blunt force hit me on the shoulder. I turned to see that Balmur had snuck up on me. Both mumbled something to the effect of me being a smart ass.

We nodded to the Druidess and left them in peace. All we knew was that we needed to go north until it got cold.

"One last thing," she said as we made to leave. "Mind the night. Nasty creatures call the night their home here in the forest. Nastier than even the nastiest day walker. Be careful, and good luck."

"Alright, thanks," I replied, following up to the party in Common, "Come on, guys. Let's get gone before they decide to put an arrow in us and be done with it."

We waited until we were well away from the city to speak again, and even then, we spoke through our earrings just to be safe. I informed the party about what I had gotten, and Bokaj told us that he had received a similar ability.

And so, we walked. By this time, our appetites had returned, so we ate and rested for a little bit and kept going. After a few more hours, dusk settled in, and we decided that sleeping on the ground was not in our best interests. The forest around us had begun to fall silent, and we wanted to be above whatever had made the insects and exotic-looking birds soften their life sounds.

I let Kayda out of the necklace, and she perched in the branches above us. I touched Yohsuke with it, and his form sifted into the stone before I used Nature's Hidden Path to get to a wide branch that he and I would share. The others managed to get to their own within easy reach of ours. We laid down with Jaken and Balmur taking first watch.

Chapter Twenty-Seven

We spent most of our time walking north. At one point, a large ursine creature—built like a bear who took steroids with every meal—with striped brown and white fur, crossed our path. That first battle was rough, though. The thing easily dwarfed my hulking thousand-pound dire-bear bulk. Jaken and I had to distract it while the others ganged up on it. Eventually, Yohsuke and Bokaj decided to try something new.

Bokaj peppered the thing's snout with arrows, and when it roared in anger at him, Yoh threw his Star Burst spell into its mouth. Its chest expanded like it was about to burp, and it actually breathed a small flame before dropping lifelessly to the ground. It gave us a really good chunk of experience, and I was also able to collect the animal as a form I could take. With this, I would be hard pressed to want to take my Dire Bear form. Bokaj set about skinning it.

"Does the skin have a name?" Yoh asked before I could.

"Ursolon," he said. "The hide is ridiculously tough, and these teeth are massive and sharp. A few of these hides, and we might be able to make better armor for our stealth and caster types."

"If we do run across any more, sure, I'm down," I said. "Besides, with that little secret play, how the hell can we lose? Good thinking with that spell to the mouth man."

"I figured it couldn't hurt to try it." He shrugged. "It's basically just a grenade spell. You swallow a grenade, splat. Same concept here."

"Smooth, man, real smooth." Jaken held his fist out for a bump. We rested a moment then continued on.

We still couldn't see the names or levels of creatures here on anything. Was it because of the secretive nature of this entire plane that these things were hidden? I guess we would just have to gauge our fights on possible or not and work out how to run, if we could, on the fly.

With the new form I had and the closeness of the humongous trees in the area, I was going to wait to play with it. I would be too large to fight something else that size and have my friends be effective in the confined spaces.

We traveled for another day in relative peace. We only saw two more Ursolons, and only one of them attacked us, so we had killed two in our time here. When we set up camp that second night, we didn't want to risk a full fire out in the open with us potentially being hunted, so I built up a wall around the flames and under the skillet. The construct helped hide the light, but the smoke had to escape. There wasn't much we could do about that.

The meat simmered as we sat in companionable silence, the night creatures making their normal noises. Once dinner was done, we ate and climbed into the trees once more. Tonight, I took first watch, along with James. He and I sat back to back a little way away from the sleeping and meditating members of the group. I watched the smaller branches move in the slight breeze. The air was crisp, not quite cold, but you knew we were heading in the right direction. At least, I hoped.

"Do you miss it?" James asked after a little while.

"Miss what, brother?"

To which he replied simply, "Home."

"Yeah. Yeah, I do," I said with a sigh. "Even knowing that there's supposed to be this time dilation where time moves so much faster here than there, I can't help but think about what's going on at home with my boy. I can't help worrying that he's growing up without me and that I've unknowingly become my father. There one day, then gone the next. I'm pretty sure Jaken feels the same."

"I hear you," he said.

"How're you holding up?"

"I'm okay. I mean, I miss my fiancée," he said. "Like, a lot. This is every gamer's dream! Even with the unknowns, this is what we've always done—you, me, and Yoh. Having you guys here makes it easier."

"I feel the same way, man. I'm glad to know you guys have my six."

"Same. Shit." He stopped. "No noise, something's close. I'll put out the all-call."

"Go ahead." I scanned the area in front of me and started trying to catch any kind of information I could. The moon, full thankfully, provided a lot of light. I couldn't see anything or hear anything out of the norm. A breeze blew from my right shoulder, and I caught a scent I had smelled before earlier on in the day. It was a muskier scent, stronger than earlier. *Telepathy only now, guys. Get ready. Whatever it is I caught the scent on your side, James.*

Tmont caught it too, Bokaj thought to us. *She thinks that whatever it is, it's close and that it is watching us. No sudden movements.*

Chances are good that it has caught that something is up. Bokaj, you and I are going to get up and walk over to Zeke and James. Act like it's a watch changeover. You guys come over toward us and see if you can catch something on your way over.

Got it, we answered.

Jaken sat up and yawned a genuine yawn before standing and tapping Bokaj. They stood and walked over to us. I stood and stretched a bit, trying to casually catch a glimpse of anything I could. Nothing yet.

"Have a good watch, guys," James said. We bumped fists and tried to keep a fluid and relaxed exchange going.

As we walked over to our spots, James and I laid down, but Yohsuke got up and made a show of stretching and scratching his neck. He walked over to the ledge closest to the direction I caught the scent of... well you know, business.

Got eyes on. Sixty feet out, yellow eyes. Bokaj, if you aim right at me from where you are and adjust for sixty extra feet? You got it, broskie. Stay still, and give'em a show.

For a tense second, we heard nothing, then a growling yelp from the spot where our observer was. The creature leapt out into the open and onto the same large branch we were on.

Before us stood a seven-foot-tall Werewolf with grey and white fur. Its slavering jaws were open with razor-sharp teeth bared in pain; it snarled at us as it walked forward. It pulled the arrow out of its chest, and the projectile clattered to the ground.

"Well, that wasn't nice," it growled in the common Prime language that we all understood. "Downright rude for a guest in someone else's territory."

"Look, we didn't know this was someone's territory," Bokaj said.

Here's hoping that high Charisma came in handy.

"Oh? Well that sounds like a personal problem." It chuckled bestially. "One that you may not survive."

Here went nothing, "We're trying to get as far as we can before the Wild Hunt catches our trail."

"The Hunt is a worthy opponent. Running is smart, but running through our territory wasn't. You'll pay for that."

"What's to stop us from destroying you right now and moving on?" Jaken asked. I was kind of taken aback to hear him suggest that, but hey, desperate times.

"Try it." The beast held its arms out. "The Pack is here, all around you. I wondered how long it would take for you to notice me, but I wasn't expecting it to be so soon. Who was it that found me?"

Yohsuke stepped forward a bit. The beast gave him a nod of what seemed like respect.

"If the pack is here, then where is the alpha?" I asked. This place was starting to wear on my damn nerves.

"I *am* the alpha."

Bullshit. "Fuck you. No alpha worth his salt would be caught dead talking to an unknown enemy right out of the gate. That's why you were watching us, to see if you could find out what we can do."

More eyes off to our right, Bokaj informed us.

Left and behind him where he was, too. Looks like he wasn't lying about the Pack being here, Balmur supplied.

"So, where's your boss?" I asked.

"Clever," whispered a voice behind me. I turned to see an even larger Werewolf less than a foot away from me.

It stood at almost eight and a half feet tall and was powerfully built with silvery-white fur. It looked at me intently with red eyes that shone in the light of the moon. They seemed to glow.

Fuck, I thought and got ready to fight. I couldn't get away by leaping back due to our first guest.

Anybody catch this thing coming in? I asked.

Everyone just shook their heads. Double fuck.

"How is it that someone banished from Prime knows so much about how an alpha might act?" it asked.

"I know things," I said. "We all do."

"Clearly," the Werewolf behind me said.

"You may go now, omega. You did well enough." I heard a snuff, then a clattering of claws.

"So, this is your territory. What do we have to do to leave it?" I asked. "Unharmed."

"Again, clever," it said. With its lips pulled back like they were, it looked like the creature was smiling. "You've been killing in our territory—that cannot be allowed."

"Look, we didn't know, okay?" Bokaj spoke up. He had lowered his bow, but an arrow was at the ready.

"Ignorance is hardly bliss here." It shrugged. "I cannot show the weakness that just letting you go would imply."

"We clearly got off on the wrong foot here," I said. I stepped closer to the alpha and offered it my hand. "I'm Zekiel. These are my friends, and we were banished here."

It looked at my extended hand before reaching out with its own clawed hand. The alpha's grip was surprisingly gentle, even if the hand engulfed my own.

"You may call me Pastela. I am the Alpha of this pack, and I have been since I took it from my lazy mate. He lacked vision. I do not."

"And what is this vision?" Balmur asked.

"To see my people thrive," she growled. "We will grow our numbers until we can contend with the world outside the forest. Then we do what we want. Starting with killing those who hunt us."

"And who would that be?" asked Jaken.

"The Little Folk and the Seelie Fae," she explained. "While we respect the Hunt, the bitch who holds the leash needs to die."

"We seem to be at odds with the Seelie Court as well. What, with them hunting us and all. Let us be on our way and deny them the pleasure of seeing their prey fall to the Wild Hunt," Bokaj reasoned.

"A sound rebuttal to what I said, Ice Elf," she nodded, "but no."

She held her hand up and clenched her fist. The yellow eyes around us swept out from the limbs of the other trees like a tidal wave of fur. I couldn't tell what everyone else was doing, but I was going out swinging.

I cast a Fireball at the fuckers swarming from my right. The explosion knocked me backward a foot, and I almost lost my balance. I saw a large, white-clawed hand swipe at me, and then I was unconscious.

* * *

When we came to sometime later, we were in a cave behind a cell door, like the metal bars had been built into the stone itself. Except it wasn't stone, it was wood. I tried to use Nature's Hidden Path, but the wood was dead, no life force to meld mine to and pass through. The bars were much too close together for me to slip through in fox form as well. I could try to bend the bars, but that would make too much noise, and I had this nagging feeling that I was being watched.

"You are awake," a deep voice rumbled from behind me. I turned to find another set of bars. They were about seven feet away from each other, like a double-sided cage. There stood a man. No, an Elf with a wild look about him. His hair was matted, and his face handsome but dirty and scarred.

"The mistress will be pleased." He turned and began to walk away.

"Where am I?" I tried to keep the building panic out of my voice. "Where are my friends? Let me the hell out of here."

He just ignored me as he walked on. I decided to take the opportunity to observe my surroundings. The 'cave' I was in was small. Two entrances, a ten-foot ceiling, and I was alone. So there either had to be more nearby, or I had been isolated for a reason. It mustn't have been too long because the moon was still in the sky.

They took everything I had been wearing while I was out, and I stared down at my nearly-nude body. At least they had left me some small clothes. I had my inventory still and my old weapons, but they wouldn't be ideal in this environment.

A short while later, after I had decided against trying to escape until I knew where my friends were, Pastela sauntered into view.

"Good, you're awake." She grinned, flashing her sharp fangs in the moonlight. "The time has come for you to join the pack. Your friends have all failed to turn, so I am curious to see if you will."

"What?!" I asked in shock. "What do you mean, failed to turn?"

"Are you stupid?" she asked after looking at me. "Did I break your mind when I hit you?"

"Answer my question first."

She chuckled, "They failed to turn. The Fae-Orc because his Goddess protected him from the gift. The Azer Dwarf because the gift burnt up as soon as it was given. Hurt one of my betas, too. The dark one... none would bite him, not even I. Dragon blood dominates all when in combination with Fae magics, so the Dragon Elf wasn't so blessed to take the gift. The marksman, he was actually clever enough to escape. Some of the pack is out hunting him as we speak. That leaves you."

As she was explaining, I felt a presence behind me. I turned to see a Dwarf, well muscled and scarred, and a human, wiry and also scarred. I was beginning to sense a pattern here. They stood safely on the other side of the bars, so I didn't pay them too much mind. My attention was on the bitch in front of me.

"Your friends will make excellent slaves and playthings. After they break like these ones did, we will gather more to join our cause. Then we will sweep over the Fae realm like a cleansing fire." She smiled at me sweetly, then touched the wall beside her on the right. "Bring him."

I hadn't heard the bars fall into the ground, but two pairs of iron-like hands grasped both my arms and carried me forward. The bars between the alpha and I lowered silently with another press of her clawed fingers in a groove I hadn't seen before, and then she led the way outside of my wooden cage.

Once we stepped out, I realized we were close to the ground in the middle of a huge clearing. It was the size of a football field, and in the middle of all of it was a campsite. An altar in the center on a dais by a roaring fire drew my attention. The thing was six feet long and covered in furs with blood spattered over it.

"I thought you said you were going to turn me?" I berated her for her lie.

"I am. That is the blood of the Bitten. Those who are turned at the altar usually have more control of the gift. Do you prefer I bite you here and now and see how the change affects you?"

I shut my fat mouth before I got myself or my friends killed. This was some bullshit, man. The two men dragged me down the sloping roots of this gigantic, dead tree into the throng of lycanthropes awaiting us. They howled when their leader stepped up onto the dais where the altar was situated. The two slaves kicked the backs of my knees so that I ended up kneeling over the altar with the back of my neck exposed and held my arms out and away from my body. I struggled but didn't budge them much.

I wish I could say that there was some kind of ceremony. That the alpha looked to the sky and offered my blood to the moon in exchange for the 'gift' she hoped for me to claim. I wish I could say that receiving the bite was as romantic as I had hoped for when I was a kid, that I thought that this was going to make things better and put an end to my problems.

Yeah, none of that sappy crap happened.

The thought to shapeshift into my elemental form, any of them, came briefly to mind, but there were dozens of werewolves here, all of them slavering open-mouthed and eager. They wanted me to run. They wanted an excuse to hurt me.

Fuck, they had my friends—if I ran, what would they do to my friends?

I stiffened and fought the urge to break free, and they must have seen it as defiance. I heard a feral growl as not just the alpha but two more creatures bit into my flesh—the white werewolf at the neck, the others on my arms. I couldn't even cry out in anguish because the teeth in the back of my neck were at the base of my skull, and I couldn't move in the slightest. I didn't dare. I was too afraid.

One of the Werewolves must have caught the scent of my fear because instead of letting go of my arm, he started to chew. He shook his head once like a dog with a favorite toy, and teeth in my neck be damned, I growled at the pain. A notification popped up in front of my eyes unbidden, so I read it hoping to distract myself from the pain.

Warning!

You have been cursed with the 'gift' of Lycanthropy. As a lycanthrope, in this case a Werewolf, there are some perks.

+4 to Dexterity, +2 to Strength, Wolf Form, and Hybrid Wolf Form.

The trade off – loss of all magical abilities when shape-shifted due to the curse and increased bloodlust and rage in shape-shifted forms. Intense emotion can cause the curse to take hold and a silver allergy to make you howl. In pain, that is.

Divine Intervention – As one of the Mother's gifted, you can eventually learn to control this curse or be cleansed of it. This is the best that can be done with you in a different plane of existence. Please hurry back.

* * *

Shit. I lost consciousness again. I had fitful nightmares reminiscent of what I had back home.

One where I was a snarling beast, ripping at my cage and anything nearby. Another where I tore into a side of meat that tasted heavenly. Each one tinged by red and hatred so deep and primal that it seemed alien to me. Granted, yes, normally, I'm an angry person in certain circumstances. I have daddy issues. Mommy issues, too. Screw it, let's just chalk it up to issues, okay? Don't judge. But this was unreal.

Sometime later, I woke up with the worst cottonmouth. An earthen bowl was shoved into my face. I took it, sniffed it, and decided I didn't care if it was poisoned. I sipped from it greedily before looking over the rim at my guest. It was a Kitsune, dark colored fur in the shadows of the tree-cave.

"The first change is always the worst." She smiled, but it didn't quite touch her eyes. She had light scarring on her arms where the fur seemed to grow patchier. None on her face, though. "Come."

She made a gesture, and the cell door opened, letting me step out. My body ached, like I'd run ten miles with a hundred pound weight strapped to me. I cast Regrowth on myself, and it seemed to help a little bit.

"Do not do that," she hissed at me. "No magics, or they will attack you. The mistress must give permission first."

"I'll do as I damned-well please," I growled back at her. She flinched, and something in me seemed to stir. Red began to cloud my vision, and I had to stop following her because I was beginning to panic. I felt a thrum through my body, and my back went rigid. It was the change. I closed my eyes and willed my pulse to slow, corralled my anger, and breathed through it. It was something I had learned to do back home on bad days.

After a few minutes of continuous breathing, the red began to recede. It was slow and took a few more minutes, but I didn't flip shit and eat my guide. Good for me.

The woman in front of me stared at me openly for another minute, then turned and motioned for me to follow her to the camp. Once we were amongst the other werewolves, I began to try and take everything in. There were no real buildings except the one we were walking toward, and that was more like a tent. Everyone seemed to be snoozing in the sun, so they were a mainly nocturnal sort of crew. Cool. There was a rather large, wooden structure away from the camp to what felt like east. It was crudely made from what I could make out. I'd have to get closer to find out what it was.

Bad news was that I didn't see my friends anywhere. I had to be discrete about how I observed everything. Otherwise, someone might gather that I was plotting something. Better to appear obedient for now, or at least somewhat. I wasn't going to make this too easy.

As we entered into the tent, more of a pavilion now that I was closer, I saw that most of the werewolves were eying me suspiciously.

Oh boy.

There was a large pile of furs over in the right corner of the roomy tent. There were potted ferns scattered here and there to really home-up the place—probably in an attempt to hide the chains on the floor, too, but you know, whatever. There was a nice brown and green rug that just pulled the whole forest inspired room together. *Very impressive,* I thought to myself sarcastically. I reached up to scratch my ear and realized that they had left my earring on! Yes! I couldn't risk being distracted right now if the Big Bad Bitch of the Wood was here, but later I would be trying my luck.

"How lovely of you to join me so soon." The figure that had been at the desk turned around and smiled at me. It was an Elven woman with alabaster skin so white you'd thought she was made of milk. Her eyes, though, were as red as her werewolf form.

"Pastela," I said with what I hoped was only a mildly venomous tone.

"That's my name." She smiled as she got up.

She walked over to me, nude as the day she was born. I took quick inventory of whether she was armed or not—and she wasn't—so I looked away. Her athletic form burned into my mind in a way that was unusual for me. Not too thin, muscled, and graceful were words that came to mind, and she wasn't so athletic and firm that she was... well, let's just not go there, shall we?

"How did you like the change?" she asked as she stood in front of me. In this form, she was only slightly shorter than I was, and she could easily look into my eyes. "Ah, you don't remember it? You were quite the savage. Injured three of the pack, bled that poor girl who brought you here pretty well, too. I had to heal her myself."

I looked at her, then in alarm as I realized how close she was; she was actually pressed up against me. I could feel her chest against my chest and arm; it made my skin crawl and my mouth go dry all at once. I looked for the woman who had brought me here, but she was gone.

"The slave has other duties to attend to," she said dismissively. "You have some here."

"Look, lady, I don't know where the hell you get off but you will let me and my friends go, or–" I began and started to step forward. The red started to edge my vision, but I was holding it back already.

"Or what?" she asked, her voice a little deeper and huskier all the sudden. "You'll attack me? Would you really? All it would take is a thought, and the whole pack will drop you, then play with your friends as you watch, helpless to stop it. Now, I am a fair Alpha. Unlike my idiot former mate, I don't kill everything that displeases me. I do, however, love to watch the hope leave someone's eyes. It's quite exciting, don't you think?"

She looked at me again, and this time, I recognized the predatory gleam in her eyes. She was enjoying this. I had come in here and done exactly what she knew I would. She was in control, and she knew it. She must have seen my realization because she smiled again and clapped.

"And I didn't even have to order you. Oh good, this will be more fun that I thought." She put her hand on my chest and began to slowly walk around me in a tight circle trailing her hand over my shoulders and back. She was looking me over like I was some kind of challenge. A prize to be mounted... on her wall.

"You are going to help me create a stronger army," she murmured from behind me. I could feel her breath hot on my neck, making my skin crawl again.

"No."

She began to laugh softly and patted my shoulder. "You are going to be fun, Zekiel. Do I need to go get your cute, little Dwarf friend? Oh! Maybe that big, strapping Fae-Orc? He looked like he would do well under my ministrations."

"You leave my friends alone, you crazy bitch," I growled at her. This time, I welcomed the rage.

She walked around to stand in front of me and smiled again; her teeth had begun to look decidedly more wolfish. "Oh-oh." She shook her head. "Can't have that, now can we?"

The burning rage subsided like a bucket of cold water had been dumped over my heart. The red tinge in my vision was gone.

"Mate and agree to teach my army your Druidic skills, or I will beat you until you decide to listen to reason." Her voice was no longer playful but commanding. "No? Fine, like I said before—I do so enjoy seeing the light of hope leave a person's eyes. Be still."

Something took hold of my body, and I couldn't move. I could breathe, and my eyes could move—but I couldn't move. I was resisting mentally with everything I had. In my mind, I was screaming, roaring at my body to move, to fight, to rip her to shreds—anything.

I stood there, unmoving as she stripped me of what little clothing—rags really—that was still on my body. Then she did as she pleased. She arched her clawed hands over my back and chest and bit into my arms and shoulders. At one point, she even lifted me by my throat, and I couldn't breathe. She beat me as many times as she pleased throughout the evening. She looked me in the eyes the entire time, laughing at my fear and pain well into the night.

Eventually, she stopped and chuckled, "Eventually, you will break down and assist me of your own free will. Without your friends as bargaining chips. Who knows—you may find that I am very giving to those who give me what I want."

She brought over one of the chains I had seen in a corner and locked it around my wrist, then my opposite leg. It was attached to the ground by magic, so when her influence wore off, I couldn't break the chains or pull them from the earth. She left the pavilion and me in it, still kneeling in a pool of my own blood. I would think that the lycanthropy would help me recover more, but her injuring me could have been keeping that kind of regeneration from taking hold.

I took a few moments to inventory my body and ensure I had full control of everything. Despite the lycanthropy questions, my natural healing abilities helped me to heal a little, but I was pretty far from okay. I touched my earring, though I didn't need to, and called out for my friends. And I kept calling. Nothing. Not a damned thing.

That meant the possibility of a few things. One, my friends had their items confiscated like mine, and they had simply forgotten to take my earring. Two, they were being held out of range for the magic to work. Three, there was some kind of magic at work in this camp that prevented communication magic. The last thing I could think of was something I didn't want to think of at all.

I heard the howls and cackling laughter of the Werewolves outside, then quiet for a long while. I thought about setting fire to the pavilion, but when I reached for my spells, it was like I was being blocked. So that meant that my theory about something interfering with magic might have some truth to it. I slept fitfully for a few hours, partly in fear of her return and another beating, the other part being the congealing blood on the floor and in my fur stank; it was hard to ignore with my heightened senses.

She returned halfway through the night, her white fur glistened red with the blood of some beast that she had killed. She offered me food, a hunk of bloody meat, but I refused, much to her delight. She gobbled the morsel up then shifted into her Elven form and wiped the blood off with the towel that she had used earlier in the day.

She laid down next to me with a warning, "Touch me in any way that I find even mildly threatening, and I kill one of your friends and cover you in his entrails." At the threat to my friends, my mind blanked and I stilled completely. "Okay? Good boy. Sleep tight!"

Needless to say, I didn't. The next day, the same woman I guess I had attacked came back to grab what she could to clean and bring me food.

"I'm sorry if I attacked you." She nodded and went about her business.

"We don't need to talk to the slaves, dear," Pastela said from her desk. "They know better than to think they rate a conversation."

"Where are my friends?"

"Mmm?" She turned and looked at me. "They're safe for now. I assume you saw that large, wooden structure on your way here? While you were planning your escape? Yes? Okay. They're there. Once a week, we like to have the slaves fight each other or a member of the pack for entertainment. If you're a good boy, I'll take you to see it tomorrow."

    I had to fight the urge to be sick—I swallowed hard—but I knew I just had to bide my time. We needed to get out of here, and I needed my friends to do it.

Chapter Twenty-Eight

I woke up to a tug on my chains from Pastela. "You were exceptionally good last night, so I will keep my word."

When she had been beating me, again, she hadn't had to order me to hold still. I stood there, taking the brutal punishment for refusing her bed and her insidious plans once more. When she had finished, I had to fight to keep my footing, but before I fell to my knees, I looked her straight in the eyes and spat a globule of blood at her. She took great pleasure in licking it off her face with a longer than possible tongue before doing more... delicate work.

I grimaced inwardly at the compliment, remembering how I had almost bitten my tongue off not to scream when she had decided my left arm didn't need the flesh that had been on it. I scowled at her and got up slowly. After she finished, she had taken the manacles off and ordered me not to move. With me free, she healed me, then took her time doing it again. Rinse and repeat. I hadn't been allowed to sleep all night.

She smiled at me, clearly thinking she was breaking me. As a 'reward', she allowed me the decency of my torn trousers. She took the ankle chain off, and I slipped them on. I still had no access to my magic, though. She bent and grasped the base of the chain that attached to the earth and whispered a word. I tried not to look like I heard anything and just stared ahead blankly. She tugged the now freed chain, and off we went.

I stepped outside to cat calls and jeering from the general populace. No big deal there. Maybe I could use that to my advantage somehow? We would see.

It took about five minutes at a decent pace to get to the arena. There was an entrance facing west, large enough to accommodate any in their hybrid forms, that led to some stands that climbed up a few rows. There were only twenty or so wolves in the arena. There were still some searching for Bokaj out there somewhere.

I looked into the pit, only about ten feet down below the bottom row, and saw my friends under an awning. They looked battered and bruised but not broken—as far as I could see.

I breathed a small sigh of relief.

"You didn't believe me?" my jailer pouted.

"Forgive me for doubting a psychotic bitch."

"Forgiven, but just for you," she purred disgustingly. "But the Dark One? He will pay dearly for that. Farlow, the Dark One shall be today's champion. Send in one of the omegas."

A wolf with black fur off to our left complied and dropped into the pit with my friends. They barely took note of him as he used a key to unlock Yohsuke's chains. Yoh stepped out from under the protection of the awning and flipped off Pastela. He saw me, chained and helpless, and gave me a small nod. He was okay.

"You, omega, get in here." The wolf then pointed in my direction, and as I gave him a confused look, a figure bounded over where I sat and landed in the pit before my friend. It was the same wolf that we had spotted the night we were ambushed.

"He's mine." I pointed at the omega. "Let me fight him in my friend's stead."

"No," she said, looking smug that she had gotten to turn the tables on me.

"If you let me fight him, I will be a willing participant in your plan."

She looked at me with suspicion. "You swear it?"

I nodded.

"Speak the words." She licked her lips and glared at me hungrily.

"I swear that if you let me fight, I will take part in your... fun." I shivered at the thought of her touching me the way she was probably thinking.

I felt the weight settle over my chest. I was bound, but I had left myself a loophole a mile wide. Stupid ass was gonna get hers. I kept my bearing as she undid the clasp on my chains. It fell away with a thud, and I rubbed my wrist on reflex; it was sore but whole. I rolled my ankle this way and that, working the stiffness out.

I stepped forward to the edge of the pit and dropped in. I landed and walked toward my friend, relief clear on my face.

"Hey, brother. I'm glad you're okay."

He swung his fist out, and it connected with my chin. It surprised me. Then he pulled me into a headlock. His earring brushed up against the side of my head as he locked the choke in. A small victory that he wore his still, but why was he so pissed off?

All for show, brother. I'm glad you're doing okay, man. They need to think we hate you, Yohsuke said.

All good, man. I thought the worst, and I am more than happy to be wrong as hell. Damn that right hook wa–I started, but he interrupted.

Here they come. Kick me away from you. Cause a scene.

Kill. I set my feet to get ready.

I roared with what little breath I had left in my lungs and flung him away from me over my shoulder. I threw him a little harder than I had meant to, but he landed the way they taught us in the Marine Corps—slapping the ground with his forearm and palm to help absorb the impact—and he was fine. He made like he was going to lunge at me again, but the Farlow wolf got to him first. The beast cold-cocked him in the temple, and my friend went down like a sack of potatoes.

"That's the thanks I get for trying to save your ass?" I yelled. The rage came a little, and I tried to keep it at bay so that it was believable but not overpowering. Luckily for me, the asshole I really wanted to fight started to talk.

"Poor little fox," he chuckled. "You'll never be one of us, and now your own friends despise you. Sucks to be you, fox."

"Oh, you have no idea what suck is, omega." I laughed. "How does it feel to be the Pack's collective bitch? I bet you get all the shitty jobs, too. At least the alpha gets to use me. You just get passed around don't you? Or, looking at your ugly ass, I doubt anyone would touch you, and she wants to have my babies? You jealous?"

It worked; he came in swinging for the fences, and I was going to really enjoy this. Time to try and learn to control this shit. I didn't let the rage go but tried to harness it. I pictured the hybrid form in my mind and urged the shift. That's exactly what it was—a shift. It wasn't like the brutal transformation I had seen Pastela go through a few times. It was my change, a quick shift and I was in hybrid form, ready for mister asshole.

I growled at him wordlessly and blocked his haymaker easily. I grabbed his blocked wrist and twisted as I jerked back on the limb. A satisfying crack came from the joint, and I let it go as I backed away smiling.

My opponent turned and threw out the limb, popping it back into place easily enough, but it looked painful. He was more cautious now, walking in a circle with me mirroring his movements.

"Don't tell me! That's fear I smell, isn't it?" I sniffed loudly before scrunching my muzzle in disgust. "Does it always smell like urine?"

He fell for it again and came at me with arms spread wide for a tackle aimed at my mid-section. I waited until the split second he looked away, then brought my right foot up and push kicked his left clavicle as hard as I could. The bone resisted, then caved, and his momentum dropped with his shoulder right into the ground beneath my foot.

I grasped the omega by his injured shoulder and picked him up until he was kneeling in front of me, staring up into the stands at Pastela. She was smiling down at us, obviously enjoying the show. Good because this was going to suck, maybe. Fuck it.

Get ready to play, you guys. I mentally whispered to my friends.

"See how she smiles while I beat your ass, you pathetic worm," I taunted. He started to struggle, grasping at my arm with his good hand, but I batted it away easily. He was in serious pain, healing or no healing.

"She doesn't care about you. You don't even rate a name. You're worthless," then I whispered so low that I hoped only he could hear it, "but your death is for a good cause."

I roared and took my clawed right hand, shoving it deep into the meat just under his shoulder blade, breaking his ribs along the way, and tore out his heart with a sickening gurgle. The look of mirth on Pastela's face turned to outrage as I threw the clump of bloody meat at her.

"Oh, my pet, you won't even get to enjoy this night."

"That's on you. I had every intention of keeping my word."

"You will pay for your insolence. Your friends will, too. I'm going to enjoy breaking all of you."

She dropped into the pit with me, and I dropped the omega's body irreverently. I shifted back into my natural fox-man form and rolled my shoulders. Yup, the urge to eat my kill was still there, and my stomach actually growled. Gross.

Incoming, boys!

I looked up to see a dark figure on the unoccupied wall behind us loose two arrows, one of which hit Pastela right in her right eye and burst into flame. She screamed and howled in furious pain.

"Duck!" I heard behind me. I saw Yohsuke throw something, then something else and moved back in his direction. Two detonations of his new favorite spell Star Burst sounded, and wolves scattered.

Balmur finished unlocking Jaken's chains, then looked up at his best friend. "Hope you brought a little more than your winning personality, man. There are a lot more of them than us."

Bokaj had gone full badass and was firing arrow after arrow into anything that wasn't us.

"Yeah, I found something that hates Werewolves as much as we do, and he's on his way. Couple minutes tops, but we gotta hold them off until he gets here."

"Sick! Let's go ham, guys," I said. Balmur had already pulled his weapons out. "How did you manage to keep those?!"

"Same way Yoh did, man." He smiled as he stabbed a slow werewolf in the hamstring. "I put them up before they overwhelmed us. Didn't you?"

"FUCKING HELL!" I screamed. This time the rage really did take over.

I grunted and fell forward only to rise again on hybrid legs. I roared, and the red tinge to my vision began to throb like the beating of my heart. As it pulsed, I began to move to that beat. Step. Swing. Connect. Elbow. Kick. Bite. Claw. Claw. Bite. Roar.

The rhythm stayed consistent until I got to the great white bitch pulling the arrow out of her eye socket.

I inhaled and let loose a roar as loud as I could at her. I didn't know why, but she was now top of my target list. I bounded forward, and she held out a hand as if one hand could stop me. I was death incarnate. Primal. ALIVE.

"Stop," she growled.

And I did. I couldn't stop my forward momentum, but my limbs froze in place. I barreled into her. The force must have made her control slip a bit because I felt her command fade as she stumbled back. It was just enough for me to regain a little control.

"DIE!" I roared loudly and swiped at her throat. Her hand was back up, and the control tightened once more.

"You forget your place!" she screamed, blood dripping from her muzzle. "Let me show you."

She came toward me slowly, then raised her clawed right hand and brought it down. It seemed to move in slow motion, inching ever closer, and I was helpless to stop it. I strained and tried to get my muscles to move, and I felt them twitch before nothing moved at all.

A whistling whine buzzed my left ear and hit her in the armpit, then another in her neck. The arrows sprouted from her so fast, I couldn't seem to comprehend how. All I knew was that I could move now, and she was close enough to get to.

I lunged forward and bit into her throat. Blood dribbled into my clenched jaws, and everything became more red tinged and brutal. I remembered tearing, eating, feasting on the flesh of my most hated enemy. My chest swelled to bursting with pride at my victory, and I howled in delight.

Then a large thing showed up, and these creatures attempted to corral me away from my kill. One with metal all over hit me with light, and it hurt. A lot. Lunging again. Biting. Trying to bite. Sleep.

* * *

I woke up on a pile of rubble, nude and sore. I shook my head groggily, then looked around for my friends. They were standing in front of this behemoth, man-shaped creature with a single eye staring at me in hatred. Each of my friends had their weapons drawn and aimed at this thing. Bokaj was trying to talk it down it seemed.

"He's the friend I told you about!" he explained loudly. The thing was twenty feet tall and would have made a brick shithouse jealous. Massive arms, well-muscled and scarred led to hands with two fingers and a thumb. In those hands, the cyclops held a huge club and looked like it wanted to use it. It stood on thick, stubby legs with the same amount of toes.

"Friend no attack other friend!" it bellowed. If I hadn't been awake already, that would have woken me up. Fucker had a voice like a freight train horn. "He bad-wolf now. Me kill him like others. You thank Grum."

I had to admit, he sounded kind of adorable in his thought process, but I didn't want to die. I got up slowly and put my hands out to my sides, palms up. I had no more clothes to wear other than dirty ones; I'd have to clean them. They were my last pair, I thought, so I just walked over naked.

Oh well.

Nudity seemed like a bit of non-issue at the moment.

"Grum, is it?" I asked, and he just growled at me in response. "Look, I don't know what you're talking about, buddy, but I don't remember attacking anyone."

"You did! You attack friend! You bad-wolf!" he cried, raising his club as if to crush me.

"HEY! WOAH, BIG FELLA!" Bokaj waved his arms in front of him. "Easy now!"

"I forgive him!" Jaken shouted. That seemed to puzzle the cyclops, but it worked because he lowered the weapon.

"I squish him for you. Flat, like bug?" Grum tested the waters a bit with that.

"No, no. It's okay, really. Friends like us fight like that all the time! He was really just playing, right Zeke?" My friend looked at me with the kind of face that I knew I had to play along.

"Y-yeah!" I stuttered then got it under control. "We attack each other all the time. When one of us goes to the bathroom and comes back, we already have a prank to play on them. It's like a game we play."

The giant being looked at us for a moment; his one eye narrowed in suspicion. "Game?"

"Yeah!" we all chorused and nodded enthusiastically.

Yohsuke took it a bit further and tossed an Astral Bolt at me that caught me in the shoulder and knocked me on the ass.

"See?" he asked, laughing convincingly. "It's a game!"

Grum nodded after a moment, as if what we had said was a wise piece of advice you'd get from an elder.

"Game look fun."

We all agreed.

He smiled. "I play too!"

We all stood still, a moment too long, as the gullible Grum swung his club at Jaken like the armored Paladin was a golf ball. He raised his shield in time to protect himself and went sailing back my way. We were twenty feet away from each other to start, and he was rising as he went. I shifted into my Ursolon form and jumped, trying to catch him, but I just missed. He landed in the rubble I had been laying on with a crash.

"Game fun!" The cyclops stomped his feet in glee at the prospect of a new game.

I shifted back and ran to my friend, casting Regrowth as I went. He laid there, groaned low, then cast a heal on himself too. He sat up, looked at me, then at Grum and back to me before laughing.

"The shit I go through for y'all motherfuckers," Jaken groaned. We all started laughing.

Did I really attack you? I asked him through our earrings.

Yeah, Jaken responded but quickly filled me in. *We were trying to get you away from Grum before he saw you, but when we tried to herd you away, you got to me. Luckily, I was able to get you to hold still long enough for Balmur to knock you out.*

Dude, I don't remember, I'm so sor–

Shut up. I meant it when I said I forgave you. That's what brothers do. Jaken smiled sincerely and gave me a thumb up.

So we left it there. His HP was recovering quickly, and he wasn't in any real danger. Plus, the danger of me getting pancaked seemed to have lessened dramatically. I helped him stand, and we walked, both a little stiffly, back to the others. Weapons had been put away, though Grum seemed to just carry his at the ready always.

"Where did you find Grum, Bokaj?" I asked.

"Oh man, me and ol' Grumpy go way back, right Grum man?"

"Grum happy, not grumpy."

"I know, buddy." He smiled his usual easy smile and turned to us. "Turns out that the Werewolves had begun to prey on things other than the Ursolons. Like Grum's goats. These things are huge, dude. The size of thoroughbred horses. Anyway, he caught a few of them hunting me and helped me kill them. Told me about his goat Bess, Bett?" Bokaj looked to Grum, who told him it was Bett. "Sorry, man, Bett. She was his first goat, and they killed her. I tracked them here. Then he followed me in, hence the rescue."

"Damn, man, that's fucking awesome," I admitted. I wasn't sure if I had the guts to tell the rest what had happened to me. I knew they wouldn't judge, but still. "So what next?"

"You got turned, man," Balmur said. "None of us did, thankfully, but are you okay?"

I looked myself over. Other than being naked, I felt fine. Hell, better than fine—I felt great. I noticed the notification icon flashing and opened it to see what it was.

CONGRATULATIONS!

You have completed a secret quest!

Biting The Hand That Feeds – You have killed the alpha who turned you, literally biting the hand that fed you. You now gain control of the former alpha's Pack. You also gain the abilities of an Alpha Werewolf.

Reward: Moon's Grace, Hunter's Call, Savage Fury. 300 EXP

Holy shit. That was a lot of abilities. As I looked through them, I began to see the ups and downs of my bounty.

Moon's Grace – Significantly decreases the risk of a cursed transformation and loss of control.

Hunter's Call – Increases the damage output of one pack member by 10%. Duration: 15 seconds. Cool Down: 3 minutes.

Savage Fury – Increases speed, damage output, and resistance of all pack members within audible range of the alpha. Duration: 30 seconds. Cost: Mobility and 150 MP. Cool Down: 10 minutes.

Those were awesome, but the downsides were huge. One, they only worked on pack members, and looking around, they were all dead. So, that was moot, and I lost mobility AND a healthy chunk of mana on that buff? That had to be pretty awesome to cost so much.

"Yeah, I'm great, guys. Check it," I said and showed them all my screen.

"Is there a pack page in your Status Screen?" Yoh asked.

"Yeah, man, the least you can do is check it out," Balmur suggested.

I nodded and acquiesced.

Name: Zekiel Erebos
Race: Kitsune (Lycanthrope)
Level: 16
Strength: 38
Dexterity: 31
Constitution: 27
Intelligence: 40
Wisdom: 34
Charisma: 17
Unspent Attribute Points: 0

Lycanthrope was actually clickable, so I tapped it and looked at it. There was the information I knew, the abilities I received, and the status adjustments, but there was also a pack tab.

I selected it, then was surprised to see I had one member. It was Kayda, since she was a part of me, technically speaking. So she was alive and well—good. There was a button that gave me the option to add members at the bottom of the page. I sent the party invites, and they all joined. Once they did, I could see their names pop up on the page. Awesome.

"Thanks for the assist, guys."

"Eh, you always were a little slow on the uptake. It's gravy though," said Yohsuke.

I chuckled with these fools I called friends. We set about searching the camp for our things that had been taken. We searched the little dens up in the tree and couldn't find anything. I went into the alpha's pavilion and searched. The desk held papers with plans to attack different settlements and recruitment strategies. Basically kidnapping a few scouts here and there, then attack when they had a larger force. Nothing else of note. Werewolves had no need of money. Under the bed furs, we found a trap door. In it was Storm Caller and all of Jaken's gear and items. I found mine in it, too, just beneath his things. Ironic that I had been on my stuff this whole time.

I equipped my items and let Kayda out to roam. She took an interest in Grum immediately. She landed on his shoulder after we explained that she was our friend, too.

"Bird play game you do?" he asked, poised to flick her off his shoulder.

"NO!" Yohsuke and I shouted in unison. The cyclops looked dejected but smiled when the Lightning Roc patted him with her wing.

"Have we figured out how far we are from the Unseelie?" I asked.

"From what the map is showing, still out of range by a few days," Bokaj informed us.

Shit.

"You want go see Unseelie?" Grum asked? "Why?"

Bokaj tried to explain things how best he could, and Grum seemed to understand.

"Ah, you try get Maebe help?" Grum asked before clapping a hand over his mouth.

"Who?" I asked.

"Unseelie Queen," he whispered. "She crazy. No say name, or she hear. Find us and come for us."

"That's what we want, though!" I cried. "We want to talk to this Maebe. See if she can help us return home!"

"SHHH!" he whispered and began to look around worried. "She hear you! Come with bad Fae to get us, like Grum mummy say!"

A few of us chuckled. We had been raised much the same way; there was always something out there to scare disobedient children before bedtime. This Maebe must have been the one here.

A breeze stirred around the group, but no leaves moved on the ground. The grass didn't stir, nor did the branches above us.

"She here," the cyclops groaned softly, almost in tears.

At the same time, the sky began to darken. Not due to clouds or night but because it had been blotted out by a writhing, black mass overhead.

"The Hunt here, too," Grum yelled. "Run!"

The baying of the hounds began, and I could begin to make out different shapes in the darkness. Black, Demon-like creatures rode atop great black steeds. They held bows and had swords at their hips. They numbered in the dozens that I could see from where we were, hundreds of feet below them. A haunting horn sounded, and the host began to dip toward us—they had found their prey.

"You guys trust me?" Yohsuke asked.

"Yep," said Jaken.

"Uh-huh," Bokaj and Balmur chorused.

Kayda screeched a challenge to the darkness above us in defiance.

"Don't ask stupid questions," I told him.

"Okay, here goes." He stepped forward and raised his hands out to his sides. "We entreat Maebe, Queen of the Unseelie Fae, for safe passage to her lands where we wish to parlay!"

The breeze became a gust, and it swirled around us, now disturbing the greenery and our clothes, hair, and affects.

I looked from my friend to the descending Hunt. I could see the largest figure of the horde galloping at the fore, his great, horned head capped in dark metal, a bow held ready but no arrow drawn. His eyes burned bright red, and his smile, in grim victory, bared his sharp teeth to us all. He had sharp features, Elven from my best guess, and he was far more muscular than even our tank was. He was massive, almost fourteen feet if I had to guess, and his mount was a beast that I had never even seen before—a horse made of pure shadow with dark, glassy eyes like a doll's, and it seemed to give off more shadow as it ran.

"I hear your call, small one," whispered a voice in all of our ears. "Come."

"NO!" bellowed the creature at the front of the Hunt. He nocked a massive arrow and pulled it back in one fluid motion, releasing it. It flew directly at the summoner of this Fae wind. As soon as it looked like the arrow would impale my brother, he was gone. Then my friends were gone.

I blinked and realized that I stood in a large, white room. It was grander than anything I could have ever imagined.

The walls sparkled like water—carved of ice, I'd have guessed—but the air wasn't cold in the slightest. I could see carvings of creatures scattered all around us. They seemed almost alive but made of solid ice. Their expressions either of fear, hatred, or resignation. There wasn't just one kind of creature but many: Elves, Kitsune, the Little Folk, Spriggans, Dryads, and even a couple of giants that didn't even come close to touching the ceiling with their weapons raised to attack.

"Beautiful, aren't they?" posed a woman next to us.

She was dressed simply in a slip of a red dress—that didn't do anything to hide her hourglass figure—and no shoes. Her pointed ears were longer than most other Elves I had seen before. They also flared out from her head a little more at a right angle. She was unique, different from the Elves I was used to seeing. It was an interesting sight. They were adorned with a dozen odd earrings and piercings of gold, silver, and platinum. It made me wonder if, with so many precious metals, this creature was allergic to iron. I had read so many books on the Fae in my childhood that the question was almost free of my throat when I was brought out of the thought.

"They are," said Jaken. The rest of us nodded, just to be polite.

She turned to look at us, and my breath caught. She was beautiful. Her skin was so dark that she looked like the night personified. Her eyes were a deep green, and her full, pouty lips broke into a bright smile. Perfect, white teeth grinned under a small, dainty nose. Her cheek bones were high, but not as sharp and angular as you might expect from someone of Fae descent. Her hair was black but with colors like reds, greens, shades of purple, and even silver highlighting throughout her hair. She was beautiful. The more I looked, the more her skin began to fascinate me. I could see little pinpricks of white scattered—like freckles—across her nose and on her cheeks, chest, and shoulders. Some scattered down her toned arms here and there. They looked like little stars, and then I realized that she *was* night personified.

"Who among you called to me?" she asked. Her voice was feminine and strong. She was used to getting her way.

"Grum did," rumbled the cyclops from his knees. "Queenship," he added hurriedly.

"Yes, I heard you. Who else?"

I stepped forward but held my tongue.

"I did, too." Yoh stepped up next to me. "I was the one who called for an audience with you."

"Yes, you did." She nodded. She walked over to Grum and looked up at him and smiled. "You were the one who uttered my name and brought it to his lips, weren't you, my precious?"

"Yes, your Queen-ness," he said, and tears began to fall from his eye.

"It seems you already know the punishment for speaking my name to outsiders? Yes, of course you do. Grum, was it? You're in luck, Grum. I'm in a generous mood today, and it seems you have at least brought me some interesting visitors. This is the only time I will do this, but good boy."

She reached out and patted him on his hand. He looked at her in surprise and faded from view without a sound other than sobbing.

"What did you do?" I asked her in horror.

"It speaks!" She turned around and seemed to glide toward me faster than a bullet. I couldn't move away from her. Her green eyes sparkled up at me from inches away. She was a little shorter than me as well. Then she seemed to grow rapidly. I looked down, and she was levitating to look down at me. She smiled.

"You see me," she said. It was an accusation as much as a statement.

"Of course I see you, you're right in fro–" I stopped when I realized what she really meant. "Yes, I see the real you. Now, tell me what you did with Grum. Please?"

Now, I knew I was out of line—dangerously so if she was anything like the queens and kings I read about—but the big lug had saved our asses. He had just been trying to help us, and that's cool with me. I like helpful people because I'm the same way. Watching her make him vanish had freaked me the fuck out—and I don't spook well. Sue me. He bled for us—with us. That's a bond grander than most in my book.

I could make more out of her actual face under the glamour she used. Glamour was a type of magic most of the Fae in my books at home were adept with. They used it to make themselves more beautiful and fascinating. Maebe seemed to be trying to do the opposite. Was this because of my True Sight ability? That let me... see creatures as they are. So she *was* hiding herself. But why?

She smiled a bit more; it almost split her face in half.

"I did something I rarely do. I rewarded him. I sent him home to his flock."

"Alive?"

"Oh, I see that you have played our games before?" she asked, delighted. "Yes, and whole. Good for you, making that distinction."

"I have heard of your games before," I admitted. "I've read books about the Fae. The game is that you will tell the truth, always but have mastered telling versions of it. Omitting information that is pertinent and telling half-truths. Power is everything to the Fae, or at least, that's what I read."

"Your books do not lie," she said simply. "Still, I don't like that you can see me. We will talk more later."

She turned around immediately and lowered to her feet. She walked over to Yohsuke and stared down at him for a moment.

"You wished to talk?" she asked mildly. "Talk."

"We want a way home. We were banished here by a spell and have no means to return on our own. We received word that, while the Wild Hunt and the Seelie queen—Zekiel what was her name?"

"If my books were right, it's Tita–" I began.

"STOP!" she screeched. "Never say the name of a Fae Queen. That summons our attention. Continue."

He stared at her for a second, clearly about to have me say the name just to spite her but must have decided against it.

"The Seelie Queen—and her gaggle of bitches—are hunting us. You aren't, so we decided to try and come to you for help."

"Oh, how I do love that word, 'help'." She clapped her hands in delight. "So few come to me these days. Why, it's been a century or more since I've even held court. Longer still since I've had a guest."

She wandered away, up steps behind us—that I failed to notice—and sat on a large throne shaped into a Dragon's maw made of ice. The body was attached, the jaws stretched wide, so that the throne fit into it perfectly. Her artist was talented as shit. It looked so life-like that it could have moved its football-field-sized body and crushed us all.

She closed her eyes and began to drum her fingers in thought while she played with her hair.

"Umbra!" she called at last, her eyes still closed.

"Yes, my Queen?" a deep voice from behind us made all of us jump. Balmur had his weapons out, and the rest of us were ready to fight, too.

We turned to see a small Gnomish man, skin as dark as my fur, kneeling behind us. He was bare chested and armed with a rapier with a thick hand guard. The blade appeared to be iron. His features were almost bland and forgettable, save for the mustache that he had twirled and twisted into handlebars.

"Summon my court. They will meet tomorrow, in the eve. We are going to have a ball," she purred. "And Zamir? See that my guests are... well tended."

"Yes, Darkest Lady," a feminine voice said from my right.

We turned our heads and noted that yet another beautiful woman was standing next to us. She was the same kind of Fae that Maebe was because her ears flared out the same way. She didn't try to tone down her beauty and ethereal looks. Where Maebe's skin was like a starry night sky, her's was like alabaster.

She motioned to us with her hand, long thin fingers waving for us to follow.

"The nude one stays," Maebe said in amusement.

I blushed and waved for my friends to go. "I'll be okay." I tapped the earring in my ear, and they nodded.

I covered myself, then turned to find the Fae Queen standing right there in front of me. She must have levitated because I hadn't heard a damn thing.

"Your earrings will not work here, unless I allow it," she said smugly. "I can see the enchantments on your items. I can see the magic all over you and all over them. Nothing escapes my sight here in the domain of Ice and Night."

She walked away from me, wandering from sculpture to sculpture. She caressed each one as she moved. She stopped and stared at a Kitsune who looked resigned and then turned to me once more.

"Are you usually so quiet?" she asked.

"No," I chuckled. "Usually, I never shut up. The last few days have been rough for me."

She looked at me, and then I looked at the ground. She walked over to me and gripped my face with her thin fingers. She stared into my eyes a moment then held her other hand up.

"Show me," she ordered.

I had no idea what she did next, but I found myself reliving the events of my time just before we came to the Fae Realm, but they were jumbled. Then the transportation and our time in the Fae Realm. In hyper speed, the events played out as I had lived them. In what felt like only seconds, she had seen it all.

She closed her eyes and digested the images I had shown her, and then she looked at me and nodded. Understanding flitting across her eyes.

"Pastela was a powerful creature," she said. "Highly entertaining to watch from time to time. She could not control you in the end, and you conquered her. Took her power for your own and did what many Fae dream of—became something better. Stronger. I can feel that while you suffered, she did not break you. Am I right?"

I nodded dumbly—it was true. I had faced a lot of hardships, both back in life and in this world. Hell, we all had, but I never let them break me. Why start now? What I had failed to realize was that while my tormentor was dead and gone, she still had a small facet of control over my actions.

Fuck that.

"This is good. Perhaps I've gone soft over the centuries, but I find you intriguing. All of you. I used to be quite the tyrant, you know. These poor, pitiful creatures," she waved her hand at the sculptures around us, "had displeased me once upon a time, and now look at them, immortal—forever frozen alive to remind those who would cross me or question my power. To remind them of their place in my realm."

I looked at the frozen Elf beside me and noted that it was true. The ice, while pure and clear, seemed to have eyes that moved in complete fear, slowly back and forth. It sent a spasm of fear down my spine.

"I won't freeze you, little fox," she said quietly from beside me. "It truly has been a very long time since I've had guests. You all are safe. As safe as can be from my people and I, as my hospitality permits. Although, if any of your compatriots do something untoward, I can make no promises."

"I trust them to keep their composure."

"Let us hope." She smiled again. "I would hate to have to add to my collection. Come, let's go see if we can't find you something cute to wear before our talk."

That wasn't our talk? Fuck.

We left the throne room through a small entrance beside the Dragon's right hind leg. Not the sculpture, an actual. Fucking. Dragon. A white one, frozen solid to be exact, and she had lovingly named him Snowball.

I had to give her credit; she had a twisted sense of humor.

The halls were made of the same material as the rest of the place, I assumed. She wondered why we were trying to fight that mage, Rowan, in the first place, so I let her in on our mission without telling her that we were from a different planet altogether. I was playing her game, omitting information and telling half truths. I'm fairly certain that she had no clue what was going on outside her realm, so I wasn't sure if she could tell I was omitting things.

"This War you speak of, could he come here?" she asked after a thoughtful pause.

"I imagine that he could. From what I have gathered after our first run in with an actual General, his people are capable of greater feats than even we are. Who knows what they can do, especially if they can use magic like he did."

"Healthy respect for the enemy is needed to understand and destroy them. Never under or overestimate them. If you plan for them to have access to the things you do, you will be better prepared."

I stopped in my tracks, dumbfounded by the wisdom of that advice. Then I hurried along after her when she didn't stop. I should have expected it from an immortal queen of the fairy realm.

We stopped in a room off to our right after a few minutes. The queen just barged right in, nothing said into a dark room.

"Hello, my Darkest Lady," a gravelly, albeit slightly feminine voice greeted us from a lit desk on the right.

"Good day, Svartlan," she greeted the figure. "Come, I have a task for you."

"Finally, you realize your views on fashion are outdated! Oh, how wondrous the clothing I shall make you! Oh, let's start with a nice green dr–"

The figure stopped talking. "Who's this fine creature?"

"My guest and your newest project. Say hello to Zekiel Erebos."

"Yes, yes he will do nicely. Oh, this darkness simply will not do," He clapped, and a light flared to life from the walls. It was blinding at first, then lowered to a comfortable level.

"Even better." I could see the Orc now, easily a foot taller than I was. He was gaudily dressed in a gold silk blouse and silver silk trousers over his bulky frame. His muddy brown eyes looked me over. I covered myself bashfully.

"No need for that." He smiled. "I've got your measurements already. I've been doing this a long time."

"What shall I do for him, Lady Darkest?"

"The works. He and three others wear cloth and leather, one in a metal shell, and the other seems to be content to just wear pants, strangely."

He stood there aghast for a moment. "Hmm. Just pants. I see. What a savage he must be, poor thing. I'll get started right away. Do you have a color preference Master Erebos? Style? Oh, how stylish these clothes will be. I will create such things of beauty."

"Nothing too complicated, please," I said, holding out my hand to stop him. "I need function, not fashion."

I saw his face fall, visibly saddened. I sighed and looked to Maebe.

"You may make all of them one fashionable set of clothes to wear should they have need of them." Maebe eyed me while she spoke to her tailor. "Color and style, so long as they are simple, are up to you."

"Oh!" The Orc grinned, his tusks flashing brightly. "Oh, you will not regret this! Darkness, please, send the others along shortly. I shall need their measurements. How long?"

"For functional wear, as soon as you can. It needs to be sturdy. Use the best materials we have available. And Svartlan? Do your best work. The fashionable clothing? It can wait until you have at least two outfits made for each them. Svartlan, do make tomorrow's outfits formidable and functional, won't you, dear? Court will be in session."

The big man was already in motion, waving that he had understood us and had work to do.

"Do you have something–" A pair of cloth trousers landed on my head before I finished the sentence. "Thanks!"

I slipped them on. Black like my fur and soft against it, too. I thought I would be keeping these.

I followed Queen Maebe out of the room and then down the hall a bit more. After a series of turns, we came to a guarded wing where every door appeared to belong to a different chamber.

We walked into the final one on the far left. A large figure stood guard at the end of the corridor outside, taking up most of the wall. It wore a cloak to blend in. I couldn't get a good look, though.

"Don't stare too long. It makes her angry," the queen said as she entered the room. "Red Caps take offense to being stared at when they are trying to remain unseen."

I remembered reading about them. Stories said that they were large creatures who dyed their hats or heads in the blood of freshly fallen foes. I shivered at the thought.

We were in a lavish sitting room. A couch of white was situated in the middle of the room before large windows on the far wall displaying quite the odd scene. On the left side of the room was a snowy, desolate waste, and the other side was a lush forest teeming with life, like the cold had no effect on the life there.

"Beautiful, isn't it?" Maebe said as she stepped up beside me. "I've always been so bent on destruction that I did not spend the time to admire the beauty of life. I allow the light lands to encroach so because it please me. It pleases me to know that every bloom, every creature that inhabits this portion of that land is alive only because I will it and that I can take that at a whim."

"Sounds like you enjoy the thought of that," I quested. Not a question per se, but a gentle nudge to continue.

She nodded, almost sadly. "I did, at one time. Over these last couple centuries, I've become bored. Morose, even. Where my art was a joy before, I find it empty. There is no thrill left for me here anymore."

"I see."

"You cannot begin to see, mortal," she said sadly as she laid a hand on my shoulder, "but I appreciate that you are trying to understand. For centuries, I have born this responsibility. I took the title from my mother, who ran her court much more assertively. There was a Fae with vision. She almost conquered the whole of the realm. Even sent a few of our kin and some slaves to the Prime realm. They were likely your ancestors. The Kitsune tend to be on the darker side of the Fae orders, since they have a more mischievous streak, and my mother did love exotic creatures. As far as I am concerned, you are one of the flock, returning to the bosom of your motherland. Welcome home."

"Sadly, I cannot claim this place as my home." I had to think of a way around this without her getting that the jig is up. "Home is where my son is. Where all my loved ones are."

She nodded. "I do not understand that, but the sentiment is not lost on me. See that you and your friends meet my expectations in the coming days. Do so, and I will see that I help you return to him how I can. You have my oath."

"And what will you require of us?"

"Be who you are, and when the time comes, which I'm certain it will, defend yourselves. That is all."

"Nothing else?"

"No, little fox. Nothing else, and though you do not call this place your home, you are welcome here. Come, I will show you to my chambers. We will dine there and speak of other, less formal business."

We exited through the door that we had used to come in; the stoic Red Cap eyed me as we walked by into the chamber across the hall.

The bedroom was truly lavish. A stark contrast from the white of the other room, it was all black. The light from the multitude of specks on the ceiling that looked like the stars kids would put on their ceilings provided plenty of light to see by, especially paired with the moon painted in the corner opposite the door. The silver light of the crescent moon shone down on the darkness and gave all the furniture a silver lining. It was exquisite. The queen's furniture was plush and looked to be only slightly used. Tables had freshly poured wine and hot food on them that smelled as heavenly as the room looked.

"Sit, please." She motioned to the first couch closest to us. I obeyed and eyed the corners of the rooms where the darkness seemed thickest. "Don't worry, Zekiel. We are alone here."

"We weren't before?" She laughed her throaty laugh, and it made me smile for some reason.

"Now, share a meal with me before we begin our discussion in earnest." Her voice took on an almost imperceptible musical lilt that I hadn't noticed before.

Was she letting go of her glamour since we were alone? I didn't think that my True Sight was getting stronger the more I looked at her.

She brought a platter of food over. Mountains of meats, potatoes, and vegetables were piled all over it. She carried it like it was a small plate in one hand and sat it just behind our goblets like it didn't weigh probably sixty pounds. Like I said, it was a mountain of food.

The goblets were both of a lighter colored metal, studded with modest gems and light filigree. She picked up her own and offered me the other. I accepted, taking my drink and hissed as it burned my palm immediately. The drink spilled in my hurry to get the offending goblet out of my hand, and it landed on the floor.

A look of concern fell over Maebe's features, then exasperation. I began to offer an apology, but she silenced me with a wave. She snapped her fingers, and a dark shadow pulled itself out of the darkest corner of the room beneath the painting of the moon. Then a second came out. Each shadow had a Goblinoid shape—long floppy ears, stubby limbs, and oddly shaped heads. She pointed at the goblet, and one of the shadows came forward, collected it, and absorbed the liquid on the floor through its hand. The shadow took the cup, then returned to the corner it had come from. The other stepped forward and offered me a golden replacement that looked almost exactly the same as the original goblet.

I took it and thanked the little creature. It seemed to look at me with its shadowy eyes, then decided that it was finished and slunk away back to its home in the darkness under the moon.

"My apologies, Zekiel," Maebe said after a sip of her wine. "My shadow servants try to anticipate my will and do their best, but they can only think so much. They didn't know that you were a Lycanthrope, as I only had a minute knowledge of the past, a mere glimpse of each scene. I have broken a deep and much abided law among the Fae. You would be well within your rights to defame me."

"I won't," I said simply as I sipped my wine. It was good, really good. The fruity flavor of the beverage was something unlike anything I had ever tasted. I couldn't stop a small gasp after I finished swallowing it.

"Shade Berries. I grow them in the hoarfrost, and they ripen rarely. I have a batch that bloomed twice in the last century. This was from the second ripening. It pairs well with the food on that platter. Let us dine."

We ate in comfortable silence. Well, as comfortable as a mortal could be with an immortal queen who could freeze him into an immortal sculpture, but hey—I liked trying new things.

The food was delicious. The meat was tender and the potatoes fluffy. The veggies lended an earthy tone to the meal that I could appreciate, especially paired with the fruity flavor of the wine. I praised the chef, and the queen opted not to share my praise, saying that she would get a fatter head than she already had. As our meal settled, we sat together and watched the stars above us. Some shifted and moved like the very cosmos themselves, radiating different colors and intensities. Shooting stars flew across the cloudless expanse—it was as breathtaking as the Fae next to me.

"So why would you ever choose to hide your true self with glamour?" I asked softly, worried my voice might disturb the stars above.

"Such impatience." She chuckled. I looked over and saw that the glamour was indeed gone. Her skin mirrored the ceiling above us. I saw what she hid with glamour in silhouette, and it was a beauty that was alarming.

Her deep green eyes sparkled in the silvered light, her dainty nose leading to thick lips that looked like pillows even though they were moving. Her jawline, high cheekbones softened by the lights and shadows. She glowed. She wasn't simply royalty or Fae—she was celestial. She chose that moment to look at me and laugh.

"You really must pay attention if you want to learn anything," she chided me gently.

I don't know what it was, but here in this place, she seemed gentler.

"This is one of the reasons. It's difficult to order someone's death and have them be afraid when they're so distracted by my beauty. Do you know how annoying it is to know that everyone in a room is imagining you nude? Fantasizing about what they would do to you, willing or no? How infuriating it is to know that and not be able to control it. Even one such as I who could crush most with a thought cannot crush that disgusting side of other creatures."

She shifted, her fingers in her hair. "There are times when it is empowering, like nothing can stop me and I have the utmost control—creatures at my beck and call for no other reason than that they admire my beauty and wish to curry my favor. Eventually, it all boils down to knowing that they see that one side, only that side, and will do anything to possess it or claim it. They want that one thing or a variation of it, and it makes my flesh crawl. Do you know how it feels to be seen that way? As someone else's fantasy?"

"I can say with absolute certainty that I do not." She laughed at my blunt honesty. "Seriously. I've never really been one to have been all that attractive to anyone. At least not in my opinion."

"That is unfortunate. That is why I use glamour to blunt my looks so that my edicts and orders are obeyed and I am feared."

"And since power is everything to the Fae, that fear is instrumental."

"Exactly. The Fae have a version of your True Sight. It's diluted and less powerful because the truly powerful of our kind used to attack creatures with it, to keep others from seeing what they didn't want seen. Over the millennia, the trait evolved into what is known today. The practice is still widely popular among the royal Fae."

"So you're going to kill me?"

"Normally, you would have been a fine addition to my collection, but the audacity you and your friends had to call upon me the way you did intrigued me. I decided to wait until I knew more. So I will learn more."

She sat up and looked at me. "What was it that you did to be banished here? Tell me of the state of Prime." I went to open my mouth to speak, but she held a hand up. "This room is warded and enchanted to prevent falsehoods. If you lie, I will know. I am asking you, though, that we dispense with the half truths as well. Tell me truthfully."

QUEST ALERT!
WHAT TO SAY, WHAT TO SAY?
The Queen of Ice and Darkness has asked you to inform her about the current affairs of Brindolla and the state of the fight against War without falsehood and half-truths. Choose whether you want to divulge this information or if you want to dodge it.

Reward: Unknown.
Accept? Yes/No

I took a moment to think, drew a deep breath, and released it slowly. I chose yes.

"I need your oath that what I tell you, you will tell no one else unless the need to do so is dire. What I am about to tell you has implications for all realms."

She seemed to think on it a moment while taking a sip of her drink. Silence was drawn out long over the span of that moment as I waited. Finally, she nodded and swore on her throne that she would divulge this to no one unless the need was great.

Much like we had with the High Druidess in Terra's Escape, I gave her the summary of our mission in Brindolla. I told her about our quest to stop War's Generals and how one had banished us to this realm, but this time, I didn't hold out any truths or information other than our being summoned here from another world.

"And with us here, Prime is in danger. Hell, all of the realms attached to this planet and its reality are probably in danger. If one of the Generals could figure out how to send us here, it's only a matter of time before they come to take the realm of the Fae too."

She closed her eyes for a moment and seemed to ponder my words. She opened them, and a steely look entered into her gaze that made my heart skip a beat.

"This is it!" she growled triumphantly. "This is where I shall make my mark in the annals of our history! This is a feeling I have not had in centuries! Oh, Zekiel! You have given me purpose again with this!"

I smiled despite the situation and put a hand out to try and calm her, then pulled it back, thinking better of it.

"As far as I am aware, these Generals can sense when the denizens of this world approach them and go into hiding. Why, I don't know, but we are their blind spots. They can't see my friends and I. That's the advantage we have—well, had. I don't know how that asshole knew we were coming, but we have to stop him—all of them—to save this planet and our own."

Maebe clapped her hands and stood up. She began to pace back and forth in front of me, thinking to herself. She clapped again and a smile spread across her beautiful face.

"If I can't do anything other than be of use to your cause, then I will do all that I can, and I will be able to have my fun. This still aligns with my plans, but there will be other minor changes to take care of. What have you and your party need of? I know of the need for clothing, but other gear? Oh, your new clothes simply must be better made than what I had coming to you."

She clapped her hands together once more, and it sounded like lightning. "SVARTLAN!"

The door to the room opened behind us, and the Orc rushed in. "Darkest Lady?"

"Scratch the order for the functional clothes. These fellows are warriors and will represent me in the Prime realm. I want you to use my personal reserve of materials as you see fit to the specifications that each will give you. You may interview Zekiel right now for his desires. Zekiel, my pet, please tell Svartlan of your capabilities. Anything you would desire for clothing and how it might best serve you."

I told the Orc about my class, several of my abilities, my combat style, and anything else I could think of. The tailor nodded and jotted down several notes on a pad he had produced from his pocket. He asked me to pull out my weapon and show him how I move with it, and the queen nodded her assent.

I equipped Storm Caller and went through several motions and movements with the weapon that I was prone to in a fight. He made a few more notes, asked me to hold a position for a moment, and asked how clothing usually felt from that angle, if it felt confining or restrictive. It was more in depth than I had ever even imagined a tailor would go. I had to admit I was even more impressed with the green man.

The queen came over to where I stood and took the great axe into her delicate hands. Like with the huge platter of food, her size didn't do anything toward letting me know her strength—because she took a couple swings with the monstrous weapon one handed,

"This is excellent work," she said after a moment.

"It was made by Granda of the Stone Hammer Clan in Djurn Forge. He made almost all of our weapons himself. It's an amazing piece. Do you want me to tell you what it does? Shellica of the Light Hand Clan enchanted it."

"No need. I can tell just by looking at it what sort of spells are laid into it. Tell me, what sort of abilities have you unlocked with it?" I informed her, and she smiled.

"Well done. Those seem potent. I feel as though my champion will be able to assist you in learning more about this sort of weapon as he is fond of axes himself. You can meet him in the morning if you would like?" I fought the urge to leap up and shout for joy and simply nodded enthusiastically. "Yes? Okay good. Anything else, Svartlan? Chop chop, dear."

The Orc left the room at a bolt, and the door slammed behind him.

"I can't wait to see what he makes," I said as I watched him leave.

"Svartlan will serve us well in this. He has been making clothing for me since I met him centuries ago. He did so well that I had to make him immortal."

I chuckled at the thought nervously. I was beginning to see that she got her way. Always.

"And you desired that we will be your what now?"

"My champions!" she said excitedly. She rushed toward me and sat me down facing her, my hands in hers. "You and your friends will go back to face this nuisance plaguing our planet with my personal backing and whatever support I can give you. In exchange, I get a few things out of this. One, a new purpose. I can both protect my realm and expand my influence into the Prime realm through you and representatives that I will send with you when you are to return. Two, I get to stick my foot squarely up that uppity bitch in the Seelie Court's rear while I do it. Oh, this is the feeling I have missed."

She looked at me then, the feral baring of her teeth showing brightly. "Thank you, little fox. You have given me purpose again. How shall I reward you? Speak up, now. Don't be shy."

I thought about it for a moment. Some might ask for riches, others for status, and all for power, but I had this nagging feeling that she expected all of those; that wasn't me. Not truly. Thinking back to our conversations and what I could gather from them, I smiled right back at her.

"I would like to be your friend," I said gently.

She looked confused. Genuinely confused. I could almost hear the workings of her thoughts, that of a Fae being long used to the political intrigue of a powerful court such as her own. Nothing was without an ulterior motive, and here all I seemingly wanted was her friendship.

"I must say that I don't know what it is that you have in mind by that," Maebe admitted while eying me down. "What do you possibly hope to gain?"

"You didn't leave anything out about those wards and enchantments, did you?" She shook her head. "No. I thought not. Did they tell you that I was lying? That my intent was anything other than what I said?"

"No, but why?"

I shrugged. "All of these conversations we've had have pointed to something glaringly obvious. No matter how powerful you are, you're lonely. All of these servants, the people you control and are responsible for, and you have no one to spend time with who you can trust or confide in. Not really. Not without having to wonder if they have a knife at your back, ready to strike when you are most vulnerable. Where I come from, there are friendships a lot like that, but the way I grew up, friends were a rare treat—the relationship a reward in its own right. I chose my friends because I see them as family."

I watched her face as she sat there, blank of all expression. Her bearing became an unreadable mask.

"I apologize if I have caused any affront to you, Lady Darkest. You told me to be honest, and I let my tongue wag too freely. I'll go. Thank you for your gracious hospitality and your time."

I stood and offered what I hoped to be a courtly bow, simplified if anything. I stepped back two paces and turned to leave, then tripped over something and face planted into another couch. I felt my cheeks begin to heat, and I hurried to my feet. A small splutter of laughter in my left ear grabbed my attention. It was Maebe. She was levitating again, her hand over her mouth trying to hide her smile.

"Stay, please?" she asked. "I'm sorry. I'm just not used to so much honesty and blunt speaking. It gave me a bit of a start."

"Blunt—sounds like me. I am about as subtle as a bear on a raft," I smiled and continued, "'bout as graceful as one, too."

She laughed again and smiled at me before landing softly on her feet and stepping forward until she was close enough to smell. Her scent was soft and alluring like the rest of her, a subtle, earthy musk with coconut finishes. It was a good scent.

"Friendship is its own reward," she mused out loud. "Then I will reward us both. I would be glad to call you my friend, Zekiel Erebos."

This was a complete one-eighty from the Maebe—no, the queen—she tried to make everyone see all the time. She seemed softer. Less likely to freeze me at a moment's notice. Maybe this was Maebe behind closed doors?

Who she really was?

"My friends call me Zeke."

"Then you may call me Mae."

"I'd be happy to, Mae."

She grinned at me sweetly. I stepped forward and pulled her into a gentle hug. She stiffened for a moment, then seemed to decide she liked the contact and returned the embrace.

"It's late," I observed. We had been talking and eating for a while, and I had to admit I was tired.

"It is," Mae agreed. "You can retire to your own room, or if you would like, you can spend the night here with me. I would like to keep my first friend close, if that counts for much?"

I chuckled. I could understand, and her bed did look rather large. Not to mention all of the spacious couches she had. I could sleep on the one we had used; the damned thing was so soft and inviting.

"Okay. I'll spend the night here."

She took my hand in her own and led me to the bed where we sat up for a little while longer and chatted about our very different lives. She spoke about some of the members of her court that my other friends and I should take note of or watch out for, and I spoke about my son. She may not have known love or what it was like to feel a parent's love, but she seemed fascinated by the stories I told her about him, about the emotions that the anecdotes evoked in me.

After a little while, she ended up using my chest as a pillow and fell asleep while I stroked her hair. Her soft breathing was comforting, especially after having been through all the things that we had been through in Brindolla—all the fighting, the death, the struggle. Every inch we fought for.

I had to admit, I wasn't as strong as I thought I was back on Earth, but my friends being here helped make me stronger. They lent me their strength, and I did the same for them, and now, I had a new friend.

Granted, yeah, she could rip my head off and use it as a doorstop. There was also the veritable army of frozen people in her throne room, but she had her own problems. We all did, and that's okay. She had me to help now; maybe I could convince her to free them. I had her friendship, too, and she was damned near forcing her help on us. I was okay with that, or at least I could be, right?

Chapter Twenty-Nine

When I woke up, my eyes adjusted to the dark quickly, and I was surprised to see Maebe sitting on the edge of the bed staring at me. I fought the urge to jump, barely, and smiled at her groggily.

"Hey, did I oversleep?"

"No, my kind needs little sleep; one so old as I am doesn't need much at all, so I've just been occupying myself."

I didn't want to ask how because I could imagine what that had been.

"Breakfast?" she asked, gesturing toward where we had eaten last night. There were cheeses, eggs, and smoked meats. I could smell it now, and my stomach grumbled at me angrily for making it wait.

"Please," I said as I swung my legs off of the bed. We ate together in amiable silence for a few minutes. Then I asked her about events to come.

"Well, as I said last night, I would be happy to introduce you to my current champion. While the two of you do whatever it is you do, I will see to the demands of my station. There is much to do before my court arrives, and I have more to do if everything is to go smoothly. It will. My staff will work diligently as I expect them to, and I will lead them into this new, glorious age of the Unseelie."

I nodded over my forkful of eggs. She politely waited for me to finish a few minutes later, and we were off. She took me through her labyrinthian hallways, out a door to our right, and we were in a brightly lit courtyard. It reminded me of the training grounds the Mugfist Clan had under Djurn Forge.

"Thogan, I've brought you a guest," shouted Maebe.

"Ye don' need ta shout, yer Majesty. I hears jus fine," a deep bass voice to our left said.

A brawny figure clad in black plate armor stepped into fire light, and I could see it was a Dwarf, but not the kind I had seen before. His skin was craggy and pitted like stone the color of midnight with diamonds sprinkled throughout it, like a mirror of the queen he served. His head was bald, and he had beard as dark as his skin. Golden eyes watched me intently before the figure knelt before his lady.

"This is Zekiel Erebos. He and his party are favored by me, and you will show him the same courtesy you would any guest of the court. He himself uses the axe, much like you, and I thought it prudent he meet you."

"Aye, Majesty."

"Good day then, Champion."

He grumbled something along the same lines to her as she turned and graced me with a smile before leaving.

Once she was gone, the Dwarf rose to his feet and turned away. There was a barrel to my left, and he went to it. He took a ladle that had been in it, served himself whatever was inside, and sighed a frustrated sigh.

"Reckon yerself good with the axe?" he asked, still facing the barrel.

"No."

He turned to eye me. Either that wasn't what he expected to hear, or he thought I was lying. He knew nothing about me, so I could probably say it was safe to assume he didn't know if I was truthful or not. He went back to grimacing at the drink in the ladle. So I tried for one of the traditional Dwarven greetings that I'd learned from my time in Djurn Forge with Brawnwynn.

"By the Mountain, that's got to be the ugliest gob I've ever seen." I smiled hopefully. It had gotten me good results before.

The Dwarf was rigid one second; then an iron axe was at my throat before I could so much as blink. I hadn't seen him move.

"I be bearin' no insult by the unproven and he who isn't me kin, guest," he growled at me. His eyes were full of murderous intent. "Been gone from me homeland for nigh on fourteen hunnerd years, and not seen kin since. Ye will nah disrespect me memory of me folk. Best be believin' me. I'll slit ye throat an' take me lumps from the Lady Darkest, I will. Mark me."

"Sir, I follow the Way," I said. Sweat began to bead behind my right ear, and it tickled like hell. I didn't dare scratch, lest he decide to make good on his word.

"Speak the tenets then, boy, and quickly," he said, his eyes taking on a crazy look.

"To use the strength of my arm to help the weak and those in need. To share the stories of my brothers over mead and sing their praises. On the Way, we are all equal."

He looked at me steadily, not budging, but not cutting my head off either.

"The hammer falls," I said softly.

"And rises again," he whispered back.

"The forge was hot."

"The mead was cold."

"The Mountain made us."

"Dwarves the Bold." He closed his eyes as the final word left his lips and dropped the axe away from my throat.

I took a risk and put my hand on his shoulder. "The Way is long and winding, brother."

A tear formed in the corner of his right eye, and he fell to his knees with a great thud before he finished the saying, "But never are we alone."

"I am Zekiel Erebos, part of the party who slew the Bone Dragon killing the Forests near a small village. Bane of Goblins and the protector to the heir of Lightning, Kayda, Lightning Roc. I am blessed by Mother Nature. I am friend of Clan Mugfist, who took me into their own and helped me take my first steps along the Way. I am friend to your Queen."

He stood with a genuine smile and pulled me into a fierce hug, heaving me to and fro with great sobs of joy. He thanked the Mountain that I knew the secret phrases of those who followed his religion.

"Yer alright, lad. I be Thogan Swiftaxe." He clapped me on the back and pulled me toward the barrel. "Share some of this piss-poor swill they call mead with me and tell me your tale."

He grimaced as he drank some from the ladle, and after having a sip, I could second his choice of naming it piss-poor mead.

"Ugh," I groaned. He smiled sadly and shrugged.

I quickly told him about everything that had happened. He asked a few questions about our time under the mountain but otherwise listened respectfully. He raised the ladle in my honor and drank deeply.

"What I wouldn't do for a taste of good, Dwarven mead." He belched loudly. "You don't happen to have any, do you?"

I checked my inventory; I didn't, but I thought I knew someone who might.

"Can you have someone go grab my friend Balmur?"

He nodded and motioned to a servant that I hadn't seen. She was an Elf like some of the ones I had seen on my way here. She nodded and left after receiving her orders.

We waited for about half an hour, discussing his time here in solitude away from the Prime plane when a light knock sounded from the door.

"Enter!" Thogan called.

The Elf servant came in followed by Balmur.

"The Mountain is GOOD!" bellowed Thogan as he bum rushed Balmur.

The two Dwarves ended up in a pile on the floor with Thogan laughing and Balmur reaching for his weapons.

"It's okay, Balmur. He's cool."

"Shit, man, warn me next time!" shouted the Azer Dwarf. "Where have you been? We thought she killed you."

"It's a long story, dude." I sighed. "I'll explain it to all of you if we can all get together, but for now, I have a question. You have any mead from our time at Djurnforge?"

He smiled and pulled out a small barrel, about two feet tall and a foot wide. He popped the cork off the top of the cask and pulled out a set of earthenware cups. He poured mead into each and handed one to me, then Thogan. The champion looked as if he was going to weep openly again and looked to us for approval. We held out our cups and tapped them together in a silent toast. We watched as the stoney Dwarf savored every last drop of his cup. Then we watched as a tear escaped.

"This be the best mead I ever had." He sniffled at us. "Thank ye, cousin."

"No problem, man."

"Now, what can I do for ye, Zekiel?"

"The queen said that you could teach me some more techniques with the axe?"

He smiled savagely and clapped us both on the shoulder. "Lad, for the gift ye just gave me, I will show ye both me clan's secret technique. Who would have know'd that Dwarves of the age'd fear magic? Strange lot. Oh well, least ways we can bring this to rights."

"What is it?" I had to admit, my gamer mind was reeling. Secret techniques were serious game changers, and we needed every advantage.

"I'll shows ye."

He stepped out into the center of the practice floor and brought his axe to bare. He snapped his fingers, and a dummy appeared to stand twenty feet away. He threw his axe at the dummy, and it hit home with a thunk. We waited quietly while he grinned at us. Then he blurred out of existence and appeared with his hand on the axe.

"Now faster!" he said and snapped his fingers again. This time, it sprouted forty feet away on the opposite side. He threw the axe, and as it sailed, he disappeared and came back holding the handle once more. He crushed it into the dummy and growled in satisfaction.

"What was that?!" Balmur asked in wonder. I wanted to be able to do that.

He said it was called something that sounded like two rocks cracking against each other. That wasn't traditional Dwarvish. I looked at Balmur, and he was just as lost. We asked him to repeat it while Balmur had his Language spell active.

"Blade Shift?" he puzzled out.

"Not so artsy as me own, but sure." The older Dwarf grunted.

"Well, how do we do it?" I asked.

"Be takin' yer shirts off, lads," he said and went through a door off to our right.

Balmur and I looked at each other than complied. When Thogan returned, he had a medium-sized box in his hands.

He snapped his fingers again, and an earthen table formed beside us. The Elven servant brought out a chair for him to sit on. He motioned for Balmur to lay down first and then got to work.

Thogan either wasn't one for conversation while he was working or couldn't afford the distraction because he was focusing all his effort on tapping the little inked needle into my friend's skin. He used a small ruler for reference, inking every line perfectly straight. After half an hour, a few sips of good mead, and a few grumbled curses from Balmur, the majority of the work was done, and I could see the outline forming. It was a pentagram about the size of a mayonnaise jar lid, but it looked different, like it was clearly missing one of the points of the star, specifically the top one. It was closed; lines closed each point, isolating them from the base of the star, but the missing portion was left incomplete. Bare.

With the amount of concentration he had for his work, I doubted that Thogan would mess up. I resolved to ask him when he stopped anyway, just to be safe.

After a once over with the ruler and a final, critical glare from the stone-skinned Dwarf, he nodded at his work.

"Excuse me, Thogan? Why did you leave one of the pentagram's points off?"

"That be what I'll use as the focal point of the spell, lad," he explained. "See here, now. Let me do me work. Ye'll see it 'fore long. Gimme yer weapons, cousin. No, no, not the wee ones, the main ones ye be usin'."

Balmur pulled out his Mountain Fangs and sat them in front of Thogan on his self-made work bench. The Dwarf picked them up and whistled in admiration at the craftsmanship of each one.

"Damned fine hammering there, cousin. Damned fine."

Thogan pulled a diamond-tipped chisel from the box and began to carve the opposite of the same pentagram into the metal back of the first weapon where the axe was widest. Rather than filling in the pentagram completely like the other, he left the other points and the base of it blank, then filled in the top point of the star.

"Together, they make a whole. This way, when ye activate the spell, yer body goes to the missing piece furthest from yerself. Beautiful magic it is."

He finished carving the first one, then handed it to Balmur. After that, he came to stand before my friend and whispered a short phrase in the grinding, earthy language he spoke previously, then touched his forehead to Balmur's for a moment.

"Now, do what I told ye, and hold it to the mark." He crossed his arms as he waited.

As we watched, Balmur pricked his right thumb with the weapon, then pressed the thumb to the carved pentagram on it before pressing it to his chest. A blinding light flashed, then nothing.

"Good," said Thogan. "Now, the runes be attuned. Ye can cast the spell. Throw it, cousin."

The dummy that hadn't been destroyed was still standing off at the other end of the room, so he took aim and threw the Mountain Fang. It hit the dummy and stayed in, and after focusing, he blurred and reappeared with his hand on the grip.

"Wooooah," he breathed. He looked at me, and we both laughed.

"Ye do tha' 'til it becomes second nature." He made a shooing motion at several more dummie's across the way that had joined the one he stood by. "I'll get yer other one done fer ye an start on Zekiel. Gimme a minute."

True to his word, he carved into this one twice as quickly as he had the other and put it in my friend's hand. He did the same thing he had to attune it but with his left hand getting pricked.

"Now mind, ye can only use one of 'em at a time." Thogan wagged his finger at Balmur. "The spell will only look for the furthest one away from ye. Use it wisely. I don't know many Dwarves what use dual wieldin', but it canna hurt to try it."

Thogan rested for a few seconds while we watched Balmur get used to the spell. He was learning much quicker than I thought I would have. It could have been due to the fact that he already had spells he could use to move instantly. Or he was just that damned good. Either way—he made it look easy.

"Lay on down, Zekiel." Thogan wiped his hands on a cloth he produced from his pocket. "And assumin' ye have a human form?"

I took the hint and shifted into my human form. I lay down on the slab and let the Dwarf do his work.

The ink he used for me was white and stood out in stark contrast to my dark skin. It stung, but having a few tattoos myself in my own world, I just tuned it out. Getting a tattoo in a lot of ways was a rite of passage in some cultures. Taking the pain to outwardly show what you had on your inside. Enduring. That my be true, and part of me really believed it because right now, this absolutely was.

The spell itself required it, and this was very much so a rite of passage to do it. And here was Thogan giving me mine.

This Dwarf, who had missed his people so much, missed the chance to grow old with his clan—to die an honorable death. This Champion of the Unseelie who had fought gods know how many battles was passing on his clan's probably-forgotten spell. The thought of it made me proud. It also added one more name to the long list of people I was trying to protect by doing what my friends and I were attempting.

After I don't know how long, the pain in my chest subsided and Thogan grunted as he looked over his handiwork. He held out his hand, and I produced Storm Caller for him. He took it into his hands almost reverently, admiring the work of a skilled craftsman. He didn't even try to make conversation over it. He kept muttering that he wouldn't harm it and the same to that effect.

He carved the mate to the rune on my chest with the greatest of care. I watched as he did it. Occasionally, gently, brushing off the metal shavings from the spot on the haft where he made the mark, he masterfully executed his art.

Soon, my great axe was back in my palm. I pricked my right thumb, touched the bloodied rune to the one on my chest and thought as loud as I could, *BOND*.

CONGRATULATIONS!

You are now bonded by blood to your weapon with an ancient form of Dwarven magic!

"And now to pass on the learnin'," Thogan said. He had me kneel and put his forehead against mine and began speaking in, what I assumed to be, Ancient Dwarvish. I didn't understand, but I received a prompt asking if I wanted to learn the spell.

Uh, hell-the-fuck yes I did!

CONGRATULATIONS!

You've learned an ancient spell. The practitioners of this spell have been gone for more than eight thousand years, and here you are, learning it. Amazing.

The realization that the Dwarf before me was around one-thousand six-hundred years old and that everyone he loved and probably their great-grandchildren were dead hit me hard. I looked, stricken, to Balmur, and he simply shook his head. I understood, though. There was no point in crushing the man. He didn't need this weighing on him, too. Instead of breaking, I stayed strong, and I read the other prompt.

NEW ABILITY UNLOCKED!

***Blade Shift** – Caster uses his weapon as a focal point for an instantaneous lesser teleportation. Range: 120 feet. Cost: 20 MP. Cool Down: 6 seconds.*

Damn. For that little amount of mana, I could really fuck shit up. Six seconds in combat was a decent amount of time, though. I would have to either plan carefully, or see where I could go with it and what I could do.

"Ye be knowin' what ta do lad?"

I nodded, selected a dummy, and threw Storm Caller; it flew true and hit the target. Then I activated the spell. I felt a tug, and then my hand was on the haft of the axe. My grip was a little loose, but I could fix that by gripping as soon as I felt my hand touch the weapon.

The transition was smoother than what I had expected. Balmur and I spent a few hours with Thogan, perfecting the skills necessary to use the spell as best as we could, and then we had lunch before practicing some more. Balmur was much better at it than I was, but hey, we can't all be good at everything.

We made decent headway when the queen herself opened the door. Thogan dropped down to his knee with his head bowed, and when Balmur didn't join him right away, Thogan dragged him down to a knee, too.

I went to, but the queen raised her hand and said simply, "No."

"Yer majesty," Thogan said from his knee. "It be rare to see you so often. What can this ol' Dwarf do for ye?"

"I came to collect my friend," she informed us. "There is much I must do yet, and I would ask his company."

"So ye were truthful then, lad," he spoke in awe.

Balmur just glanced at me and shrugged. To him, this was kind of par for the course. I was a naturally friendly person. He knew I would explain things when I could. I hoped.

"Of course, my Lady Queen." I smiled at her. "Thogan, thank you for blessing me with your spell and your help. I appreciate it in the fight to come."

He nodded and smiled back, "Lad, ye gived me the best gift of me life. Ye did me the honor. Yer kin ta me. And Balmur too. If ye could come back again and share a drink or out there in the hall—I'd be happy."

"Of course. Balmur, I'll join you and the others later. Okay?"

"Got you, man."

The queen allowed me to exit, and we walked to her room once more. On the way there, she told me about some of the preparations that had come to pass. Food was made and the throne room cleared. I asked what she did with the people, and she explained that she had a room for them to be stored.

"You said that they were no longer as interesting to you, right?" I asked, reaching that she was feeling generous.

"Yes," she answered as she put some leafy greens on her own plate from a platter brought out by one of her shade goblins.

"Why not free some of them?" She stopped to look at me for a moment, so I continued, "Not the ones who did something truly bad to you or yours—I'd never think to release them—but what about some of the others whose crimes were minor enough to be forgiven?"

She placed her hands in her lap and stayed silent still. Either I had her interest, or she was trying to decide if there was a hidden agenda on my part.

"Everything I told you thus far has been truth. I want your friendship, but I also want to have you seen in the right light or shadow if you prefer. This is the new age you so desired, right? Why not thin your art collection of the less desirable pieces and focus on the future? Your cold night in Prime? Ushering in a new era. From what I gathered on our way here, everyone assumes that you're crazy. Evil. Vile. I know that you don't mind that, but what if you could show them better, that you are what they need. How many more Fae would swell your ranks from the enemy if they knew you were capable of such cruelty to those who cross you and forgiveness for those who are deserving?"

Before she could answer, I said what I thought could possibly sway her, "Wouldn't it drive that Seelie bitch insane to know that even in secret, her people might prefer you?"

"Oh, you are good," she said simply. Her smile was slight, but it was there. "Cunning minded, my friend. Very cunning. Oh, but were you here a century ago, we would have had our fun. Come."

I nabbed a plate that had been made for me by the shade goblins and hurried along after her. We walked for possibly fifteen minutes until we came to a large room, larger than the throne room that was full of the living sculptures. We walked in, and she lifted us with a pillar of ice so that all of them were visible.

She held a hand out and flippantly waved to our left then our right. Rows of the sculptures began to crack and shatter. There were groans and rumblings of some of the larger creatures accompanied by the flutterings of the smallest creatures. Fairies and pixies, I thought.

"Speak to them on my behalf, Zeke," she said with a smile. "Tell them of my—how did you say it?—ushering in of a new era?"

I sighed. I hadn't seen this coming at all, and I hated public speaking. I was never all that good at it. Shit.

I looked out at the now thawed creatures sprinkled amongst the still frozen creatures. They looked up at us, some with hatred in their eyes, many with confusion, and a few with hope. Hearts and minds, win the hearts and minds.

"Eyes!" I spoke loudly, accidentally falling back on the first word that got my attention for some time in the Marine Corps. I took a steadying breath, then used my chest to amplify my voice. "All of you who now move freely have earned something I'm certain you never thought you would—forgiveness! Today, the day of your freedom, marks the beginning of a new era for the Unseelie Fae. Your crimes—whatever they may have been—are forgiven, and for that, you have Queen Maebe to thank. In the coming days, no, hours—change comes. With her leading the way into a new era of prosperity and power, you will all gain tremendously."

Some grumbled so low I couldn't hear them, but one of the Elves who looked like the queen spoke up quite loudly. He just looked like a jerk and carried himself like one too. "And what kind of power would she offer us? Frozen, watching her languish over these last centuries, I have my doubts that she could provide anything."

Dude, I'm trying to do you a solid here, I thought anxiously. *If I don't come off hard enough right now, she may just say fuck it and freeze them all or worse, kill them and none of them will be spared. Time to talk tough.*

"The power to keep your life, should you but hold your tongue and do as you're told, asshole."

Some of the others laughed, and the Elf just snickered and made a rude gesture. I saw movement to my right, and suddenly, Maebe was standing in front of the offender. She thrust her palm forward and plucked it back almost faster than I could follow. The Elf before her fell to the ground, horrified with his mouth agape. She put something in his mouth, and then he froze solid once more. The queen looked over her freed subjects with a cruel smile, then leapt onto the pillar with me once more. She pulled a handkerchief from nowhere and wiped her palm and fingers clean.

"His heart," she said by way of explanation when I looked askance of her.

After a second, it hit me that she had fed him his heart. I looked at the ground and saw the small smattering of fresh blood and the frozen pool of it inside the ice. I looked at her, and she smiled sweetly.

"He will make an excellent centerpiece for the feast later." She looked back over her subjects, then back to me.

"Go back to your homes and families, if you have them. Those of you who don't may see the queen's folks and see about work that needs to be done. When the call comes, answer it," I pointed to the newest addition to the art, "or end up like that."

They fled. Hell, I didn't blame them; I would have too. If it did come to that, could I back it up? I thought back to the little boy that Rowan had slaughtered to send us here. One who had been close to my own son's age. That was someone's kid. If I had to be a little harder—more brutal and savage than was normal for me—so be it. If a few needed to pay for their inability to cooperate just to keep more safe, I would have to live with that. I didn't have to enjoy it—just endure.

"Will you accompany me to my throne room?" she inquired brightly, despite the grizzly act.

"Sure?" I answered with a shrug.

We walked back slowly; she was going over the things I had said. She praised me for using the Fae love of power against them while making her appear generous.

"You would have made a wonderful, terrible Fae." She chuckled throatily. "That threat at the end? Delectable."

We came to the throne room, entering by way of the same door we had used the day before to leave. Inside, it looked much the same as before, but empty except for the giant Dragon with the throne in its jaws.

We walked to the front of the giant beast. Maebe snapped her fingers, but rather than the simple sharp pop the action would normally give, it sounded like an iceberg breaking in half. The ice on the Dragon's body begin to cloud, then crack and fall away in great chunks.

The Dragon's eyes opened behind the ice on its head. Great orange orbs focused on Maebe and then myself. A rumble and a crash, then the Dragon shook the ice off its body like a dog might shake after a bath. Ice flew at the walls before falling harmlessly to the ground to shatter. Her throne it sat down gingerly.

"Messy as ever, Snowball."

The Dragon raked her with a look of annoyance and yawned to the point that I found myself joining in. It smacked its lips, then reached a fore claw up to scratch its chin. Now that the ice was gone, I could see that the scales weren't what I thought they'd be—smooth and rounded until the point at the bottom. No, these were jagged, white scales that looked like flat icicles, some at least several feet wide at the largest coming down to a point almost like a rapier on some. His jaws were covered in some more jagged, long scales that dripped cold water that froze before hitting the ground as ice shards. Now that he was here, the pleasant warmth of the room had dropped to what one might expect in a palace of ice.

"You're much too old to call me that now, little one," it rumbled to her. The voice was deep but somehow wizened, like an older man's would be in his later years. "You know my name. I would appreciate you using it. Where is your mother?"

"She hasn't ruled for five centuries," Maebe said.

The Dragon nodded and smacked his lips again. "A five century nap? Well, it has been a while. What have I missed?"

She began to fill him in on some events I didn't understand, but he seemed to because he nodded along and asked a simple question here and there. After a while, she began to tell him of the latest situation to arise—my party's arrival to their realm and the fight against War.

"I see," he grumbled with his eyes closed. "And you have summoned me for counsel?"

"Yes and no." Mae sighed. "They are to be my champions in the Prime realm, and I wished to aid them how I could. I have yet to impart what I can to them, but it cannot wait for some. Your presence is two-fold. You being awake shows that I am serious in what is to come, but I wanted to know if you would be willing to help outfit my new champions for the cause."

"Nothing is without a cost, child," he rumbled; he seemed to be enjoying that she had come to him. "You know my price."

"I do," Maebe said, looking slightly defeated.

She stepped forward, so close to the maw of the Dragon that it dwarfed her. Was he larger than before? The tip of his nose was at least a good foot and a half taller than me, so it was huge to her. She walked around the side of the Dragon's head to just behind the jaw line. She then began to scratch him roughly with both hands. A sigh of relief almost pushed me off my feet, and the shaking coming from his back leg thumping the ground didn't help either.

"Please, Uncle Winterheart, please help me with my champions?" she said it with so little enthusiasm, that this had to have been something that he asked for all the time when she was younger.

How old was she?! Damn, man.

"That wasn't believable at all, but oh well. A daft old uncle like me has to take what he can get, right?" He chuckled and ice began to fall as his breath froze. I hadn't noticed it before, but the air seemed to grow cold to the point where my breath began to show, and the sound of ice cracking resounded around us as he lifted his head from where it had frozen to the ground.

"I remember when you were but a small, smiling creature but only a dozen centuries ago. You used to climb my scales and pester me about Ice Magics all day—begging me to teach you how to fly." He sighed theatrically before muttering, "The good old days."

He looked at me then for the second time since his release. "I have been frozen a long time, but the time has yet to come where one would be so rude as to not introduce themselves to an ancient Dragon, such as myself."

"Forgive me, Great One," I said as I attempted to bow as I had to Maebe. "I am Zekiel Erebos, come to help defend this land from War and his minions. While I did not choose to come here, I have found a great friend in Maebe."

"YOU WILL CALL HER QUEEN, MORTAL!" the ancient Dragon reared to his full height and bellowed at me. The wind whipped, and I felt the cold fury of his words slap against my skin. "BOW YOUR HEAD AND BEG FORGIVENESS AND I MAY ONLY EA–"

"You will do no such thing!" Maebe's voice carried over the roar of the great mister before me. She stood before me with her fists to her side, staring down the confused Dragon. Well, staring up the Dragon, anyway.

"What?" he gasped. "He blatantly disrespected you! He thought himself better—calling you by name! Him! A subject!"

"He isn't a subject. He's my friend," she explained calmly. I was just trying to stop my teeth from chattering noisily.

The temperature had dropped significantly, and I was cold and terrified. Thankfully, I didn't have to go to the bathroom beforehand.

"Friend?" He tilted his head to the side in a dog-like manner. "What use has a monarch for friends?"

"Someone to talk to who won't stab me in the back. Someone I know who will listen to me and treat me with respect because they want to, not because they have to. Zeke has treated me better in a day than any subject has in my entire life and at no cost. The gifts I give, I give freely because he doesn't ask. He doesn't demand. He simply wanted my friendship, and so he has it. He has given me new purpose, Winterheart! He has helped me find something to help wile away the years unlike before."

"If you needed a companion, why did you not come to me?" The great Dragon, this primal being of ice and death, suddenly reminded me of a jealous, sullen child.

"Would you want someone who lectures you on etiquette all the time to talk to? Someone stuffy and crotchety?"

"I most certainly am not crotchety!" he cried indignantly.

"Who was it that froze a servant's entire line because their meal wasn't cooked the way they hadn't remembered to request for it to be?" He looked at her in shock. "Yes, I knew all about that, Uncle Winterheart. At the time, it was slightly entertaining, but no more. I like to think I have matured past that."

Winterheart looked at her with his giant, orange eyes a moment longer, then sighed in defeat.

"Okay, I can be crotchety at times, but do you know how hard it is to be frozen so long?" He stood on his back legs and stretched, his head bumping the ceiling. Something cracked, and he groaned in relief.

"You can't even tell how long you've been frozen!" Laughed the queen. It was a magical sound.

"It's so hard on my achy joints, child!" He feigned injury and lifted his offending leg.

"How about a deal, then?" she asked, a smile on her face. He looked at her in careful interest, the ridges above his eyes raised slightly.

"You give my friend and his friends who qualify for your aid what you can, and I will let you out more often."

"Done," he blurted out before she could recant the deal. No bartering, nothing, Damn.

"What can you offer them?" the queen asked sweetly.

"I would have to see them first," he explained. "Bring me the ones who have an affinity for the cold. Oh, and also, food, please. A lot of food."

Servants left, some coming back with freshly cooked haunches of meat, larger than even I thought was possible. The Dragon ate heartily while the other servants went to fetch Bokaj and James.

While we waited for my friends, I watched Winterheart eat. It was amazing. I had fought a Bone Dragon, sure.

That was cool as hell.

I had even been turned into a werewolf.

Again, cool as hell.

But here, not forty feet from me, was a feasting Dragon. A living, breathing Dragon.

"I knew her mother, you know," he said after throwing a large side of ribs into his mouth whole and swallowing another seconds later. "She raised me. Thought me as a pet until my intelligence began to rival even her own. That's when she taught me magic, and I took to it like, well, a Dragon to the air. Her magics focused primarily on the cold and darkness. My focus was always the cold. It changed me over time. Made me look like this. More powerful than my peers, though I was already that."

He chuckled and then picked up a table full of large meats and vegetables, tossing the whole thing into his gullet. "Oops. Sorry about the table, my dear."

"Of course you are, Uncle. I know how hungry you get. Remember, we hold court tonight."

"Yes, yes," he muttered, sucking on a clawed digit. "Just a small snack to hold me over."

By my calculations, he had eaten a small farm. The shock must have shown because he chuckled again, and Maebe smiled at me.

"He ate for three days once, stopping only to belch and berate a servant for tardiness. It was quite a show."

"Oh I remember one of the giant lambs you brought to me. Oh!" Drool dropped from his mouth and shattered on the floor. "How succulent it was! So tender, and the spice of it was divine!"

My friends came in moments later, while a debate on how a rack of lamb should be spiced raged, and they stood aghast at what they saw.

"A Dragon! Holy shit!" James shouted.

"It's rude not to introduce yourselves," I chided. Winterheart smiled at me.

They introduced themselves, and then the ancient Dragon did the same. He looked to Bokaj first.

"You are of the Ice, born of it. Changed by it. You, I can work with." He laid down in front of my friend, then breathed onto him, a great gust of arctic air cut across the forty foot distance and lanced through him. The air circled once, twice, then engulfed him in a tornado of ice shards and cold.

After a moment, the air current died down, and Bokaj fell to the floor, unconscious. I started to move forward, but the Dragon stopped me. "Let him lay. He has to cope with the blessing. Come, I turn now to you."

He reared back his head and roared loudly, almost deafening us all. Ice erupted from his body, then crashed into me, sinking into my skin. It hurt, at first, and my health dropped by almost three fourths, but I actually stayed conscious for this one. Then I went numb.

WARNING!

Your spell Frozen Dagger has been lost to the fury of the storm that is Winterheart, Ancient White Dragon.

What the fuck?! He took the spell I had relied on so much? That spell had gotten me through tough times and had saved my ass more than once. Not to mention, it was one of the cheapest spells in my arsenal. That fucker had cheated me!

CONGRATULATIONS!

You have been blessed with more insight into what it truly means to use true cold to attack your foes. You have been granted the more powerful variant of the Frozen Dagger spell – Winter's Blade. This spell has the same limitations of the original spell but does twice the damage for only 10 MP.

Bow and scrape before the bender of the frosts to his will, the powerful and majestic Ancient White Dragon, Winterheart!

I'll never understand this world's sense of humor, I thought to myself as I stood and cast Regrowth on myself.

"Thank you, Winterheart," I said, attempting to bow again.

"Show me," he said simply, curiosity in his eyes. "Hit me with it."

I smiled and complied willingly. He would pay for fucking with me. First, I started with the normal shot. I motioned like I was throwing a knife to cast the spell. Rather than a small blade of ice shooting forward, a large, three-foot-long sword of ice that radiated cold energy flew from my hand and crashed into the side of the Dragon where it exploded against his side. He smiled at me.

"That all?"

Oh hell no. I decided to charge the spell this time. I activated my ability, then waited for the spell to charge the full amount and thrust my hands forward. The sword that appeared this time was a great sword, roughly the same size as a certain buster sword from a favorite game of mine. I sent it speeding at the scales I'd hit a moment before. It thunked into his hide and exploded with a small concussive whomping sound before he laughed, again unfazed.

"That was very nice!" He grinned at me and looked over to James who was just standing there kind of lamely.

"Come touch my scales, little Dragon Elf." He spoke like he was trying to call a dog. James walked right up to him and touched his chest with his hand already encased in ice. The fist glowed white for a moment, then dulled and flared once more.

"Awesome," James whispered while looking at his fist. "It explodes now, and I can freeze my opponents. Well, there's a chance to anyway."

"Good. That is all I can provide for you."

"Excellent, thank you, Uncle Winterheart." This time, when Maebe scratched his scales, it was genuine.

Chapter Thirty

We were all excused to meet and prepare for what was to come. Maebe said she would be along after a while, giving me time to talk to everyone. A servant walked us to a larger room with chairs and a table with food on it. Yohsuke and Jaken were there already. We all sat down and waited for Balmur. He showed up a few minutes later with Thogan to guide him. He nodded to me and paused to look at our Fae-Orc as if he wanted to speak to him but left us after a second.

"Everybody alright?" I asked. They all looked okay, but you could never truly know.

"Everyone seems to be going out of their way to be sure that we're comfortable, but no one will speak to us unless it involves having to go somewhere," Yohsuke informed me.

"It's been a smooth day, man. What have you guys been up to?" asked Jaken. "And what was the deal with the queen?"

I told them everything that happened, careful not to say anything about half truths and anything I omitted. I held up a hand when someone would try to correct me on something and simply pointed to the walls, then my ear. We were probably being listened to, so best just to let me speak and catch them up as best I could.

"Then we saw the Dragon, received his blessings, and here we are."

"Woah, a real Dragon?" Jaken whispered in awe.

"Yeah," I couldn't help grinning at his expression. "She mentioned having something for you too, Yoh, but she didn't say what it was."

"Cool, man," he said. "She pissed me off when she interrupted me, but I'm glad she's cool with us for now. I wonder what our gear is gonna be. I know we gave him some instructions, but there's a vast difference between taking an order and trying to fill it, you know?"

"I hear you, man. Svartlan will do what he can. He reminds me of the guy at boot camp who would just sit in that chair and tell you your sizes for everything. Dude was crazy good at his job." I nodded at the door. "Shouldn't be too long now. The court will be gathering soon, and she will want us to be presentable. There will be food and whatnot, but you can be sure that whoever is there will be trying to pull some power-game shit and you will likely be a pawn somehow. Be on your toes."

Ten minutes later, someone was knocking at the door. I opened it, and Svartlan rushed in with servants in tow. He presented each of us with something to wear; he even gave Jaken new clothes to wear under his plate-mail—a striking, black material shirt that looked pretty damn good with metallic blue of his mithral armor.

To Yohsuke, he gave a pair of black breeches and a matching, long sleeved, black shirt with red trim along the seams. Then he handed him a cloak of the same material and color with Ursolon boots dyed black and red.

"Thanks, man." Yoh smiled at him as he looked them over.

"The material is Black Dread Silk," Svartlan explained before presenting Balmur with his little parcel. "The Lady Darkest demanded you have the use of it. This is to be your battle attire. You will find the defense a marked improvement. Not to mention, stylish."

True to form, the armor that Balmur pulled out had the Dread Silk shirt and a leather vest that looked both simple and stylish to wear. The leather was almost as dark as the silk but dyed to the same black and purple color of the Azer Dwarf's beard and hair.

"The leather is also from her personal supply. The animal that hide belonged to, the Belgar—a large, horned creature—has a hide that is nigh impenetrable to most weapons and highly resistant to magic. It's also in your breeches as the pads, young Dwarf. You're welcome! Moving on!"

He stepped in front of Bokaj, who took his gift with a grin and a thank you. Bokaj pulled out a white, thin material that looked like a hoodie from our world, put it on, then pulled out a matching pair of breeches. Last was a pair of boots made from the same material.

"These were a good deal of fun to make, though why you wanted your cloak like that, I don't know." He sniffed as if insulted. "Anyway, Shadow Lizard membranes. These creatures are called that for their stealth capabilities, obviously not for their skin tone. If you pull the hood up, you will find that you blend into most environments and are harder to see. Dear Balmur, don't look so disappointed. I have the utmost faith in your abilities as a sneak. Plus that armor will look dashing on you. That color, Oh! Brilliant."

He turned to me, and an almost sinister grin split his face. He pulled the next parcel from the servant behind him, who quickly scurried away.

"A vision came to me while I labored over this, a dark and terrifying vision. Her name shall not be uttered, for you can probably guess whom it was, but she bid me make this—special."

I took the package and opened it. It was the same dark material my friends had but thicker.

"She decided to gift you with her own personal touch. The material inside that is the hoarfrost—ice of her making infused with dark magic so as to never melt or soften. It will lend you extra protection. The breeches are the same. Ursolon boots, dyed black to match, with a slight personal touch and the same with the shirt. I took some liberties to make it more attractive. I think you will like it."

I held the shirt up in front of me and saw what he meant. Emblazoned on the front of it was a blue hued Lightning Roc, like it was my symbol. My crest.

"It's beautiful, Svartlan. Thank you." I shook his hand. "I will thank this mysterious benefactor myself."

He shook his head in amusement before finally turning to James.

"Ah, the savage." He frowned slightly. "Simple, inelegant, and quite uncouth. You were my favorite to work for. I made yours specifically to spite you. Just breeches. HA! Svartlan will make style come to you, and you will like it!"

That last bit was shouted in a bellow of challenge. He huffed for a second, obviously enraged at the very idea of it all, but he ran his hands over his head and breathed, visibly regaining control. He flicked his wrist at the Monk, and the last servant dart forward, her parcel held out.

James grabbed it and tore it open. Inside was a pair of the same sort of padded breeches that Balmur and I had been given. Underneath was a pair of sandals that looked like our Ursolon boots.

"Demitrinus!" Svartlan called.

An Elf servant, almost indistinguishable from the others that had come along, stepped forward. Seriously, the guy looked average as hell for an Elf. Forgettable even. He bowed slightly as he stood beside the Orc.

"He makes art. Under my watchful eye and with your approval, he will make art of your bare upper body," Svartlan explained.

"How?" James asked cautiously.

"Tattoos, of course. Yes, yes, I know you feel that your scales will be mussed, but I assure you, it will be fine."

"If it's just to look stylish, no." He shook his head at the tailor.

"His inking may look good, but it is so much more. He uses the blood of monsters and other alchemical creations to give his artwork power. You would be well outfitted, and, according to my research and that of my servants, there are many Monks who sport such artistry."

He looked uncertain, then looked back to the rest of us.

"I'm kind of jealous, but I'm branded already, so I'm good. I say go for it," I said, showing my palms and the elemental marks on them.

"Dude, love tattoos." Bokaj grinned and touched his arms where he had several in our own world. Jaken nodded along.

"It'll help, right? Go for it, man," Balmur finished.

"Better be cool as fuck. What kind of ink were you thinking?" Yohsuke asked.

"We have some made from the blood of some of the animals who made your new attire, and we thought that defensive would be best."

"Hey Zeke, think Kayda would want to make a contribution?" James asked.

"We can always ask. Let's take this party to Thogan's yard. He should be able to make us a table."

We left the room we were in and went on the track to the Stone Dwarf's haunt. When we arrived, Thogan was swinging his axe in practiced, precise motions through a complicated and deadly-looking form. I'd seen work like this back when I had practiced martial arts.

"Thogan, you mind if we kick it here for a while?" Balmur asked.

"Don' know what ye'll be kickin' but aye, ye can stay." He smiled at us. Jaken came in last, and the Dwarf eyed him before walking over to stand in front of him.

"Yer Clan Mugfist then?" he questioned him in a low tone.

"Yes I am."

The Dwarf eyed him longer this time. The silence was thick in the air. The rest of us had seen what this small man was capable of. I'd been at the end of his axe myself. This was going to get ugly if it did.

Thogan put his hand forward, and Jaken took the offered handshake. The Dwarf pulled the larger man down into a very awkward hug and hopped from foot to foot in glee. He began to sing a Dwarvish tune in his gravely bass voice. He raised a table like the one he made before, and James sat down.

I touched my necklace and willed Kayda to come out and stretch. She shook her long feathers out and greeted the party briefly before taking wing in the little space this room had to offer.

"Oh, she be a real beauty, lad," Thogan said with wonder in his voice.

"Yes she is! Oh, she's perfect! Tell me her name, Zekiel." Svartlan almost jumped onto my shoulders trying to get me to answer him. "Kayda? Oh, it's so simple it hurts, but she wears it so well! Come here, darling!"

I called to her through our bond, and she came to land beside me. Svartlan made to touch her, and before I could warn him, he made contact. The shock I expected to come simply didn't. Curious.

He called me beautiful, she explained in my mind. Ah, that made sense. I see that flattery worked well with her. Gonna have to have a talk about that. *Jealous,* she crooned softly.

I blushed and pushed her playfully. She pecked back but missed me on purpose.

I explained the situation, and though the idea of pain didn't seem attractive, she consented.

"How much do you need?" I asked Demitrinus.

"Freely given? Not much, maybe enough to fill this small jar." Even his voice was bland. Wow. He held out a small cup made of glass like a jar slightly larger than that of a thimble.

He pulled out a box, similar to Thogan's own, and laid out his tools on a cloth he pulled from it. There was a needle, much like the one used on me and Balmur, then a larger one, too. Both were made of diamond and looked sharp. Expertly made.

"This will take time," the Elf stated.

"Why don't you all go get dressed, and we will meet you soon?" Svartlan said.

"I'll stay. You guys go get dressed, and then Zeke can come back and trade me," Yohsuke said. He gave Svartlan a look that brooked no argument.

We complied. We took our time, bathing before we got dressed. The water was scented with oils and perfumes. Enough to hurt my nose, but at least we smelled good.

One of the servants took me, now dressed in my new gear, back to my friends. Yoh was standing near the door and nodded to me as the servant took him back to get ready. I stood vigil in the same place, leaning against the wall and eyeing the proceedings from my spot. A grunt here and there, sometimes a soft curse. It was pretty boring.

I must have dozed off for a second because I felt a thud and I was sitting on a raised stone bench. Thogan sat next to me, a smile on his face.

"He's almost finished up now. Yer bird's been watchin' over him like a, well, bird," he said sheepishly. "Ye can go an look now, if ye like."

I nodded and wandered over. What I saw was interesting to say the least. Not ink I would have chosen.

The first marking I noticed was the one on his back. A set of black wings with gold feathers that started in the center of his upper back, rose to his shoulders, and then swept down to his lower back. As I moved closer, I walked to my left to get a better look at the rest of his upper body. His arms had spiraling blue bands that began on his inner arm at the crease of his forearm and wrapped around, intersecting and crossing until they stopped at the wrist. His stomach had two grey tattoos, one on each side beside his abdominal muscles that looked like horns, thick at the bottom and curving into a wicked, pointed tip. The final markings I saw were two black swirls on his pecs, darker than the scales that covered some of his body. They were about six inches wide, and the lines were an inch thick at the widest.

"Pretty wild, huh?" I chuckled at him. He grimaced and nodded slightly. The process was going quickly enough; Demitrinus was sure in his work and was very dexterous from the looks of things. He chanted under his breath as he went, and the ink seemed to spread a little wider and farther than just the point of his tools. Magic at its finest right there. Could have done with that on my own tattoos. Rite of passage aside, it still stung like hell, and the healing process was a pain in the ass.

"What do you think, man?" James smiled slight, then grimaced as the Elf finished the right arm and moved back to his kit. "They picked specific parts from the animals, and the designs on my chest and arms are to help channel energy into what I want. Uh, theoretically speaking."

"I think they look good, man. It's not what I would pick, but it's not my body." I raised my eyebrows and sent a telepathic Mental Message reminding him that it wasn't his real one either. He nodded back.

I glanced and noticed that the he had moved on to Kayda's blood in the little cup. He muttered a few words, made a symbol with his hand and began to pour liquid from a small flask into the cup. Stirring it, he muttered a few more words, and it began to glow before changing to a now-blue color. The shade was the same as Kayda's feathers.

"What did you do?" I questioned, my curiosity piqued.

"The spell makes the blood more pliant to the reagent additive I put in," Dimetrinus droned. "The reagent makes the magical effect the blood gives permanent, or at least last as long as the marking lasts. Some markings may fade over time depending on the race, abilities of the individual, and the skill of the artist, and before you ask, I have not had any of mine fade."

"Fair point, man. Please, don't let me interrupt you."

The artist just grunted before dipping the tip of his needle into the concoction and going about his business.

"Best to let him work, Zekiel." Svartlan yawned. "This last bit will be tricky."

I nodded and payed my friend a smile before I went back over to Thogan. We sat, and he asked me to tell him about my time with the Dwarves. I recounted it all to him, and he smiled at the stories. Even laughed with me when I told him about the crone who taught me to enchant. He did get a little quiet when I told him what happened with Garen, the racist Dwarf.

"That was a great dishonor that he paid his clan and our Way," Thogan said. "Got to apologize for that, lad. There are some of all races and creeds who don' like outsiders or other races. That doesn't reflect well on any clan, let alone under the rules of hospitality. That's a grave disrespect. She would be well within her rights to kick him out on his arse."

"Oh, whatever she's doing, I'm certain he's paying for it right now." I smiled, probably more cruelly than I should have, but it was genuine. "She's a cruel bitch, she is. She was just training me, and I wanted out of the clan. I can't imagine what it would be like to actually earn her wrath."

Thogan laughed heartily at that. "Think I should like to meet this'un."

"Oh, I doubt that." I laughed and clapped him on the shoulder. "Wanna lead me through some great axe exercises?"

He nodded eagerly and pushed the range of the room away from the working guests. Once we were far enough away, he had me bring out Storm Caller and go through some motions that I had seen him doing slowly and with purpose. He corrected me on a few things: widened my stance a bit on an overhead chop, had me lean back a bit on a wide, horizontal swing, hand positioning, and even some theories on movement and attack styles. He remarked that it was uncommon for a Druid to use a weapon like mine, and that gave me pause. Granted, I knew why from a gamer standpoint, but I wondered why he thought as much, so I asked during a small break.

"Well, yer usually one fer casting spells." He splayed his hands like he was casting. It made me chuckle. "What I knows about magic users is they tend to not be as, er, burly as yerself. They don't like the front lines."

"They're squishy," I interjected.

"Exactly!" He clapped. "They takes a beaten like a wee fruit, no offense meant, lad." I smiled and waved it off. "That, and they tend to spend all their points fer mana and spell strength, not that I blame'em."

"A term we like to use is 'Glass Cannon'," I suggested. The ancient Dwarf looked at me as if I had gone daft. "You might be able to fire it a couple times to great effect, but it doesn't take much to destroy it."

"Aye, lad." He nodded his understanding. "If ye know'd that, why are ye swingin' the axe? I mean no disrespect, ye swing her well, but it don't make sense."

"I like to be a little more hands on than a lot of magic users, I guess." I didn't want to divulge things that I couldn't, but I tried to put it to him in a way he would get. "I like to be as well rounded as I can. I wasn't always with my party, either, so I didn't want to be so easily done in. Since I found that I would be working with my friends, I've kind of been trying to fill out whatever role it is that the group needed. I can heal a little bit, fight up close and from afar, and I even picked up enchanting to help my friends with their crafted goods. My role is kind of fluid and ever changing. It seems a bit more fun that way, you know?"

"No, I don't." Thogan grinned. "My lot are warriors. We live and fall by the blade or good mead... or a good woman... or a bad one—we are only so picky. But the wee bit of magic we know, we use to our advantage in battle, but it be scarce. Not many of me brothers would be able to do what ye do so selflessly. Ye be a good lad, Zeke. Ye be well along the Way."

I felt my face heat for a moment at his praise. Was it selfless? I didn't know about that; it was kind of what I would do in almost any game my friends and I played. I was too lazy to pick a play style and stick with it because I was too curious about other ways of doing things. Well, I don't know about lazy, more indecisive, which sounded a lot more *me* than I should have been comfortable with. Whatever.

"I don't know about that, but I am a team player. I was taught a motto by my leaders—Semper Gumby. It means 'always be flexible'. My ability to fill in the gaps for my friends makes me happy." I gave the Dwarf a cheesy grin and laughed. He joined me. We spent a few more minutes refining my technique while we waited, then the rest of the group joined us except for Yoh.

"Where's Yoh?" I asked.

"The queen came and nabbed him before he could bathe and change. Something about a gift that he may find worthwhile?" Bokaj supplied.

"I have no idea, but has anyone checked up on him?" I questioned, suddenly worried.

"Earrings aren't working." Balmur shrugged. "He can handle himself. Seems like he freaks a lot of people out. I know he did with the werewolves. They didn't even want to fuck with him too much."

True, I thought to myself. Yohsuke could be a scary motherfucker if you got on his bad side.

"Gonna have to wait and go with the flow then," James said and winced as he stood from the table. "Finally done. Can I heal myself?"

"Yes, actually. Ki would be best used, due to the magics in the ink itself." The Elf cleaned and cleared his tools from the stone slab of a table. He stood and bowed to us, then looked to Svartlan who dismissed him. We thanked him as he passed, but he didn't seem to genuinely care.

"Our Darkest Lady will return from her sojourn with your friend as soon as she can," The Orc smiled at us sweetly. "She has taken him to her private study."

"Where is that?" I asked.

"The dungeons," he shrugged, "or at least right next to them."

"Oh FUCK no, Snake," I cursed and crossed the space between us. "You will take me there. Now."

"She said you may worry and that you alone could come. The others will stay with me and learn the appropriate etiquette for this evening's affair. Thogan will escort you."

I looked to the Dwarf who had his great axe in hand and a grim expression on his face. "Business be this, lad. Let us go."

The others in the party looked toward me and gave me nods of approval, and I took off behind my guide.

We jogged through the labyrinthian hallways and passages until we came to a guarded door. Two suits of armor covered in frost—no, *made* of frost—stood on each side of the double doors with their halberds crossed before it. Thogan grunted at them inarticulately, and they moved out of the way with a small dusting of ice shavings falling off where they moved, like the joints had frozen in place.

"Gotta know how to talk to 'em," he chortled. Then adopted his business-like countenance. "Ready yerself. It gets a mite bit dreadful from this point on."

I gave him a terse nod and waited as he opened the door on the right. When he did, a wall of stench burst forth and hit my nose like I had actually sprinted into the side of a building. "It gets worse, lad. So much worse. Come."

I followed Thogan into the dark, dank depths of the stairwell we were in. As we walked on, the door we used to enter slammed shut, and I'd be lying if I said I didn't have that whole 'cartoon horror movie' vibe going on. I felt the darkness around us begin to creep in on us and had to fight my body's natural reaction to freeze and look for threats. I was the threat here. We took the stairs slowly, as they were unevenly spaced and crudely cut. It seemed like a defensive tactic that, if I weren't about to shit myself due to fear, I might have appreciated.

"It's not a natural fear, lad," Thogan said. "It be a sorcery. Allows the queen to make magic of the prisoners' suffering."

Moral conundrums aside, it seemed industrious, but I just couldn't bring myself to care until I knew my friend was safe. The moaning and groaning was low and constant. I could hear voices crying, cackling laughter, and mumbling from the insane, infirm, or both. It was not a pleasant sound. The whole place felt like it was festering.

We came to the bottom of this set of stairs, then took another off to our left. Five minutes later, we took another set that seemed to break from the wall and go into open space. The closest wall on each side was fifteen or so feet away. There was a landing that branched off in three routes: one in the center that lead straight down, and the others branched away from that set at an angle left and right. Those two looked more faded and foggy. False stairs—they were an illusion that my eyes found. I stayed quiet about it, though.

"False stairs here, they be illusions." Thogan grunted and moved on.

I grinned and followed along. That must mean he trusts me. Or he trusts his queen's choice in friends.

Eventually we came to a door covered in runes and locked shut. "We're at the door, Mae," I whispered, and it opened on its own. It creaked open loudly, louder than even I thought it should have, and we walked in. The inside was brightly lit in comparison to the rest of the surroundings. It was almost to the level of a hospital's fluorescent lighting. The ceiling was covered in bright ice, and a center spot of black in the middle was situated over a deep basin that flowed into the floor. A drip left the black spot, and it fell into the basin and drained away.

"Hello, my friend," Maebe greeted me warmly from her seat to my left. I looked, and there were shelves with books and bottles that were clearly labeled behind her; her desk was very neat as well. The room smelled as clinical as a hospital as well and had a wooden door in the rear that stood slightly ajar.

"Hi. Where is Yohsuke?"

"He is in the next room, communing with a Demon."

"Oh oka–A FUCKING WHAT?!" Her tone had been so nonchalant that I almost shrugged it off, too. I didn't even wait for an answer—I began to move toward the door.

She was in front of me almost instantly with her hand on my chest. My feet moved and slid, but she didn't budge. "You may go in and observe, but if you interrupt or go into the circle, his life will be forfeit. Swear to me that you will not intervene, and I will not stop you."

I looked down at her and scowled. "You swear?" She nodded.

"Then I give my word that so long as he is safe and I think he can handle it, I will not intervene."

"Witnessed," Thogan said from behind me.

"I will allow you then. Please, be quiet, though." Maebe turned and led us into the room.

Chapter Thirty-One

This room was larger, about forty-five feet squared with a raised floor in the center where a circle and pentagram you would see as the go-to symbol for a lot of occult worship on it. In the center of the circle stood my friend. His old cloak was hanging off to our right on a rack; he wore red shirt and some black breeches. His hands were out from his sides a bit, palms forward and slightly raised, as if to encourage someone to come at him. His breathing was quick but steady.

"What is he doing?" I whispered to the Fae queen.

"He is communing with the Demon. When it is ready to be seen, it will show itself. Quiet." She nodded to the raised floor, and I realized that it was a circle within another, larger circle.

"I consent to the terms of our agreement to negotiate. Show yourself," Yohsuke ordered and looked up, dropping his arms.

"So be it," an ethereal, cultured voice replied.

The air rippled in front of the Grey Elf in the circle, and there stood an honest-to-goodness Demon. He stood an easy ten feet tall, not including the scaly, curved horns that jutted out of his forehead coming to a pointed tip a foot above him. His face was stunning: eyes with glowing red irises, a masculine nose above blackened, pouty lips that let a little bit of fang peek through. His jawline and cheekbone would have made a male model jealous and most women weep with joy. His body was slim and athletically muscled, but I got the feeling that was a lie. Most beings like him had some serious supernatural strength going on; I had read it in dozens of books and seen it in all kinds of movies and shows. Just because he looked like a beefier track runner didn't mean he couldn't hand out some serious whoopin's.

His tail whipped back and forth behind him like a cat about to pounce on a mouse. At the end of it, no it wasn't a little cartoon devil tip, it was as sharp as a javelin and pulsed a sickly green light. He stretched his wings to the edges of the barrier and yawned dramatically.

"You called me forth for this one, Maebe?" it posed the question as it took notice of us. "You could have used my skills for anything and you chose a broken mortal?"

"Who you calling broken, fuckface?" Yohsuke spat. "Your negotiations are with me now, not some imaginary conversation piece to try and break my focus."

"Oh my, this one has bite!" It clapped and smiled at the tiny man before him. "Tell me, little one, what is it you desire?"

"I want the power to take out the Generals of War," he said calmly but forcefully.

"I don't know who that is, but oh well, I will play along." He actually took a knee so that he could stare the Grey Elf fully in the face. "And what is it that you believe you could provide me, mortal, that I would part with any of my strength for your cause?"

"Information and safety."

"Oh, information I can work with. Let's start with that. What can you tell me that I don't already know and that you think I might care about?"

"Someone is leaking information on how to summon Demons," he said simply.

"This is not new information, Broken One. Demons put forth that information often. It's a way for us to play on the Prime realm and prey on idiots who don't follow instructions well. A broken circle? My kind gets a new soul to play with. A miscanted word? You could very well end up a toad or some other nature of undesirable thing."

"They're giving the real deal to Goblins and probably other lesser beings." Yoh crossed his arms and smiled as fury crossed the Demon's face.

"Lies," it spat venomously. "No Demon would allow himself to be summoned by a filthy Goblin willingly."

"I'm in the Fae realm dude. Can't lie." He smirked. "And I think I know who might be doing it and why."

"Tell me who," the Demon demanded. His wings flared out, and I could smell sulfur from where I stood.

"Put your damn dick away," my friend commanded flippantly. "You know that's not how this works. Tit for tat."

"Fine, what will you protect me from, if you need power so badly?" The red being looked at him contemptuously.

"Two things: the being who is leaking the spells and summonings to lesser beings," Yoh explained, "and me and my friends."

"What makes you think I would ever fear you and your pathetic friends?" The Demon actually laughed at him.

"Because when we come to the infernal plane to take care of the motherfucker sending that shit topside, we're coming for them and anyone in our way." He growled and came dangerously close to the edge of his protective diagram.

I bit back the urge to shout a warning and brought Storm Caller out at the ready just in case.

"And when I say anyone, I mean *ANYONE*, including the slimeball who kept me from them. That looks like you if you don't give me what I want."

The Demon inched close to the barrier where my friend's face was, not an inch away and laughed. Just laughed. Yohsuke started to laugh, too. It was genuine. Then his right hand shot forward, breaking the barrier, and caught the Demon by its face. A bright, golden light flashed, and the Demon recoiled as if in pain. Yoh kept laughing.

"OATHBREAKER!" it hissed at him. "I will devour your soul and torture you for eternity!"

I started to rush forward, but Mae and Thogan grabbed me. I looked to Maebe, and she put a finger before her lips in the universal sign for quiet.

"I broke no oath," Yoh said calmly. "I agreed that no harm would come to me during our negotiations. You were the arrogant puto who thought he wouldn't be harmed and didn't feel the need to say so before the terms were deemed worthy. And if you thought that was bad? There's plenty more where that came from because I'm going to be so much stronger when we come knocking down your fucking door. Either help me or hide because I will get what I want."

The look of outrage on the infernal being's face quelled, and it started to smile. "Call your man off, Maebe, and let that one go. I am no threat to anyone in this room. At this time, no one will die. I so swear."

"Witnessed," I growled.

I stepped forward to the edge of the raised floor, to the side closest to the Demon and across from my friend. I nodded to him, and he nodded back.

"I will give you the power I can on condition that you provide safe passage for me and two of my minions and the information you have on the traitor."

"You and both minions provided they aren't helping the traitor in any way, shape, or form."

The Demon's eyes narrowed, and it nodded in begrudging respect. "I can agree to that stipulation."

"Good, because here's another." Yoh smiled, and it looked dangerous. "You are to tell not a single being, soul, minion, Demon, or anything or anyone else about our mission or that we are coming. You are not to share with anyone or thing, directly or indirectly what you have learned and will learn should this deal be struck."

"I won't tell anyone," the Demon promised sweetly.

"Oh no you don't." Yohsuke laughed. "That's a stipulation in our agreement and contract. I'm not taking anyone's damned word on that shit."

"I really am beginning to detest you, mortal."

"Deal with it."

"Did you want anything, little fox?" The Demon asked sweetly. "Maybe you and I could strike a deal? Hmm?"

"He's your man right there. I have a feeling my new friend would take umbrage to your trying to take me from her. Not to mention, I'd just give you the works the same way he did."

It looked to Maebe, and she smiled at him the same way she had her newly freed subjects—all feral and deadly.

"I shall pass on you then." It looked back to the Elf before it. "If that is all you want, then I suppose your soul would be too much to ask for? Not even an option? No? Fine. I agree to your terms."

"The deal is struck. Bring forth the contract."

The Demon stood up, and Yoh let him. He snapped his finger, and a piece of parchment appeared.

"Blood to bring the words into being," the Demon intoned as it pricked a finger and Yohsuke did the same. "Touch the page to form the contract, and say the Oath to form the Pact."

"I, Yohsuke, bind myself to this contract until its fulfillment or I die the final death. In exchange for the power to defeat War's Generals, I will give this Demon information and safe passage for two of his minions—should they prove not to ally with the traitor—and they keep their silence of what he has learned this day. That he will keep his silence to all of what he will learn today as well as our coming to the Hells."

As my friend finished, so did the infernal being. The sheet of parchment glowed red and black a moment before words materialized. The Demon read it first to check for errors, then passed it to Yohsuke, who read it carefully.

"Don't you sneak shit about getting my soul, you bastard. That will cost you extra. Fix it and fork over more of your power because that wasn't in the verbal agreement."

"Can't blame me for trying, can you?" The Demon waved a wickedly clawed hand over it, and the soul bit left the page. He read it again and saw that it was good.

"Scaling powers and more gained upon leveling up rather than a single transaction? That's agreeable."

"Figured as much. Your thumb print in blood at the bottom seals the Pact. Mine is there already."

He pressed his thumb on the opposite side of the Demon's, and the page doubled. "Your copy and mine should we need reminders. The item is soulbound so you can never lose or misplace it."

"Good," Yoh said.

"My payment?" Wings snapped shut and the Demon looked ready to pounce again.

"Your traitor will be either the advisor to or an imposter of a General of the Infernal Nobility. Think of someone who, up until recently, may have been occupied in their vices or 'work' and has become more vocal to the community about spreading discord and chaos. More so than normal at least."

The Demon closed its eyes as if in thought and nodded before looking back at Yohsuke.

"Hold still," the Demon said.

It leaned close to Yohsuke and whispered something even my sensitive ears couldn't hear. Then lightning fast, struck a clawed hand into the Grey Elf's chest and lifted him up. The ward around the outer circle flared to life and stopped me from getting inside. I started swinging my axe with wild abandon while the two beings outside it tried to stop me.

"Power through pain was never not agreed upon, little mortal. You should have stated that!" it bellowed its laughter.

The pulsing, green-lit tail raised behind my friend like a viper and stabbed him in the back where his heart was. I watched as the sickly light entered my friend's bloodstream, and his veins turned black.

In a plume of sulfurous smoke, the Demon vanished and left his victim to fall to the ground from nearly twelve feet. I watched helplessly as his health bar began to plummet. I cast my healing spells on him until my mana went dry, but nothing was working. Green foam was frothing from the side of his mouth as he coughed and sputtered. When I could do nothing else, I tried to get to him again.

I raged against the barrier in front of me as tears flooded from my eyes. The edges of my vision started to glow the tell-tale red of rage, my Lycanthropy curse coming close to triggering. I fought it back, screamed my fury to the realm, and pounded my bloody fists against the wall before me as I fell to my knees.

Finally, he stopped moving. His health bar drained to one hit point. "No no no no no," I whispered.

Prayed.

I didn't want to lose my best friend. The guy who had taught me so much about myself back home. The man I served with, who saved my life in my darkest times. How could I face his wife if he didn't make it home? None of us was promised that if we died here we would respawn or go home. Even the damned gods didn't know.

"I'm not... dying... yet," I heard and looked up to see my friend smiling weakly at me. "Puto."

I laughed at him; it was one of our favorite things to call each other when we were gaming.

I sniffed a bit, "Get up then, fucker. We've got hell to raise and a party to crash."

"Fuck, that shit hurt," Yohsuke groaned and sat up. He pulled a potion out of his inventory and downed it. "God DAMN those taste bad."

The barrier chose then to fall, and I rushed forward. I pumped a Heal into his body, and his HP jumped up by seventy and continued to rise with the potion he used.

"Let's go get you cleaned up, bud," I said as I helped him stand.

"Fucking shitbag-ass Demons and their love of wording, bureaucratic, motherfucking..." The man cursed the Demon until we got to the changing room where he bathed himself and changed into his new gear. He even threw in some classic insults and curses just to see me grin. I was glad to see he had made it.

"Let's go fuck with some Fae, dude."

Chapter Thirty-Two

"So, the spell worked for you, brotha?" Jaken grinned at Yohsuke. "Glad to hear it!"

"So that's what that was!" I put my head in my hand and sighed. "A stored holy spell of some kind?"

"Yup, Ring of Storing is definitely going to be the bane of quite a few more baddies' existences," Yoh chuckled. "Where's her Lady of Darkness-ness at, bro?"

"I'm not sure. I can't believe nobody thought to go with you, man, and how the fuck did you know to do all that? Where did you get your information?" I started to grill him.

"Woah, dude. Can't give all the tricks away, and you knows I do okay solo styles. The information? I got that from a little trick my instructor taught me. I can commune with the dead. Spirits and shit. I don't do it much because those fuckers are creepy, and they look all gross and whatnot, but it can help sometimes. After we found out that the Goblins were summoning Demons, I figured I should dig up what I could. Turns out someone high up in the food chain in the Infernal realm has been doing some shady shit, and that was my in."

We turned and came into the throne room at last and joined the rest of our friends. The place was set up for a huge shindig. Tables at the sides held food and refreshments. There was a floor to dance and congregate. It was lovely.

"As far as the summoning itself, well, Maebe provided that. I guess the Demon owed her a favor. She knew his true name."

"Names and power. Got it. Fuck, this is all so fantasy."

"Video game world, brother." Jaken elbowed me playfully.

I grunted and began walking a bit faster over to the rest of the group. We filled them in on what had gone down, and everyone agreed that they were happy that Yohsuke had made it through.

"And this soppy bastard starts the waterworks."

"I was pissed off that you were going to die before I could kick your ass at a video game, motherfucker."

"Shit, I might as well be immortal." We all laughed at that.

"I am glad that you all are well," came Maebe's voice behind me, "and you all look so good, too. Intimidating, I'm sure."

We all turned, and what I saw nearly floored me. She wore a tight fitting, black dress that seemed to writhe on her body like living shadow. Snowflakes glinted along the top near her shoulders and thinned out toward the bottom midway down her calves, and it looked much like a winter night sky. Her black hair was up in a braid that had the highlighted portions woven in. She was stunning, alluring even though she still had her beauty-dampening glamour in full effect. The others were still taken by her, but I got the full effect of her true self.

Wow.

"The festivities will start soon. I take it that Svartlan went over some of the formalities and explained things to you?"

"Yes, my Queen," Balmur supplied. "He also said that someone may challenge us?"

"As my champions in the Prime realm, they very well may. They could also try and win you over with honeyed words, promises of power and glory. Some may even seek to destroy you simply because you have my favor. You will need to be on your guard. I will have servants placed strategically around you, loyal to me of course, who will help if you truly need it, but I must warn you, any aid on my part, except in a few circumstances, would be seen as weakness on your part. That would hurt their support of this coming venture."

"Got it. Schmooze, but do it classy," Jaken said with a hand in the air for a high five.

"And don't get seduced by the ladies, or gents, looking at you, Balmur." Bokaj snapped his fingers and gave Jaken a high five.

"Har har, you know me, man, all about the dudes." Balmur rolled his eyes at his best friend and shook his head.

"And try not to kill anyone unless you are challenged to a duel. They may see an unsanctioned death as an affront."

"There might be duels?" I voiced my skepticism.

"It hasn't happened in some time, and I doubt it will as this is the first time I have held court in centuries. They may take issue with me, though. You may see... things that I have to do to strike fear into their hearts. Earn their respect. I may seem cold and indifferent—more so than usual, yes Yohsuke—but I want the best for you, and you have my full support. I do not say that often."

She graced us all with a radiant smile and stepped away with her eyes on me a moment longer than I thought necessary. I walked over to her as she began her journey to her throne.

"Excited to see your people?" I asked softly.

"I am excited to usher in a new era for my people. Whoever makes it through tonight, that is. I feel there will be a challenge. Where it will come from, I do not know, but it is coming." She stopped as we reached her throne; the Ancient White Dragon behind it snorted at me by way of greeting, and I nodded to him. "When the challenge comes, will you stand with me?"

"That's what friends do." I gave her a genuine smile and reached my hand out to her. She grasped it, and I gave hers a gentle squeeze. "We've got your back."

"Why would you have my back?" She looked genuinely puzzled. "It is on my person, and I dare say you cannot 'have' it."

I looked at her in shock for a moment before I burst into laughter that I couldn't stop for a beat. She looked like she was hurt that I was laughing at her. "It's a saying where I'm from. It means that whatever you may face, I'm behind you to help and watch your back."

"Ah, what a delightful, barbaric saying." She patted my shoulder comfortingly. "Thank you. I have your back as well."

"Well said."

She sat on her throne and waved me to her right. Winterheart rested his head on her left.

"The court may enter," she ordered to the servants at the door.

And they did. There were creatures that I had read about walking, moving, and giggling across the floor in their own respective ways, but all knelt once they came to stand before the queen. They kissed hands, they sought knowledge behind veiled questions, and more than a few eyed me hungrily for where I stood. Maebe was phenomenal. She gave as good as she got, even dismissing a few before they could pay their respects.

After they paid their respects to the throne, they ate and chattered among themselves. My friends roamed the floor, watched by Maebe and I. Some of the Fae would speak to my friends, especially Bokaj; his high Charisma must have made him more appealing to them, but nothing outright bad happened. Quite a few of the guests stood grouped closely together and whispered with their eyes on the throne. Eventually, the eating and whispering began to decline.

Finally, Maebe stood, and the royal Fae spoke, and I broke away from my staring into the crowd for any potential threats.

"Welcome, Court of the Unseelie. My court, long have I overlooked you due to a lack of interest. I was lost to my despair without a sense of direction. I had become bored of the doldrums of daily duty and withdrew. But not you. You have done your duties, taking care of my lands and my interests while I have contemplated the next step in forward progress. Step forth, my champions of the new era!"

My friends separated themselves from the crowd of Fae, and I stepped forward to stand to the right and slightly behind Maebe at her shoulder. The throng burst into chatter, some even boldly stated that a new era was a surprising idea from a sullen child. She didn't even so much as blink. She let the skepticism build until I thought that someone may outright question her—then she continued.

"These creatures, my champions, will be marching toward a new goal in the Prime realm. They will go forth on their quest with our aid and support and will escort a few chosen Fae to act as catalysts for change and as ambassadors to a few larger cities once through. They will also be protecting our interests while in the Prime as I instruct on occasion." She stepped closer to the crowd and smiled at them, all teeth and predatory glances. "Their judgement is my own, as they are my friends, and I am theirs."

The volume in the room devolved into whispers about this being someone completely different and that there was a usurper on the throne. That she had gone soft and who in their right mind would befriend mortals let alone anyone. She was Fae royalty—what need had she of friends, when all should simply be satisfied to serve? Again, Maebe said and did nothing. She let them speak as they would, which was new to me, but then again—politics.

Am I right?

She didn't need to ask anyone for help; she was queen. Anyone who stood in her way or in the path to her goals would be demolished, and that's exactly the look and vibe I got off her in that moment. I couldn't help feeling like I had bitten off more than my friends and I could swallow. Wouldn't be the first time my eyes were bigger than my stomach.

"As time goes on, our foothold in the Prime realm will grow stronger and our influence will carry over. People will see how we aided our champions, and their people and our influence will grow further! Soon, we may shed our chains here and usher in a new era of prosperity and change for the Unseelie. No longer will the lies spread by the so-called 'Court of Light' be able to curse and slander our people. We will let our actions shout over their whispers. Stand with me, my court. Unseelie and we stand to gain so much more. Power unrivaled."

The crowd muttered some more, and then all in attendance knelt quickly. Maebe looked triumphant, her smile radiant against her dark, starry skin.

"Soo–" she began to speak, but a cold, cultured voice interrupted her. I turned to see someone seated on her throne. Not even Winterheart looked up at the individual.

"I am so glad to see that you have finally made some friends, little queen."

He was tall, or long in this instance, as he lounged over the hand rests of the throne lazily. One leg draped in green rested over the armrest, and the other sprawled in front of the throne closest to us while his head and upper body leaned over the side closest to the White Dragon. He wore a matching green shirt of the same color and material that looked almost like satin. He propped his bald head on the knuckles of his left hand while his right drew patterns on the seat under his stomach.

I looked to Maebe for some clue as to who the hell was in her domain and saw that she, too, had bent the knee to this man. His gaze shifted to me, and his ears, much like Maebe's, longer than a normal Elf's but angled up and out rather than straight out like the queen's, twitched. I felt a gentle but insistent tug at my hand and looked to see Maebe was trying to pull me toward her.

"Leave him," the man commanded. The pull vanished.

"Who are you?" I asked. No sound escaped from any of the Fae, but I heard footsteps as my friends began coming closer.

"Mortals and their need to name things." He smiled sardonically. "You've been told that names carry power here and yet you ask. Some would see it as an insult that you demand they define their being and declare it to you. I choose not to, for now. I am called many things. You may call me Samir, Zekiel Erebos. Bokaj. Jaken Warmecht. James. Yohsuke. Balmur. You are many things. Many names, but I will bestow upon you a title that none before have had here—wrong."

My friends had gathered to my left and right, and I felt comforted by their presence. I didn't know who this guy was, but this wasn't looking good.

"Your being here is wrong. You do not belong." He stood and every movement seemed simultaneously languid and dangerous. He stepped closer to us, and I could see more details in his face.

His features were striking: high cheekbones and such a chiseled jaw that I swore to myself silently that being around these manly-ass men was going to give me a complex. His eyes were purple, vibrant and swirling inside his head like whirlpools.

"You may join us, Maebe." He waved the queen over with a gesture, and she hurried over.

"My friend, you must not speak to this being so." She looked genuinely worried. "He is the physical embodiment of the very realm itself."

"A what now?" Jaken asked.

"I am a manifestation of the will of this realm of Fae. Magic is powerful here, and our only God here is the realm itself. That is why your Prime realm's Gods have not been able to come to your rescue or aid you as they have, presumably, before. I mean to remedy that."

"Please, Great One, do not end them," Maebe pleaded quietly.

"I will not. I simply want what is not meant to be here gone. All of them and another who tampers too much." His swirling eyes alighted on all of us. "I mean none of you any ill will. You were sent here by blood sacrifice. Exiled. The queens have the power to right that wrong."

"I had planned to–" Maebe began, but Samir held up a hand.

"I know well of your plans, child." He sighed. "They are ambitious, ill thought, and mediocrely planned." He grinned at Maebe as she frowned. "I approve. Chaotic and far reaching. You do your ancestors proud. No, that is not why I've come. I want the interlopers gone and the hunters who came by mistake. It took time to find it, but I did. Titania? Come."

He snapped his fingers, and flash of warmth, light, and the scent of summer filled the air for a brief moment before an Elf the almost exact opposite of Maebe stood behind us. She was six feet tall with a slim build, and her ears were the same as the

Unseelie queen's. Her skin was almost the color of gold, long, wavy hair of pure white, and her irises were golden with white pupils. It was unnerving and captivating at the same time. Then I started to notice that she wasn't as beautiful as her glamour made her appear to be. She was working hard to be more than "supermodel" gorgeous.

That was kind of sad, but weren't we all trying to appear to be things we weren't?

Oh well.

She quickly knelt before Samir, her face a mask of serenity that I doubt I could ever pull off. "Lord of All Summers that Were and Are to Come," she acknowledged him.

So he did have many names, but damn, if that wasn't a mouthful.

"Rise," he ordered. Gone was the understanding he had bestowed upon us. His whole visage held wrath and scorn. The material of his clothes began to move slightly, and I realized it was the same grass that we had woken up in when we first arrived in this realm.

"What can I do for you, Great One?" she asked, clearly uncomfortable calling anyone but herself superior.

"You have allowed one not of this realm to poison your mind and my land. No more. Call forth your advisors."

"I have been trying to kill the beings not of this realm, Summer Sun. Please, they are there. I could finish them now if you would let me?"

"Raise a hand to my champions, and I will waste your entire court!" Maebe screeched and began to march toward her opposite.

"Enough!" Samir ordered and gravity seemed to shift. It was suddenly impossible to stand—so all knelt in that moment. "Call your advisors, Titania, or I go hunting myself."

She looked horrified and scowled before following his orders. She clapped her hands twice, and the scent of ozone and the sea breezed in around us as three pale, wizened Elves in pale, bone colored robes appeared appeared next to the Seelie queen.

Samir surged forward and gripped the middle one by the throat and lifted him effortlessly off the ground.

"You dare attempt to spread your cancerous poison to my realm?" he growled and flecks of spittle splattered across the victim's face.

He struggled, then struggled more as a sizzling sound began. Where the liquid product of Samir's outrage had landed on the Elf's face and clothes, the skin and material began to burn and melt as if eaten by acid. Then the screams began and were cut off a second later by an angry jerking motion from the bald being. The old Elf no longer struggled as the grass that made up Samir's shirt had crept forward and grasped it by the broken neck. The body was dissolving, and the grass was absorbing it as it liquified.

"This creature's council you kept and made sure to implement. It has been causing me no end of pain, Titania. I keep out of the Seelie and Unseelie politicking because seeing you feud brings me amusement and provides both factions function. In return, I give you magic, longevity, and status." His face turned into a scowl and moved mere inches away from her. "THIS is how you repay your realm? You would see the very lands and peoples you are supposed to rule die? ANSWER ME!"

She cowered before him and actually stepped behind her advisors. "I didn't know! I didn't think that it could–"

"You lie? IN MY REALM?!" Samir shook with rage. The grass had long since finished its meal of whoever that poor bastard had been, but now it was longer and seemed to move like snakes toward the now sobbing woman.

The physical manifestation froze, then smiled coldly. The grass shrank and settled back around him as the same clothes he had worn and moved over to stand in front of Titania. He looked down upon her dispassionately and caressed her cheek. Her glamour faltered, then was gone completely. Everyone saw that she wasn't what she led them to believe but stayed quiet because Samir was still close.

"You will pay, little child. You will pay, but first, you are going to help your enemy send her champions to the Prime realm." He hushed her with a finger to her lips. "Ah, silence." The sound of her sobs and pleading voice were gone. Her lips moved, and her shoulders shook, but nothing reached our ears.

"Now," he turned his purple eyes toward us, "a reward on his behalf." He closed his eyes and touched us, two at a time, on the forehead. As he put his hand on my head, I felt a rush of energy and got a notification that I had reached level 17.

He allowed us a minute to allocate our points appropriately. I pumped three points into Constitution; that put me at an even thirty and three hundred HP. With the other two points, I evened out my strength and put it at forty. Maybe swinging my axe a bit harder could help; we would see.

We murmured our gratitude, but he simply waved it away.

"For her crimes against me, Titania will be assisting Maebe in teleporting you back to your realm. Tell me, who was it who exiled you to my domain?"

"He calls himself Rowan, but he is a stronger entity than the one you just destroyed," Balmur explained.

Samir stepped forward and looked into Balmur's eye a moment, then closed his own. "I see. It has been four and a half weeks since you were banished."

"Fuck!" Yohsuke, Jaken, and I growled in unison. Not only had we only leveled once while we were here, that fucker had plenty of time to dig in and gather his power.

"Do not despair." Samir smiled comfortingly or at least attempted it. It looked mostly predatory and came off disconcerting, but we tried to rally.

"I can help you, but it will take time." He looked to the still kneeling crowd, then back to Maebe. "Are your delegates here?"

"No, they are preparing for the journey. They will be ready by dawn."

"Excellent. Then they leave tomorrow at noon. Until then, Titania is my prisoner. We will be using your throne room here as the location for the ritual."

Maebe nodded and knelt before Samir. "Dismiss your court Maebe. I sense you have won their support, and my approval has bolstered that."

"Thank you, Deepest Shadow," she whispered reverently. She waved her hand in a dismissing gesture.

Once they had cleared the room, no one but us, Samir, the queens, and Winterheart remained.

"Do you have any questions for me, mortals?" Samir turned toward us and eyed us with mild interest.

"Many, but I'm more concerned with getting the bastard who killed that kid and sent us here," Jaken said. It was the first time I'd heard his voice deepen in anger.

I looked over at him and saw the fury in his features and realized that he was as angry as I was, if not more so, because he was still new to fatherhood. Not that one needed to be a parent to want revenge for child victims.

"You would have made an excellent Fae, Paladin. Too bad that your allegiance lies elsewhere. I will see to it that your vengeance is facilitated, at least in that you will be able to attempt exacting it. Past that, I cannot aid you. Magic, even as powerful as mine, has its limits, and my aiding you will cost me dearly."

"Everything has a price," I stated, dreading the answer to my next words. "What is yours?"

The bald Fae imitation, or was he actually a more true Fae than any of the ones here—fuck that train of thought. The headache that would likely be induced by a rabbit hole the size of Texas like that would have killed me. Samir looked at me, and his eyebrows, purple like his eyes, rose a little in surprise.

"You would have made an excellent Fae as well, little fox." He stepped closer to me, passing a horrified Maebe to stand before me.

"Thank you." I looked up at him, not defiantly but just firm. He sniffed me like a dog would scent an offered hand.

"I smell your realm on you. You have the attention of the land Herself and Her protection. She has blessed you. I also smell something else." He looked at Bokaj. "You have a companion, do you not?" Samir looked back at me. "And you? Call them forth."

I looked to Maebe, who just stood there gaping at me and back to him. He just stared at me expectantly. A deep bass rumbling sounded to my left, and I felt Tmont brush past my leg.

"Ah, a panther." Samir knelt in front of the great cat and looked her in the eyes. "I feel your strength, little one. Tell me, do you believe yourself strong enough to assist your master in what is to come?"

She sat once he asked and looked to her master for a moment.

"Don't worry T, whatever comes, I know you have my back."

She looked back at the Fae before her and hung her head. I got the feeling I knew her answer without needing to cast a spell. She was worried.

"I see." Samir clucked his tongue and wagged a finger at her teasingly.

His voice rose slightly in a lyrical manner and took on soothing tones. Tmont raised her head and began to sway a little with the rise and fall of the sound. I couldn't understand the language it was spoken in, but I could almost feel the melody unfold in my chest. Finally, he reached out and tapped the panther on her head, and I saw her whole body ripple with waves like you would see after throwing a pebble into water.

When the ripples moved across her, her body began to change. First, her fur darkened to a deep black, like Maebe's shadows. Then her bulky frame began to slim down, and her muscles bulged a bit more. She wasn't fat before, by any means, but you could tell she had a little extra slink in her. Now? Now she looked like a gym paid her to work out there. Her ears had tufts of long, black fur growing from them now that twitched as the song died.

She purred and butted her head up against Samir's left leg and wandered back over to Bokaj.

"My, my, Granny T, what big teeth you have!" The Snow Elf teased his friend. "Oh shit! They are bigger! Damn, Tmont–" She swatted at him before leaning up against his legs, "Put the roids down, bruh."

I put my hand on my I necklace and willed Kayda to come out. She materialized from it and looked around brightly.

"Oh my, a Lightning Roc," Winterheart rumbled from where he was sitting. He craned his neck so he could get a closer look, and Kayda cried a warning. "I mean you no harm, youngling. I am Winterheart. I haven't seen one of your kind in a long time."

He brought his head back a bit, and she settled once more. "You didn't... take her from the nest, did you?" the Ancient asked with a hard glare.

"No. He and I rescued her from a Goblin raiding party that had killed her mother. She died to give her life and entrusted her safety to my brother here," Yohsuke spoke for me.

The Dragon nodded and looked to Samir, "If you will have it, Fae Lord, I would offer my strength for this one. The Druid has proven honorable, and my darling niece adores him. I would further show my support for this cause."

Samir looked to Winterheart and nodded, then back to Kayda. "Roc. You do not look the imposing figure I imagine your mother would have been."

The way he said it pissed me off. Kayda hadn't asked for what happened. She hadn't asked to be pressure cooked the way her mother and I had had to do, fighting to give her life. I was about to tell him to shove it when Maebe touched my hand. My familiar called at him, her chirps and whistles clipped and almost bitter sounding.

"You aren't whole, and you worry that what has made you feel broken makes you weak, that your deformity will hamper your master. Am I right?"

Kayda shuffled forward and stopped a foot away from Samir and called, long and hard. At first, in rage and anger. Then it turned to fear—the fear that he was right. I could feel her emotions in my chest and berated myself for not knowing this before. I looked up from my frustration in time to see Kayda look back at me sadly with her lightning yellow eyes. She'd tried to hide it because she knew I'd be like this. I didn't deserve her.

"You deserve to spread your wings. You deserve to grow. You, who have fought to survive and thrive, deformed by your very birth, but didn't let it stop you." He stooped until he was eye level with her. "You, Roc, would have made a most excellent Fae creature. This realm would have been more splendid than it is with your addition. Winter Dragon, lend me your frost."

The embodiment of the Fae Realm stood to his full height and reached his left hand toward Winterheart. The Ancient Dragon stood as much as he could and reared his head back. The temperature dropped dangerously, and then his head shot forward with a concentrated burst of ice and freezing snow bursting from his maw. The sound of it was like the wind of a category five tornado in a tiny room—it was deafening. The energy from the breath weapon funneled into Samir through his hand and once it stopped, the Dragon collapsed and huffed. The Fae lord brought the energy from within himself and then into his bare hands. It flowed like a contained blizzard in a small ball with streaks of green and purple, like a snow globe. It was still loud as hell.

"Do you seek power, Lightning Roc?" Samir called loudly. "Do you wish to continue to thrive?!"

Kayda let loose a cry that sounded like thunder and spread her wings wide. She puffed her breast, and the energy shifted. She was engulfed by the light and sound.

The light went from blinding to bearable in seconds. Then it faded completely. Kayda ruffled her feathers after and bowed slightly to Samir. She turned to look at me, and I took in the view.

She was now two feet taller, putting her at six feet, and her body was a bit bulkier. Her azure blue feathers now had shorter, more pointed feathers of a lighter blue that resembled scales like Winterheart's mixed in around her breast, back, and the bony ridges of her wings. She had been cute before, but she was even cuter now. I looked at her stats and saw that a small bump in her charisma had helped with that. I looked over her other stats and my jaw dropped. Her race had changed!

Name: Kayda
Race: Storm Roc
Level: 12
Strength: 16
Dexterity: 20
Constitution: 25
Intelligence: 14
Wisdom: 10
Charisma: 10
Unspent Attribute Points: 0

Oh man! What would this mean for her? What would she be able to do? Would she be able to use other elements as well as lightning? We would have to see when the time came. For now, she still only had her two main spells, and her next would come in three levels. I broke from my thoughts when I felt a brush of cold but familiar thought against my mind and noticed Kayda looking at me.

Okay? she asked me, clearly concerned.

"Yes, love," I assured her. "I'm okay. How are you? How do you feel?"

Different. I could tell that the concept was new and confusing to her. She ruffled her feathers and shook herself out. Static emanated and dispersed along her feathers in small, beautiful sparks and arcs of white and blue.

"Mesmerizing." Samir stole the word from my mind as I was thinking it. "She is even more beautiful, and now she may not be whole, but it will not be the product of her matron's folly."

"The fuck did you say?" Yohsuke asked incredulously. He looked like he was ready for war, and I couldn't blame him because I was there with him.

"She told me everything you know of what happened," he nodded to Kayda where she stood, "and you corroborated it. She failed to protect her nest and must have been careless in her hunts to have been tracked that way. Even if the Goblins had stumbled upon her, she should have been more than a match. She was not. She failed. Her young died."

I was honestly lost for words. Few times has that ever happened to me, let me tell you. My friends would back me on that, but this asshole had just spouted all that, and I didn't have a rebuttal. She should have known better, and maybe if she didn't have a nest to protect, she could have fought harder. I would've made that argument, but he continued speaking then.

"Regardless of her inability or whatever else may have factored into her demise, her progeny was deeply affected by it. Instead of allowing the creature and her young to perish as I would have, your realm's deities and Nature itself saw fit to give it a chance. As have I. Take better care of her than her mother, mortal, for she is beautiful and welcomed here if she should wish to stay."

"Her mother sacrificed her life for her, you st–" Yohsuke began, but Kayda spread her wings in front of him and cooed at him.

"Let it go, brother," I translated. She was feeding me her thoughts and feelings now. "She understands what was given, and she doesn't hold her mom responsible."

Yohsuke looked from me back to Kayda and nodded once before turning and walking away a few feet. Kayda followed him, and I knew it'd be okay when my friend started cursing at her softly and called her a stupid bird when she tried to peck him playfully. She must have been trying to cheer him up.

"Thank you for your assistance and gifts, Samir. They are appreciated," I said.

"As I know, mortal. My request is that you keep those creatures out of my realm as best as you can. If I find another, I will destroy it and turn my sights on the Prime for retribution."

"This is a fight for all the realms, not just your own," Jaken informed him. "We're fighting to stop these guys, and yeah your help is appreciated, but we can only do so much. Help the other realms and find a way to tell us should you find another, but don't needlessly lower the defenses of the Prime realm when it would just do more harm than good."

"Be that as it may, no more will come here, or the price will be steep. Now, I must really prepare if I am to get you to when you need be. Until tomorrow."

He was gone then, faded from sight, taking Titania with him.

"There are no preparations for me to make. I bid the rest of you to retire for the evening and ready yourselves for tomorrow. Good night." Maebe hurried off out the door before any of us could speak. When the door clapped shut, we all turned toward each other.

"That guy was a dick," Balmur stated flatly. The rest of us laughed, and a horrified Winterheart just looked on while shaking his head.

Chapter Thirty-Three

A servant led the party to their various rooms, and I was led to a room at the end of the hallway across from Yohsuke's room on the right. It was about the same size as my room at the inn in Sunrise. It was comfortable enough with a nice bed and little in the way of furniture other than a sturdy dark wooden chair.

We all went about our evenings, served good, warm food, preparing for gods knew what was to come the following day in our own ways. Kayda perched over in a corner near the bed and slept with her head on her chest. Keeping her cooped up all the time wasn't fair. I laid on the bed and tried looking at my newest spell and ability but couldn't focus on it. It'd have to wait.

All I could think about at first was how shaken Maebe had been. I guess being ordered about and seeing the closest thing to a Fae Queen's peer being laid low like that would cause her reaction—but damn.

After a while, my thoughts drifted to Rowan and what he had done. My last thought before going to sleep was the look of terror on that boy's face before his final grizzly moment. It sent a shudder down my spine. After that, the dark of slumber claimed me, and I knew no more.

I don't know how much later it was, but I felt a shift on the bed and opened my eyes to see that it was Maebe.

"Hey," I greeted her groggily. She hushed me with a finger to my lips and slid under the blankets with me.

"If you would pay me a boon, I would sleep here with you tonight. Our guest and his... actions have unnerved me, and for once, I do not wish to be alone."

I nodded and scooted over. We all had bad dreams and fears. If someone could take my power, what kept me safe and whole where power was everything, I'd have shit myself. She had put on a much braver face than I would've.

Eventually, I nodded off a couple of times. The queen was quiet, but she must have been alright because she had been still with her eyes closed before sleep claimed me.

I woke up to her staring at me on a chair once more. I jumped a little in surprise, and she smiled. Kayda cooed at me from beside Maebe where the queen was scratching her head absently.

"G'morning," I mumbled at them both. Maebe nodded and Kayda just turned her head to a more advantageous position. *Goofball*, I thought to myself with a harrumph.

"Time?"

"Is still relative," Maebe answered with a small smile, "but it is mid-morning and close to time to leave. You have food that your chef has been outfitted with, and the rest of your new travel clothes are ready as well. They have been packed in a sack, but we do not have the time to appreciate them as my doting tailor wishes. Come, we must gather."

We left the room; Kayda would've been difficult to bring through the corridors so she went back into my necklace with the promise of letting her out as soon as I could.

We entered into the throne room again and sat at a thick cut, beautiful, wooden table with food all over it.

"'Bout time, ya sleepy bastard," Yohsuke shouted as we walked through the door.

All the party was there eating. Winterheart opened a ridged eye and looked us over before Yohsuke finished his thought, "Hurry up and eat, fucker. We got shit to do."

I grinned and joined them at the table. I let Kayda out to fly and eat some as well. The whole table took to throwing bits of meat up to the bird as a game. She was doing so well, in fact, that even Winterheart was impressed with her accuracy.

He began to question her and speak with her in his own way and she back. While they spoke, we tried to plan for what may be to come.

"Do we have a window of time on when we could be sent back?" Balmur asked. Maebe shook her head. "Okay, so our plan is going to be worthless."

"Not necessarily," Bokaj objected. "We know where he is and where he's likely to be. I'd say if he was going to hole up somewhere, it's going to be where he can get anywhere in the city as quickly as possible. That leaves the rock—it's centralized and easy to see as a base."

That's fair, I thought to myself and nodded. It was a very fair assessment that I hadn't been concerned enough about. Shows where my head was at.

Right up my ass.

"Okay, so dislodging my head from my rear here," I grunted. "He thinks we're gone, so we may have the element of surprise. He won't be able to exile us from the plane again, so that option is gone. If we get the drop on this guy, we have to go all in. Hard as fuck."

"Anyone get anything good on that last level?" Jaken asked. "I got a couple of good abilities that I can try out and one I wanna keep in reserve if shit really hits the fan."

The others nodded and began to explain some of their more recent spell acquisitions. Yohsuke had gotten a strengthened version of his Infernal Body buff and a spell called Hellfire Arrow, plus the ability to speak and understand the Infernal language in all forms.

James got some movement buffs for water walking and some kind of kung fu flying steps like the old movies. Bladed Limb sounded pretty cool; it let the user's body became even more of a weapon. His limbs would become as hard and sharp as mithral for a short time. Not to mention ice-type abilities courtesy of Winterheart.

Balmur got a little house spell that seemed cool, his own fireball spell, and another utility spell I hadn't opted to get of my own—polymorph. It turned a targeted creature into a less threatening creature—here's hoping I get to see a chicken!

Bokaj wanted to leave his a surprise but did let us know that his were some heavy hitters and a trap, so we left it alone.

My own, though, mine seemed interesting. One was called Star Fall; it summoned a shower of stars in a thirty-foot radius. Seemed like a crowd control spell to me. The other was a fear spell called Predator's Call. It instilled fear in a target and potentially caused them to lose focus or be unable to move. The first spell was intensely expensive at three hundred MP. One cast and I was down to a fourth of my total mana. Predator's was much more manageable at fifty MP per cast, but it had a one minute cool-down time. So, I did what I believed right and channeled the new spell into my ring of storage. While I was thinking about it, I had Bokaj give me a few of his mithril-tipped arrows. While I meditated and recovered my mana, I thought about a way to store spells and trigger them on impact.

Sure, I could give these arrows elemental damage, and that would be really nice and all. However, if I could store a more powerful spell and have that be unleashed without the direct mana cost to me, that would give us a huge advantage.

I looked at the ring on my finger. The design was simple—a circular swirling pattern around the stone that held the mana of the stored spell inside, which then led to where the focus was inside an unbroken pentacle—like the one Yohsuke used to summon the Demon. I mimicked the design of the ring onto the arrow, taking my time to get everything right. The swirling lines I engraved went up and back away from the tip of the arrow but circled it much the same.

I didn't have the stone necessary to "store" a spell. The trigger for our rings was intent. You focused on the spell stored in the ring, and the mana gets released in the form of the desired reaction.

With the idea I had though, maybe impact could be the trigger. The spell would be stored in the tip where the impact would "break" the pentacle and act as intent and release the spell. I was going to kick the shit out of myself if this worked and I could've been doing this all along.

I took a deep breath and envisioned the pentagram perfectly positioned with the center being penetrated by the tip of the arrowhead. After looking over my work, I filled the engraving around the pentagram on the tip. It was steady, grueling work, and my training with the hag paid off because I didn't screw it up. The mana I was going to be using to fill the swirls around the arrowhead itself would come when the spell was cast onto and "stored" in the desired location.

"Ah. Pleasant spell theory there, little Druid," Winterheart grumbled at me. He was looking over my shoulder, and I had been so focused I didn't feel his presence. "Humor a curious ancient, what do you intend to use that for?"

I explained my thoughts to him, and he nodded sagely.

"Close the pentagram except for a small portion before you try to store the spell, then as you store it, close the circle. That may help keep the spell there and from leaking out before the desired time."

I thought about what he meant and tried it out. It took about ten or twelve arrows before I finally managed one; I lost count—don't judge me.

I was so excited that I moved too quickly and jabbed my thumb with the tip. My stomach lurched, and I swear I was the asshole coyote on the wrong side of the cliff before the fall in that moment.

I felt the electric jolt from the stored Lightning Bolt shoot through my body, and I fell to my knees. I stuttered a mild swear and fell to my face. The arrow disintegrated and blew away.

"Fuck, man, you okay?" Jaken asked. He put a hand on my shoulder, and my health leapt back up to mostly full.

"I fucked up. Okay. I got this. Gimme six arrows, Bokaj. I got some shit here for you, brother." I sat up with a grunt and held my hand out.

"You're killing my stash, man. Shit. Gimme some of that stuff, though, and I'll be good." He smiled and handed me six arrows and left me to my work.

I made another of the Lightning Bolt arrows, then looked at Winterheart and grinned.

"Wanna help me test this one out, big guy?"

"I am not a 'big guy,'" the Ancient Dragon huffed indignantly, "nor am I a target to be shot at by a tiny archer."

"Oh." I gave him a defeated look and nodded. "You're right, I apologize."

"It's cool, Zeke. He probably couldn't handle the damage I'd cause anyway." *Yes,* I shouted in my mind. Bokaj swaggered forward to take the arrow carefully.

"You think you could even penetrate my scales, tiny Elf?" Winterheart chuckled, and ice shards fell from his chin and shattered on the ground.

"Guess we'll never know." He sighed and looked at the Dragon then back to me. "It's okay for people to be scared, man. Judgment free zone with us."

There was a dangerous rumble from Winterheart who stood as large as he could. "Strike me, puny mortal, that I might laugh at your attempt."

Bokaj just smirked at me, then as humbly as he could, nocked the arrow and aimed for the Dragon's chest. He loosed, and it streamed off, invisible the second he let it go. It struck true, and it slid between the scales and slammed home. At impact, you could see that the spell was released on the target to some effect before the projectile turned to cinders and fell away. Winterheart took the damage stoically and held his head high. Rightfully so, that was no easy spell to take, and he had barely blinked at it. That went a long way to show how much health he had and how far we needed to go in order to stand a chance against an Ancient Dragon.

He eyed me and Bokaj a moment and nodded before settling back down. "Well done."

We high-fived, and then we heard, "It tickled."

That motherfu–*stop.* I controlled my thoughts and refocused on my task.

After about another hour, I managed to create the five arrows I really wanted. One of the Call Lightning arrows, three Fireball arrows, and the hardest one which was my newest spell. It was hard to let go of the mana, but oh well. It may come in handy. Who knew how much firepower we would need to take this bastard and whatever forces he had amassed.

I gave them to an excited Bokaj who slipped them into his inventory rather than this quiver. Just to be safe, he assured me. I smiled and threw a piece of meat up to Kayda as she had grown bored of trying to play with the White Dragon who seemed only interested in talk. She was a bird of action, and I could appreciate that. Balmur approached me about maybe enchanting some of his throwing knives to hold spells. He seemed less crazy about it when I told him that the spell could ruin his weapons upon use.

We waited in amicable silence after that. Maebe sat next to me and ate small bites, chewed methodically, and swallowed.

"You okay?" I asked quietly. She looked up at me, and she smiled sadly.

"I will miss my new friend," she admitted. "I know you have to go, and I know that you have a mission. I also know that we have only just met, but you have been one of the kindest people I've ever known. The few conversations we've had have been insightful, and I think I will miss them as well."

She looked around the throne room as if for the first time. "This... emotion is foreign to me. Is it always like this? Friendship that is?"

I smiled back at her gently. "It can be hard to tell a friend goodbye. Especially if you feel like they are a good one. I'm going to admit there are times that you scare the absolute hell out of me. You are so strong and feral. It's terrifying, but at the same time, you are inquisitive and capable of feeling things that to others are so strange that they don't give it a chance. I like our conversations, and if I'm being honest, I'll miss those, too."

She nodded slowly and quietly.

"I know you don't mean to frighten me. I respect that," I continued. "I'm proud to have someone so strong and amazing as my friend. I just hope I can make you as proud for you to be mine. Thank you for being my friend, Mae."

She blinked at me, then smiled softly. Maebe stood and clapped her hands in the air, and an Elven servant rushed into the room. The queen spoke to her for a moment before the she sped off out the door once more.

"Zekiel Erebos, stand," Maebe ordered me, her tone soft but firm.

I stood in front of her, genuinely confused, but I trusted her.

My friends stood and gathered close enough to be within easy reach.

"As you have asked for nothing more than the boon of my friendship where others would have sought power, standing, wealth, or all three, I see fit to give you something better. Kneel, please."

I knelt in front of her and looked at her face.

"To you, I bestow the stars." She pulled an ornate dagger from the small of her back. I first noticed it when I was following her this morning and wondered how long she had been carrying it.

I heard Winterheart's head lift from the floor swiftly, but I didn't look away from Maebe. I had to admit the dagger made me a little nervous.

She slipped the blade across her palm, and dripped the pooling black blood onto my forehead. I was instantly even less comfortable with all of this. I closed my eyes and just barely won against the urge to wipe it away. Then I felt it begin to warm until it was hotter than I could bare, and I brought my hand up to the spot and felt the sticky blood on my middle fingertip. I brought it to my eyes in time to see it be absorbed into my skin. A heartbeat later, my flesh began to tingle. It began at the spot on my forehead, then worked its way from there to the rest of my body.

I looked at my hand and watched transfixed as white dots began to form and streak from the spot like a meteor shower through the night sky. I looked at my other arm, and the tingling swept down it the same way it had from my finger up. Soon, the feeling subsided, and I could stand again. I looked at the notification that popped into my view in stunned silence.

KNOW THIS!

You have been given a Blood Rite, the Rite of the Stars by the Queen of the Unseelie Fae, Maebe! This Rite has altered your existing race from Kitsune to Celestial Kitsune.

CONGRATULATIONS!

You now have the ability to learn Celestial spells and the language of the higher beings!

I dismissed the prompts and looked to my friend.

"What have you done, little Queen?" Samir's cultured voice queried from behind her. She turned and knelt before the equivalent to her realm's entire being personified.

"I have given my friend the one thing I know he would never ask of me. Something to show how much his companionship truly means," Maebe spoke with dignity and respect, but you could tell she was afraid. She looked like she had a metal rod in her spine, she was so stiff.

He eyed her and stepped around her to get to me.

"Well then." He looked me over in an appraising manner. "I did say you would make a wonderful Fae. How delightful. You truly will make a wonderfully entertaining Queen, Maebe."

She nodded to Samir and smiled at me.

"You do know that, though he has passed the Rite, he cannot be your successor?"

"I am aware," she acquiesced. "I value you, Zeke. And you all as well. This will allow me to stay in contact. You will also be treated with the same deference as I will in your realm.

Who knows, I may come and visit you myself if the way is prepared enough for me."

She took a parcel from the servant she had sent off earlier and then turned to give it to me. "Ah, thank you, Genera."

It was a book. Two books, actually. A thick one that was on top of a thinner one, maybe the size of a diary.

"The larger tome is a spell book, Shadow Speak. It will allow us to communicate using the darkness that now makes up our beings."

I lifted the heavy book and opened it. Dust fell from it and while it settled I got a prompt asking if I wanted to learn the spell. I chose "yes" and placed my hand on the first page. The pages began to warm to my touch and after that, the book exploded into a shower of pages. They began to burn and my vision flashed white. Suddenly, I know the theory behind whispering to the shadows and having them act as messengers. It was also possible to pass messages from one realm to the another if both recipient and sender were familiar with shadow magics.

"The smaller book is to assist you in the basics of the Celestial language. My apologies, it is the best I could do."

I reached out and took her hand before pulling her into a hug. "You've done plenty. Thank you."

"We are family now," she whispered. "Bonded by Blood. I will speak to you as I can, as often as I can. Stay safe and know that I will miss you."

Samir nodded, stepped away from us, and raised his hand. A shackled Titania materialized beside him. Her hair was disheveled, and she looked like she had been crying a lot. Moments later, hooded figures joined us, the emissaries that we were supposed to take along.

"It is time," he said simply.

I hadn't noticed that there was a large set of glyphs arranged in a circle where he stood with a triangle striking through it. Each tip of the triangle held more runes. To our left knelt Titania in the tip of it there, Maebe on our right in her spot, and Samir at the top.

"Empower the circle, Titania," Samir ordered. She began to sob, but put her hands on two glyphs. Her hands began to glow and fed blue-white light into all of them.

"Maebe, begin the chant to open the portal." The Unseelie queen began to sing in a language that was incredibly beautiful. It ebbed and flowed like the tides of the oceans. It was hard not to sway with it. You could feel the power thrumming through the air around us.

"I will be guiding the spell to constrict and rewind the time you lost as much as possible. Be prepared, I do not know when you will be arriving. Good luck."

He held his hands first at his side, then raised his left hand and arm straight up. The air around him began to shimmer as if with heat. The glyphs brightened and began to pulse in the rhythm of Maebe's song.

I looked to Titania and noticed that she looked older by the second. Her features began to wrinkle and slacken. Her hair greyed from the tips and worked inward—as if the glyphs were siphoning her very life force. Which they probably were. This may have been her punishment from Samir.

I didn't get the chance to really focus on it because Samir finished his now quickening complex motions and frenzied tones from Maebe took my attention. An audible tear sounded over the spell circle, and I saw a rent in the air before it begin to shape.

"Leave this realm and only return of your will and with my blessing. Go!" Samir ordered.

With one last look at my newest friend, the party surged forward into the unknown before us. The air was sucked from our bodies, and the falling sensation stole my sense of direction from me. It felt like hours that we went through the feeling. My lungs crushed until I thought they would implode from the pressure I felt and lack of air. Then we fell through a white portal, and all discomfort was gone.

After catching our breath, Jaken sighed and voiced what all of us had on our minds, "Fuck that."

Chapter Thirty-Four

Looking around, I saw that we were inside the gates of the city we had visited days ago, Maven Rock. Well, days in the Fae realm. We were in an alleyway between the wall and a few tall buildings. There was a large crowd gathered nearby based on the commotion I heard, and someone was speaking. Balmur motioned for quiet and waved for us to follow him.

Yohsuke looked at our three guests and just held out a hand to make them wait there.

"We'll be back for you. Just stay out of sight and don't die." The lead one nodded, and we left. Learning more about the mysterious cloaked figures would have to wait.

We had an asshole's day to ruin.

The party moved cautiously around the corner of the building to our left and peeked around. Our target, Rowan, that greasy snake fucker, stood and spoke to the same crowd that had stood helplessly watching that boy die.

"The enemy is gone, my faithful puppets," he assured them, "and soon, those of you who still have your free will here, will learn that War and his Generals are generous masters. Soon, you will know nothing of poverty, pain, or suffering. You will only know the elation of being a part of the One. My agent left on swift legs to find my brothers and sisters, and soon we will claim this world."

There was a murmur, but I realized it was only from select portions of the crowd. Those closest to the speaker had slack faces, devoid of any emotion or understanding.

"Let's go get his bitchass," I grumbled. He didn't have a single drop of blood on his fine clothes, and I could still feel the gore on my skin.

"No," Jaken responded in a whisper. "We wait. Too many bystanders."

"He thinks we're gone, man. He's relaxed. Soon, he will move along and fuck up. Then we strike," James suggested.

Balmur nodded in agreement, and Yohsuke put his hand on my shoulder.

Trust me, brother, he said using our earrings. *I want his ass broken and dead, too. We just gotta do it smart. Minimal blood on our hands.*

To all of us he said, *You guys think it's weird how some of the people over there look like no one is home?*

Yeah, Bokaj patted Tmont's head. *T says they smell dead, and I can't help but feel like those are the ones he was talking about when he said "puppets." Think those are the people who were disappearing?*

Makes sense. Balmur shrugged. *All we need to do is wait.*

Okay. Wait it is. I huffed quietly.

"My loyal subjects, go and collect the meal and bring them to me. Let me share our insights with them that they may begin serving our master. Go."

The crowd nearest him began to shuffle off. Some of the more lively ones, the ones that may be unaffected by him, still just dispersed. A few of the larger, better armed, stupid ones stayed, though. Including Rowan, there were ten total. They looked like they would've been part of the city guard. They wore plate of lesser quality than our Paladin's and carried long and short swords.

Balmur, see if you can't sneak ahead or above and find a good place for an ambush. Bokaj, you go with him. You hear some booms, you know what's up. Jaken began trying to help us plan as we went.

We began following and tailing our target from the shadows. While he moved Rowan, began speaking to people, and usually when he did, he would touch them and their expression would slacken. He'd move on, and they would just stand there a moment before shuffling off. The further he walked, the closer we got to the large rock that the city was named for.

So he builds his army this way. We have to stop him. Soon, or we may be overrun, I warned.

Up ahead and on your right there's a larger roadway. We can set the honey pot there. There are a couple people there he could speak to. May be our best option if we need to start sooner rather than later, Bokaj reported.

Good shit, man. Let's go get into position. Crowd control to start with, then move in. Jaken, you stay off to the side, man, Yoh advised. *Let's assume that the zombies are just done for and put them down swiftly.*

The big Fae-Orc nodded and moved off as quietly as he could.

At this point, it was going to be a matter of time before an innocent was caught in the crossfire again. I couldn't think about it, and I didn't think my friends wanted to either. I couldn't blame them. We left the bastard there and moved on to prepare for the attack.

It took about ten minutes for him to get to our position. Yohsuke, Bokaj, and I were on top of some of the lower buildings with oddly shaped roofs we could use to our advantage. Tmont, Balmur, and Jaken were hidden at street level where they could enter the fray safely. James followed our target to feed us information.

As he walked up and hailed the two civilians beneath us, Yoh and I dropped the world on top of his head. I unleashed my stored Star Fall, and then Yoh cast his Black Snow area of effect attack. There was a flash beneath us, and an opaque shell appeared around Rowan and his posse.

None of us had left our positions in hiding, just peeked out and cast before ducking back.

"Who dares attack a General of War?!" the mage shouted in outrage. "Show yourself, coward!"

I snickered and snuck to the rear of the roof and around to the other side. I shifted from my Kitsune form to my actual Fox shape and slunk forward as low as I could get. When I looked over, he was standing almost directly in front of me facing toward where Yoh's hiding spot was. Since our return to the Prime realm, our notifications were working perfectly, and although his level was still high at fifty six, all of us may stand a chance if we got lucky.

His attention was on Yoh's roof with his shield still up, so I backed up out of view and switched to my fox-man form once more.

Shield is still in place, I informed the others. *Balmur can you get in there?*

I already am, came the cool reply. I edged closer and saw motion for a split second, and one of the armored cronies went down in a heap. Not dead but with what looked like a serious injury to his legs. I hadn't seen the Dwarf behind the largest of the puppets.

The General and his crew turned to look, and another one from the right dropped. Rowan raised his hand with a mutter, and a pulse of energy rippled from him. Balmur's stealthed form cleared, and he was visible to all.

"Well, well. Looks like I missed one!" Rowan clapped his hands before him.

Shit. Get ready to run, man. I'm gonna try and fear him. You guys drop the roof on his ass.

I activated my newest ability—Predator's Call—and felt the mana drain from me. I opened my mouth and a roar so forceful leapt from my throat that it startled even me. The opaque shell around the enemy stuttered, then dropped completely and all hell broke loose.

I heard the thrum of a bowstring and two nova-like bursts of fire rocked the group on opposite sides below us. That was two of the Fireball arrows I'd made at work right there. Holy shit that was sexy. There were three of the guards down in a pile of cinders, and the others looked to be in rough shape. Another fireball hit the mage dead on and detonated around him. Another guard fell, but Rowan came out unscathed.

"Your spells are useless against me!" He laughed.

Ah. I see, I thought to myself. *He very well could have resistance to magic or some kind of buff against it?*

I couldn't see one under his HP bar so I decided against it, even though it was still possible.

Another Fireball arrow took two more guards, and the Star Fall arrow took care of the remainder. So far, I didn't think he had even seen us. That left only Rowan, but who knows how long before the other puppets came. Time to preserve mana. I brought Storm Caller into my hand with a flex of will and began to step from my hiding place when I heard a clash of metal on metal.

"Remember me, bitch?!" Jaken roared. I stood just in time to see his whole body shaded in red. Rowan had eyes only for him at that moment.

Drop his ass! I roared to my friends. The image of that poor little boy jumped into my mind, and my vision tinged red for a heartbeat before I leapt into the air.

Jaken surged forward and hit the mage with his shield. A small sliver of health left his bar. Maybe two percent. This was gonna be rough. I hit him like a freight train. Storm Caller smacked right into his back with all my strength, and he stumbled forward, bouncing off my friend's shield once more. That did a paltry three percent. I noticed a slight glow around his body, and I knew I was right.

He has wards for damage guys. Be cautious.

We know it, asshole. Yohsuke laughed at me. *Shut up and swing that axe.*

"Dick," I said to both my best friend and the asshole in front of me.

"That's hardly appropriate language for a dog," Rowan sneered.

"Oh, I'll show you a dog," I seethed. "I'm gonna make you pay for what you did to that kid."

"We all will!" Balmur cried. He came out of stealth behind the man sandwiched between the rock and a furry place and slashed the hell out of his back, his Mountain Fangs twirling almost as fast as saws. Blood began to show where the Azer Dwarf struck, faster and faster.

"Enough!" Rowan pushed out with his hands, and a force like a tidal wave hit us all and pushed us back and onto our backs. The health I lost left me a little angry, but ten percent was manageable.

Bokaj was there instantly, raining down a hail of arrows that would have left Robin Hood himself feeling a little envious. Sparks flew from where they hit and bounced off. Some disintegrated upon impact, but the damage was stacking slowly. His distraction gave Jaken time to stand and get back in there. Yohsuke sent a javelin of Hellfire at Rowan's exposed back. It hit, and the resulting cry of rage and pain was like music to my ears.

I let Kayda out to play, and as soon as she saw the asshole, she dropped a Lightning Bolt right onto his head. More points gone. He was down to about eighty percent of his total health now, and I could hear shuffling behind me.

I risked a glance and was rewarded with the sight of another three townsfolk moving toward us.

"We got company!" Balmur shouted before stepping into shadows behind him. A bolt of flame followed him, but he was already gone.

I threw Storm Caller at the folks behind me, and the weapon slammed one into another behind it. They went down in a heap. Balmur was there as soon as they landed to finish those two off, and arrows sprouted from the third. He fell down with a crash, and I called my weapon to me.

A black streak blurred past me, and James was on top of Rowan beating his fists into his head. The asshole was flat on his back with his hands up to try and defend himself, but it wasn't working too well.

Back up. At least thirty-five feet. It's time to hammer him. I held up my hand and cast Star Fall on him. While the heavens fell on him and thirty feet around him, I downed a couple of mana potions, and my MP jumped up a little bit. Spell time was over for now, I guessed.

Yohsuke was there with James, stabbing his Astral Spear into the openings as Jaken moved toward Rowan's legs. Balmur patrolled the areas behind us looking for more puppets, and Bokaj held his shots. I stayed back and tried to watch for any signs.

His health was down to sixty percent when the mage slammed his fists on the ground, and another wave of force pushed my friends away. James ended up flying onto the roof behind me that I had been hiding on. Yoh hit a wall to our right and lost a pretty chunk of his health but was still kicking, and Jaken slid back a few feet because he had braced for it.

 The man stood and brushed himself off, as if wiping his sleeves and pants off would hide the fact that his nose was freshly bloodied and he was definitely tussled.

 "Enough play," Rowan growled menacingly.

 He held up a hand, and a large bank of storm clouds began gathering above us. Kayda looked up into the sky and banked into the clouds. I tried to call to her but she just took off with a thought sent to me, *Save.*

 If that fucker hurt my baby, death would be a reprieve. He turned toward Jaken who had begun to glow red again, and I took the opportunity to put my great axe away and shift into my Ursolon form. I trundled up behind Rowan and swatted him into the same wall that he'd flung Yoh against. The clouds didn't disperse when his chanting turned into a gasp, so that must have meant the spell was finished or, at least, that portion of it. He slumped to his knees before the wall, and Yoh started hammering him with his Astral Sword.

 Bokaj let arrow after arrow fly into the vulnerable mage. One arced into his body and looked to have an electrical charge, but it didn't dissolve like mine did. Then a flaming one hit. Two more. The shield that had been around Rowan up until now was beginning to fade, and his health was getting lower. I brought myself to stand in front of him when a bolt of lightning caught me in the stomach and threw me off my feet. It took about ten percent of my health, but that was to set me up for the big show.

 I opened my eyes to see a large bolt of lightning arcing through the sky like a laser beam aimed at my chest. Before the beam could hit my body, Kayda intercepted it. She didn't even flinch. She cried out in anger and angled herself to shoot toward the offending caster. When he was in range, she unloaded her Lightning Ball spell at him that looked like it was empowered from the Lightning she had absorbed. It hit the caster and stuck for a moment before he could dispel it while standing painfully.

That gave Balmur time to fire three more arrows into his body that knocked him to his knees once more.

"Sorry, all, but you really shouldn't be here. If at first you don't succeed and all that, right?" He grinned and began a complex casting, and his fingers twitched in time with this words. I had just stood when I felt the familiar lurch of teleportation take me like it had last time, but then it stopped. I stood where I had been, and Rowan's face was slack.

I lunged forward as Yoh laughed.

"We aren't going anywhere, asshole," Yoh sneered, "but you can go to Hell!"

I reached the mage as Balmur appeared behind him. Yoh threw another Hellfire Bolt that struck him in the head, and the man began to scream as the flames stuck to him. Balmur struck then, his Mountain Fangs piercing flesh and bursting into flame. There was a small popping sound, and finally, all was quiet.

The General's HP had hit zero, but he wasn't dead—not quite. "Well, I couldn't send you away, but him? Him I can do. Hell is a new concept, but I wonder how he shall do there."

He grabbed Balmur, barked a word, and the Dwarf was gone in a cloud of sulfurous smoke.

Afterword

We hope you enjoyed Into the Light! Since reviews are the lifeblood of indie publishing, we'd love it if you could leave a positive review on Amazon! Please use this link to go to the Axe Druid: Into the Light Amazon product page: geni.us/IntotheLight.

As always, thank you for your support! You are the reason we're able to bring these stories to life.

Author's Note

Well folks! That brings this book to a screeching halt, and true to form—who would I be if I didn't have a final word for you all, eh?

I'd be an idiot. Well, a bigger one. Thanks for taking this journey with me and my friends. Thanks for your patience. Thanks for the facepalms and for laughing with us. Or at us—be that way.

But regardless—thank you. I'm beating myself into writing shape trying to get book number two to gods knows how many cranked out for you, and I hope you enjoy them as much as I do.

With all the love I can possibly muster for you—you lovely reader, you—I bid you to love each other and pick up another book.

Respectfully, and irreverently,
Zeke

About Christopher Johns

Christopher Johns is a former photojournalist for the United States Marine Corps with published works telling hundreds of other peoples' stories through word, photo, and even video. But throughout that time, his editors and superiors had always said that his love of reading fantasy and about worlds of fantastic beauty and horrible power bled into his work. That meant he should write a book.

Well, ta-da!

Chris has been an avid devourer of fantasy and science fiction for more than twenty years and looks forward to sharing that love with his son, his loving fiancée and almost anyone he could ever hope to meet.

Connect with Chris:
Twitter.com/jonsyjohns

About Mountaindale Press

Dakota and Danielle Krout, a husband and wife team, strive to create as well as publish excellent fantasy and science fiction novels. Self-publishing *The Divine Dungeon: Dungeon Born* in 2016 transformed their careers from Dakota's military and programming background and Danielle's Ph.D. in pharmacology to President and CEO, respectively, of a small press. Their goal is to share their success with other authors and provide captivating fiction to readers with the purpose of solidifying Mountaindale Press as the place 'Where Fantasy Transforms Reality'.

Connect with Mountaindale Press:
MountaindalePress.com
Facebook.com/MountaindalePress
Krout@MountaindalePress.com

Mountaindale Press Titles

GameLit and LitRPG

The Divine Dungeon Series
The Completionist Chronicles Series
By: Dakota Krout

A Touch of Power: Siphon
By: Jay Boyce

Red Mage: Advent
By: Xander Boyce

Peaks of Power: Beginnings
By: Paul Campbell Jr.

Pixel Dust: Party Hard
By: David Petrie

Coming soon!

Ether Collapse: Equalize
By: Ryan DeBruyn

Skeleton in Space: Histaff
By: Andries Louws

Fantasy

Coming soon!

The Lost Sigil: Insurrection
By: RAYMOND BECKHAM and DARIUS COOK

The Black Knight Trilogy
By: CHRISTIAN J. GILLILAND

Appendix

The Good

Zekiel Erebos (Zee-key-uhl Air-uh-bows) – Marine who loves gaming as a civilian with his buddies who are still in. Class: Druid. Race: Kitsune, has a tail.

Yohsuke (Yo-s'kay) – Zeke's best bud/brother from the Marine Corps. Overlord, yeah you read that right. Class: Spell Blade. Race: Abomination (halfbreed Drow and High Elf)

Jaken Warmecht (Jay-ken) – Zeke's friend who typically needs help catching up in the games the group places together. Class: Paladin of Radiance. Race: Fae-Orc.

Bokaj (Bow-ka-jh) – A friend from the gym who loves video games and is in a pretty wicked band! Class: Ranger. Race: Ice Elf.

Tmont (Tee-M-on-t) – A panther with a taste for tails who happens to not just be a walking bag of assholes but is also Bokaj's pet. Mainly that first one, though.

Balmur (Ball-mer) – Bokaj's best friend and another good buddy of Zeke's who loves to game! Class: Rogue. Race: Azer Dwarf (Fire Dwarf) HIS BEARD IS A FLAME!

James Bautista (Really?) – Another Marine that Yohsuke and Zeke know and game with often. Class: Monk. Race: Dragon Elf.

Kayda (Kay-duh) – A pretty little bird with a shitty past and, hopefully, a bright future.

Locals

Sir Willem Dillon – Owner of the tavern in Sunrise Village (the starter town) and Paladin of Radiance. The first guy the group meets and doesn't try to kill. (Or do they? MUAHAHAHA—No really, do they?) Jaken's trainer.

Dinnia (Dih-nee-uh) – An Elven Druid who takes pity on poor Zeke and brings him into Mother Nature's good graces. Zeke's trainer.

Sharo (shah-row) – Another panther who assists his partner in crime, Dinnia, in training her student. Not a walking bag of assholes.

Kyra – Queen of the bears and good friend of Dinnia's. We like her.

Marin (mare-in) – We, uh... we don't talk about her. 10 out of 10 though. Kick ass dire bear.

Tarron Dillingsley (Tair-run Dill-night-slee) – Gnomish enchanter who—let's face it, shall we?—sucks as a teacher for various reasons.

Rowland – Blacksmith in Sunrise who decides he likes the travelers, especially the one with the tail—no bias.

Maebe (may-buh—soft buh—if she hears you talking shit, I'm not responsible, yeah?) – Unseelie Queen of Winter and Darkness who somehow gets thrown into the mix.

Thogan (ThO-gun) – Champion of the Unseelie Fae and a rather clingy Dwarf with a rough complexion.

Titania (tih-tah-nia) – Queen of the Seelie Fae who has a predisposition of being a raging bitch to anyone and everyone she doesn't like. Like outsiders.

Shellica (shell-oh-cuh) – A Dwarven enchanter who, let's face it, is probably coo coo for Cocoa Puffs.

The Bad

War – Galactic conquerer who probably suffers from only child syndrome. Probably needs a hug, or he will keep trying to take over the universe.

Minions of War – Not the lovable minions everyone loves. You know, not the yellow ones, or that fish from that one Will Ferrell animated move. These guys seek to undermine the strength of the gods by eroding the world around them slowly, and they serve the other assholes in this list.

The Generals – A number of War's better warriors capable of taking out the strongest people upon the planet—and together they did. Dick move.

Rowan – I'm not gonna say much about this guy—read the book then you'll know what a dickbag he is.

Pastella (Pahs-tell-uh) – Crazy Elven woman with a taste for torture and violence.

And The Ugly

Insane Wolves – Think crazy wolves, but you know, crazier and angrier for some reason. Due to proximity to a minion of War, the minds of these animals have eroded to nothing but the drive to kill and eat anything that is not them or another wolf.

Undead creatures – As you can imagine, due to proximity to a minion of War, these poor bastards rose from the dead in order to protect their alien masters. Even the stronger versions are worthy of a small bit of sympathy—they sure as hell didn't get any, but they are worthy of it.

Bone Dragon – I mean, pretty self-explanatory, right? It's a Bone Dragon! No skin, no muscle—all bleached bones and hate for the living.

General of War (Blight) – The asshole who did some truly terrible things, sent us on a supposedly one-way trip to the Fae realm, and got his ASS kicked. Yeah. That guy.

Ursolon – Think of a giant, striped bear with an anger management issue the size of North Dakota. Yeah. Now go fight one.

Werewolves – The heroes in some tales—but not this one. Oh no. These guys suck, big time! Hairy, needy pieces of crap.

Alpha Werewolf – The jerk in charge of the other jerks above. Bigger, badder, stronger, and usually *way* more cunning and ruthless.

The Wild Hunt – A flock of assholes (read Demons) who patrol the realm of the Fae and take out anything they believe doesn't belong there.

And other random jerks too unimportant for now to mention—they know who they are. Bunch of assholes.

Made in the USA
Lexington, KY
22 April 2019